How many hours do we spend in loving?
I don't know, I don't care.
We're lost in a maze of fevered loving . . .

Mandarin Orange Sunday
The luckiest day of the week

Mandarin Orange Sunday

Angelique Durand

BANTAM BOOKS
TORONTO · NEW YORK · LONDON · SYDNEY

MANDARIN ORANGE SUNDAY
A Bantam Book / November 1981

This is entirely a work of fiction, and its characters and events
are wholly fictional. Any similarity to past or present persons
or events is purely accidental, and no identification with any
person or event is intended.

The Author

ISBN 0–553–14709–9

Published simultaneously in the United States and Canada

Bantam Books are published by Bantam Books, Inc. Its trademark, consisting of the words "Bantam Books" and the por-
trayal of a rooster, is Registered in U.S. Patent and Trademark
Office and in other countries. Marca Registrada. Bantam
Books, Inc., 666 Fifth Avenue, New York, New York 10103.

PRINTED IN THE UNITED STATES OF AMERICA

0 9 8 7 6 5 4 3 2 1

This is for . . .

> Jon-Torben—for his words.
> Frank R—for his help.
> William—for helping me make it
>   through my life.

*If the fool would persist in his
folly he would become wise.*
William Blake

Mandarin Orange Sunday

1

The car, the man, and my weekend disappear from view.

I lean against the cool stones of the porch wall. My body feels weak, slightly sore, tired. I need to sleep—by myself. To feel the luxury of aloneness.

He waved, briefly. Tall, cool, blond, impeccably dressed. Even his slight wave was suave, cool.

I watched him climb into his MG. He smiled and waved once more. He blew me a kiss. I blew him a kiss.

And then—no more man. Only me . . .

I go into the house, close the door, and lean on it. With relief, I feel the smile leave my face. I go and get myself some coffee and wander slowly out onto the side terrace. I gently lower myself into a lounger, and for the first time in forty-eight hours I can *relax*.

I met Steven at a party on Friday night. An account executive—advertising. Very trendy: Cardin suit, silk shirt, Gucci loafers with matching wallet and briefcase. The first man I've brought back for the weekend whom I didn't actually know. I'm sure that my being a well-known writer with a super pad in a secluded part of Malibu helped him decide between me and the jiggly-boobed blonde.

Still, I didn't mind: I felt I needed the experience of a Steven.

He certainly tried hard enough to impress me all weekend. All that stamina—strength and length! Perhaps I should have applauded when he told me he'd read *The Joy of Sex* three times.

I sip my coffee, wondering whether I will ever want to see Steven again. I stare out over the garden. I've just had it landscaped—it's all rocks, Japanese shrubs, bonsai trees in special pots. Gulley, my cat, is asleep under the young willow tree.

I ought to get dressed, but I like the sensual, warm feel of the peach silk kimono against my naked skin.

1

What I *should* do is some work. I'm in the middle of a chapter, and I haven't written anything for over forty-eight hours; it makes me feel ashamed of myself. I normally write six to eight hours a day, usually in the afternoon and evenings, sometimes even all night. I *always* write.

But now I haven't written anything for two days, and I feel sluggish and lazy: I hate that. I go and take a shower. I stand under the water for a long, long time, washing away the remembered sex—forty-eight hours of sex instead of writing.

I've never been to bed with a *trendy* guy before. Not with someone who *works* at being trendy. So much Gucci everywhere. When he pulled it out, I half expected to see the green and red Gucci stripe along it. I've never before been fucked whilst the guy was telling me about how impressed his boss was with him—a raise *and* a promotion due next month. It got *him* off, anyway . . .

"I *love* your beautiful eyes," he told me. (My eyes are green, with flecks of gold). "So . . . beautiful!

"And your name, too. I adore your name. Is it your own?"

I explained patiently that it was. (My name is Solange delaMer. That's the name I write under, I should say. I was born Solange delaMer Osborne. American father, French mother.)

"Does Solange"—he complacently mispronounced it, stressing the last syllable, 'So-*lange*'—"actually mean anything?" He was leaning over me munching on an apple, bits of it falling into the bed. He picked up a piece that had fallen on me.

" 'Sol' means 'sun,' " I glared at him, "and you pronounce it like that, too—'sol' as in 'doll,' not 'so' as in 'doughnut.' And *anzh* means angel. *Sol*-anzh!"

"A sun-angel—how sweet!"

"Thank you," I said dryly, with a falsely sweet smile. (My ex-husband used to call me "sun-angel.")

I stop daydreaming—I don't want to think about Steven anymore, even though he was an enthusiastic lay, and I love to get laid. I wonder—am I all *that* desperate for someone to share my bed? Am I *that* lonely for company? I come back to the present, with the shower head set to massage, water gently pounding on my back. I turn the dial, then give one last rub at my pussy hair. I don't want Steven's sex left on me.

Yet I know I have a need for the sex of someone I love to

be on me—in me. What I want is *my* man. I wonder where he is? I think that maybe he's given me up waiting for me, has gone and got himself married to someone else. If he has, well ... it's me he should be with. Me, who has the same loves and interests as he does. He's one side of a puzzle and I'm the other—put us together and we fit into each other so exactly, so perfectly.

Stop daydreaming, Solange! Ah. ... but Solange *loves* to daydream!

I dry myself, enjoying the velvety feel of the towel. I rub Fluid B-21 all over my body and splash myself with l'Heure Bleue. I feel clean once more—revirginized. ...

I climb into a faded pair of cutoffs that barely cover my ass; put on a tiny bikini top that barely covers my boobs. (Barely is the word.) I feel like a California beach girl.

I brush my blonde-streaked light brown hair. It's slightly wavy, parted in the middle, and just past my shoulders. Thank God for Vidal Sassoon and Rene Furterer! I care so much about how I look to men. Equal rights for everybody, I say—but I love to be a female who's *being* female.

The door buzzer—roses, from Steven, my Gucci-striped stud. How sweet! Then the phone rings. It's Steven, thanking me for a beautiful weekend. I thank him for the roses. He wants to see me again on Friday. He asks enthusiastically— even pronouncing my name correctly.

I smile: a conquest—how delicious! "I'll get back to you, Steven. ..." But I know perfectly well that I won't. He's just not my type. Still, I enjoyed trying him ...

Oh, Solange!

*　　*　　*

I fly to New York. Justin Markham, my agent, meets me and drives me to his spacious apartment on Central Park West.

I've written three books so far—all highly successful. All of them are about a witch called Pandora. I can totally immerse myself in Pandora. It is a much-desired metamorphosis: I make her the person I so very much want to be—I become the person she is.

Justin and I have tea together. I observe him carefully: He's a suave, forty-two-year-old, good-looking, and sexy smoothie, who reminds me of William F. Buckley Jr. Justin's a softy—except for business, that is, when he becomes a veritable Mr. Jaws, wielding his diamond-studded ballpoint.

3

Justin smiles, gives his dark blue blazer a brush with his long fingers. He's talking about royalties and taxes, but I'm not really listening—business isn't my forte. I leave business to him and my ex-husband.

"I'm seeing Rand next week," he says with an inquiring glance, tucking away a strand of his graying, golden-brown hair.

"I didn't know he was coming over." I feel slightly annoyed that Rand hasn't let me know; it shows in my voice.

"He's not," Justin continues soothingly. "I'm going over for a couple of days. Can't turn down a few days in the South of France, can I?" He smiles his "tolerance of females" smile—I know it well—and rolls his eyes heavenward. . . . I know what's coming, that smile has telegraphed it: "I should say, *Anna* can't."

Anna is his tall, thin, beautiful ex-model wife. She makes me look and feel fat, but despite that drawback we get on very well together. I can *talk* to Anna, and I know she doesn't tell Justin. Well, I don't *think* she does. . . .

Justin looks at me tolerantly, and again I know what's coming. "I'll never understand why you and Rand had to go and get yourselves divorced." He shrugs and leans closer, as though trying to glean the answer from my impassive face. "Why *you* divorced Rand, that is."

"Well, don't worry. It won't interfere with business. Your ten percents will still ring up regularly." (Justin handles both of us.) "We're still the very best of friends." I stare at him very deliberately, then grin. "Why, we even fuck now and again." An eyebrow shoots up, and an amused smile crosses his face.

Bootsie, Justin and Anna's basset hound, sits in front of me and woofs quietly. I give him a quick cuddle: we're old friends.

Justin lights a cigar. I watch the ceremony. It fascinates me: his little silver clipper thing, the way he wafts the flame around. Somehow it's very sensual—those long slim fingers of his, his cool suaveness. Perhaps I want him to perform a similar sensual ceremony on me? He keeps a boxful of cigars on the coffee table: Romeo y Julieta. "Aren't they illegal?" I ask with a smile of complicity.

He grins back. "Yes—just like that stuff you occasionally smoke. . . . Oh yes, love, before I forget." He takes out his wallet and hands me some tickets. "They're for two performances of the Jan-Toby Axelsson Band at Madison Square

4

Garden, tomorrow and the day after. Anna and I are going to both of them." I hastily move the tickets out of Bootsie's reach—he's partial to important pieces of paper.

A teasing light appears in Justin's eyes. "You two—honestly! You don't *really* like that stuff, do you? Haven't you grown out of it *yet?*" I think he must practice that incredulous look—he uses it a lot on me. "I don't know how you *could*, that is. *Like* it, I mean. You're so very fond of *good* music, Solange. It's one of your natural categories of communication, a frame of conceptual reference you early acquired. . . ." He shakes his head wonderingly.

"You sound like Rand."

"Rand and I *appreciate* the importance of good music, the way it functions, that is, as an intellectual lingua franca. I don't know how you can listen to that teenage pop stuff."

"Justin! One, I don't listen to teenage *pop* stuff, as you call it. And, two, Jan-Toby Axelsson is *not* a pop singer. His music *is* good music." I feel irritated, because he's downing one of my favorite guys.

He gives me his tolerance-of-women look again. I return a friendly glare. "He's a poet," I say, "like Dylan and Cohen. Like Kristofferson."

Justin makes a choking noise that develops into a guffaw. "Well, if you think that rock singers are poets, God help me as your agent." He rolls his eyes heavenward.

"No wonder you and Rand get on so well." I pout at him.

He pats my hand, raises his eyebrows, and looks down his nose at me. "Well, enjoy youself, sitting among all those screaming hippies and groupies. But are you *sure* you'll want to come and hear string quartets on Sunday?"

"Of course—they're beautiful. You know I adore Bartok."

His eyebrows, still raised, and his slight shake of the head express a profound incomprehension. Justin and Rand find it hard to understand how "*that* kind of stuff" could hold any attraction for me when I love classical music so much. And I do, having been raised on it by my cellist father. I write my books listening to Rachmaninoff and Stravinsky, Mozart and Debussy. I adore Papa Haydn and Johann Sebastian, am ecstatic over Walton and Vaughan Williams. I truly believe that Justin and Rand think there must be something wrong with me, some sort of dread psychotropic disease—incurable, obviously.

5

I look noncomitally back at Justin. We smile at each other and finish our tea.

* * *

Justin has an appointment with a publisher. As he goes, he tells me to be ready to leave after lunch the next day: we're going to see Gerald, my editor.

I go to my room, shower and change. Anna comes in as I'm dressing. She seems even taller and thinner than when I last saw her. She's five feet nine and has a perfect 32-22-32 figure. Her hair is dark, cropped short; her eyes are brown and look very slightly slanted. She's so beautiful and sophisticated and poised. Next to her I always feel so gauche.

And I think *dumpy* must be accurate: I'm just five feet three. Why couldn't I have been a *willowy* five feet nine? No—I had to have boobs that measure a full and bouncy thirty-seven inches (and oh, do they bounce!). And my waistline is just over twenty-five inches (on a good day). And as for my hips, I'd make a great peasant—they nearly match my boobs for inches.

Solange wants to be tall and willowy, not little and curvy.

The only good thing about it is that *men* seem to like my little and curvy body: From their viewpoint, short is a plus—it makes *them* all seem tall. And as far as boobs go—let's face it, the American male is obsessed with mammary glands as sex objects!

Anna's telling me something about her mother, but my attention is still on her thinness. I wonder if I should have a tit-tuck and lose some of that bounce, like I once planned.

That was five years ago. I had it all arranged: I went to *the* specialist in Geneva and set it all up to have $3,000 worth of tit-tucking. A perfect 34C, that's what I'd be.

Rand found out!

What was I thinking of, arranging to pay money to mutilate his property? He didn't want me to lose *any* of that lovely busty substance!

Anna comes over as I'm slipping into my slim, black suede boots; she touches my black silkdress, running her fingers along the shirring of the elasticated top, on which are embroidered tiny pink French knots. "You're so *lucky*," she says with a smile. I give her an inquiring look. "Having such beautiful full breasts, I mean. I'm going to Geneva next week, to have an implant—a perfect 34C."

I can't help giggling. Perhaps I should have offered her two inches of mine? I can see it vividly: two operating tables,

6

Anna on one, me on the other; the surgeon gingerly transplanting two inches of squeezable, wobbly tit. . . .

I explain to Anna and she adds her giggles to mine. "Oh, Solange, leave your tits *alone*. It's mine that are the problem. They're too dark; but of course, they can't make nipples any lighter." I see she's serious. "Look," she says, unbuttoning her silk shirt and baring two tiny mounds with big brown nipples and brown areolas. "I'd like to have pink ones—those lovely rosy *pink* ones. All melty."

She's really getting herself enthused. I've never heard a woman extol tits so much. Maybe she's gay? No, clearly not. Bi, perhaps?—*"semeye-gay"*—as the Texan linebacker calls them in a very funny book I once read.

"Yours are pink, aren't they?" She reaches out and gently pulls my dress top down to my waist, easily, because of the elastic. "They're *beautiful*," she sighs, touching one nipple, then the other. "See—yours are all pink and rosy. All *melty*."

"Oh." What more can I say, standing here with my boobs hanging out and my nipples standing up? We look at each other.

"I think you're very beautiful, Solange. Round and soft. Men *love* that. I'm all angles, that's why I'm having my tits done at last. It'll make Justin happier."

"Oh?" I'm beginning to feel like a moron. Can't I think of anything else to say? "Oh." Obviously I can't. She comes closer, and I wonder what's going to happen next. After all, these days every free and liberated woman is obliged to have a lesbian episode. Her hands come towards my boobs again. I look at her and think I almost could, with Anna. . . . She pulls my dress up to cover my boobs, giving me a wistful, gentle smile. "I'll meet you here tomorrow, for the concert," she says as she leaves the room.

"Oh," I say to myself. "Oh. I wonder . . ." I wonder what it would feel like, her lips on my "pink melty ones." I wonder— what would her large brown ones feel like between my lips?

*   *   *

I've walked into the party scene from *Shampoo*: back to the late sixties—flower power, peace and love, psychedelic music, strobe lights, sweet-smelling candles, and, permeating all, the lovely smell of pot. It reminds me of ten years ago, back in Oxford. There's actually a Beatles song playing: "Lucy in the Sky With Diamonds."

I'm at the party with Matthew, a close friend, who happens to be gay. The party's in a huge, sprawling apartment. Very

7

modern, geometric lines and playpen furniture, Art Deco and Beardsley prints. Matthew takes my hand—he's wearing a burgundy-colored Cardin sweater, with the little Cardin symbol on the roll-neck. His hair is dark blond, naturally curly, and falls down to just beyond his collar. He's got beautiful blue eyes. I adore his good looks.

He spots some friends across the room and pulls me through the crowd. The group of half a dozen men greet him; he introduces me. They all behave with great friendliness, in fact two of them kiss me on the cheek like a long-lost friend. They're all *so* pleased to meet me. Three of them have read my books. "I *do* love Pandora," says one; but another says he doesn't believe in all that supernatural nonsense, and he thinks my books are just simply *dreadful*. I give him my sweet and sugary smile that clearly conveys he's an asshole.

"Come and meet Webley," says a tall, auburn-haired man, taking me by the arm. "Webley works for Simon and Schuster, or Harper and Row—one of those, anyway. So you have lots in common, don't you?"

"We do?" I trot to keep up with him. I become terribly aware of the strobe lights and the grass smell. Auburn's hand on my arm feels thin and bony. I notice a *super*-looking man as I fleetingly pass him by. I wonder if *he's* gay? Christ, I hope not! Why am I being dragged to the *other* side of this huge room? I may never see my adorable man again. And I need to get myself laid: to be sexy and feminine—a softness for some masculine hardness.

"Webley." Auburn smiles.

I meet Webley. Short, sandy-haired, in a bottle-green corduroy suit. Webley edits cookbooks. Oh, Christ! I smile fixedly at him as he happily chatters on about writing. His expertise, he informs me complacently, isn't confined to cookbooks. He'd be only too happy to look over any of my new stuff.

I flash him a false smile. "I must go and pee, Webley dear." I squeeze his arm and quickly disappear, leaving his baffled look behind me.

I find a bedroom, flop onto the huge bed. The room has more Art Deco, plus Andy Warhol soup cans. I don't think I could sleep here.

I wonder just what I *am* doing here. I don't really enjoy parties all that much. Is being single, free and liberated really worth it? Worth what? I don't know—I'm still trying to find out!

Is being single and free what I really want, anyway? I guess it must be—I divorced Rand, didn't I? Rand didn't want the divorce. Rand was just indulging my capricious whims because, as he said, he knows I can't really manage without him, and I'd be back. He's given me my wings only because he knows it's not really like I think it is out there in the big, bad, cold world.... Perhaps he's right. He normally, infuriatingly, always is!

Rand *let* me get the divorce. Is that what you really want, Solange? Why don't you just go off by yourself for a bit? There's no reason for a divorce, no need for it *really*, is there? Is life with me *that* intolerable, Solange? If you *need* to have a few affairs, then *have* them. You really *do* want a divorce, then, Solange. No, I won't stand in your way, Solange. I love you, Solange. His eyes like those of a hurt little boy....

Perhaps if he'd gotten angry....

What's the matter with me? Am I really *that* selfish?

But here I am: divorced. Liberated. Rich. Beautiful.

I look around the bedroom. Perhaps I'd better get myself back to the party and that gorgeous guy....

My attention goes to the low, ornate nightstand at the side of the bed: there's a book on it, *Go It Alone* by Patricia Wells. I glance at some of the turned-down pages, and see that someone has been rereading all the gorgeously sexy bits. Thank God we females can write erotic, sexy literature these days. I really do hope Jessica found happiness with her lovable painter Mickey, although I think *I* would have taken Lance, the rich Texas cowboy whom she left high and dry.

I've never had a Texan. Everything is supposed to be bigger in Texas. I wonder if *everything* is?

I'm forever *thinking* about having lots of divinely sexy affairs, only I never seem to work my way around to having a *serious* one. I think I really would like a once-or-twice-a-week secret lover: a rich married man in a slinky motel. Magic fingers. X-rated movies. Yes, I really *need* the experience. After all, wasn't that why I got divorced—to play the field and have lots of divinely naughty sexy flings?

I go back to the party. Shit! The gorgeous man has his arm around a young girl with long blonde hair.

I go and find Matthew.

"Aren't you enjoying the party?" he asks, seeing my glum expression.

"Not really, Matthew dear. I think I'll just go back to Justin and Anna's."

"But you haven't given it a chance yet." He smiles cheerfully.

9

"I don't really *want* to."

He nods, smiles. "Come back to my place, then. I'll make us something to eat."

"I. . . ."

"We'll watch a movie and get stoned."

"Well. . . ."

He puts his arm around my shoulders. It feels nice, protective. I think I'd like Matthew to protect me.

I like Matthew's apartment. It's large and almost sparse, except it isn't. There are piles of huge cushions everywhere, and honey-colored velvet modular furniture. A couple of huge paintings on the walls—Matthew's. I like them. He did one for me, reminiscent of Ben Nicholson; I've hung it in my dining room.

Matthew Gardner paints. He does a variety of artwork to earn money, but basically—he *paints*.

I follow him into the kitchen. It's bright white and shining. Everything—a beautiful array of copper saucepans, mousse molds, wooden utensils—hangs in its exact and proper place on the wall.

I always feel at home with Matthew. I grind the coffee and put it on to drip as he starts to scramble us some eggs, *Matthew* style: precisely, correctly, perfectly.

I go to the bathroom, fiddle with my makeup and hair. By the time I come back he's got everything set out on two trays in the lounge: French bread, salad, the eggs, and a bottle of Moet NV. The lights are out, and he's lit some perfumed candles—how romantic! He's sitting there rolling a thick joint in his slim fingers.

He hands me the joint, and I toke as he pushes a cassette into the TV recorder and turns the set on. He grins at me—it's a gay film. I've never seen one before. I've seen a few silly sex films, of course, but never a totally gay film.

"Who's supposed to get turned on by this?" I ask Matthew as we eat from the trays on our laps. I'm mesmerized, by the two gorgeous, hunky, suntanned Adonises performing on the screen in front of me.

I'm aware of myself sucking a large piece of French bread as I watch the Adonis on his knees swallow, to laryngeal depths, the *huge* cock that had been advanced towards his face by the other gorgeous Adonis. I give a sort of squeak. How *can* he do that?

"I threw up," I tell Matthew, who returns a puzzled frown. "I did—when I first tried that. *All* the way down, I mean. I

10

tried, but I threw up—all over Johnny's hot, steamy cock." I toke and giggle; move my face closer to Matthew's. "Can you . . . um . . . ?"

"Now, wouldn't you like to know?"

"Mm." I nod enthusiastically. But Matthew's not telling. He smiles at me, enigmatically. I bet he *can*. . . .

The uncomed Adonis is fucking the comed Adonis now, over a huge pile of pink and lavender cushions. How sweet! I'm still sucking on my French bread. Not much of a substitute! Matthew hands me back the joint, and I throw the soggy piece of bread down onto my plate.

Matthew moves himself around and stands up. "I'm feeling deliciously horny," he says with a wry grin.

I stare at his bulging trousers. "You look deliciously horny—even if it's not because of me," I say drily. He has that enigmatic smile on his face again. "Why don't you blow the candles out? Then I can blow you." It seems exceedingly funny. "Or you can ass-fuck me, and you won't be able to tell I'm a girl. Well, you can *try* to pretend you can't tell. I mean, with *my* figure!" The idea is making *me* feel deliciously horny.

"Solange . . ." He stares at me.

The thing is, it must have been inevitable that Matthew and I would get around to trying it, one of these sunny days. We've known each other for nearly two years.

I stand up, swaying slightly, giggling. "Matthew, have you *ever* made it with a girl?" I pull my dress down and stand there in my tiny, black, lace-sided, silk panties, and my boots.

"Keep the boots on," Matthew says, inspecting my body carefully.

I stand watching Matthew pull his sweater off and climb out of his pants. I firmly squash an urge to giggle: men always look so *silly*, standing in underpants and socks. He quickly takes the underpants off, and I very nearly *do* giggle: men look even *sillier* standing in socks and a hard-on.

I wiggle out of my panties. Matthew takes them from my hand, looks at them, presses the silk against his cheek, then presses the underneath part to his lips. It turns me on that he's smelling my female smell.

"Can I keep them?" He looks at me seriously, earnestly.

"Yes, of course."

"Don't take the boots off," Matthew repeats almost pleadingly. He comes closer: we're the same height now that he's taken his shoes off.

11

"Have you? Ever made it with a girl?" My giggle isn't from embarrassment or shyness; and he knows I'm not giggling at him. I'm just feeling deliciously stoned.

"When I was . . ." He thinks, pulling at a strand of his blond hair, "eighteen, that's twelve years ago. Twice. Two different girls. Skinny things—like boys. It was *awful*. I only just got inside and I came."

"Poor *baby!*" I giggle, then reach for his cock—erect, but not yet steaming. I take another delicious toke, glance at what's happening on the screen. "Matthew," I tease, "that's disgusting! A nice boy like you having filthy movies like this." We watch in an awed, reverent silence as the other Adonis comes. "Hell," I say to Matthew, gently rubbing his cock in my two hands, "that's given me *a touch of the eager creamies.*" We both smile: Matthew knows my private expression for getting horny.

"Thought it would."

"Matthew, you did it on purpose!"

Matthew grins, then says seriously, "I wanted to try it with you, someone I know and love. I think it will be worthwhile with you. You understand . . . how it is with me."

"Oh, Matthew . . ." There are tears in my eyes for some stupid reason. But then, isn't that me?—little Ms. Sentimental Ass.

We sink onto the carpet as if in slow motion, kissing. It feels nice: warm and gentle.

"Can I touch you?" he asks.

"Yes, of course."

"You're so round and beautiful. You have a *lovely* body, Solange. I've never touched a *woman* before." He reaches for my breasts.

Matthew's touching them gently, squeezing them, feeling them as if they were marshmallows. Circles the nipples with a gentle, tender index finger. "They're so firm and *full*, yet they're so soft, and so *pink*." He buries his face between them. I feel a mouth over a nipple, his fingers on the other one; I let out a moan—the touch almost shocks me. How does he know how to do that? It feels so good! He stops, moves down my body to feel my stomach, then my patch of curly hair. He kisses it.

"You smell so nice." I smile. It's the smell of me and l'Heure Bleue. "Like your panties." He kisses my pussy hair. "Turn over." He feels my ass, kisses it—pushes into it with a finger. "It's lovely. Round and lovely. Everything's so silky and soft. . . ."

"You can fuck it," I tell him.

"I want to fuck your cunt," he says, to my surprise. The word sounds so startlingly crude coming from Matthew. I feel a delightfully warm and loving glow—I'm the only woman he's ever said that to.

He lifts my bottom up, kissing it, and pushes into me, waiting and creamy, from behind. I'm resting my arms on the sofa.

"Why haven't we done this before?" I cry out to him.

"I've never wanted to fuck a woman." He pushes into me, deep—it hurts, it feels good.

"But you're fucking *me*." His fingers grip around me. I push them down to my button. "There, Matthew. *There!*" Of course, he wouldn't know about fingering clits and eating pussy. . . . I move against him. His fingers taunt me and I feel an explosion, a nerve-flash. I cry out loudly as I come— almost a scream, the feeling is so intense. I sense that he's surprised, even startled. Doesn't he *know* that women come so violently, so loudly?

The night is long and beautiful—I almost want to write a poem about it. I haven't felt so satisfied for such a long time. Not since Johnny. It goes on, and on. . . .

His mouth is warm and insistent as he eats me again. He does it so expertly, so sexily. And he's never eaten pussy before!

I cry out as I come again. It feels so damn *good!*

And at last we cuddle up in the fresh, cool bed. The dawn is just peeping through the blinds as he kisses my face and my hair. My body feels so electrical, so deliciously tingly.

Perhaps the feeling will never go. . . .

We fall asleep.

*   *   *

I awake dreamily, sleepily, and let my head rest drowsily on the pillow. I remember where I am. Matthew isn't in the bed. I hear some Bach playing in the lounge. The small alarm clock says 10:30.

I want to see Matthew, to touch him, to talk to him. What will happen between us? We'll always be friends; but will we be lovers again?

I go into the lounge. He's sitting at his work table under the huge, high windows, sketching at something. He sees me and smiles, quickly rises and comes over to me, takes me in his arms and kisses me gently.

"You'll get cold, Solange." He takes my hand and kisses it,

13

leads me wordlessly back to the bedroom, helps me into a short white terry robe. I pull it tightly around me. He smiles, kisses me gently, then runs his fingers through my long silky hair, smiling as he carefully pulls at a tangle. "My come and your silky hair." He kisses me again.

He gets me some coffee and sits watching me drink it. I feel rather like a pet. I don't know what to do, what to say.

"Are you hungry?"

"No, I never eat in the morning."

"All that liquid protein has filled you up." He smiles his lovely smile, soft and gentle, at me.

"Oh, Matthew . . ." I hug myself to him.

"It feels strange." He kisses the side of my neck.

"What does?"

"Feeling soft, soft boobs against my chest."

"Don't you like it?"

"I like yours, Solange." He holds my shoulders, looks closely into my eyes. "I don't think I'd like it with anyone else, though."

"That's 'cos we're friends."

"Yes."

"I can't stay long," I tell him. "Justin and I have a meeting with Gerald." I place my hands on his chest. "I've got to get back to change." Leaning forward, I kiss his lips tenderly.

"Later," he asks. "What are you doing later? For the weekend?"

"I'm going to a concert with Anna tonight and tomorrow."

"Don't tell me!" He grins—he too knows my passion.

"Yes."

He shakes his head, laughing, and pulls me close to him. We hug quietly for a few moments. He looks at me seriously. "I think I haven't had enough of you yet." He runs his fingers slowly through my hair, pulling gently at another tangle, and smiles.

"Oh, Matthew. . . ."

"I don't know what this is, Solange. You know how it is with me, my life-style. I never thought this would, could happen. I don't know what it is. But I don't want to lose it yet. Not yet."

"Do we have to lose anything, Matthew? And even, do we have anything to lose?" We look at each other with funny, lost expressions. There's so much for us to talk about, but we know that now isn't the time. We need time for ourselves— time to think it through.

14

Later, the meeting goes well. The paperback will be out soon. And my fourth book is nearly finished, too.

Pandora is beautiful. Why can't I become Pandora . . . ?

* * *

Madison Square Garden. Packed to capacity, both nights. One night becomes the other: déjà vu. Well, I've certainly been here before. . . .

I take no notice of the screams and the shouts echoing around me, the stamping and the clapping. I take notice only of him. I listen to his words. I listen to his music. How can he stand so near and yet be so far away? How can he, Jan-Toby Axelsson, poet and rock star, who loves words as much as I do, be so totally disconnected from me?

Anna grins at me as we share a joint, and for a moment I think we're both wondering what we're doing here, among the masses.

Long hair. Short hair. In-between hair. Hippies and bikers. Screaming groupies and teenyboppers and neat little schoolgirls. Fifteen-year-olds. Forty-year-olds. Babies papoosed in backpacks. Toddlers randomly toddling. Men and women—overgrown toddlers—too stoned to toddle.

Anna and I take another toke. Everyone around us seems to be smoking. We listen to the band do a number on their own.

I feel that I'm being stared at. I look, for the first time, at the person next to me: a fuzzy, long-haired hippie in an old Afghan coat. He smiles. I smile and hand him the joint, tell him to keep it. He tokes, smiles in delight at the quality, and hands it to his friend—also fuzzy and long-haired—but this one's slightly Neanderthal, weirdly atavistic. I light up a fresh joint. I notice that they're staring fixedly at my gold cigarette case (18 karat, with my name on the front: a present from Rand).

"Great shit," my fuzzy hippie whispers in my ear. His Neanderthal friend leans over, also interested in my goodies. Am I going to get mugged?

I open my case again and give them one each, with a smile. They grin at each other serendipitously: Who is this crazy rich chick in her white silk shirt, French jeans, and Italian handmade leather boots, handing out happiness? "Shit! Thanks, lady." The hippie grins and pecks a warm, furry kiss on my cheek. I giggle with Anna.

The clapping, stomping, and cheering start. *He* walks onto the stage. Jan-Toby Axelsson: thirty-eight. Poet. Well over

15

six feet of great body. Dusty blond hair hanging to his shoulders, falling into his eyes. He's wearing tight jeans and a cream-colored shirt open nearly to the waist. He plays something on his guitar, and a cheer goes up from his fans; he starts to sing, in his deep, husky voice . . .

I feel wiped out. I sit smoking, hiding behind dark glasses, hiding my tearful, stinging eyes as everyone leaves. The fuzzy hippie and his friend invited me and Anna back to their pad. We declined; neither of us felt partial to fuzzy, atavistic Neanderthals.

Especially me. Not now. Not after *his* words.

It's always the same—it was the same the night before, too. No matter how many times I see him, it's always the same: his words, his poetry, his music always find their way right to the center of me. It's like I've always known the words he writes. It's a puzzle to me, a strange puzzle. And it's only with him, not with any other poet, any other singer.

Both nights, I go back to Matthew. He makes love to me. I'd always thought of Matthew as slightly feminine—soft and gentle, qualities I admire. But he's not at all. When he makes love to me, he becomes the most masculine man I've ever had. . . .

I'm living in a happy daze.

Bartok's fourth quartet is still echoing around in my mind from two nights ago.

"You'll be late for work," I tell Matthew. Hell, I sound like a wife! How domesticated . . . how utterly ridiculous! I watch Matthew closely, across the breakfast table, as we sit eating yoghurt and sipping grapefruit juice that he's freshly squeezed. He looks up from his copy of *Christopher Street*.

"It's all right." He touches my hand. "You *are* going back today, are you, then?"

"Yes, Matthew. I have to."

"Yes."

"I don't want to spoil what we've had, Matthew. Our friendship. I should go—I stayed an extra day, as it is."

"Yes." He looks unhappy. I think I do too.

"Matthew, you're gay. And that's nice for you—*right* for you. What we've had—it's because we're *us*, not because we're man and woman. *We* needed to love each other. If we cling to it, it might spoil, Matthew."

"You're not upset about it, are you?" He touches my hand

16

again: his hand soft and warm against the silky smoothness of mine.

" 'Course not, Matthew. It was too nice to be upset about. But—you have your life and I have mine. You couldn't, and shouldn't change your lifestyle, Matthew; you'd hate anything else."

"Yes, I would."

We sit in silence for a while, finishing our yoghurt, sipping our fruit juice. He takes my hand in his, and pauses.

"Let's make a baby together, Solange?"

I gasp. I stare. I don't know what to say. I sip some juice, my hand slightly shaking.

"I'd like a baby, Solange. It's something I really *want*. I'd feel safe with you having my baby. I know you'd look after him, love him—that he'd always be my baby, too."

"Matthew. . . .?" I stare confusedly into his beautiful blue eyes.

"I don't trust anyone else, any other woman, Solange. Not in *my* position."

"Oh, Matthew!" I sink to my knees in front of him, and he cradles my head, kissing it over and over.

Matthew and Solange—Solange and Matthew. We gaze at each other, both knowing that we have to get some space, some distance, between us to be able to think for ourselves, without each feeling the immediacy of the other's presence.

2

Gulley and I are eating shrimp. We like to share. It's warm and dark—an evening full of velvet night, jeweled with stars. The sky, soft, warm, velvety, would be nice to make love on. . . . Why am I by myself, when I want to make love?

A tear falls onto one of Gulley's shrimps, but he doesn't seem to mind. Gulley: the man in my life. My protector and companion. Gulley: a large fluffy ball of marmalade-colored fur. Gulley and I understand each other, love each other.

I feel restless. Should I call Rand? Should I call Matthew? Johnny—perhaps I need to talk to Johnny?

Gulley finishes his shrimps and curls up to sleep on a chair on the terrace. I go for a walk along the beach. I love the warm darkness. I watch a few people jogging past; see a young couple kissing in the sand. Solange, proving she can make it on her own, everything a woman could want to be.

Why are you crying, Solange?

I can see the lights in a few of the houses. In the house next to mine, there's Bill Seagram, famous movie star, and his wife Ginnie. They *adore* their "little farm," as they call it: six kids, dogs, cats, one goat, and some chickens. They've become my friends. My only friends around here, really.

Perhaps I keep myself apart too much. I like to be alone, quiet, playing my records. Writing my words. Reading books.

I *like* being alone in my little secluded house. Perhaps I should get out more, go to more parties, cultivate more friends. I have plenty of opportunities; but people stop asking after a while if you keep on turning them down.

I like my house. The movie star who sold it to me had it decorated in "Fake French." Now, it's modern gentle and warm, nothing garish or ostentatious. Thick shaggy white carpets, Roche-Bobois furniture. Silk walls and a hanging Chinese carpet. Matthew's painting; Blake's engravings. Cacti and bonsai. And books—so many books, books all over the place; I can't live without books.

I leave the warm sand and the warm dreamy night and go home. Climb into bed, listen to Dylan and Axelsson; listen to Vaughan Williams' *Job* and read some of my beloved William Blake.

I should live in Blake's City of Golgonooza—not in Malibu. . . .

*   *   *

Well, this is it. Solange being sociable and her most beautiful: slinky white silk dress, eyes kohled and mascaraed, cheekbones perfectly defined, mouth peachy and pouty, hair Rene Furterer shining and healthy. And gold—gold and diamond earrings; gold chains around my neck. A few gold chain rings for my fingers. One huge black opal on my right hand.

Oh, Solange . . . how can you not get laid tonight?

Solly Steinberg, well-built, fiftyish, jolly, and balding. A pussycat. Successful literary agent—as famous and as well-

18

known as the writers he handles. Sarah, his wife (his third): early thirties, tall, raven-haired, with big brown eyes. Partly Cherokee. Wholly, extremely beautiful.

Holmby Hills—need I say more? The house is elegant—Solly's present for Sarah on their marriage two years ago. He had the house three doors away—three worlds away—when he was married to wife number two.

I'm talking to Sarah. Sarah's pregnant: a son for Solly. My future is secure, she tells me. Gentle Sarah, I'm sure *her* future was *always* secure. . . .

The party is loud and boisterous. His loud, boring bash of the year, Solly jokes, giving me one of his bear hugs. Solly and Justin are affiliated somewhere along their miles and miles of business connections. "Why aren't you at home writing, making us some lovely money?" he jokes.

"You would like me to leave?"

"Never to darken my doorstep again, huh?" Solly laughs: everything wobbles. He hugs me once again before leaving to talk to some other guests. "I'm very glad you came, Solange."

I sip my gin and tonic as I wander around. I see people I know, many people I only recognize: rock stars, country stars, movie stars. Even some writing stars.

Gaylord Christian, literary genius, holding court: outrageous, outspoken, deliciously biting and sardonic. I'd love to talk to him, but I'm sure he doesn't talk to females who bash out popular erotic novels about a sexy witch and the supernatural; not even if they're on the best-seller lists for months and receive great reviews.

I edge my way around the crowd. I talk and chat, even dance with a few people. Solange coming out of her shell, Solange being attractive and witty. Solange wishing she were at home with a book, with her music, with Gulley, feeding him shrimps.

A warm hand touches my naked shoulder, and I turn, slightly startled.

"You do not have a drink."

I look up into the eyes of a tall, impeccably dressed, *very* good-looking man. Late thirties, with a suntanned olive skin; thick black hair down to his collar. An inviting, friendly smile. I think I recognize him, but I can't place him.

He pushes a drink into my hand. I take it and smile. He clinks his glass gently against mine, making the action seem intimate and sensuous. "I've read your Pandora books."

"You have?" Bright, professional smile. Who *is* he? He's certainly not a writer, I always remember them. Business?

Did I meet him with Justin someplace? With Rand? Oh, shit!

"Yes. All three."

"I hope you liked them." Am I *supposed* to recognize him—is he one of *those* celebrities? I feel foolish.

"I thoroughly enjoyed them. I think, too, I would thoroughly enjoy Pandora." Warm, sexy, come-on look from those warm, sexy, come-to-bed eyes. Oh, so that's it! Getting a lay is the name of the game. His accent—it's very English and educated; but behind it. . . . Italian? Spanish? Turkish? Not French, definitely not. Somewhere around the Mediterranean, though.

Those slightly slanted brown eyes are mischievously smiling into mine. What does he want, besides the obvious? And why *me* for starters? There are so many beautiful starlets here—Solly brings them in for his parties, seems to have them on tap.

"I am being rude." He takes my right hand in his—kisses it *firmly;* warm lips on warm flesh. "Daxos Christophidou."

"Oh." I smile sheepishly. I *do* feel foolish. "Hello. . . ." Now, of course, I know who he is: business, Greek, son of Spyros Christophidou.

"I thought it was nice to talk to someone beautiful who *also* knows who Electra and Penelope are. Euripides and Sophocles also." He grins disarmingly. "I get so immensely bored and tired of giggling females, beautiful though they may be, asking me about my yacht and my plane, about my father's island and how much money he has—how much I have." He laughs. Is he making fun of himself, or me?

"Pandora consulted the Oracle of Delphi," I say, "so that makes me eligible to talk with you, does it? Do I pass the qualifying test?"

He looks at me quizzically, but doesn't reply; instead, he takes my elbow and, with gentlemanly grace and panache, ushers me out onto the patio. Tables of food in the garden, a rock band. Me and Daxos Christophidou. I notice other females looking and whispering.

We stand on the flagstones. He looks down at me, his head to one side. "Having a beautiful figure makes you immediately *eligible,*" he smiles.

"It does?" I ask dryly.

"Indisputably so," he grins. "Good figures are good for a good lay—that's my philosophy." He takes a sip of his drink. "But most of them aren't good conversationalists. *After*wards,

20

that is. So, yes—Pandora consulting the Oracle *does* make you eligible."

"What for? A conversation, or a. . . .?"

"Well, *both,* of course." He smiles his come-to-bed smile again.

I burst out laughing. I don't believe this conversation is real. But all the same, I'm enjoying it.

We stroll over to sample some of the caterer's expensive offerings. We're discussing Plato—that is, *he's* talking about Plato. We talk about Irene Papas and Electra. The *Lysistrata* of Aristophanes. He mentions a little place he knows—fantastic couscous. He must take me there—immediately.

"Where is it?" I laugh.

"Athens," he states simply.

I smile lazily back. He's obviously making fun of me again.

"So—we shall leave now?" He's looking at me earnestly—he's really serious

"You're *serious?*"

"I *never* joke about couscous."

My mouth is open. Solly passes by, touches my arm, says something to Daxos. They talk money for a minute. I think I should get out of here. I don't like to be made fun of. But maybe I'm putting *him* down. He must have so many dumb blondes and dizzy redheads. Perhaps he really *is* recognizing me for what I am—for what I want to be: intelligent, witty, educated. Solange—someone's at last recognized you!

He turns to me as Solly ambles off. "We will go now." He takes my elbow. Close up, his cologne smells slightly musky and sensuous.

"But I can't just go off to Athens with someone I don't know." What a lie, but I protest a little, for form's sake. I have of course gone off with someone I didn't know, a couple of times. "You can't be *serious?*" I gaze up into his laughing brown eyes.

"I am very serious." He looks coolly at me, takes a slow sip of his drink. "You're not married. You're not a virgin."

"No. But that's not the point."

"Is it that you don't like *Greece?*" he asks incredulously.

"I love Greece."

He smiles once again. "What part of Greece do you love?"

"Aghios Nikolaos. That's my very favorite place. I feel really at home on Crete."

21

"Ah. . . . Knossos and the Bull Dancers. The Minotaur and the palace of King Minos. Pandora again."

I look composedly at him, but I don't feel in control anymore. I wanted an affair, didn't I? And *what* an affair this one could be! A sexy, classy, rich, sybaritic fuck. Mmm. . . .

"Come—we go, then." He takes my arm once more, insistently. "You have a free week or two, yes?" His hand is warm, inviting. So inviting. . . .

"I'm writing."

"I have a typewriter."

"I . . . ."

"Come—we go to your house to pack. Or, we buy you things."

"But. . . . I. . . ."

"You will be brought back safely. You will be well looked after. *I* myself will see to it that you are looked after."

"I'm sure. . . . But. . . ." One little last protest. He presses my hand. I'm going. . . . I'm going. . . . I'm *going!*

"Daxos!" We turn. Three men and Solly surround Daxos.

"Business, darling." Solly smiles and pats my arm. Daxos is spirited away.

He turns to me as they start towards the house. "Don't go *anywhere*. I'll be *back*."

He smiles. I smile.

I feel weak and wobbly. Phil Westing comes and talks to me. He works for Solly—handles TV dates out here for all us prolific writers bursting to get our books on the best-seller lists. He gets us onto the Carson show, the Mike Douglas show, and if we're lucky, a program with Phil Donahue. We wander into the house.

"I want to read it, Solange. You must let me. It'll be *months* before it's out in hardback—I can't wait." Phil squeezes me in a hug. Dear Phil, he's a close, close friend, and a lover.

Some people join us; I'm introduced, but I don't really take in their names, their faces; I'm miles away, staring at an empty doorway. . . .

A form is filling it, a tall, muscular form. Black trousers. A white silk shirt, close fitting, open nearly to the waist. Dusty blond hair to his shoulders.

I watch the image in the doorway: Jan-Toby Axelsson walks—so ordinarily—into the room.

He stands, hands on hips, quickly scanning the party. I notice a few of the many females in the room become immediately attentive. Their eyes light up—even from here, I can read their minds and the signal they're putting out: How can I *get* to him? And I wonder if they'll be able to. I hide a smile as I watch him looking over a few of the girls, very quickly—an expert surveying the prospects, obviously.

"Hey! Mother!" shouts one of the men standing with Phil. Jan-Toby Axelsson stares, recognizes, smiles, then comes over to hug him.

"Whereya bin, cowboy?" Jan-Toby Axelsson slaps him on the back.

"Jan." Phil shakes his hand. Phil *knows* him?

"Phil, ol' buddy." Jan-Toby Axelsson shakes Phil's hand. Slaps him on the back, too. Tokes on Phil's joint.

"Jan. Meet Solange," Phil introduces us. "Solange delaMer —you know, the writer."

"Sure do. Nice to meet you, Ma'am." He takes my hand; his hand is firm and warm. "Ma'am"—how genteel and polite.

I smile. "Hello." Oh, God, those eyes. . . . large, *very* large —and startling. They're a deep amethyst. Beautifully sexy and penetrating. I've always been a totally weak-kneed female for blue eyes. But his. . . . What really fascinates me about them is that they shine with intelligence. There's a real person in there, keenly *using* them to further his awareness. We're staring at each other, and I can't move my head, my eyes.

"Pandora," he says with a smile and a slight nod. "Literary fantasy. From a Literary Lady." He smiles down at me once again, rocks back on his boot heels. I return his smile. I feel easier: I liked his words. But then, I always do. . . .

He turns slightly. The men talk together. I hazily listen.

"I see you have your eyes glued on the beautiful Beverley, Jan-Toby," Phil says, and Jan-Toby Axelsson grins broadly at him.

I watch them both drooling at the tall, *thin*, raven-haired beauty. She has a blue dress on that's slit up the front—*all* the way up the front—showing off her long shapely legs.

"Solly likes to please his guests—and she won't say no to *you*," Phil continues. "If it's famous she'll fuck it. And anything else you might want her to do, too."

Is that a manic gleam I see in their eyes? They both laugh and I pretend I haven't heard.

"She's rather dumb," Phil goes on confidentially, "but shit, laying *that*—who cares what she's got in her brains?"

Chauvinistic bastards! But I guess that when you're a *superstar*, with all the girls that must throw themselves at

23

your feet (your cock, I should say) you can afford to be chauvinistic and choosy. . . . I see the girl take notice that she's being stared at by Jan-Toby Axelsson. She quickly gives him an interested smile. I guess he's going to get laid tonight!

"Shall I make the introductions?" inquires a grinning Phil. Jan-Toby Axelsson looks evenly at him. Phil winks and says, "Hey, don't put it down until you've tried it. She has one little trick—" He whispers into Jan-Toby Axelsson's ear, and they both burst out laughing. Chauvinistic bastards!

I need to get out of here, to go somewhere quiet and safe. I hurriedly cross the room, noticing on the way that Daxos and Solly still have their attention enmeshed in earnest conversation—it must be about money. Daxos is being eyed by a tall, striking blonde. He doesn't appear to notice her, much less me. Should I go over to him? But I had my chance and I lost it; I don't think I will get any couscous tonight.

My quiet, safe place: Solly's library, where else? Walls full of books. Old-fashioned, with a casual, slippered, smoking-jacketed comfort. Solly knows I love it, and he won't mind my being where I always end up when I come to his house. I shut the door and shut out the party, then flop into one of the brown leather chairs to relax for five minutes before I go home.

I pick up a book lying on the small gilt table next to my chair: Dylan Thomas. His words make me feel myself again:

> Let me escape,
> Be free . . .
> Live self for self,
> And drown the gods in me . . .

Oh, yes, escape! That's what I want—doesn't everybody? That's why I came here, to escape. But escape *to* what? And even, *from* what? Am I just trying to escape from my own fears, my own panic, which may have as their real cause trivial misunderstandings and unreal uncertainties? Philosophical Solange. How come there aren't any great female philosophers? (I asked Johnny that once. He laughed and said that "female" and "philosopher" were mutually exclusive terms).

I read the lines over and over. The door opens and closes behind me, but I don't even turn; I haven't the strength. Only strength enough to keep looking at the words on the page in front of me. Party guests wouldn't bother with the library, anyway.

"I wondered where you disappeared to." A deep resonant voice behind me. I turn, startled; I thought someone had just looked in and gone away again.

Jan-Toby Axelsson comes around the chair and stands in front of me. He peers at the book, smiles. "The Literary Lady likes the Welsh Bard." He raises his full glass and sips from it. He sways slightly, I think he's a bit stoned.

I close the book and watch him walk to the brown leather chesterfield. "Come on then." He pats the sofa behind him. "Come and let's talk—don't get to talk to Literary Ladies much."

He's putting me down. Putting me on. Teasing me. Playing *some* kind of game.

"Come *on*." He beckons impatiently.

I go over and sit, not next to him—he's sitting in the middle of the long sofa—but in the corner, where I feel safer. "I was just about to leave."

"We'll talk a whiles first." He smiles and nods affirmatively.

"What do you want to talk about?" I ask him calmly, as if I've been talking to Jan-Toby Axelsson all my life. He seems different in person, no longer on some stage, miles from reach. He finishes his drink, then carefully places his glass down on the Persian carpet.

"I like Pandora."

"You do?" I wonder if he's telling the truth.

"Sure do, Ma'am."

"I'm rather partial to *your* words."

"Let's form a mutual admiration society, then." He grins lopsidedly, then lights up a handmade cigarette he's been holding in his hand.

What else can I say? "I was in New York last week. I saw your concert. I enjoyed it."

"Which one? Should have come and said hello." He hands me the joint. I feel his fingers next to mine as I take it.

"The Saturday one." I can't tell him *both*.

"That's good. Went better than the Friday one."

I nearly protest, but keep my secret. I toke on the joint, feeling like a stupid little girl, liking it because *he's* toked on it. I hand it back. "Do you *really* like Pandora? My books? I mean, people say they do, but when you ask them specifically, you find that they were only being polite."

"Yeah," he laughs quietly, "That happens to me too. They

25

haven't even *heard* the words, never mind related to what I'm *saying*. But I honestly like what you write." He rubs his finger along the side of his nose.

"I wouldn't have thought that Pandora would be quite your literary, excuse the cliché, cup of tea."

"Oh, wouldn't you have thought. . . ?" He eyes me up and down, a lazy smile on his face. "She's one cool little lady. Does she take after you?"

I stare at him blankly and he hands me the joint again. I'm not sure about this conversation. "Pandora is Pandora," I say dismissively, asserting my ability to stay uninvolved. I puff at the joint once more and hand it back. There's a smile in his eyes—I have the feeling that he's amusing himself with me. That makes two men in one night, teasing me for their own amusement.

"Is there going to be another book about her?" he asks.

"Oh, yes. I've nearly finished it—giving it a final edit."

He smiles gently. "I'm in the middle of an album, too."

"Oh." Again, what to say?

He nods and says, with an affirmative flick of a finger, "I'll get a copy to you."

I take a quick look around the library. He's looking at me with those sexy eyes, and it makes me feel vulnerable. I don't like feeling like that; I don't, often, in fact. I think I should leave now.

I stand up. "I really must go. It's late and I've got a lot of work to do tomorrow."

"Pandora?" He smiles again. Is he genuinely interested, or is it just some more teasing?

"Yes."

He stands up, next to me. "You came in your car?"

"No. Solly sent one for me."

"Didn't know who ya'd be leavin' with, huh?" He looks down with a sardonic grin.

"No!" I glare back angrily; but I think of Daxos. . . .

"Hey! I'm sorry." He shrugs his shoulders. "Didn't mean to offend no Literary Lady." He smiles that sardonic smile again.

I calm myself. "You didn't offend me."

"No—just presumed. I'm sorry."

Observing him, I conclude that he really is. My smile's to show him I'm classy enough to take his teasing good-naturedly.

"Of course you have your old man at home waiting for you?"

26

"No! There's no man," I say slowly, my heart thumping. Why am I feeling nervous and excited? "And if there were, I wouldn't make him wait." I hold out my hand. "It's nice to have met you. I listen to your words a lot. It's always nice to meet someone whose words one likes so much."

He's keeping hold of my hand—it feels so small in his large one. "That's what I think, too, Ma'am."

I pull my hand away. I never actually thought I'd ever meet Jan-Toby Axelsson. I certainly never dreamed the meeting would be like this. It feels out of place, out of time, and decidedly *odd*.

I take a few steps. "Thanks for the chat. It really has been nice to meet you, Jan." I extend my hand again.

He takes it, with the ghost of a bow, a nod. "Nice to have met *you*, Solange." He pronounces it perfectly, with a grin. "A Sun Angel—of the Sea. . . ."

We look at each other, holding hands and start to giggle. *Both* of us.

He laughs. "Lady—you're somethin' else!"

I'm smiling, I can't help it. "Thanks for the chat." I'm feeling warm and glowy as I walk towards the door.

"Hey! Wait up. Where ya goin'?"

I turn. "Home. It's late."

"I'll drive you."

I turn cold.

"Look," he comes over beside me, "I only live a little ways from you, don't I? Can't be but half a mile. I've seen ya."

"You have?" Why don't I admit I know all this?

"Sure thing, Ma'am." He's grinning again—teasing? "Playing with Bill Seagram's kids on the beach."

And I've seen *him*: jogging along the sand, early mornings. "Please . . . I don't want to put you out. I'll get a lift." I continue towards the door. Why does it seem so far away? As I open the door his hand comes up, pushes it closed, holds it shut demandingly. "I'll drive you, Ma'am," he repeats slowly in his measured Texas drawl.

I glance up at him. He's looking at my slinky dress. Does he want a one night stand? Why not the ravishing Beverley? Perhaps he really does prefer brains to long legs. Is *that* what I'm to be, his token, short and curvy, classy and brainy fuck?

"D'ya have some objection to bein' driven home by a friendly neighbor?" He sounds slightly cynical.

"No . . ." I close my eyes for a moment. "Look, I didn't mean to be rude—I just don't want to put you out, take you

27

away from the party—I'm sure it'll go on for hours yet. I just want to get home. I'm tired."

"I'll drive you home, Ma'am." His hand on my shoulder, insistent, authoritative. His skin against my skin: it feels so good, so sensuous, except that there's not *enough* of his skin against enough of mine.

"Thank you," I murmur.

He drives an old, dusty, beat-up black Porsche; slowly, safely. I don't know why, but that surprises me.

"I've just finished reading *Prodigal Father*," he suddenly says as we're nearing home.

"So have I. I really have—just the other day. It *was* good, wasn't it?"

"Expensive." He laughs, then glances at me—a sort of puzzled yet pleased look. I wonder what he's thinking?

Silence.

"It's this next house along," I tell him.

"I know."

"Oh?"

He grins sideways at my surprised look. "I'm *nosey*. I know most faces around here—who goes where. Quite a few are friends, of course."

Of course. . . . I think as he stops. "Thank you." I'm holding out my hand again.

"Don't I get invited in?" He grinning again. "For a drink, or somethin'. See your etchin's? I'd like a drink, please Ma'am."

I look at him with a carefully neutral expression. The scene is familiar. "Shouldn't you be getting home to your wife?"

"She ain't there." He regards me with his head on one side. "I've been let off the leash for a few nights." His tone is cynical.

"Thank you for the lift." I quickly get out of the car. He's out of his side and standing in front of me.

"I won't try nothin'. Promise!" He flashes me a disarming little-boy smile.

"That's not the point at all."

"What *is*?" He's grinning again.

"I really am tired. I really do have a lot of writing to do tomorrow." I stare at the dark blond fuzz on his chest (I love fuzzy chests). He's so close to me that it's about an inch from my face. I suppress a smile and look up at him.

"I wanna see your house. Where you work. You're a fellow writer—I like that." He looks serious about it, too—but is he? "And besides," he grins, "Like I said, I'm just plain *nosey*."

He looks from the house to me. "Swear to God." He puts his hand over his heart. "A quick look, one drink, then I'll be off."

I look up at Jan-Toby Axelsson: that long, dusty-blond hair, those large amethyst eyes. I've loved his words for eleven years, ever since his first big hit single and album. What the fuck's the matter with me?

"One drink." I smile. "One *quick* one."

"Swear to God." He follows me along the path to my house.

Gulley runs to greet me, and I introduce them. I don't think Gulley's very impressed, though.

"Shit! This is *great*." He stands looking around the split-level lounge. Strolls lazily—oh, so lazily—down into the lower section, lets himself flop back onto one of the sofas.

"No fuckin' frills and bows and things *wives* like."

I feel pleased and excited that he likes my house, that he likes *me!* "What would you like to drink?"

"Scotch, please, Ma'am."

"I have Chivas Regal." I nervously chatter on as I clunk ice into his glass. "I don't drink much. I've got a large selection, but I'm not really sure what they all taste like."

"You don't need a selection if you've got Chivas," he says with a wide grin.

I pour it for him; he smiles, lifts it to me, takes a sip. "Where do you write, then?"

"In my study."

"Can I see it?"

"Ye-es. . . ."

He follows me. I can feel his eyes on me. Is my ass wiggling just right? A sexy, *classy* sort of wiggle. Damn! Who's giving whom the come-on now, Little Ms. Classy-Ass?

He looks around observantly. "Shit, this is *great!*" he repeats himself. *I* think so: it's spacious, modern and white, with books everywhere. A huge modern desk: typewriter, papers, books, but *no* telephone. He sees the stereo unit; there's an album of his leaning against it.

"I was playing it earlier," I tell him shyly.

He goes over and sees a tape of Dylan's half pulled out of the 8-track. Kristofferson's *Easter Island* lies on the floor next to Dylan's *Street Legal*. An album of Van Cliburn playing Rachmaninoff's second piano concerto. Another of Ashkenazy's.

"I don't know much about classical." He shrugs. "A simple cowboy, that's me." He goes over to my desk, picks up some

29

of the typed pages. "Hey—I like this. It flows good." He turns and looks at me, puts the pages down. There's a slightly puzzled look on his face. I feel a warm happiness permeating me. He likes my words.

"You can see, I *am* in the middle of a lot of writing." I feel awkward and shy. I just want him to finish his drink and go.

He follows me back to the lounge, sits down, flops back into the corner of the sofa. I watch him finish his drink, and then he waves the glass at me. "Do I get another?"

"I said one. A quick one."

"That was half a one, Ma'am." He winks.

"Ma'am"—no one's called me that before. Such Texas cowboy gentility! And I *wanted* to meet a Texan. I take his glass, throw some ice into it, pour in some more Scotch, hand it to him. "Perhaps you shouldn't drink so much."

"I don't. Just at parties—*when* I go to one. Or the occasional binge with Joel and the boys when we're on the road. I ain't one of ya stereotyped boozin', pill-poppin', coke-snortin' rock stars, ya know. A clean-livin' cowboy, that's me," he adds complacently, patting the sofa next to him; and, as I can't think straight anymore, I sit down next to him.

He looks around the room. It's slightly untidy, as usual. Books everywhere—in units around the walls, as in my study and bedroom. Plus the odd one on a table, on a chair, on the floor.

"So many books. It's great. The Lady obviously reads a lot."

"Don't you have a lot of books?"

For a moment he looks irritated. He crunches some ice, takes a sip of his Chivas Regal. "Everythin's so fuckin' *tidy*."

"I'm by myself. It's different. I can have things as I want."

"I've got a nice den, my study. Built it myself," he says into his drink. He's nearly finished it and I'm *not* going to give him another one.

"That's good. Everyone should have some space for themselves."

"I've got the fuckin' space. But it's the fuckin' *time* to myself I don't seem to get." He looks around him again. "Where's your bedroom?"

Oh, no! "It's in a handy place," I say drily. "For when I need it."

He grins. Looks at me for a moment. Takes a sip on his

drink. Looks at me again. "I wanna fuck you." He reaches out, touches my face gently. Trails his finger down my neck, my shoulder, my arm.

"Pardon?" I pull myself away from his touch. I'm beginning to feel slightly sick. I don't want this to go any further. I want him *gone*.

"I said, I *want* to *fuck* you." Suddenly as he brushes some hair out of his eyes, he looks like a little boy.

"I think you should go home. I think you need some sleep."

"Let's fuck and then sleep—together. I'd like that, please, Ma'am."

"I really would like you to go."

"I don't want to!" He finishes his Scotch.

"I'm sorry," I smile, directly but dispassionately, "I don't go in for one night stands. And especially not with married men."

He just sits there and looks at me—looks, with those beautiful amethyst eyes of his. What's the matter with you, Solange? You know you want him. "Please go. . . ."

"You really want that?" He rubs the side of his nose, contemplatively.

"Yes, I do. Please."

He stands up. "Didn't want to offend ya none, Ma'am."

"You haven't. Honestly." I reach out and put my hand on his arm, smile up at him. "Let me see you out."

He follows me to the front door. "Thank you for bringing me home." He looks at me. I don't think he's quite sure what's happening, why I'm asking him to leave. "I really do appreciate it." I touch his arm again.

His hand on the doorframe, he stands and looks at me with a lopsided grin. "The Literary Lady *is* a lady. . . ."

I return the smile. I don't feel that he's teasing anymore—he's serious.

"The Poet's a gentleman," I reply hopefully, pleased with myself for thinking of it.

He takes me by the shoulders, gently rubs his hands up and down my arms. I know he's going to kiss me. He does. His kiss is hard. His lips are hard. I think I'll always feel them. . . .

"You're one beautiful lady." He turns and walks away, gets into his car. We look at each other for the longest moment. He nods once, drives away.

Jan-Toby Axelsson—neighbor: good deed done, to drive a stranded female home.

31

Jan-Toby Axelsson—back on his pedestal: poet, rock star, father, husband.

I walk into the lounge, flop down onto the sofa where he was sitting. I'm still wondering why I sent him away. I pick up his empty glass, smile to myself: "I'll never wash it again," I say, giggling, and wonder what he fucks like . . .

*　*　*

I'm aware of something warm, tickling me, as I come up from a dream. Up from sleep. Up to daylight, to an approximate consciousness.

Gulley's standing on me, purring. His whiskers are what's tickling me. He wants his breakfast.

"Hello, Gulley." I sleepily rub his fur. He purrs and nuzzles his nose into my neck.

I stretch out languidly; I really don't want to get up yet. Gulley knows this: He meows, pounds up and down on the pillow next to my ear. "Oh, Gulley"

As usual, he's won. Some liberated female I am! Even my male chauvinist cat can do anything he wants with me!

I get Gulley's breakfast, make myself some coffee.

I hear the front door and Miriam comes into the kitchen. "Well. . . . Some sight for *sore eyes!*" she says. "Good job I'm not the *milkman.*"

"Hello, love." I watch Miriam, so bright and bouncy, pour herself some coffee. Her dark brown eyes seem extra shiny this morning.

"*Hadn't* you better put something *on?*"

I only realize what she means when I look down and see myself naked. "Mm." I finish my coffee.

"Enough to turn a girl *gay,*" she jokes as I exit.

"Wanna give it a try?" I poke my head back around the door.

"I *have,* darling—but I just *can't* do *without* that seven inches."

"Know what you mean." I giggle, and head for the shower.

Miriam Hedgeworth. My secretary; self-appointed housekeeper and food-buyer, but most of all my friend and confidante. She used to work for my publisher in New York but decided she wanted to give California a try. She came to me originally as my secretary—I get so much mail—and also to type my manuscripts. But Miriam likes organizing, loves running everything, and always *has* to be doing something. She got into dusting and polishing, tidying and rearranging, even though we have a lady (Elena, and she's become a friend, too) who comes in twice a week for the cleaning and laundry.

Miriam has a room here but goes back to her own little expensive pad and her own lovers in Venice most nights. She's twenty-nine and divorced; a hundred and two pounds of slim prettiness, with dark brown curls and a beautiful, glowing, coffee-colored skin. Needless to say, Miriam makes me feel fat; however, we still get on wonderfully. We never have to tell each other things—what to do, what not to do, things like that.

After my shower I find her sitting, reading some mail, on the seafront terrace. She's in a billowy yellow cotton dress. She pours orange juice for us. I sit down and stretch out my legs, put them up on the coffee table.

"Are they *new?*" she asks, nodding at my tight black cotton gauze pants, my wooden high-heels (so very high), my rose-pink, shirred cotton gauze tube-top.

"It's all new. Picked them up at Bloomy's when I was there."

"About *time*. You *never* buy enough *clothes*. I *mean*, a good day's *shopping* to you is raiding a *book* store! Christ, if *I* had your bread, I'd *never* stop buying clothes!"

She hands me one of the letters: Some sweet old lady has sent me an incantation for a love potion. You have to chant it at full moon (what else!) over a small fire in a graveyard on a Sunday at the hour of Venus—shit, 4 A.M.! I turn the page. The love potion recipe is written on the back. I read it out loud: " 'A handful each of rosemary, myrrh, coriander, mastic, verdigris, and broomstraw from a graveyard.' Oh, and 'cumin.' "

"Mustn't forget the *comin'*," Miriam giggles—an upward arpeggio.

"Shall we try it out?"

Miriam considers. "How about O.J. and Billy Dee . . . Or *Kris?* Or *Warren?*" She goes dreamy-eyed.

"Let me know if it works," I say, grinning again, wryly.

"You look *tired*."

"Do I?" I do still feel tired, actually.

"Did you go to that party?"

"Yes." I tell her about Daxos Christophidou.

"What!!" She swings herself around, leans her elbows on her knees, props her glasses up on her mass of curls so that she can observe me closely. "You *mean* you came *home?* Alone? You didn't go with *Daxos Christophidou?*"

33

"No. I'm still here."

"Solange, you're *crazy!* What's the *matter* with you?"

"I don't know . . . the moment sort of slipped by."

"Slipped by!" She grabs my arm, astonished and annoyed with me. "My *God!* You could have been giving him *head*—all the way to *Greece!"*

I laugh.

"Listen," she says, "I'm going to be off after lunch. Up to Frisco, for my two days."

Miriam has a rich businessman in Frisco. Her rich, white, dudie stud, she calls him. She spends a few days a month up there with him. He likes her to give him head—to eat her (Miriam enjoys telling me these details). He won't have actual intercourse with her—he doesn't want to be unfaithful to his wife!

I wave Miriam off and go and do some work.

Pandora. How I love writing about her. Pandora is me in another time, another place. She would have gone with Daxos without the slightest hesitation. Pandora would have fucked Jan, there and then. She would have given him so much love, so much perfect sex, so much of herself that he would never have left, would have stayed and stayed for . . . an eternity . . . ?

Can I *really* be Pandora?

The phone rings. It's Johnny Brandigan, friend and lover, the one time passion of my life.

We talk, and it's like he's standing right there in front of me: I see those blue, blue eyes, deep set and always smiling, his beautiful black hair, down past his shoulders, thick and lustrous, wonderful to grab hold of when we're fucking. He has a mustache and a tidy beard; I've never seen him without them.

"I'll be seeing you soon, then?" I ask.

"Yes, poppet." He always calls me that, among other endearments, has done so for twelve years. His voice is deep, with a soft, Irish brogue, somewhat Americanized now.

"Take care." I smile.

"I'll be comin' soon, me little darlin'."

What was it that happened to Johnny—to me? Why didn't we succeed and make it together?

I feel restless, without being quite sure why. I try to do some more work, only to angrily tear it up.

34

The door buzzer jolts me. I pause, thinking maybe they'll go away, but it keeps buzzing, one solid wall of sound. I rush to the door, nearly tripping on my high heels, to fling it open.

"Ma'am." It's Jan-Toby Axelsson, a long-stemmed rose in his hand. He presents it to me.

"Thank you." We stand looking at each other. I feel surprised, startled; I didn't expect this.

"No hard feelin's?" He gives me an easy smile.

"No—why should there be?"

"Just thought I angered you up some, Ma'am." Those twangy Texan vowels of his sound so nice.

"No. Really, you didn't."

He leans on the doorframe, swinging his gold-rimmed aviator sunglasses around in his hand. Dressed in jeans and tight black tee shirt, rocking back on his boot heels.

"I was an asshole. Doin' my macho number. I'm not really like that. And you don't come on to a *lady* like a fuckin' groupie."

"You're not the first man that's come on to me that way."

"Don't think I'll be the last, either, lady."

I look at him and can't help smiling. "God, I hope not."

He grins. "I didn't see your etchin's last night."

"Mm?"

"I said a drink and a look at your etchin's. I had the drink . . ."

"I don't have any etchings." I inhale the rose's gentle perfume, keeping my eyes fixed on him.

He looks at me carefully, thinking, rubs his finger along the side of his nose. "That's that, then." He smiles, nods, says, "Ma'am," then walks away.

I feel the proverbial sinking in the stomach: a moment of sheer blind panic.

He turns back and looks at me. "Nice knowin' ya, Literary Lady." He turns away, a sardonic grin on his face.

I breathlessly watch him begin to walk to the gate; the panic presses in on me. "I have some *engravings*," I manage to say.

He turns back quickly, stands still. Staring at me.

"Would you like to see them?"

He puts his head back, stands with his hands on his hips, frowns slightly. "Lady . . . I thought you'd never ask." He follows me inside. Helps himself to a drink. "Where's these *engravin's*, then?"

"In my . . . bedroom."

"Handy."

"You think so?"

"You never can tell."

"You can't?"

"Not with a Literary Lady."

I stare up into his teasing eyes, but I know I'd better not do that. How could you say no to those eyes?

"Who did these engravings?"

"Blake."

He stares down at me, gives a slightly puzzled frown. "Better show them to me, please, Ma'am." He takes a drink. Looks at his glass; empties it.

"This way." I can feel his presence close behind me; I feel awkward, because I know he's watching my classy-ass as we climb the open-work stairs.

"Jesus, you look pretty," he says behind me, and I can't help smiling. I do love his work: his words, his music. He's a shiny hero from afar. But I *won't* be used, not by him or any man.

I angrily fling open the door of my bedroom. It's a huge room. White—so very white. Everything's tidy, I'm relieved to see.

"There they are." I point to the far wall: my engravings and, also, actually, illuminated etchings. They are originals and very, very precious. I quickly go over to the stereo and tidy up the few records lying around. I watch him go over and stand studying the engravings.

"I went to the exhibition of his work," I say. "In London. I went day after day. I think the guards thought I was planning a heist. If only I could have. . . ."

He laughs. "They're incredible. Which is your favorite?"

I go and stand by him, look up at him, my head just reaching his shoulder. "This one." I point to the man with the baby angel on his shoulders—the frontispiece of *Songs of Experience*. "And this."—Blake's *Vision of Creation*, Jehovah using the compasses. "And of course this one especially"— *The Tyger*. Then I point to the sixth engraving—the baby angel hatching out of the egg. "And I adore this—it's been my *special* favorite since I was a little girl. It was the first one my parents gave me—because I was a sun-angel. I'm so lucky to have them; his work is priceless, of course. They were my grandfather's."

He looks down at me with a smile, and says, "Little, ain't ya?" He seems to be puzzling over something. He moves,

36

suddenly, quickly, striding over to the bed, where he picks up a few of the various books of poetry lying around on the floor. Blake. Milton. Coleridge. Moore. Scott. Auden. Yeats. He stares at an old, leather-bound volume of Conrad.

"I always seem to have those ones near me," I say defensively, again feeling a stupid, confining shyness. He's looking at me with that puzzled expression again, a rather beautiful expression, actually. But I wish I knew what the hell he's puzzling out.

He picks up a book of Macniece's poems, looks at a page, smiles, puts it down, picks up another book. "You like John Brandigan?"

"Yes. Very much. I met him in college."

"He's older than you," he comments as he turns the pages, reading a little here and there.

"Yes. Ten years older. I was in my first year; he was a Fellow."

"Got yourself a first class honors."

"Yes." Oh, that inane shyness again! He must have read that detail from a book jacket of mine.

"Clever little lady," he grins and winks, "ain't ya?"

"That's nice—coming from a magna cum laude, Phi Beta Kappa."

That lopsided grin again. "I met Brandigan once at Berkeley. Long after he'd left Oxford, of course. I went back there for a reunion, and he was on a lecture tour. I went and listened in. I like the man's words."

"So do I."

"Do you see him?"

"Occasionally. Actually, I was talking to him on the phone only just before you came. He lives in Monterey."

He slowly smiles that lazy, lopsided smile. "You two fuck?"

"You've *seen* my engravings," I tell him haughtily, ignoring his question.

"What else ya got to show me?" He reaches down and smoothes the honey suede of the waterbed's frame. "Shit, this is nice!" He looks around, still smiling, caresses the suede again. "We have one of those brass things—with a canopy, all fuckin' pink lace and frills." He rubs his nose and regards me steadily. I'd better get him out of the bedroom.

"Would you like some coffee? Anything to eat?"

"I'd like to eat *you*." Intently staring at me.

I feel myself blushing. The breed of man that calls you "lady" also seems to be the breed that's very direct. I first

37

encountered this directness with Johnny. The first month I knew him, I went around with a permanent blush on my face—or it felt like that at nineteen, when I was totally naive and innocent. All the same, I think with a private smile, I rather like that breed of man.

"Hey! I'm bein' an asshole again," he winks.

"I'll get some coffee." I walk quickly from the bedroom; I can feel him striding to catch up with me. He grabs hold of my arms, pulls me around.

"I'm sorry," he insists. But his eyes are still shining with amusement. Arrogant bastard!

Keep your cool, Solange! Be the lady—the Literary Lady!

"You smell good," he says. "What is it?"

"L'Heure Bleue," I reply in my perfect French accent, then realize he may not know what it means. "The Blue Hour."

"It's sexy." He rubs his hands on my arms and I tense automatically. "Like your accent."

"*I* don't have an accent. *You* have an accent."

He laughs. "You do *so*. What is it?"

"I guess it's a mixture of refined English and aristocratic French," I say with a grin.

"Sounds *sexy* . . ." Teasing me again. "Soft and gentle. You say soft g's and long a's. *Classy!*" Another grin. "Or should I say, *clahssy?*"

"When I was little, I used to talk in French *and* English, all mixed up." Why am I telling him this?

"Your ma's French, huh? I read that. A writer, too."

"Yes." I'm surprised he knows this. "She's *very* good."

We stand looking at each other. I don't know what's going on. "How about I get us that coffee?" I ask.

"Okay." He follows me into the kitchen and watches me put the coffee on to drip, his fingers drumming on the huge silver concho buckle of his wide leather belt, which also has smaller conchos all around it. The buckle, I notice, is engraved and beautifully inlaid with carved turquoise.

"Why don't you go and sit in the lounge? I'll bring it in."

"Sure thing, Literary Lady." He leaves the kitchen. I think he realizes . . .

I take the coffee into the lounge, but he's not there. I find him in my study. I'm a bit annoyed: he's reading some more of my new writing—more about Pandora's private life. Private until *I* publish it, that is.

"Do you write much a day? How many hours do you work?"

I answer these and further inquisitive questions.

"Jesus, lady, that's great! I wish I could." His smile says he means it. He's rubbing the side of his nose again, a habit, like his sexy, lopsided smile.

"Come and have the coffee."

We go back into the lounge and I pour the coffee. Gulley comes in and stares at us both, very indignantly.

"Why d'ya call him Gulley?"

"His full name's Gulley Jimson."

"Of course!" He claps his palm to his forehead. "Joyce Cary—*The Horse's Mouth.*"

I grin, pleased that he knows. "I couldn't resist calling him that. Gulley Jimson is one of my very favorite characters. Actually, I'm totally in love with him." Gulley yawns at me.

"I like him too. He's got to be a cool dude, thinking old Billy Blake was the greatest Englishman that ever lived."

I laugh lightheartedly—the first time I've been able to with this man. I feel, suddenly, altogether easier, knowing that from that moment we've become friends. I feel so pleased: I don't find too many people who even know of, let alone *worship* Blake, as I've always done since a child.

We drink our coffee, talking about Blake, Yeats, and the biography, *Prodigal Father*. He suddenly looks at me for a long time. Puts his coffee cup down.

"It's so good to talk to somebody about something I love. Don't get a chance to do that often." He smiles. "Well, not to a beautiful Literary Lady, anyway. I haven't had a discussion about literature with a lady since I was at college. There ain't that many people, especially ladies, into Blake, Yeats, and Auden. Faulkner and Conrad—they're my *special* favorites."

"Yes, they're *my* special people too."

He gives me that look again; we continue to stare unabashedly at each other, smiling, enjoying each other's company, and enjoying the spectral company of the writers we admire.

"I want to fuck you," he says quietly.

I can feel tears coming to my eyes. "I don't want you to. . . . I couldn't handle it." I look awkwardly around me, feeling so utterly foolish at my admission.

"Why not? Why couldn't you?"

"You're a married man. A *happily* married man. I couldn't handle that." Why am I saying these things? Me, who only a few days ago was hoping to get involved, *wanting* to get involved, to have a brief delightful affair with a married man. I guess it must be because, as usual, I've picked the wrong man: I'd want an *everlasting* affair with *this* one. "It's nice being friends, talking about literature," I add.

39

"Haven't you ever fucked with a married man, then?" Oh, why doesn't he *drop* the subject?

"Y-yes. . . . but that was different." George, a publishing executive, but he was just a sexy weekend in his New York apartment, never to be seen again. He wasn't someone I'd admired from afar. No, this is different; this could, with a terrifying power, expose me to emotional stresses that I know I couldn't handle.

"I'm sorry, Jan." Saying his name—it seems so strange, his being so close to me, me calling him by his name. "But tell me, Mr. Axelsson, just what *are* you doing here? *Why* did you come back?" He flashes me a puzzled frown. "Ah—it must be my amazing intellect! Didn't I hear you say on Johnny Carson once that you belonged to Mensa, too?" I tease. "Of course . . . didn't you say to Phil that you wanted something brainy and classy to fuck for a change? Is that it? Am *I* your token classy and brainy fuck?" Oh, *why* is he giving me that special, lopsided grin?

I go over and stand by the French windows, watching Gulley, asleep under the willow tree. "Do you want some more coffee? I begin, but he comes over, stands beside me. I turn and look out at the side garden again. I've somehow got to turn the conversation around to his going, so that he *will* leave, so that I can be safe again. I can feel and hear my heart thumping away.

He encloses me in his arms. I'm trapped, but it feels so good. He puts his hands over my breasts, feeling them through the thin material, giving me small, electrical, tingly shivers.

"I want to fuck you." He kisses the side of my neck, and the shivers and tingles increase. He swings me around and pulls me closer still. He's kissing me. "I want to make love to you, Solange."

I push myself away from him. He's touching my bare arms, his hands still electrical. "Make love to me?" I ask slowly, terribly aware of his hands, of his skin on my skin.

"Yes." He kisses me again, his intolerably persuasive hands on my bare back. His voice is a whisper as he pulls me even closer. "I *want* to make *love* to you. . . .

I look at him. *"That* you can do," I whisper, just before he kisses me once more.

*　　*　　*

I'm in a dream world—a world of sensuous feeling, where everything is so perfect.

It's not just our bodies that are fucking, but our minds. It's *all* melding, everything we have, everything we are, deep, deep inside, because he's Jan and I'm Solange. We've found each other again. Two sides of a puzzle—together and fitting exactly. Our words tell us that. I always recognized his words; he always recognized mine. *So why did we take so long to recognize each other?*

I can't move. I'm cradled in his arms while he's asleep. I can feel his gentle breathing. I feel damp and sticky, disheveled and oh, so perfect. Everything smells so sexy. He wakes up and kisses me.

"Are you hungry?" I whisper.

"Starved," he replies.

"I'll make us something."

"Yes, please, darlin'." He caresses my ass.

He gets up and goes to the bathroom; I follow him, watch him pee. Behind him, I lean over and kiss his ass, reach around him and stroke him as he's peeing. He laughs with delight. I caress his ass once more, kiss it—it's a great ass.

Back in the bedroom, he climbs into his jeans; I put on a long, slit-to-the-waist, cream silk caftan.

He sits in the lounge browsing through the Iris Murdoch book I'm rereading, listening to Dylan, while I'm scrambling eggs and making salad. As we eat, we chat like two excited children: he likes Iris Murdoch too. And he digs Tom Robbins and Ashbery as much as I do. He's even *heard* of Louis Macniece and Philip Larkin. He likes Tom Moore too. And our mutually favorite Kipling is *Kim*. By an unsurprising coincidence, neither of us knows quite what to make of Ezra Pound, but Jan tends to the opinion that he was a "pretentious old mystificator," which makes me giggle.

How can two people from such different backgrounds be so similar? A loving intimacy is engulfing us, surrounding us with its persistent closeness. I wonder how long it will stay, and if we'll ever have it again.

It's very late, and we're smoking some grass, cuddled up on the sofa, still talking about books, writers, poets, poems, even about our doctoral theses. I grin at him with a fluttering of eyelashes, "I'll show you my thesis if you'll show me yours."

"Let's go to bed," he whispers as we finish the grass.

"Yes, please. . . ." He carries me there.

It's a dream: when I awake, I'll hear his voice singing; I'll still be in New York, watching his performance—

No, that's not it—

It's a dream: but when I awake, I'll still be in Sollys' library, having fallen asleep reading Dylan Thomas. Jan won't have come in—he won't come in.

No, that's not it—

It's a dream: but I fell asleep over my work after Miriam left. When I awake, he won't return, won't offer me a rose—and himself.

No. . . . no, that's not it either. . . .

"Easy, now. Slowly. *Slowly.*"

It's *his* voice. It's whispering in my ear. I can't move, he's heavy, pressing me beneath him, holding my hands above my head. Our bodies are moving together. The bed won't let us stop; it's moving us. Why is he so deep inside me? No one's ever been that deep inside me. Perhaps I've never let anyone. . . . Perhaps I've never given so much. . . . Am I trying to take *him* inside me?

He stops, kneels up, and I look at him—his hair all around his face, his eyes almost wild. His chest hair is wet; beads of our mingled sweat running down to his dusty-blond cock-hair and onto his cock, glistening and wet.

He watches me as he kneels between my widespread legs. His erection—perfection—sways slightly as we move.

His fingers caress me. He presses a finger onto my magic button of happiness, and an electrical shock, so great that I cry out, runs through me.

"I want to *see* you come," he says. His voice sounds hoarse. I think I hear a hint of wonderment in it. "Jesus, you look so beautiful when you come—you blush so pink." Why did he say that? You don't *have* to say things like that to one-night stands!

I can't think anymore. I can only feel his fingers; the pressing, the rubbing, the stroking, the fondling. I'm not me anymore, there's just feeling—beautiful feeling. I cry out as I come, moaning loudly and pushing against his hand as it pushes against me.

How long does it take me before I settle down? Perhaps it just seems like a lifetime.

I'm lying still; he's kneeling between my legs. I look into his eyes for a moment, and have to close mine. It's his mouth, his tongue between my legs. An intimate meeting of flesh. *No—don't do that!* I can't come again! I just can't. I can't. *I* can't!

He laughs, leaning up on his elbows, looking at me. "I've never felt a woman come before. I could *feel* it—it's incredi-

42

ble." He kisses me. We're chewing at each other, enjoying our mouths, the sexy taste.

"You melted. . . ." Telling me all this seems to delight him. I wonder why? He's looking at me with that puzzled expression again, and I'm trying to puzzle out what he's thinking. He kisses me quickly. "Shit, lady, you certainly can't fake that!"

"I've *never* faked a come," I tell him, breathlessly but indignantly.

He kneels back on the bed, pulls me into his arms. The bed wobbles violently. "You come so *easily*—so *much*. Jesus, lady, I could become addicted, I tell ya." I wonder how many women he says that to, and then I immediately wonder why I'm being cynical at a time like this.

He moves suddenly, pulls me with him, kissing. We tumble onto the floor. "It's better here," he whispers and pulls me into his arms, kissing me again. He's gently rubbing his cock against my sticky little button.

"Come into me," I cry out, impatient. I want to feel him inside me. . . . and besides, how long do we have, a few more hours?

He pulls me, my legs up around his waist. "Oh!" It hurts, it went in so deep. It's a violent feeling, fucking on the floor. No gentle moving, no gentle giving, no waterbed wave motion. Each thrust comes as a sudden shock.

We're looking at each other. His hands are on either side of my head, his arms outstretched. I don't think I've ever looked at someone for so long. We're just looking; but it's as though our eyes are fucking. It's not fair! *It shouldn't be this good with someone I can't have!*

It's hurting me, I'm burning. But he doesn't stop. Every woman's dream: an everlasting fuck. I scream out involuntarily—my happy little cunt's coming again.

He's kissing me, chewing on my neck, chewing on my lips. I feel so sore. I need his soothing come: balm for a hurting little pussy. I grip his sexy ass; I feel him tense, and he cries out hoarsely; I feel his warm come, beautiful soothing come, inside me.

He completely smothers me and I only wish that I could stay smothered by him. Suddenly I'm crying.

He rolls over, pulls me into his arms. "Why are you crying?" His voice, so deep, is gentle. "What's the matter, darlin'?"

"Don't you know that women cry sometimes when they've come?" I'm sobbing and he's caressing my hair.

43

"I've read that. Never had it happen before, though. . . . It's nice," he says quietly, kissing me.

I put my arms around his neck, cuddle him as closely as I can. I don't care anymore what he thinks of me. I can't control my feelings, anymore, not after what we've just shared. I'm still sobbing slightly, my body, on top of his, melting into him, clinging, and becoming him.

"It feels like we're sharing the same skin," I whisper. Then I realize what I've said—and that he may not want me to say anything so intimate.

He doesn't say anything, he just *looks,* with that puzzled little lost look of his. One of my tears plops itself onto his chest. He touches it with his finger, then licks it. I try to smile through my tears: I don't want him to think that I'm *stupid,* crying because I love what he did to me, what I did to him, what we did to each other, crying because I love . . . him.

I kiss and lick his lips, his face, his eyes. Why is he smiling at me so? I move down his body, kissing and licking. I take his fucked-out cock, all limp and sticky with his come, in my hands. I lick it clean for him, then crawl back into his arms, only to see that puzzled, dreamy look in his eyes before he closes them. He's smiling again. . . .

*　　*　　*

I awake. Where am I? I move, and the bed wobbles. I suddenly remember everything, every little detail. But why am I on the bed, then? He put me up here, obviously. But where is he?

I sit up, and the bed wobbles violently. I realize: he's gone—a tactful exit. Leave the chick's pad while she's asleep. No need to say anything then. No need for polite, banal chatter then. No embarrassment; no feelings; no nothing.

A great night; a great chick; a great lay. Next groupie, please! I feel my chin wobbling as my eyes fill with tears, unwelcome and unwanted tears.

What *else* did you expect? Love and roses forever? Just because you've admired him from afar—that doesn't make any difference to him. Just because he's no longer Jan-Toby Axelsson, superstar, to you, but now Jan, friend and lover—*that* doesn't make any difference, either. Two halves of a puzzle, indeed! Maybe he just doesn't want his half to fit your half. Just remember *him* as a great night, a great lay; if you're lucky, that's how he'll remember you.

I was right, though: I shouldn't have fucked him. I knew I

44

would feel like this—and I shouldn't have done it if I couldn't handle it.

But *that's* stupid and childish! Why *can't* I handle it? Ms. Classy-Ass could handle the other brief encounters, the other delicious little fucks; so why not this delicious little fuck?

Everything smells so sexy; I'm so sticky. The sheets stained with his come. I kneel up, his come runs from me. I touch it, taste it on my fingers. I stand up. I feel a bit shaky: so much fucking and coming, I feel a bit achy from it all—how masochistically gorgeous!

I rub my sticky little pussy, angrily. His sex—in me, on me. Need a shower; need some coffee. A good strong dose of caffeine, that's what I need. I glance at the clock—8:30. Gulley will want his breakfast. Better get it for him, before he does his bullying, male chauvinist cat act on me.

I look back at the bed. Why didn't he say good-bye? I sniff hard—I'm not going to cry! At least the puzzle fit together for a little while. . . .

"Gulley," I call to him as I near the kitchen door, "break . . ." I stand startled, paralyzed.

"Mornin', Ma'am. Didn't wanna wake ya. You were sleepin' so perfectly."

My mouth open, I stand looking at Jan, who sits at the breakfast nook table, with Gulley washing his paws next to him.

Jan smiles. "I put you back on the bed. *I've* slept on quite a few floors in my time, but I didn't think you had." He stands up and comes over. He's naked, but that's okay, so am I. "Don't you have anything to say to me?" He gives a sudden wicked grin, holds my shoulders, gives me a quick kiss.

"I thought you . . . I thought you'd gone." We stand looking at each other.

"Hasty retreat, huh?" He pulls me to him, and we're kissing. He rubs his hands on my ass, grips a cheek in each hand; it feels nice. I can't move. "I wouldn't go—not like that. Not with you."

Not with me? What does he mean by that? I let myself be led over to the chair and pulled onto his lap. I hug myself to him; his arms are tight around my waist. "Listen," he says against my neck, "I can guess what you're thinking: another one-night stand. Another chick to lay, give me head, get my rocks off. But it wasn't—it wasn't like that, no way. I can always get that—I *do* get it, whenever I want it. But not you. Not with *you*."

I look up into his eyes, searching. I think he means it, but

45

what's he *really* thinking, sitting there so close, looking so inscrutably inscrutable?

Okay, Solange, get yourself together. Show him you're the classy-assed Literary Lady he thinks you are. That you're enjoying this quick fling as much as he is—and *as* a quick fling, nothing more.

He kisses me.

That's it, Solange, you've got a chance at one more day and maybe one more night. Take it, don't mess it up.

We shower together. I dress in a long, strapless, billowy pink gauze dress, make myself look as beautiful as I can. I make us fresh coffee, take it out onto the terrace for us. We sit sipping coffee and reading my mail. He's laughing at some of the letters.

"I thought I received some dippy mail—but some of these, Jee-zus!"

It feels nice, just sitting out here doing something as ordinary, mundane, as reading mail.

"Here's a guy who wants to fuck you." He looks sideways, grins, flips the letter across to me.

I read it and giggle. "I guess you must get your share of offers, too?"

"You better believe it." He grins sidelong. "Some chick, last week, she sent me her panties to jerk off into and return to her."

"What!" My mouth's open again. He laughs, traces it with his finger. "Are you serious?"

"Swear to God," he laughs, holding his hand over his heart.

"Actually, I can believe it." I'm suddenly blushing.

"What?" He leans forward, amused. Pulls me toward him and showers my face with kisses. "Tell me."

"A guy, he sent me a bottle full of come. Special Delivery. I mean, to *this* address—God knows how they get my address. It was a half pint bottle and full; he'd been saving it up for me in the fridge. Thought I might like to use it for my complexion." Jan falls about in helpless laughter. "It's true— Pandora uses her lover's come for her complexion."

"So he thought . . ."

"Right." We're both laughing uncontrollably, and he pulls me onto his lap.

"How's *your* complexion? In need of any assistance?"

"Don't tease me!" I hit his bare chest—he's only put his jeans on.

"Who's teasin'?"

We're kissing and cuddling, laughing and chewing again. It feels like we've been lovers, friends, for years. How I *wish* it could be years! I hug myself to him. Silence: I'm not talking, Jan's not talking. It doesn't seem we're breathing, even. . . .

"What you said . . ." He speaks quietly, hesitantly. "About feeling like . . . like we're sharing the same skin. I liked that."

"You did?"

"I *did*."

"Why?"

He doesn't answer, just kisses me.

I sit up straight on his lap, smile as I touch his earrings. He has two tiny beaten-silver hoops in his left ear. He smiles back at me and touches my earring, to complete the circuit. I touch the thick-linked silver chain around his neck. There's a turquoise bear claw hanging from it. And at the top of his left arm there's a tattoo—a sort of stylized Aztec eagle. I touch it, and he smiles and caresses my face with his left hand. I notice for the first time that he doesn't wear a wedding ring on it. I rub my palm on the fuzz of his chest. His skin's so suntanned; mine, light gold, looks pale against it.

The phone rings, startling me. It's Matthew. Jan continues reading my letters and listens to my conversation. I look out to sea for a moment as I put the phone down, leaving it off the hook. Jan's staring at me inquisitively.

"A friend."

"A lover?" he grins.

"Matthew's gay, but we have, actually."

Jan raises an eyebrow, grins that lovely lopsided grin of his. I tell him about making it with Matthew the last time I was in New York. "Actually," I say, "he wants me to have his baby."

"What!?"

"He does. He says he doesn't trust anyone else. That there *is* no one else he could make a baby with."

"You ain't gonna do it?" Jan looks shocked at the idea.

"Well, no one else has ever asked me. I *would* like to have a baby, lots of them, before I'm too old."

"You ain't too *old*. What are you? Twenty-seven, twenty-eight?"

"I've just turned thirty-two."

"You don't look it."

Beatific smile from Solange for that boost to her ego. I

47

don't look it—and I'm extremely, smugly pleased with myself about the fact. "Well, I am. And I really would like some babies before it's too late."

"Well, that's a good idea if it's what you want. But not *that* way." He frowns, shaking his head. "Sounds like a stupid, dumb idea to me—dippier than those letters of yours."

"Well, it's really nothing to do with you," I reply haughtily.

"That ain't the point. It'd just plain be a mistake."

"Why?"

"Babies should be made in love."

We look at each other, right through each other.

"Why, you're nothing but a romantic—all Byron and Shelley." I try to sound flippant, but I'm feeling sick. "But what you said sounds like a great song title."

He stares steadily at me for a moment, then says quietly, "Don't do it."

"It's none of your business!" I add bitchily, "After tomorrow, I'll probably never see you again."

"I know what's dumb and what ain't!" He shakes me, quite fiercely. *"Don't do it.* It'd be *wrong* for you!"

"How the fuck do *you* know what's right and wrong for me? You hardly know me!"

He stops. "How long does it take—to get to know someone?"

I see the gentleness in his eyes, but what does *that* mean? I dare not ask.

We look at each other. He pulls me closer to him, and we sit in silence for a time, but I want this closeness *gone*. I don't want it for only a few short hours.

"Do you fuck a lot of women?" I ask, letting him know that he does, and that I know that's how he's thinking of me—a quick lay, no more than that.

"No . . ."

"I don't believe you."

He laughs, but without embarrassment. "Actually, when I'm on the road without Meliss', I have my share of the chicks."

"Oh, don't tell me," I tease. "Fantastic little groupies. Sixteen-year-olds who give *great* head."

"Ya looked!" We laugh. "That's about it. A chick to blow me. Since I've been married, though, I've never had an *affair,"*—he says the word with sarcasm—"nothing like that. Less complicated. I'm needin' an easy life. Nothin' heavy or involved. Only quick, nameless fucks that don't mean anythin'. A chick'll come and service the whole fuckin' band." He looks cynical. "Starfuckers!"

What am I suppose to say to all this? A quick nameless fuck—is that what I am? I think he's trying to get a tactful message across to me, and I'm suddenly angry. "Is that what you think *I* am? A *starfucker?*"

He looks angry, but then suddenly grins. "You're a famous lady—maybe I'm starfuckin' you!"

Why am I laughing with him?

I reach out and touch the tiny lines around his eyes, rub the palm of my hand on his face, which is scratchy and stubbly. He's shaved his beard and mustache off recently—I wonder why.

"What about you, Ma'am?" Grin. "Many men?"

"I don't have one a night." I smile at the thought. "I got divorced to liberate myself from a dying, cloying marriage. I really did *think* I'd fuck around much more than I actually do. It was my big plan, being liberated and adventurous. But when it comes down to it—well, I can't get into bed with just *anyone*. I don't, I *won't*."

He asks offhandedly, "You come a lot for the men you fuck with?"

"Why? It's none of your business." I'm irately indignant. Johnny, I remember, asked me the same thing the last time he was here. Is it some sort of male ego trip, keeping score? After all, who's counting? And why do I solemnly answer his dumb question? "A lot? Well, it all depends. With you, it's easy. . . ." A smile brightens his face. "If I loved someone, I mean *really* loved someone, who loved me the same way— you know: commitment and sharing, which I've never really had yet—well, I think he'd just have to look at me and I'd come." He looks at me, and we both grin.

"You come so *easily!* I'm getting a hard on just thinkin' about it." He pulls my hand down onto him. He's right.

"Wanna hear a confession? Ya gotta promise not to sell it to the *National Enquirer*, though." Lopsided grin. "I ain't made a chick come for two years, since before I married Melissa. I mean, I ain't had *that* many chicks since. Well, not many for me." Wry grin. "Only when she hasn't been around, which ain't much. To give me head—Meliss' won't gi. . . ." He stops himself suddenly, serious-faced.

What do we say now? I'm feeling awkward. He knows that I know what he was going to say: Melissa won't give him head. Why not, I wonder? After all, it's a rather delicious experience.

"Melissa-Sue and her Ma are fundamental Baptists—born-again Christians," he answers my unspoken question.

"Oh?" Religious convictions? Is giving head—or coming, for that matter—anti-Christian, then? He looks away, and the conversation is closed. I'm glad—it was getting too intense, anyway. I don't want to know about him and his wife. Maybe he'll tell me next that his wife doesn't understand him!

I put my arms around his neck, holding myself close to him, making it all right for him. He's been honest with me, and I like that. I kiss his cheek; he looks at me, so I trace his mouth with my finger. I can feel a sort of angry pain inside him, and I wonder why it's there. I wish I knew *all* about him—his life, his feelings—and that he knew all about me, too. I've only gazed at his photographs, read the few notes on the sleeves of his records. . . . I know nothing about this man. My eyes slowly fill with tears as I gently touch his face.

"Make love to me," I whisper. "I love you."

"Love me?"

"Yes."

"How?" His face has grown dark. He turns away.

"I mean. . . ." I stare at him for a moment. "We belong together. I've found you again. I *love* you. I think I would be complete with you."

He's looking at me again, with his puzzled, lost look, still not telling me what it is he's puzzling out.

I hit him on the shoulder. "And now you've made me say things I don't want to say to you—that you'd obviously rather not hear." I touch his lips, feeling exposed and vulnerable.

"Solange . . . I . . ."

"If you want to go, leave. Just go. I'll understand—you wanted a quick one-night stand, a quick lay. Someone who doesn't *mean* anything." I calm myself down. "I should never have said that, just now. But I just couldn't hold it in. I couldn't—not now, not after what we've shared. Like you said yourself: How long does it take to get to know someone?" I feel like an idiot child again. "Oh God, I feel so *stupid!* I'm sorry, I didn't mean to make things awkward for you."

"You want me to go?" he asks slowly, with an even look.

"I *want* you to make love to me. Eat me. Fuck me. Everything me."

"That's what I want, too."

"It is?"

"Sure is, Ma'am," his slight smile becomes a serious look.

"I can only stay until tomorrow morning—you understand, don't you?"

"Yes. That I understand. Twenty-four hours away. So much can happen in twenty-four hours. . . ."

He pulls me close and kisses me.

"Listen," I eventually say, "I *do* understand. No strings. A quick lay. You're happy. I knew that when I let you in."

"There's a lot of things you don't know, lady!"

Why his angry, bitter look? "What does that mean?"

"Nothing I'm going to get into with you now." We stare at each other.

"You've opened me up," I cry out, hitting at his shoulder, unable to stop myself. "No one's ever done that before—not like *this*. I feel so helpless. I feel there's nothing I can do. . . ."

"I'm sorry. I'd never want to hurt you." He gently cradles me in his arms, kisses me.

"It's not a hurt, only regret." And it is. Regret for tasting something I can never have.

* * *

We're eating dinner. Solange giving him something beautiful to remember her by, apart from the adorable fucking. He's eating a huge steak, enjoying the Bearnaise sauce I've made (thank God for a French maman!). I've lit candles all over the dining room, and it looks dreamy and romantic.

I've decided that I'm going to play at being the perfect mistress for these last few hours: Nana incarnate, Anna incarnate, Emma incarnate. *They* weren't perfect, but *I* will be. The *perfect* mistress. And I suppose I shouldn't forget 'O', as well. Hm! That perfect, I won't be!

"I think I'll report daily for my dinner," he says with a grin, engulfing a huge piece of sauce-covered steak.

"Dinner is for being such a good lover."

"Hey—you're good for my ego, Ma'am." He reaches out and touches my hand, takes my index finger and dips the tip of it into the Bearnaise to lick it. I smile and lean across to kiss him. Those stark, awkward moments of this morning, when we both seemed to open up each other, have completely vanished; now there's only intimate enjoyment, an evening full of loving feelings.

I want to finish off the few pages I was working on when he arrived yesterday. We're in my study, I'm working, and Jan's browsing through the countless books I have lying around the place. The feeling is one of quiet intimacy. We feel so much at peace with each other, so totally familiar with each other, how could we have known each other for just a few short hours? I think we've known each other for a very, very long time.

"You've got a lot of magic and witchcraft books," he says, replacing the grimoire on the shelf.

"Yes. For Pandora. So you'd better watch it—I might cast a spell on you, make you fall in love with me forever."

"See—what did I tell you, I *knew* you were really Pandora."

And I'm feeling a warm glow of happiness, because he's right, of course.

"You've got so many first editions. Beautiful old leatherbound ones."

"Yes, I've been collecting them since I was a child. I got quite a few of my grandfather's, when he died."

"You must have everything ever written on Blake. As well as all his stuff, of course. You've even got an 1808 *Illustrations to the Grave*."

I smile delightedly. "That was my grandfather Osborne's as well, like the engravings. They were *his* grandfather's. He was English—Sir Richard Osborne."

Jan smiles that puzzled smile of his and reverently turns the pages of the book.

"I'm glad you like Nobledaddy too," I add.

"Who?"

"Nobledaddy—that's what I've always called my beloved William since I was little and became intrigued with his concept of 'Nobodaddy'. So what else could I call him? I really do consider him the noblest daddy of them all."

Jan laughs. "Shit, that's beautiful, lady."

"I'm glad you approve."

"*Approve*, I . . ." He stops. And I wonder why. But I don't think I'm going to find out. "You haven't got all that much American literature," he says.

"No, I guess I should collect more. I adore Faulkner, though. But I'm sure you know far more about it than I do."

"I was always readin' when I was a kid."

"So was I. But, don't tell me—I can guess what *your* favorites were."

"You can, huh?"

"*White Fang* and *Lord Jim*, no doubt."

52

"Shit! Jesus fuck! You're *right*."

I laugh in delight again. "Of course I am—it's obvious."

He laughs and kisses me. "And you . . ." He looks me up and down, that puzzled look on his face again. "*Jane Eyre* and *Lorna Doone*, I bet."

"Right!" We laugh and cuddle and kiss.

It feels so exquisitely good being with him like this, even though it makes me ache to know it's something I can't grab hold of and keep. I go and put some music on for us.

I'm writing, correcting a page I wasn't too happy with. The music's playing and Jan's writing; the peaceful, contented feeling is still with us.

"What's the music?" he asks.

"Rachmaninoff's *Variations on a Theme of Paganini*."

"Jesus, it's great!" He grabs the record sleeve and copies the number from it.

When it comes to an end, I put more music on.

"What's that? What's that?" He reaches for the sleeve.

"Prokofiev—his first piano concerto. Ashkenazy doing it with Previn."

"That's fantastic! I've never gotten into classical, not beyond recognizing the famous bits everyone knows."

"I knew you'd like them."

"How?" He's staring right through me. "How did you know I'd like them?"

"Because of your words—and the melodies you put them to."

"Jesus fuck! You knew! And you're right, of course. Just like with the books." He regards me with the same look again, puzzling it out. He puts his hands on my face, kisses me quickly, then goes and sits on the floor in front of my collection of records and tapes. I watch him for a moment, enjoying his genuine delight, before returning to my work.

The record ends; I put another on. "Ralph Vaughan Williams—*Job*." I explain. It's a sort of ballet, except it's more a series of tableaux; a '*Masque for Dancing*,' he called it."

He looks at the cover, with the William Blake engraving on the front. "Shit! It's fantastic! And. . . . and I've never before heard these things! What have I been doin' with my fuckin' time?"

"I was brought up on classical music—my father was a cellist."

"A cellist—really? Shit! But this music, it even *sounds* like

53

Blake—like your *Nobledaddy*. That's some composin'!" He looks amazed, delighted, and a little overwhelmed. "Your collection, it's nearly all classical."

"Yes, afraid so." My turn to grin. "I have all yours, though. And all of Bob Dylan's. Oh, and Kris Kristofferson's and Leonard Cohen's."

"You must like us."

"*You're* all right," I say dryly. "Room for improvement, perhaps."

He gives me that beautiful lopsided grin of his, and he's kissing me again.

"It's no good giving me a touch of the eager creamies. I want to finish this off first."

"Touch of the *what?*"

I explain my pet name for getting horny. He laughs and cuddles me, kisses my face, then goes back to whatever it is he's writing, stretched out on the sofa.

And suddenly a morose unhappiness hits me. Solange and Jan, lovers—I can't seem to grasp it or understand it. It's something I want; yet it's something very painful, with its promise that contains its own ironic denial. I wanted to be free to have affairs, to fall in love. Is this also part of freedom, falling in love with someone who doesn't love me, whom I can't allow myself to love? I haven't really freed myself at all. It's just a different sort of trap, with different furnishings.

It's after midnight when I stop writing. I smile brightly, trying to put the mean unhappies behind me. "I hope you don't think I've been ignoring you?"

"No. You're working, and that ain't ignoring." He holds his arms out to me, and I go and cuddle with him on the sofa. "It's been so good," he says, "just sitting here. Listening to those sounds of yours, and working. I can't believe it—I mean that. I've never had an evening like it. I never knew it was possible. It's so fuckin' *good*. I wish. . . ." His voice trails off, and he gives me a sad look. Sad, but with a hint of defensiveness. "I don't just wanna be a rock composer and singer all my life. I think I'm ready to settle down and do some heavy writing, too. I've been on the road for thirteen fuckin' years. I want to write some more poetry. And I've got a fantastic idea for a novel I wanna write. You know, I wrote a book of surrealist poetry once, but it was rejected all over the place. It's *good*, though. That was after I left college, when the band and I were battlin' to make it. But I keep it to myself, and I add to it occasionally. Not recently, though. Not since before I ma—" He stops, stares at me.

"Your songs *are* poems, Jan, and they're so good. You say so much. Why don't you do something now with the poetry you've done? Now that you're known, you could easily get published. Or, write some fresh. And a novel. . . . oh, Jan."

I'm getting that lost, puzzled look from him again. What the hell is he figuring out? He pulls me to him, kisses me for a long time.

"I. . . . I don't have the time to myself, Ma'am," he states simply. "You need peace for writing poetry. Like we've had here tonight. It's. . . . I wish. . . ."

There're actually tears in his eyes, and again I'm feeling a deep pain within him. Why? Oh, hell, I wish I knew all about him, could be his friend, could help him. I wish. . . . I wish I could *love* him, that he'd let me.

We sit and cuddle, like babes in the wood. "I'd love to read what you've written, Jan."

"It ain't. . . . I'm not sure about it, anymore." He glances at me: again that defensiveness. "I guess I wanna be Blake." Oh, that beautiful, wistful little-boy smile!

"Perhaps you are. I know what you mean, though, I'm never satisfied with what I produce. Not any of it. I changed my ideas completely when I started to write. At Oxford I was scared, among the literati. So I told myself, Solange, you'd better write like that, do it properly. My first Pandora manuscript was so flowing and *literary*—everything I'd learned, writing essays and dissertations. It was all *wrong*. I realized I didn't *want* to write like that, except for Pandora's poems. I wanted my writing to be snappy and modern—classy-assed and smart-assed, like Pandora herself."

"See," he interrupts, "I keep tellin' ya, I'm right—you *are* Pandora, all classy-assed and smart."

I can't help but laugh with delight. Solange likes having her ego patted on its classy ass.

We kiss, gently subsiding along the sofa. Undressing doesn't take long. It's rather nice to make love in my study. I've never done it before. And I'm so glad it's him I'm doing it with. . . .

* * *

I'm awakened by kisses. On my face, my neck, my nipples, my pussy hair. I see that it's just morning. We make love again. How many times during the night? I can't remember,

55

and it doesn't matter. The last time, before we slept, seemed to go on for hours, a forever fuck.

And again we're looking at each other, fucking and looking at each other. We're hardly moving: just enjoying being part of each other. A good-bye fuck. And as we look at each other I think we both realize that it's no longer *just* sexy, sensual fucking; we're making love. Making *love*.

He's lying in my arms. We're both in that lovely dreamy not-quite-asleep state. How long do we lie like this? All I know is that it's morning and he'll be gone soon.

It's so unreal to me—he's leaving to return to his wife, to a family he loves. To a woman he loved so very much—to want her to be his wife, to have his baby: such an intimate thing. Lucky lady. . . .

We shower and I make coffee. We don't talk; there's an uneasiness in the air, a slight awkwardness. I want to say so much—and I know I can't. Does he want to say anything, I wonder . . .

He leaves me in the kitchen as I talk to Gulley. He comes back five minutes later, with his boots on and carrying the papers he was writing last night.

"I'll see you out," I say in a whisper.

At the front door we stand looking at each other. It's very hard not to cry when you want to.

"Try and do your writing, Jan. You *must*. I think you need to." I reach up and hug myself to him, kiss the side of his neck. We smile at each other.

How simple: it's all over. All over. . . .

"It's been nice knowing you, Literary Lady." His voice, even though it's soft and gentle, cuts through me. He holds my face in his hands, kisses me.

I watch him turn and walk along the pathway, away from me. I go inside, and just as I'm about to shut the door a feeling of desperation comes over me. I open the door quickly— I *have* to see him again, even if it's just for one more second, even though he's walking relentlessly away from me.

He's just *standing* there. Looking at the house. The door. Me.

"Jan!" I cry out, and run into his arms.

We're kissing—chewing at each others' mouths.

"I'm sorry . . ." I pull myself away. "I couldn't let you go without . . . without . . . I don't want you to go. Not now that we've found each other." We're kissing again. I look at him and touch his face. "I *love* you."

He holds my face in his hands, just as he did when he was

56

leaving, and I see that his eyes are shining and misty. "I . . . I love you, too. . . ."

We look at each other for a long, long time. The tears feel so hot on my cheeks.

Jan-Toby Axelsson turns and hurriedly strides out of my life. I wonder whether, next week, he'll remember me—remember my name, what I looked like, what I fucked like, how much I love him. I go into the house, close the door; I lean back against it, find myself crumpling into a little heap on the floor.

What the fuck am I crying for, anyway . . . ?

I climb into my cutoffs, put on a bikini top, and decide to go for a walk on the beach. The tide is out; I sit on the washed smooth sand, idly tracing with my finger the print of a dog's paw.

Why is it that all the motivations and interactions of my characters are totally transparent to me, and I can analyze them with precision, whereas when it comes to my own life . . . it's a matter of impulse and unmanageable emotions?

The sea is slowly creeping in. This very early in the morning the sun looks nice and inviting; I want to warm myself, and have the sun melt my hurts away. I look back at the sea.

Malibu. So different from Cap d'Antibes.

Cap d'Antibes. That's what I need.

I walk slowly back. Miriam will be returning today, to look after Gulley for me. Yes—I'll go to France. Home!

3

Rand meets me at the airport.

He takes me in his arms, kisses me gently and quickly on the mouth. We don't talk much. He says that he's pleased to see me. I believe him, for Rand would not lie.

At the house, I unpack my few things in my room. I take a quick shower and put on a strapless, pink-flowered dress. I comb out my hair, shake it, put on my sunglasses.

Rand is on the terrace. It's small, with rock gardens all

around it, the Mediterranean far below. When I'm away, I forget how much I love this house. Eight years ago we found it, bought it, decorated it.

"Well?" Rand looks at me inquiringly as Hortense brings us coffee, croissants, and butter.

"Well what?" I pout—a mannerism I can't seem to kick; I can remember being three, using it on my Daddy. It got me whatever I wanted. I know Rand can tell something is wrong. I also know I'm not going to tell him, that I *couldn't* tell him. He would think me even more stupid and childish than he already does.

"You've missed Justin and Anna by two days."

"Oh, yes . . ." I face him, realizing that I'm pouting again. I pout a lot with Rand. Maybe it's psychological—Freudian or something? My mind associating Rand with my father?

He reaches out and brushes my fingers. "Something is wrong. What is it?" His look is almost harsh; then his face softens, and he pats my hand condescendingly.

Rand Farraday, apart from being my ex-husband, is my friend. He has been my friend for a very long time—eleven years—and I guess he will always go on being my friend.

I look into his brown eyes as he gently runs his fingers through his hair. He wears it quite long and it tends to fall into his eyes. He has this habit of absently brushing it aside. It's dark brown, but it's going gray now, making his good looks even more distinguished.

I busily start to eat a croissant, as usual putting far too much butter on it. "Am I stopping you working?" I ask.

"Yes."

Why the hell is Rand always so direct, so honest!

I give him a half-hearted smile. "Sorry . . ."

"You always are." He drinks some of his coffee and watches in silence as I eat the rest of my croissant.

"I just needed to get away. I won't disturb you. Go and write—please."

"Will you be all right? Is there anything you want to talk about?" His voice is precise, low, very English, very educated.

"There's nothing to talk about, really. I just needed to get away. You know I won't disturb you."

"Yes."

"I fucked someone I shouldn't have, and I'm a bit down in the dumps."

"Oh?" He looks very slightly annoyed. No. Amused. No. Tolerantly *understanding*. He pats my hand again and raises

58

an eyebrow. "It's all part of being a free and liberated female, isn't it?" His cynicism is icy.

"I just needed to be here for a bit. It's warm and safe here." How stupid, idiotic, to say such a thing! But it's true, all the same. Rand has a warm softness about him. I suppose, to be really honest with myself, I'm not *really* out there in the big bad world all on my own, am I? I'm holding myself snug in the safety of Rand's shadow. I wonder . . . have I the guts ever to really leave it?

"Do free, liberated young ladies need to feel warm and safe? I thought they were demonstrating that they didn't. That's what you got yourself divorced for, wasn't it?" He smiles sweetly, falsely, as he stands up. I glare back at him.

"I'll see you later, then," he says. "I'm in the middle of a chapter." At the house, he turns. "Don't play the stereo too loud."

Rand always makes me feel like a little girl. I realize I'm pouting again. Maybe I *did* marry Rand because I wanted to fuck my father.

Being divorced for two years hasn't made me any less dependent on Rand. Something goes wrong, and I run to him. Just like I ran to my father. I married Rand right after my father's death. I'd known him for just three weeks.

I was twenty-one then and ecstatically happy at being no longer an undergraduate, having achieved a first class honors degree in literature. I was also totally heartbroken, unable to shake off the grief enshrouding me, the grief of losing the two most important men in my young life: My father, in an air crash. And Johnny, when he went off to discover himself and the world.

I divorced Rand just before my thirtieth birthday, after nine years of being totally engulfed in his life.

Rand is fifty-five. He's tall—just over six feet—and has a beautiful, firm muscular body. He looks to be in his late forties and is immensely pleased about it.

As I stare at the Mediterranean far below me I become aware of him standing by my side again.

"Why don't you stay, Solange darling? I'd be much happier if you were here, with me."

I look up at him. He's very tanned. He's taken off his shirt and stands there in his faded blue jeans. "Don't smother me, Rand."

He glares at me. "You're still a child. One day I hope you'll find out how to grow up." He turns and leaves me; inwardly, I can do nothing but agree with him. I wonder whether he'll want to make love to me later on. I know Rand—yes, he will.

Rand "makes love." Rand "sleeps with." Rand does *not* "fuck." As far as Rand is concerned, I do not have a "cunt." Nothing so crude for Rand. "Pussy" isn't *too* bad—he's used that, sort of jokingly. Yes, "pussy" is acceptable. Let me touch "it." "It" feels nice. Rand has an "it," too. "It" wants you, etcetera, etcetera . . . How genteel. Rand tolerates my joking about hot steamy cocks and drippy cunts, but we don't actually have them.

When we "make love," Rand comes with a slight shudder and a gasp. But I really don't understand how anyone can come quietly—I come hoping that I haven't disturbed the neighbors. Do they realize I'm coming? Or do my loud cries make them think I'm being beaten up? Not in France, anyway: *vive la petite mort!*

All in all, a very pleasant sex life, very comfortable, loving, and gentle. I always came; he always came. Did it matter, really, that there was no excitement?

*   *   *

I'm lying next to Rand, in his bed. In his room. It's a platform bed. The room is very simple, very masculine. Clean lines, no fuss. Nothing feminine.

I fucked. Rand *made love* to me. But I couldn't come. I can hear him snoring gently, turned away from me. I dreamily touch myself; I still can't come—I don't think I want to. I wonder why I can't come for Rand, with Rand, and I think about the time I first met him . . .

. . . A party. Weston-on-the-Green, a tiny village just outside Oxford; at the Masons'. George Mason plays viola and had often played with my father, who played cello. Now that my parents had gone back to France to live, George and Hilary Mason, whom I'd known since I was a little girl, were keeping a gentle eye on me.

It was summer and surprisingly hot for England. I was still totally and delightedly immersed in the realization that after three hard-working years of study I was no longer an undergrad, I'd *gotten* my degree. I felt grown up for the first time. Me, with my tiny, extremely expensive, rented cottage.

The only thing that marred this happy, carefree feeling was the sudden wrench of Johnny's leaving. Johnny, my love, had gone, taking so much more than he knew. For weeks I had sat in my tiny garden, listless, lifeless, unable to do anything, even to read my beloved books or to think about my impending postgraduate work.

So Hilary Mason, over tea, realizing the anguish I'd been going through, had invited me to her party. "But you *must* come to meet someone new. You *must*."

I was the youngest person there. "Come and meet Rand"— Hilary guided me to the other side of her beautiful Georgian living room. Rand Farraday, famous writer. Physics Ph.D; I was in total awe. He was good-looking, well-spoken; he'd won awards for his science fiction writing. And Rand Farraday was talking to *me*.

He rang me up the next day (he was staying with George and Hilary) and took me out to dinner—an elegant dinner at the Weston Manor hotel, which was once a sixteenth-century monastery: the perfect place for a romantic little girl to be wined and dined by a famous writer. And that night we went to bed together. He spent three whole days with me and we went to bed a lot. I didn't come, though. What would he think of me if I demanded that he make me come? It wasn't a bit like Johnny and me, and the way we feasted on each other.

The afternoon of the phone call. I was in the garden with Rand. My mother, speaking from Paris, told me about the awful plane crash. I went to Paris, and we buried Daddy there. Maman went to the South, to the sea—she wanted to be alone. And I returned to Oxford, to my little cottage.

Rand came down from London. He stayed with me; he consoled me; he loved me. And, two weeks after my father's death, Rand married me. Rand was six years younger than my father, and three years older than my mother.

For a time, I found a peaceful haven in Rand's arms and in his bed. I worked for my doctorate. Rand wrote another book: *The Mask of Time*. I was still in awe—impressed, overwhelmed. Rand received the Nebula for it.

Rand became my shelter from the world. My two men had deserted me. Johnny had walked out. My father had been killed.

. . . .and now I'm lying here in Rand's bed, unable to sleep. Am I *still* using Rand as a peaceful haven . . . ?

I get up and go into the lounge. Biscuit-colored carpet, modern Italian leather furniture. Rand hasn't changed it since I left. I set the stereo volume low and play Prokofiev's first piano concerto—I adore it—and play it again.

I go and raid the pantry: a croissant and too much butter, a large peach, and a glass of wine. The sun has begun to rise, and I'm listening to Debussy—the piano music, Book I of the Preludes.

I wonder how long I can stay here. I should be writing. I'm only really happy when I'm writing.

I become aware that nothing is playing on the stereo. Lying on the floor in front of it is a pile of a dozen tapes. I feel light-headed, and I eventually realize that I haven't slept properly for days. My tiredness is making me irritable, but I feel too tired to sleep.

I pick up one of the tapes—Jan-Toby Axelsson's last album. I start to cry.

I hook my little finger under the tape and pull it out of the cartridge, yards of it. I pull it, stretch it, destroy it. With a pair of scissors I cut it into small pieces.

Still crying, I go into my bedroom, pull my silk kimono off and fling it angrily on the floor. I realize that I'm in a foul, perverse, unreasoning, unthinking mood. Beneath the stereo unit I notice four records—all Jan-Toby Axelsson.

I'm still crying—and I don't know why, I really don't. What is there for me to cry about? I feel light-headed, vertiginous once more. I pull the records out of their covers and throw the disks onto the floor. The covers all have close-ups of his face. One with his mustache; he's smiling. One clean shaven with sunglasses. One with his mustache and beard—he's sitting between his two German shepherds. And lastly another with his mustache and tidy beard, with his band behind him. They're all drinking Coors.

I tear up the covers until there are no faces left. I open the French windows, step out onto the balcony, and throw the records out onto the rock garden. I throw all the pieces of the album covers onto the garden too—scattering them on the wind like ashes.

I hate him! I hate me! I throw myself onto the bed, crying.

I think about how he fucked me. My fingers go to my eager little pussy, and I think about him—eating me, fucking me, coming in me, coming over me. I think about his body, his eyes, his cock—how it all tasted. At last—a touch of the eager creamies . . . and I come.

I fall asleep, cuddling up to my pillow, pretending it's Jan-Toby Axelsson.

* * *

I awake at noon. It's after one before I'm showered and ready to face the day.

Rand is on the terrace reading *Le Monde*. It's his lunch time. He likes his lunch at one—exactly. Salad, crispbread, cheese, French bread, fruit, and wine. Then coffee. It's always the same, always has been. He reminds me of Phileas Fogg. Rand likes things stable, predictable, and secure. Dare I say, *dull*.

I kiss the top of his head. He smiles at me.

"Did you sleep well, darling?" He's so sweet and caring, and it makes me feel so *guilty*. He *loves* me, and I love him too. But . . .

"I got up and played some music. I went into my room, I didn't want to disturb you."

"It was nice." He looks sideways at me as he turns a page.

"What was?"

"Our love." He smiles approvingly once more, then disappears into his newspaper.

"We *fucked!*" I cry out.

"It's more than just *that* between us, isn't it?" he asks gently, humoring me, sensing that something is wrong. I almost feel as though he *knows* what is wrong.

"Fucking is fucking," I glare at him.

"Yes, dear . . ." He eats Brie on crispbread.

Hortense, our—*his*—housekeeper, always wears a black dress and her hair plaited into a chignon at the nape of her neck. She brings me some French bread and *thon,* which she knows I like for lunch. I thank her and pour myself some *vin ordinaire* and water. When I was little I was given, as most French children are, a mixture of wine and water. I guess I've never completely grown up—I still like it that way for *déjeuner.*

We eat in silence for a while. I'm watching the sea; it's beautiful—crystal and glinting. Cap d'Antibes seems so different from Malibu, almost like fairyland, never-never land. I don't think I'll ever grow up while I'm here.

Hortense brings the broken tape to me at the table, stands there with it in her hands. "Madame Solange?" She puts it down next to me, and Rand looks. "Is broken, yes?" She smiles, pleased with her English.

"Yes, Hortense." She nods and leaves it there.

Rand looks at the tape, smiles—he knows my passion for Jan-Toby Axelsson. "Why did you do that? *Did* you do that?" He looks over the top of his reading glasses.

"I, um . . . I got angry," I say glibly but unconvincingly.

"*Destroying* things won't help!" he snaps, sternly. Chastised, I pout, poke my tongue out at him. Yes, I'm still a child. . . . Why is he always so *right?*

Hortense returns, looking worried. *"Madame Solange—les disques, ils sont tous éparpillés là-dessous, dans le jardin."*

"Scattered—yes, I threw them there. *Ça va, Hortense—laissez-les rester là, s'il vous plaît."* She nods dubiously; she won't touch them, now that I've told her to leave them, even though they offend her Gallic sense of tidy orderliness.

Rand nods to Hortense, shrugging. (After all, the French *know* that the English are really all mad.) She goes off again, and he asks me, "What *is* this all about, Solange?" He neatly folds up his newspaper (he won't let me read it until he's finished with it).

"It's not about anything," I lie evasively, incorrigibly vague —a number I do on him quite often. Of course, it *is*—I *want* the records and the torn covers left right there. I want the sun to *melt* the discs, to make nothing of them, to melt them down into a zero, a nothingness that can no longer hurt me.

"You're behaving very oddly. You arrive here out of the blue—not that I mind that, of course. But something is wrong. You say you slept with some—"

"Fucked!" I interrupt him. "We *fucked!"* I start to cry.

"Well, something is obviously wrong. You destroy your records . . ." As I continue crying, Rand suddenly looks at me—right at me. Through me. Inside of me. He looks at the broken tape and then back at me; and somehow, by some leap of inductive intuition, he *knows.* Improbable though this knowledge might seem, he accepts it. He deliberately takes a sip of his wine before speaking. "It was him, wasn't it? That's it, isn't it?"

"Oh, shut up!"

"Solange . . ." He shakes his head, smooths his hair. "Now perhaps you'll understand why I didn't want you going off on your own, being all alone, no one to look after you. I *like* looking after you. And now you've got yourself hurt."

"Shut . . . up!!"

Rand thumps his fist down hard on the table. It's not often that he gets angry, but when he does it goes on and on, he stays angry and disgruntled for days. "You're so *stupid* at times, Solange! I could hit you, I really could." He looks as though he means it. If only he really *would* hit me—*fuck* me! "I don't understand you," he goes on, "I really don't. You wanted this . . . this *ludicrous* divorce. I didn't stand in your way, though you failed to convince me of the necessity for it—you failed to produce any good reason for it, either. And now, exactly as I expected, you've hurt yourself. God, you women! So ridiculously illogical, impulsive, not to mention spitefully, wantonly destructive. So childish! *Why* behave as a spoilt child, Solange? You don't really need to, now do you?" Condescendingly, he gives me a look of wearied patience.

"At least I'm getting myself *fucked!*" I burst out at him, pouting. "Some men *like* eating me, *enjoy* me, think I taste beautiful and sexy. They enjoy me enjoying *them*." Yes, I'm really trying to hurt him now, claws unsheathed, no pussy-footing. My shouting brings a startled, hurt look to his eyes. Good! I *have* hurt him!

"Solange . . ." Gentle again. It annoys me even further.

"You can't give me what I want, what I need!" I cry at him. He flinches. I've hurt him again. Good! I run to the edge of the terrace, gripping the white wrought-iron rail, kicking the post: the spoilt selfish brat in me coming out.

Why is it, with Rand and me, that it always comes down to sex? In everything else, we're friends. It was only in sex that Rand couldn't give me what I needed.

And apart from all that, I wanted a child—children. I want a baby growing inside me; I need that, I need to feel it. Not because I think a woman's not a woman unless she's had a child—that's stupid. But I just want to have that experience. I want to make a baby with someone I love, to have part of him growing up inside me. And also I want the experience of bringing up a child in the way a child should be brought up—in happiness and love, as I was; finding delight in things they're learning. Never being in fear of their parents or other grownups. But Rand already had a son and daughter by his first marriage, so he never wanted *me* to have his children.

Rand and I—we're both totally compatible and totally incompatible. Our friends and family couldn't understand it when we divorced—when *I* divorced Rand—and now, they don't really understand our friendship.

"How did you come to . . . um, get together?"

"At a party. We talked. He likes the poets and writers I do. Then we just drifted home; he was a bit stoned, I think, and needed a friend, someone to talk to. So did I. So we fucked. We sort of just . . . go together. Fit together." *Belong together,* I'm thinking.

Rand just looks at me. He's very good at that—just looking, sometimes with a quizzical lift of an eyebrow, saying nothing. "And you *hated* yourself the next morning," he says after a suitable pause.

"Bastard!" I hit out at his stomach, over and over.

"The trouble with you," he says, stiffening his muscles and ignoring my attack, "is that you're a dreamer. It's little girls who fall in love with rock stars. Not grown women. You really *are* a child, aren't you, Solange?" he comments with a self-satisfied smirk.

"I'm *not* in love with any rock star!" I protest. "Loving someone isn't being 'in love' with them. Anyway, he's a person. A *person.* Someone has to be a rock star, and famous, just like someone has to be a lawyer, a milkman, a writer. I married you, and *you're* a famous writer. Oh, really, Rand!" I hit at him again in my fustration with his deliberate, pretended obtuseness. "Just because he writes songs and poems doesn't mean he has no personal life. Can't you see that? There's a *personal* side to him. It doesn't matter to me that he's a rock star—that's got absolutely nothing to do with it."

"No? But you can't deny that you've always *worshipped* him," Rand says superciliously, "like a stupid little teenager."

"Bastard!" I hit at him again. "It's his *words* I love." I pout and turn away.

"Trite rubbish. All that those so-called rock poets turn out is trite junk, pretentious trash—or even just *trivial* trash." He smirks again, and I hit at him again, futilely. Are we both getting some kind of perverse pleasure out of putting each other down? It's a common enough pastime, after all.

"So—you let him sleep with you." He turns me around.

"He *fucked* me!" I yell. "He *fucked* my *cunt!* What's the matter with you? Can't you say those naughty words? Oh, you bigoted prude!"

"Yes, very well . . ." Rand looks amused, his head on one side, his left eyebrow raised. "So?"

"So *what?*"

"Did you enjoy it?"

"Yes. . . ." I whisper. "Oh yes. . . . Yes!"

"Well?" Rand raises his voice.

"Well what?"

"Why are you in such a state, then?"

"I'm not in a state."

"Oh yes you are!"

"I'm not in a fucking state!" I scream.

"Bloody hell!" Rand thumps his fist against his forehead.

"I'm never going to see him again," I state, haughtily throwing back my head, trying to regain a facade of coolness.

66

A facade behind which I'm annoyed—angry with myself, ashamed of myself too, for not having been able to make what happened between Jan and me the "quick, nameless, unmeaningful fuck," the one-night stand, that it obviously was for him. But I *must* make it mean no more than that to me. I must. I *must!*

"Never? Oh, all right, then. No more to be said, is there, in that case?" He's regained his air of tolerant amusement.

"Oh, shut up!" He's so infuriating!

"Yes, dear. . . ."

"*I love him!*" I burst into tears and sink to the concrete, and Rand kneels, concerned for me. "Why doesn't he *remember?*" I cry out.

"Remember?"

"Yes, remember—that we've been together *before*. That we should be together *now.*"

"Oh, Solange! Not all that reincarnation stuff again, please! I know we put it in our books, but in real life it's a different . . ."

"But it's *true!*"

"So *you* say."

"It *is* true!" I *believe* in reincarnation—no, more than believe. I *know* it's true, that it's how things are. I *can* remember things. All my books are about it. I know that I've loved Jan before, that he's loved me before, and I've always felt as though I've been just waiting for *him* to come along. Of course, wouldn't you know it, when he did, he was married to the wrong woman—I was too late finding him.

"Solange . . ." Rand being soft and gentle, hugging me to him. "Stop living in a dream world. Come back to me here, let me look after you properly—you *need* looking after. You'd be much happier then, wouldn't you? Just writing, instead of making yourself unbearably miserable as you're obviously doing at present. And anyway, how *can* you love someone you hardly know—someone who hardly knows you?"

"How long does it take?" I say and then start to cry again.

"Solange . . ."

I suddenly want to hurt him again for being so understanding—so condescendingly, patronizingly understanding. "He and I shared more in our sex and our loving in those few hours than you and I have ever shared," I tell him bitchily.

"Hm . . ." Rand draws away. "Does that make you feel better, telling me that?"

"Shut . . . up!" Oh, shit, just look at me being the spoilt, tempestuous, sulky, weepy child! What the hell would my readers think of me if they saw me like this? Where's the cool, chic, beautiful Solange disappeared to? Why do I *allow* her to disappear and be replaced by this tearful, gawky monster?

Rand has his arm around my shoulders. "We were happy together, weren't we?"

"No. I don't know. . . . I suppose so," I grudgingly admit.

"Well, then—why not come back, darling?"

"Don't smother me! You always *smother* me!"

"It's not *me* doing that. Are you sure it isn't *you* doing it?" he asks me enigmatically.

"See . . . ! *That's* what I mean!"

He scrutinizes my face intently, then shrugs. "I find you a bit prickly, just now. But I *know* it'll work, if you come back."

"Oh, you do, do you?"

He lets me have the last word.

* * *

The records stay in the rock garden, warped by the sun, gathering dust that covers his voice, his music, his words, him. . . . It helps, somehow.

And I sleep in my own room. I like my room. It's soft and gentle, all in white. We always had separate rooms.

I take my baby Fiat and drive to Villefranche to see my friend Marie-Claude Leboux.

Marie-Claude is one month younger than me. We went to school together for a time and became the closest of friends, the sister neither of us had. Marie-Claude has a beautiful little house. A high, whitewashed brick wall enclosed part of the garden, where we sit watching the sea, sipping wine, eating shrimps for lunch. Marie-Claude is very chic, very beautiful, with blue eyes and blonde hair that hangs straight down to just past her chin. A cheeky fringe somehow makes her look very French, and she is. To me, Marie-Claude is perfect—and at times, she almost makes me wish that I were gay. She's five feet five, with a 34-22-34 figure. We love each other—a close, appreciative love.

Marie-Claude wanted me to come and live with her in her little house so that we could become even closer sisters. She doesn't *work*, not in the usual sense of the word—she's a professional mistress. She has six men.

We talk and talk, in French of course, and I open my heart

to her and tell her all about Jan. Marie-Claude and I always share, always tell. We understand each other. And I know that if anyone can sort me out, get my head put on straight, she can.

Marie-Claude's solution to this is, of course, simple—and typically French. "Why do you not become his mistress, ma chérie?"

"Oh, Marie-Claude . . ."

To Marie-Claude, It's the obvious answer and, moreover, a civilized, eminently sensible answer. (I think Rand would see the logic of it, even.)

"I don't think I'll ever see him again, Marie-Claude."

"Then you must take many lovers—you do not take *enough* lovers, *ma chérie*," she smiles. "Yes . . . ?"

"Oh, Marie-Claude, I don't know. I know that here that is how these things arrange themselves. . . . I don't know. D'you think that *is* maybe what I need—lots and lots of lovers?"

She takes my hand in hers. "I think perhaps that it would do you much good. . . . You have seen Johnny recently, yes?" she asks, watching intently for my reaction.

"Not for about six weeks," I reply offhandedly.

"You are still in love with Johnny?" Am I? How did she deduce that? "Perhaps he is the man you really want, Solange?"

"No, I don't think so. No, Marie-Claude. I love him, yes—but *in* love with him? No, definitely not." As I speak I realize it's true: I used to feel a passionate love for him, but it faded when he left me. "I was very young then. It's different now. Now, my love's just for a dear friend, no more. I know there couldn't be anything stable for us, not now."

"But you still let him make love to you."

"Yes, of course, when he visits me. We both enjoy it. We've *always* enjoyed it."

"Then that is good." She smiles and pats my hand. Marie-Claude is so sensible about love and relationships. I wish I could be like her. Her men are rich, good-looking.

She smiles at me. "So, why *not* become Jan's mistress?"

"It was only a one-night—no—two-night stand on his part. He doesn't want more than that."

"But are you quite sure of that, *ma chérie?* How could a man not want more of you?"

"Yes—I'm sure. If he had wanted that, or even wanted to see me again, he'd have said so. He's that type of man, Marie-Claude. But he has a wife."

She studies me seriously. "In that case, *ma petite*, you were rather foolish to allow yourself to fall in love with him, were you not?"

"Oh, Marie-Claude, you are so right! Except—except that I didn't *choose* to fall in love with him."

"But you did, *ma chérie*," she says practically.

"Yes, I did." My eyes fill with sudden tears as I think of Jan and me that last night. That morning before he left— making love. And it *was* love we made.

Marie-Claude leans close and grins cheekily. "You have fucked with Rand?" she asks.

"Yes."

"The same?"

"Yes."

"*Hélas, c'est la vie.*" She shrugs; we giggle in unison. "We go buy things?"

"Yes, let's go and buy *lots.*"

We take Chou-Chou, Marie-Claude's Afghan hound, with us and set out to spend lots and lots of money. We spend a hilarious hour in the jewelers in Nice, buying earrings. We both belong to what we've christened "The Three-Earring Club"—we have three earrings in each ear. We suddenly decided, in the spring of '75, that one per ear wasn't enough. The new fashion hot from Paris was another earring—stud or hoop—next to your usual hoop, so we had it done at M. Joubert, an Antibes jeweler. One night, very stoned on champagne and pot, we reached the momentous conclusion that another hole in each ear would greatly expand the range of permutations, and a beautiful diamond stud, a smaller hoop, and a large hoop would have that esthetic *je-ne-sais-quoi* that two holes would never give us.

The assistant in the shop in Nice is young and good-looking. He watches us closely as we try to decide on the earring we really want. Not studs—we each have a quarter-carat Cartier diamond stud for the top hole. There are some beautiful filigree crescent hoops. We explain to him that we want a large and a small hoop: two sets of each so that we can have the same. When he returns with them, Marie-Claude flutters her eyelashes and we both give him the come-on. But I think he must have given *us* the come-on: leaving the store, we find we've bought eight pairs of earrings and spent nearly a thousand dollars each. But who cares! I look at it this way: what the hell do we have earlobes for, if not to hang things on!

We sit in a sidewalk cafe and eat enormous ice-cream

sundaes, unable to take our eyes off each others' new earrings, giggling like little girls. I suddenly think of Jan—when we touched each others' earrings.

It's late when I drive home. I'll see Marie-Claude again before I go. She's visited me in Malibu three times—but she's very French in her attitudes: she thinks America can hardly be called civilized.

Maybe I do need to come and live with Marie-Claude. Maybe I could have six men, too. . . .

* * *

It's been nearly two weeks. Rand's been talking to me again about staying. How many women would *love* to have a Rand taking care of them! So why *don't* I sell the house at Malibu and just come back here? I love it here; I love *la belle France*. And I'd be near Marie-Claude, whose friendship is precious to me. My mother's in Paris—I'd be nearer to her. The life-style here in France suits me; and I love the wine-dark Mediterranean and the dusty, dark-green hills. I even love Rand—he's my friend. So why can't I just return, be safe again and secure in Rand's shadow?

I stand in my bedroom, looking from my tiny balcony over the rock garden towards the sea. I can see the warped and dusty records, the torn covers. I wonder what *he* is doing. He said he was busy recording. How long does that take him, to record a new album? Does he take his wife with him when he's recording? I suddenly hate her, and then I feel stupid: I don't know her, but she *must* be a nice person. She must be, because he married her, he's in love with her. She's so very young, and very beautiful in the few magazine photographs I've seen of the two of them together.

She doesn't read much, he told me: that, at least, is something I have that she doesn't, I think with a very smug smile. He told me she *tried* to read books he'd suggested, insistently suggested, but she didn't finish them.

But feeling smugly pleased with oneself, though gratifying, doesn't actually get you anywhere. Actually, I'm in fact more puzzled than smug: to me, Jan and his wife don't seem to fit, either emotionally or intellectually. And yet they are together. Well, she's beautiful, that must be it. And he loves her—that must be it. She must be fantastic in bed. . . . But on the other hand, Jan said she won't even give him head!

If I stayed here, I'd never see Jan again, and maybe it wouldn't hurt anymore. Should I stay? Rand would be happy.

I'm sure Gulley Jimson wouldn't mind moving back to France, he knows this house already. Maybe Miriam would even like to come.

Oh, how can I *start* sorting out these convoluted feelings?

Rand comes into my room. He looks at me as I lie naked on the bed, smiles. "The Thorntons have just rung—they want us to go to a dinner party."

"When?"

"Tonight. Come on, Solange—you'd better start getting ready. You know how bloody long you always take."

Immediately I'm feeling smothered again, and I know for certain that I *have* to get away from here, from Rand.

* * *

I kiss Rand good-bye. There's sadness behind his impassive expression; there are tears in my eyes. He seems to want to say something, but all he says is, "Come back soon, Solange."

The taxi takes me to Villefranche, to Marie-Claude's; I'll spend a few days with her before I leave.

"Don't leave so soon, Solange. Stay a little longer," she says as we're having dinner at the Carlton.

"But I have to go, Marie-Claude. I *need* to go."

"Then come back. Stay with me. We'll share some lovers."

We smile wistfully at each other. Maybe that would be nice; we've often talked about the two of us with one man, but we've never done it. I glance across the crowded restaurant, and my gaze is held at one particular table.

"You are thinking of Johnny, yes?"

Marie-Claude has read my mind, as she quite often does— as I quite often do with her. "Yes . . ." My gaze returns to that table, where two young girls, *très chic*, are with two elderly men. It was at that table, some two and a half years ago, that I started my quest for freedom, my search for liberation. I suddenly realized—and it was an almost visionary experience—that I was buried in a marriage that had become a warm and happy friendship.

"Solange . . . Solange!"

I grin at Marie-Claude, embarrassed. "Sorry . . . I was miles away."

"Thinking of Jan, *ma chérie?*"

"No! Yes. No . . ." I take a sip of my wine. "I'm trying to make the love go away."

72

"Then stay here, Solange."

"And share . . . ?"

"You would like that? It would be better for you."

"Would it?" I'm still unsure. But to have no emotional ties—*that* would be better, certainly.

"I think it would." She pats my hand. "Of course it would," she continues. "Much better than being by yourself and lonely in California."

"I think I'll go and see Maman first, before I go back home," I tell Marie-Claude. She gives the tiniest shrug and smiles happily.

* * *

Paris. My mother meets me at the airport. We hug and we kiss—it's been six months since we last saw each other, when she came and stayed with me for a few weeks. We talk excitedly as she drives me to her home on the Rue Benouville.

"You look so beautiful, darling," I say, staring in awe as she drives the cream Mercedes. Her long fingernails, beautifully manicured, are painted a dark browny red.

She smiles sideways at me. "I have a beautiful daughter, too, *ma chérie.*"

My maman is the epitome of the beautiful French woman, French chic. She is taller than I am, with a wonderfully firm, youthful figure. Her face is beautiful and aristocratic. Her eyes are large, hazel; her hair is blonde. Since as long as I can remember she's had it blonde, worn long, either tied back with a velvet ribbon or in a graceful chignon. I've inherited, thanks be, her beautiful high cheekbones. She's fifty-two now, but doesn't look a day over forty-two. She's had one face-lift and one tit-tuck. I didn't think she needed them, but *she* did, and she went ahead and had them.

I adore having her for a mother, because I can *talk* to her. I always could.

Véronique delaMer is one of France's leading writers. She writes for women about women (but she's in no way a "romance" writer). Teasing, I tell her she fits in somewhere between Françoise Sagan, Anaïs Nin, and Pauline Réage. I love her books (all in French, of course, though Penguin Books are bringing out English translations). And what pleases me greatly is that she loves my writing.

She remarried five years ago. Philippe de Courcy is a banker, forty-one, extremely good-looking. He's every woman's dream of the typical gorgeous Frenchman. As we near the center of Paris, I begin to feel alive again.

* * *

The next week is an exciting and happy one. I forget my depression, that I had the awful blues and the meany-mean reds. If I'm lucky, they won't return.

As always when I'm in Paris, we spend a day in the beauty salon having our faces, bodies, and hair done. And we spend days shopping—Saint Laurent, Givenchy, Cardin, Dior, Chanel. We buy something from each. We're like happy sisters, not mother and daughter. I feel revitalized, repaired, reborn.

I tell her everything about Jan-Toby Axelsson.

"*Ma chérie*, it is unwise, foolish to give your heart so completely to one who gives little in return."

"Exactly, Maman. I know. But I'm *over* it now. And being here with you has helped." It's true, it has—her warm love always helps.

"You will not see him again?"

"No, there was never any question of that."

"And you do really feel settled about it all now?"

"Yes . . . I think I do. but I'm hoping I'll still feel the same way when I get back. So close again, near to him."

She continues benignly informing herself about my relationships—not prying, just interested, with a practical awareness that her own experience may be worth putting at my disposal. She makes my interests her own—but not with any intent to live vicariously through her offspring.

"You have no other lovers at the moment, *ma chérie?*"

"No, not really. Well, nothing serious."

"Get yourself some."

"Yes, Maman." We smile. My maman is very similar to Marie-Claude in her outlook; both are completely and utterly French, of course. Only a beautifully French maman would tell you to take lots of lovers.

"And you will not return to Rand?"

"No, Maman." My face, I'm sure, betrays my immediate feeling of obstinate resistance.

"Maybe you should have stayed with him," she insists, wistfully.

"No, it wouldn't have worked. I need to be on my own."

"Perhaps you are *too* independent, *ma chérie?* It must be the American in you coming out," she smiles.

Even though my father was American, I've never considered myself to be. He was from Long Island—his family had an estate at the Hamptons. I was born in Paris, where we lived for the first two years of my life; then, until I was four, we lived with my grandfather on his estate on Long Island. I remember the huge grounds and the swimming pool where Daddy taught me to swim; and Granddaddy Osborne, tall, stooping, soft, and gentle (he was a historian). And after that, back to Paris until I was eight, and then to Nice, where Marie-Claude and I met and became best friends, until I was fourteen. And from Nice we went to London. We lived in Hampstead, in a big, rambling house on The Bishop's Avenue.

I finished my schooling in England. I got a place in a private school, a school where I found that I enjoyed learning, that in fact I had a passion for learning, a compulsion, an addiction—except that unlike an addiction there was no coming down from it. It just went on and on. I found myself—for doing what I enjoyed most—being given honors in Certificate exams, "O" level, "A" level, even Royal Society of Arts. Then, ecstatically, I heard I'd got a place at Lady Margaret Hall. I was to be—and was, before it had really sunk in—an undergrad at Oxford. (I'd considered the Sorbonne, where my mother went, but English literature attracted me more than French. I didn't, for even one minute, consider Harvard, where my father had been. I've never considered myself to be an American.)

"Darling?"

I come out of my reverie. "Yes, Maman?"

"Darling . . . I am going to have to leave you for the night. Until tomorrow afternoon."

"Oh?" I stare into her hazel-brown eyes.

"I go to Jean-Paul."

"Oh?" I bite my bottom lip. Jean-Paul was my mother's lover before she married Philippe; he's married, twenty years younger than she is, raising a family; but he and mother have a gentle love for each other—and see each other regularly.

"Does Philippe know?" I ask cheekily.

"But of course, *ma chérie.*"

"And does he too have . . . ?"

"But of course, *ma chérie.* Though we never speak of them to each other, that goes without saying." She shrugs, "It is always taken for granted. And you, Solange, you will be all right?"

"Of course, Mummy," I say in English for some reason. I go with her, and she packs her overnight case.

As she's leaving, she puts her case down, turns, and takes my hand. *"Ma chérie* . . . there is something I should tell you."

Oh? A confession? In her long white strapless evening dress she looks beautiful, too beautiful to have anything to confess.

"Philippe and I . . ." She hesitates. "We are separating."

"Separating?" I'm amazed.

"That way, it is better. . . . We will talk of it tomorrow, if you wish."

After I've waved her good-bye, in her cream Mercedes, I watch television for a while: reruns of my favorite historical series, *Les Rois Maudits*—The Accursed Kings. Jean Piat, the actor who plays the king's cousin Robert d'Artois, is gorgeous and sexy—I fancy him like hell.

I put on a slinky black nightgown I bought earlier with Maman, then go to the kitchen to raid the larder. I pour myself some wine, get a croissant and some grapes. Walking back up the stairs, I feel voluptuously sexy in my slinky gown.

The main staircase, wide, with thick blue carpet, divides into two at the top. The left-hand branch leads to my room. On the top stair, I'm startled by a voice.

"Solange?"

Coming up the stairs towards me is Philippe. He's in evening dress, and has a broad smile on his face.

"Philippe? I thought you were away?" I still feel startled, unsettled.

"I have returned a day early." He comes to stand in front of me on the landing and smiles again.

"Maman. . . ." What can I say, how. . . . ?

"I *know, ma petite.* I know where Véronique is, of course. It is of no importance. *Ça n' importe rien.*"

"Oh?" Why do I feel awkward? The American in me?

He smiles down at me, takes my shoulders, kisses the top of my head. He's tall and slender. His looks are beautiful rather than handsome. His hair is dark brown, collar-length; his eyes are dark brown, too. Somehow he doesn't look a bit like a stepfather.

"You are going to bed?"

His quizzical smile makes me suddenly realize that I'm standing here in next to nothing. Well, with him looking at me, that's how it feels. Thin black silk, the lace just covering my nipples. Thin, thin straps.

I turn and walk towards my room. I don't feel like a

stepdaughter at this moment. At the door I hesitate. My hands are full with the glass of wine, croissant, grapes.

"I will open the door for you."

"Thank you."

"Goodnight, *ma petite*."

I turn and look at him. "Goodnight, Philippe."

He smiles and quietly closes my door. I breathe, with a sudden realization of how gauche and shy I felt. Is it because he will soon no longer be my stepfather?

I find that I cannot eat the croissant or the grapes. I get into the huge bed. The covers, which match the curtains, are of dark and light pink silk. It's very beautiful—very French. I drink my wine and then lie down, smile as I notice the mirrored ceiling. What a waste, though, with me alone here.

I wish it were tomorrow and that my mother were here. Why are she and Philippe separating? My thoughts jump irrelevantly to Jan—and it doesn't hurt too much.

I'm not feeling sleepy. I'm lying here, just looking up at myself in the mirrored ceiling. I push the covers back so that I can see my body. The black silk heightens the pinkness of my skin. I recall lying here naked, masturbating. I think I'll get a mirrored ceiling put in my bedroom at home.

Just as I sit up to take off my gown, the door opens. I freeze. I'm minutely aware of myself as I swallow and touch my throat, heart pounding. Philippe has closed the door and stands looking at me. He's in a short, dark blue robe and has two tulip-shaped champagne glasses in one hand; in the other is a bottle of Dom Perignon.

"I thought you might like a nightcap."

"I've had some wine." My voice is hardly above a whisper. Why am I so nervous? Why am I feeling so *excited*?

He comes over, in a very leisurely manner, and puts the wine and glasses down on the night table, then sits down next to me. I'm on the side of the huge bed nearer the door; I'd thrown the covers back to the other side, and I realize that one minute later and he'd have walked in on me fingering myself.

He takes my hand, kisses it. All form, no genuine warmth. Philippe de Courcy, I realize, has an empty soul. He takes my face in his hands, kisses me. "You are beautiful, Solange."

I can't say anything. He pulls me closer and kisses me. I can't even respond. Or pull away, either.

He smiles, stands up, takes a gold lighter from his pocket and goes around the room lighting the various candles in their silver candelabras. At the huge, ornate fireplace, he kneels and lights the logs. He returns to me and turns out the bedside lamp.

I'm now kneeling. Sitting back on my heels, I look up at him.

"Tell me to leave, and I will go." He gently brushes my face.

Why can't I answer? I watch him open the champagne, pour me a glass. He nods slightly and drinks. My hand is shaking as I drink; he notices, smiles, takes my glass from me.

I'm aware of him gripping my arms, pulling me steadily from the bed until I stand before him. He slips the tiny straps from my shoulders, and the gown slithers down my body, draping itself gracefully around my feet.

His hands go to my breasts. As he fondles my nipples, I close my eyes and allow myself to give in to the always-enjoyable sensation. . . . One of the logs crackles and startles me. The candles flicker; the room has many lights and shadows.

I'm suddenly unsure of where I am—or even of *who* I am. The candlelight, the log fire, have transported us to another time, another place. He's not Philippe, and I—I'm not Solange, not anymore.

Instead, he becomes transmuted into one of my favorite fantasies: my seducer and lover, la Bête. I, la Belle, stand before him; only this Belle would never have treated him so coldly, so cruelly. This Belle would have allowed, *encouraged*, la Bête to ravish her, seduce her, love her, do anything he wanted with her. The face of Jean Marais floats before me, and I change it into the face of Jean Marais as la Bête in Cocteau's film. As Avenant, the hero, Jean Marais was handsome; but as la Bête . . . Oh, how beautiful, how sensuous! Am I the only woman to dream of la Bête taking, fucking, *loving* her? If I had been la Belle, I would never have wanted him to change back into a mere mortal. To lose myself in that beautiful Beast . . . I can envisage the sensual sexiness of it. And the fucking—it would be glorious. When I dream of it, it always is.

I don't understand how any woman could see la Bête and not fall in love with him. And am I the only woman who went to see *Star Wars* and fell in love with Chewbacca? Wookiee-Nookie—how *divine!* I always wonder where he keeps *it*. Is it telescopic, only to be seen when he gets turned on? A turned-on Wookiee—gorgeous! I bet he could go on forever!

And Darth Vader—am I the only woman to have watched his stride with a swirl of his black cloak, and wonder what he *fucked* like? Ravished by Darth Vader . . . I wonder what his is like—as big, dark, and ominous as he is? What would an analyst make of my sexual fantasies, of la Bête, Chewbacca, Darth Vader . . . ? And who next—King Kong? (I try to imagine what it's like—King Kong *coming!*)

I know people get turned on by animals—bestiality. But I'm not one of those, *that's* not my dream at all. For la Bête is not an *animal*—la Bête is . . . magic.

How I wish I could really find *ma* Bête, the one for me! In a lonely chateau we would live and love. . . . read literature, write novels and poems. And I would have his babies. . . .

Ma Bête. . . . où es tu, ma Bête? Where?

The kiss on my pussy hair brings me back to reality. The stark reality of the situation before me, Philippe, on his knees, gently kissing my pussy hair, my thighs, my legs, my feet, my toes.

What *is* this? I can't let this happen! *I can't fuck my mother's husband!*

He kisses my pussy hair again, gently feels between my legs. Slips a finger between the already moist lips of my waiting little cunt. "You desire me!" he laughs.

"Philippe, you're my mother's husband. Her *husband!*"

He sits back on his heels and smiles insolently, making me blush. I feel so stupid! I feel like his little stepdaughter. I go and stand in front of the fire, and he comes up behind me.

"Please, Philippe." He doesn't move. "Please. It would be best." He still doesn't move. I turn to face him, and he takes his robe off. His cock is huge: fat and huge. All I know is that I want to feel it inside me. . . .

He puts his hands on my shoulders, gently pushes me to the floor. I'm lying on the carpet, my arms and legs spread as he's battering away at me. I watch the flickering shadows, smell the burning logs. I close my eyes slightly, and the room becomes a magical world. . . . I want only la Bête's face to be there. The face of la Bête: blond and gorgeous. Why does it look like Jan-Toby Axelsson's face, as he looks when he had his blond mustache and beard? Can *he* be ma Bête?

I claw at his back as I come, and he still goes on fucking me. Whose back? La Bête's? Jan-Toby's? Yes, yes. . . . not Philippe's. *Never* Philippe's.

He grunts and exclaims as he comes. He kisses me. We look at each other, lying close, saying nothing. After a while I sit up and move closer to the fire. He comes behind me, encloses me in his arms, kisses my neck. And then he eats me again, and I begin to ache from all the coming.

He leans over me. "We make good sex together, Solange."

"Yes. . . ." I whisper.

"I knew that you would be like this, just like this. So beautiful to make love to."

"Did you?"

"Oh, yes. A man always knows a woman worth making love to." He looks at me again. "I would like to hurt you. You would like me to hurt you?"

I gaze up into his brown eyes. When he smiles, they look slanted. . . . I think of my latest novel, in which Pandora fucked Lucifer himself.

"Hurt me?" What is it he wants to do to me?

"Would you not like to be owned—to be hurt?" He laughs, joyfully. "You have read 'O'—*l'Histoire d'O?* Every sensuous woman has read 'O'."

"Philippe?" I struggle to sit up, but he grabs for me and holds me down, pinning my arms above my head. *"Please. . . !"* I panic. Can he really mean this? This kind of thing has never happened to me before. I've never *wanted* anything like this—not *real.* "If you hurt me, I'll scream," I tell him in a husky, nervous voice. "I'll cause a great deal of trouble for you."

He laughs, unruffled, and kisses me. "I will not. Have no fear, my little one. Evidently, you are not one who enjoys herself, who satisfies herself, with being hurt."

"No!"

"Not even a little bit? Not even the aching from so many orgasms?"

How did he know that? "That's different."

"Ah . . ." His smile, complacent. *"That* pain you desire. *Vive la petite mort!"*

He kisses me and we're suddenly laughing. We roll over, and I sit on top of him, to lower myself onto that wonderfully *fat,* erect cock.

"Ah . . ." He holds my waist, pulling me down onto him.

"This pain you love, *ma chérie."*

How can I deny it? *Is* there a little masochism in all of us? And how far could we let ourselves go, bit by bit, little by little? Until we are enslaved, like "O," by our own deviant desires?

"Wait. I want you the other way." He shrugs me from him, jumps up and grabs the pillows, roughly pushes me over

80

them. "I want you *this* way." I cry out as he pushes, too impatiently, too quickly, into my ass. He feels for my button —and I explode again.

*　*　*

Morning. I've never woke up feeling guilty before, and I don't like it.

At least Philippe—thank God—isn't here. And thank God my mother isn't here. How can I face either of them, ever again?

And what the fuck am I crying for?

The room is dark. I get out of bed and pull the cord to open the drapes. The sunlight dazzles me. I turn away from the window and look around at the debris of last night's guilt. The candles are all burned out. The fire, cold ... no, a slight smolder.

Oh, shit! I feel sick and, oh Jesus, I feel so wretchedly *guilty*. I pick up my silk nightgown from where I left it on the floor last night, and toss it onto one of the chairs. The bed sheets are crumpled and stained—oh, hell! I feel like a guilty child—how can I explain stained, crumpled sheets? The bed smells so sexy when I go and sit on it. Madeleine, the housekeeper, will make the bed, and she'll know someone's made love to me. I wouldn't mind that, of course, but she's not so stupid she won't realize that there was no one here last night but Philippe. Oh, hell! *Will she tell my mother ... ?*

I dash to the dressing table, return to the bed with my bottle of l'Heure Bleue and empty half of it onto the stained sheet. That conceals the sexy smell, but not the stain. The *stain* ... Ah! I grasp the bottle of Dom Perignon, still half full of flat champagne, and pour it lavishly over the sheet, then rub and rub at it, to rub away the stain and the smell ... and my guilt with them, perchance. There ... I accidentally spilt the champagne, and some perfume, too. Oh, Solange! What a clumsy deceiver you are! But it's all I can do; improvisation is exhausted.

I lie in the bath. I've poured more *parfum* and body shampoo into the water than I usually use. I rub angrily at my sore little pussy. My bottom's sore; I massage it gently. I'm still crying a little, on and off.

But at least *something* has changed. There's something, at least, to be said for this horrendous feeling of guilt: It's taken my mind completely off Jan-Toby Axelsson.

I settle back and relax, almost disappearing beneath the

water. I've filled the bath too full; it spills over onto the thick pink carpet. My hair, bubbly with shampoo, is piled on top of my head.

Yes ... I have to relax, calm myself. It's going to be all right, Solange. Maman will never know. She'll never know that we awoke at dawn this morning, after a few hours' sleep, and made love once again. Made love? No, not that, there was no *love*. We *fucked*—as crudely as the word can sometimes sound. The fucking and the coming: enjoyment limited to the bare physical functions, that's all. We lay side by side, not sleeping, not talking, until I finally blurted out: "You won't mention anything to Maman?"

He laughed, hugging me gently to him. It almost seemed caring. He kissed my face. His gentleness puzzled me.

"Non, ma petite. I shall say nothing to Véronique, I would never be so insensitive—I adore her too much." He kissed me. "And I adore you, too."

"Tell me—why are you and Maman separating?" I sat up and looked at him. Lying there with his arms behind his head, he looked so insolent.

"The idea—it's Véronique's, not mine."

"But *why?*"

"It is Véronique you must ask." He smiled, caressed my face. "My ... how shall I say? ... preferences ..." He waved his hands, enigmatically, in a small circle. "Maybe it will be better this way."

Preferences? Oh!—he wanted to hurt me.

He pulled me to him, kissed me. Turned me over, pressed me beneath him. "Why do you not return to France to live, *ma chérie?* To Paris—or to the South? I could see you—you could become my mistress." He smiled; but his lazy smile isn't like Jan's, it's cold, icy cold, empty of any love or even of affection. "I think I would like you for my mistress—I could teach you so much."

"Teach me?" Teach me what? "Wasn't I good enough?"

"You know you are good enough, more than enough," he laughed. "You are very good. But ... *other* things ..." He kissed me, then scrutinized me at arm's length. "Are you quite certain that does not intrigue you just a little?"

"What? What exactly are you trying to hint at, Philippe?"

"You would look beautiful in a collar." He caressed my neck with a proprietorial, assessing touch. "A collar of solid gold, of thick gold links."

His manner, intense, obsessed, with an undertone of ecstatic excitement, frightened and repelled me—but also fascinated. How much, I wondered, *would* I do for someone I loved? Would I let Jan inflict pain on me because he loved me and I loved him?

"No? It does not intrigue you? You are not in the least tempted to know what it can feel like?" His subdued, resonant laugh sounded to me like an echo of a boisterous Dionysian orgy: a world where orgies and sadism were taken for granted and, therefore, inescapable.

Why the fuck would he think that I would like his nasty world? "I don't think I'd enjoy having a ring through my pussy," I told him angrily. "I *enjoy* sex and loving too much to turn them into a pathetically degenerate sport for sadists, for people who have to have someone else's pain before they can get off."

Philippe grinned wryly. "Perhaps there *are* uses for man's inhumanity to man—or woman. . . . But, *ma chérie, you* are indeed not a woman to be made into a slave—not completely so. All the same, I think you would love to be *owned* by a man whom you love—a man who passionately loves you."

"That's not the same thing."

"But the line between is so thin; how can one distinguish the difference?" He laughed and kissed me. *"Ma chérie,* you—you are made to cherish and love. You are made to give babies to."

"I am?" In Philippe's eyes, this was clearly a great compliment.

"Yes, truly," he nodded, smiling but solemn. "Why have you not yet found your man and had his babies?"

"I . . ."

"Is there someone whose babies you want to have?"

I closed my eyes. "Oh, yes . . ."

"Well, then?"

"He's married. He loves somebody else. He gave his baby to her. I met him too late."

"What a pity! Yes, *ma chérie,* it would be nice to give you babies."

"Oh, really, Philippe!" I said angrily. Never, never would I want Philippe's children.

"Yes, really. It would arrange itself very well. Now that Véronique and I are parting, I will remarry. Someone younger. I will have children."

I began feeling guilty again, as soon as he mentioned Véronique. "I don't wish to discuss you and Maman."

"Why not?" he said in surprise. "You and I—we have always been friends, haven't we?"

83

"I know." My eyes filled with tears. "But now we have *fucked*," I cried. "How can I ever face Maman?"

He cradled me, kissing my hair, so gently it surprised me. For someone who'd like to hurt me, he was so considerate, so solicitous.

"There is no need to make of all this a convoluted emotional riddle. We have loved. *Ç'est la vie*. I enjoyed it; you enjoyed it. There is no need to feel guilty. *Never* feel guilty about love, *ma petite*—never about love. Only about hate. Hate is what really merits feelings of guilt."

We kissed again. We fucked again. I remember Philippe's last words to me, as I was falling asleep: "You would be so beautiful to hurt, *ma chérie*. Think about it, consider it well. Come back to France, be my mistress, be my lover. Let me love you. Let me hurt you a little, just a little. . . ."

I suddenly awake. I must have fallen asleep in the bath: the water is lukewarm.

Dried, with my hair finger-combed, I suddenly realize what I must do. To me, at this time, it is the *only* thing I can do.

I write a note to my mother explaining that I have had an urgent phone call and have returned to California. I book a flight to L.A. via New York.

As I fly home, all I can think of is, *why* didn't I send Philippe away, refuse to have anything to do with him? Why did I enjoy it all?

4

"Gulley!"

Gulley and I cuddle, delighted to see each other. Miriam smiles at me; we hug each other briefly.

It's so good to be home in my own little house. I rush to the sea terrace. The sea is why I could never live in Paris, in New York, in London.

I sit down and Miriam brings me some coffee. Gulley jumps up onto my lap and settles down; I find his "Tyger" purring, his "Tyger" furriness, very comforting.

I feel safe again. I'm *home!*

"Did you *enjoy* yourself?" Miriam's face is ecstatic as she talks in her usual excited, italicized way.

"Everything was great," I lie and smile.

"You saw Justin? He's been going crazy."

"No, I stayed with Matthew for two days."

Miriam chats on, gets me up to date so everything as my bath runs, and I sit and soak and read some mail. Miriam perches on the side, still chatting away. A letter from Johnny: he rang but I was away, he'll come when he can; and why was I away when he wanted to come?

Oh, Johnny . . . I whisper to myself.

Miriam gets us some dinner. We sit on the terrace and eat it, enjoying the warm September night.

"Oh *yes!* I *forgot!*" Miriam says excitedly. "You have *two packages.*" Before I can say anything she goes off, to return with a box wrapped in gold paper, with gold bows. "The other's big and heavy." She disappears again and returns, pulling and pushing it. The huge box is wrapped just like the first, all in gold.

"What *is* it?" I exclaim.

"I've been *dying* to open them for *weeks.*" She claps her hands. "Quick! *Hurry!*"

I can't help but laugh at the little-girl look on Miriam's face. "You open the big one," I tell her. She expertly demolishes the gift wrappings. I'm filled with curiosity and excitement myself, and join her on the floor on my knees, unwrapping the packages. We uncover a sealed carton. Miriam runs a long fingernail along the taped edges until finally the lid can be opened. "God, I hope it's not a fucking *bomb.*" We both look at each other, frozen for an instant, then burst into uproarious giggles. We pull back the flaps of the box.

"Records?" says Miriam, giving me a quizzical look. "My *God!* Did you *order* all *these?* There's got to be *fifty,* at *least.*"

We look through them. Willie Nelson. Waylon Jennings. The Rolling Stones. The Allman Brothers. Crosby, Stills and Nash. Neil Young. Leon Russell. Jackson Brown. The Band. . . .

"My God!" Miriam scratches her head. "There's *got* to be *every record* these dudes ever *made! Who* are they *from?* You *know, don't* you?" She shakes my shoulder. *"Who?"*

"I, um. . . ." I rub my palms together—they're wet.

"Quick! Open the *other* one." She's pulling the wrapping off the smaller box.

"No—let me!" I take it from her, pull the lid off the box, which is gold also. There's a letter on top; Miriam grabs for it.

"No!" I snatch it back. "It's *private!*" On the front of the envelope is written LITERARY LADY, and it's sealed. I suddenly don't want to read it yet. Not with Miriam here.

I place it on the glass table behind me. "I'll read it later."

Miriam looks at me with intense curiosity. "Special, huh?"

"Yes."

"When did this all *happen?"* With her head to one side, she looks pert and cheeky.

"You know when I went to that party?"

"The *Christophidou* one?" She rolls her eyes up, renewing her reproach.

"Mm. Well, the guy who brought me home—it's *him.* He came back, the day you went up to see Frank. He stayed a couple of days. That's why I rushed off to France."

"Oh . . ." She sits back on her heels, gives me a puzzled look. "It's *off?"*

"It was never on," I sigh. "He's married. It was a one, *two,* night stand."

"What's all this, then?" She nods at the records and the other gift I haven't looked at yet. "A thank-you present?"

"I don't know."

"Open it, then!"

"Oh, I *can't!"* I find myself terrified, crying, unable to touch the contents of the box, unable to face what they might cause me to feel.

"Let *me!"* Ignoring my tears, she dives into the box, pulling at tissue paper. "My *God!"*

She hands me a heavy necklace of silver and turquoise, mother-of-pearl and water opal. "It's a *squash blossom,"* she says. *"Indian."*

"Yes . . ." I examine it. Hummingbirds, it's beautiful. I'm still crying, but now it's because those feelings, undammed, have flooded in and swamped and overwhelmed me.

"Jesus *Christ!* Do you *know* how much they *cost? Shit!"* She soon has everything laid out on the table: Another squash blossom—flowers. Some necklaces of silver and turquoise. Rings and bracelets of silver and turquoise, and a collection of earrings too.

"Jesus . . . fucking . . . *Ke-rist!* There's several *thousand dollars'* worth here!" She gapes at me. I've managed to stop crying, but I can't seem to stop trembling. *"Shit!* Some fuckin' *thank-you* present!" she says, awed.

I pick up the necklace of hummingbirds and gently caress it. "It's so *beautiful.* Oh, God . . ." I'm crying again.

. "What the fuck did you *do* for the dude?"

I huddle down into a little collapsed ball, with my head on my knees, crying my eyes out. The necklace digs into my cheek, but I don't move.

"Solange . . . Jesus, girl!" Miriam cradles me in her arms. "It's all right." Gentle, sweet Miriam. She continues to comfort me, "Fuckin' *hell!* The dude sure *got through* to your little *pussy,* didn't he?"

I'm still crying.

"When are you going to *learn,* girl? So ya *lost* ya little *head* and ya little *pussy* to a *married man?"*

"I thought I'd get over it," I reply, looking up at her regretfully. "I mean, we're not going to see each other again."

"Who *is* this dude?"

"It doesn't matter. . . ." I pick up the sealed envelope. "I think I'll just go to bed. . . ." I can feel Miriam's curious, solicitous eyes on me as I leave her on the terrace. I hold the enevelope in one hand and the hummingbird necklace in the other. I turn, uncertainly. "Um . . . I'll talk to you tomorrow. And . . . thanks . . ." I go back to her; we peck a kiss at each other, and she gives me a comforting hug.

I'm too exhausted even to wash my face. I pull off my caftan and climb into bed. The necklace is next to me. I'm wondering why he sent me all those things. I look at the envelope for a full minute before I open it. I read it, and cry. Then I read it again.

To my beautiful Literary Lady:

I thought your rock album collection could do with some improvement, and being an expert. . . .

The jewelry? I thought it would surprise you. It's what I like—I just hope it's what you like? I rather think it is. (Just as you know *what music I'd like.)*

I want to write, to say, much more to you than I'm going to. But if I did? Well, my life would become impossibly complicated, and it's that way enough already. I only wish it could be some other way.

I hope I haven't hurt you. And you know that I love you. (Between us we've got some rotten lousy timing!)

There's one more album I've got to get to you. (I

*finished it last week). It's not pressed yet. Hey! I bought
the records you played for me. (I play them in my den.)
Getting me some class, huh?*

*Literary Lady, don't be angry with me, and for God's
sake don't hate me. I can still hear you telling me (and
you do too have an accent) that you love me. I think of
other things too—but if I wrote them down, you'd
accuse me of pornography.*

*I've been writing some poetry, in my den, listening to
the music you knew I'd like.*

*This had better be it, my beautiful Literary Lady.
Perhaps I should call you Heloise and sign myself
Abelard.*

*Don't be angry with me. Don't be hurt. And please
don't hate me.*

I love you, my Literary Lady.

Jan

Could I really have been crying for hours? It certainly feels
like it. But I can't cry anymore, and I'm wondering if there
can be anything left to cry about.

I wish I could write him a reply. But how can I? I know he
only wrote that letter because he thought it was the right
thing to do, that I would like to read it.

It's no damn good loving someone who doesn't love me.
Even though his letter says he does, his letter is mere
politeness. He *doesn't* really love me. He never did.

*   *   *

The next few weeks are hectic but very enjoyable. The
third Pandora book is out in paperback.

Me, sedate and beautiful, on the Johnny Carson show,
plugging the book. I was worried about the show. Why? Only
because Jan, in between making love, had told me that he
often watched the Carson show, that he exercised with his
weights while watching it.

I had bought a new dress and boots for the show. And now
I wonder why the hell I bothered, and why I'm feeling so
nervous, especially when everything is over with Jan. But it's
just . . . just that I want him to see me on the show, looking
beautiful and being witty, intelligent, charming. I want him to
realize what he's missed out on.

Besides all this, I've finished the fourth Pandora book.
Miriam and I Xerox it, and I take it to New York. Justin's

delighted with it, and so is Gerald, my editor. It will be out in hardback on the spring list.

I stay with Matthew for a few days. We discuss—again—the idea of having a baby. I tell him that I'm still thinking about it, but that I need more time. Dear Matthew, he understands. My friendship with Matthew is precious to me, it's like having a foot in another dimension, a dimension where relationships between people can be more honest without being at the same time less sexy. I don't want to hurt him at all. I know that by delaying a decision on this question, I'm hurting him a little, but it's just that I *do* need more time. I can't bring myself to say a flat "no," that it's nonsense, that it wouldn't be fair to the child, all the other escape clauses.

* * *

Back in L.A. The morning after my return I have a visitor. It's Johnny, down for a few days.

Johnny Brandigan. Every time I see him it's like the first time. I stand there, just gaping in amazement at his Irish good looks, the improbable architecture of his animated face, and feeling like a foolish little girl.

I watch him climb out of his TransAm. There's a layer of dust over it, covering the big gold eagle decal on the hood. Where can he have been to get it in such a state?

He stands and looks at me, and smiles. I can't help myself; I run into his arms, and he catches me, swings me off my feet, kisses me. He carries me into the house and kicks the door shut. We're still kissing, and go on until I fidget to be down.

"I'll get you some coffee," I say, hugging him.

"I want *you* first, *mavourneen*."

"You have the coffee first!" I smile up at his blue eyes, those *bloody* blue eyes! I think it was those eyes that first did it for me. . . .

. . . It had been raining hard and it was cold, that damp, bone-chilling English cold. I was irritable, headachy, period-achy, and worse, I was late. As I was still in my first year I was very punctilious, usually, about not being late for tutes and lectures.

I don't know, even now, how it happened; it was all so fast. My attention was focused on my lateness. I remember that I cut (illegally) across a corner of the slippery, soggy, wet grass of the quad. There was a silly rhyme that had kept on echoing all morning in my mind: "March winds will blow, and we shall have snow." It had been windy and rainy, but now snowy. I hated this corroding cold, which the stupid little gas fire did nothing to keep at bay.

Then suddenly my feet were elsewhere, and my poor little ass came down hard on the squidgy turf. "Shit!" I looked around for my books.

"I'm thinking you could be doing with a little gentlemanly assistance," said a deep voice from behind me as two arms yanked me to my feet.

That was the exact moment when I first looked into those deep set, blue, blue eyes; they smiled at me in the friendliest way. He began picking up my books, and handed them to me one at a time: Fry, Gilchrist, Erdman, Wilson. And then my mud-smeared notes. And lastly the complete Blake, Keynes' edition, which I always carried everywhere like a talisman.

"I don't need to be asking what you're reading, do I?" It was only then that I realized that he was Irish.

"I was ... um ... late." I felt asininely foolish, idiotic, *stupid*, standing there with clammy mud oozing through my jeans.

"You must have been! Or do you make a habit of infiltrating the forbidden fringes of the lawns?" He leaned over me, getting his handkerchief muddy wiping the back of my leather jacket.

"Oh! I'm so sorry." I blushed, back of hand to mouth.

"But I won't tell on you. We don't want you being sent down, do we?"

"Sent down?" I echoed, my voice full of alarm. "But ..."

He burst out laughing, and I realized, too late, that he was teasing. I wasn't used to Johnny's teasing then. To ease my embarrassment, he asked, "Now why is it I don't have any beautiful little ladies at *my* lectures?"

I'd never talked to any of the staff except at lectures or tutes. He seemed to tower over me, those blue eyes occupying half the gray sky; I bit my lip as I smiled back timidly, a pusillanimous, weak-kneed female, watching him rub his black beard and stroke his black mustache. "Thank you" was all I managed to get out. I clutched my portable library and ran for my life.

I didn't see him again until three days later. I was out shopping with my roommate, Cynthia Greenham-ffinch. William Morton, a third-year student reading Greats, kept on asking us out—both of us; we were trying, hilariously, to analyze his motives. With an armful of packages, I was turning towards Cynthia, walking almost crabwise. Bump. I dropped the parcels . . . and again I heard that laugh and found my field of vision totally occupied by the blue of those eyes. I'd have sworn he could expand them, like those birds that can inflate their cheeks. I stood there with my mouth open and stared at him as he picked up my parcels.

"D'you think fate's maybe tryin' to tell us something?"

"Oh! Um . . ."

"At least it's not raining this time."

"No . . . No, it's not."

He carefully inventoried my boots, my jeans rolled up to the knees, my white arctic fox fur jacket; and my hair, long and streaked, with a fringe. "You'd better be bein' more careful, me little darlin'." He winked and with a wave of his hand as he walked off.

"Do you *know* him?" Cynthia demanded.

"No. Not really. I bumped into him the other day. Well, no . . . I, um, I slipped in the quad, and he picked me up."

"Well, lucky *you*, darling."

"Who is he? Do you know him?"

"He's Johnny Brandigan, that's who."

"What's a Johnny Brandigan?" I asked dryly.

"Fellow of Balliol. Goes with Valerie Barnard."

"Who's she?"

"Professor Barnard's daughter."

"Oh."

"All the girls get their knickers in a twist over him. He is rather more-ish."

"Mmm . . ."

The next Saturday afternoon, Ben Simmons and I were walking down the High Street after buying some albums. Ben was a sort of steady—my only steady, in fact. In fact, the only guy I went out with at all, though we didn't see each other more than once or twice a week. Ben was from Wichita, Kansas, and over in Oxford on a Rhodes scholarship. I *liked* Ben; above all, because he was studying English literature, but also because he had a lovely sense of humor. Besides, he was quite good-looking, with bright hazel eyes against dark brown hair and beard.

We went into the Honey Pot to have tea and crumpets. We were laughing about a party we were going to later. Ben had got hold of some grass and persuaded me to buy it for us, a lid of the best Moroccan being affordable to rich me and not to him on a lowly scholarship. We were on our second cup of tea and Ben on his fourth crumpet, when who but Johnny

Brandigan came in and sat at the only free table—the one next to ours. He smiled broadly and made a few remarks to Ben, whom he evidently knew; but he kept his eyes cheekily on me. Defenseless, I had to wait a thousand years for Ben to finish his tea and crumpets.

I really wasn't surprised when Johnny Brandigan turned up at that party; but he said nothing, just grinned wolfishly at me.

I wasn't even surprised when he turned up at a smaller, private little dinner party given by George and Hilary Mason, my parents' friends who lived just outside Oxford. Again he kept staring at me, as though he wanted to devour me . . . and my little panties got quite wet.

One week after that dinner party, Johnny persuaded me to go away for the weekend with him. We stayed at a beautiful little pub of pale gray stone in the Cotswolds. I'd never been made love to so much; I'd never even spent the whole night with a man. I'd only had two men, anyway—the first at sixteen (the boy next door) and the second, Ben Simmons, both of us so quiet and shy.

Johnny Brandigan was the first man to eat me. The first man to teach me to eat him. The first man that ever fucked my ass. And, best of all—the first man who'd ever made me have an orgasm . . .

. . . Johnny had his coffee and took me to bed. We spent the rest of the day fucking and talking.

It's two in the morning, and I'm lying along Johnny, my head on his shoulder. He's holding me tightly; it feels so comfortable, this body I know every single inch of. He's sun-tanned all over—his garden is evidently secluded. But his appendix scar is white, as is the tiny scar on his right shoulder. He has a scar through his left eyebrow, too. I touch it and kiss it. It was from a drunken brawl in Hong Kong, he once told me.

"I've missed you, me little darlin'."

"Have you?" I'm used to his Irish blarney; I don't know whether to believe him, not anymore.

"Yes." He slaps my ass, then grips it in his large hands, smiling. "And who have you been offering that delectable little cunt to?"

"Don't talk like that!" Me, all prim and proper.

"You *haven't* been fucking?"

"Don't use that word." I say peevishly.

"What word? 'Fuck?' "

"Yes! You make it sound so *dirty*. And *I* make love."

"Oh, do ya now, *macushla?*" He slaps my ass again, fondly. " 'Fuck' isn't dirty, anyway." He grins, knowing I'm teasing him. " '*Fuck*' is Chaucerian." At this, we dissolve into Chaucerian laughter, and he rolls me over and kisses me. "I've missed you so, me little poppet . . ." And he's eating me again, and of course, I'm coming again . . . and again . . .

We go for a walk along the beach the next day, holding hands like a pair of young lovers. He's got me wondering again why we didn't make it work. We just walk along the beach, not even talking, just enjoying being with each other, and I keep on thinking of our years in Oxford . . .

. . . I fell in love with Johnny Brandigan the first night he took me to bed. I was in total awe of this man: my first big shiny hero. I worshiped him and I wanted to go on loving him forever. But the first time he tried to go down on me, how I squealed and wriggled! I was nearly nineteen, but so naive!

When that mouth of his and that tongue of his started to do all those delectable things to my little pussy, I gave way to all that gorgeously electric erotic feeling and came, screaming. I dove into the pillows, hiding my face and crying—I was so *embarrassed*. How *could* I have screamed out like that? And that feeling—what was it? My daintily fingered little orgasms had never been so violently, so shatteringly sensuous. I only knew that I wanted more; and Johnny gave me much more. We spent the summer together, and Johnny Brandigan turned me into a woman.

Then my second year with Johnny. Not living together, of course, for he was a Fellow of his college, and I was only a lowly undergrad. We spent our weekends together in the Cotswolds, at Stratford-on-Avon, at Warwick, Banbury, Cirencester, Malvern. The next year we went even further afield: He took me to Dublin, and I was enchanted. I don't know how many plays I saw at the Abbey Theatre, all in their true and original flavor.

I met some alluringly antisocial poets at a little pub Johnny took me to somewhere among the grimy back streets of Dublin. One of them wouldn't even talk to us. Johnny had sold out, he said, "bein' a bloody fuckin' lecturer in *English* at Oxford." I giggled, and Johnny surreptitiously pinched my ass. And there was Johnny's childhood friend, Kerry O'Don-nel; I never found out what he did, but he didn't like to be seen around much, and he asked me if I'd give him a "contribution for the Cause" when he heard I was Johnny's rich bitch. He frightened me at first, but then we took him to dinner and he turned out to be witty and sardonic and charming. He was very pleased I wasn't British, anyway. Another childhood friend of Johnny's, Liam O'Shaughnessy, was a first officer on a merchant ship; we took him to dinner, too. Such a *man!* Yes, I rather liked Ireland.

And then came my graduation, with first class honors! Johnny fucked my ass off that weekend in celebration. He was as pleased and proud of me as I was. Actually, I think his pleasure meant even more to me.

That's when I rented the cottage. I'd still attend Oxford, but *now* for my two years' postgraduate work. It wasn't that I really *needed* a doctorate in literature, I just wanted to have one. Johnny and I in our little cottage ... of course, the happiness didn't last for long ...

... "What are you thinking about?"

Startled, I stop walking. "Just about us in Ireland. At Oxford. At the cottage.".

He lifts my face up. "Why the fuck didn't you *wait?*" he asks angrily. His anger rebounds from mine. We both know it's too late now.

* * *

I watch Johnny. He's sitting on one of the sofas, with Gulley curled up next to him; an air of domesticity surrounds them.

He's just on his second large glass of whiskey. This worries me. He's always been a social drinker, but he's drinking more than ever—two whole bottles of Scotch in the two days he's been here. I wonder what I can do.

"It's been over two bloody years," he suddenly says.

"Two years?" I go over and sit next to him.

"Since you've been here."

"Yes."

"And you're happy, poppet, are you?"

"I guess so. In my own little way. I don't know. . . ."

He reaches out and touches my arm, touches my throat, my breasts. His hand is warm and firm. Finally, he grips my face, his thumb on my chin. "You're being bloody cryptically perverse, aren't you?"

"No, I am *not.*"

"You are." He pulls me closer and we fall back on the sofa with me pinned beneath him. He kisses me. "My immensely fuckable little darlin'..." He kisses me again. "But you're unhappy. And you know you bloody well are. I can tell."

"You can?" I wriggle unsuccessfully to get free.

"Of course. What's up, eh? Tell me."

"It's nothing. *Really*." But he doesn't believe me.

"I never meant to hurt you," he says.

"You didn't. You haven't."

"Yes, I did. You wouldn't be here if it weren't for me."

"Yes I would!" I protest. But would I?

...In France, two and a half years ago, I committed adultery with Johnny Brandigan. Not that I paid any heed to the legalistic niceties, but I *was* married to Rand at the time.

It doesn't seem that long ago. Marie-Claude and I were having dinner in Cannes before going on to a yacht party. I was gazing idly around the restaurant until I noticed *that* table and the man. I hadn't seen him for eight years. Johnny and I stared at each other.

"Ma chérie, what's the matter?" Marie-Claude asked. "You're so pale, like you'd seen a ghost."

Oh yes, how did the ghost manage to walk across the crowded restaurant and stand smiling before me?

"Johnny! It *is* you. I thought...." It was hard to speak, my throat was still so dry.

There were tiny lines around his eyes. He looked older, but it was still *him*, witty and lively, shining from those blue, blue eyes. His black hair, still no gray in it, hung thick and straight, longer.

"It's been a bloody long time, me little darlin'."

Oh, that beautiful Irish brogue! But not quite so Irish as before. "Yes, it has...." I pulled myself together and introduced Marie-Claude.

"Darlin'," he told me, "I'm in a bloody boring business meeting, but I *must* see you later."

"We're just about to leave," I lied. I didn't think I could stand the stress of seeing Johnny again.

"I want to see you later, *mavourneen*." He smiled, squeezed my hand.

"What about your wife?" I asked bitchily.

"What about your husband?" A ghost of a smile from Johnny Brandigan.

"He's at home. I'm staying with Marie-Claude for a few days."

"Well, me darlin', Amy's at home too."

I wondered why I couldn't take my eyes from his. And did I look all right? But I knew I did; Marie-Claude and I had face masked, hair washed, nail lacquered, primped, and preened all afternoon. And my dress, many shades of pink, was from Givenchy: peasant style, bared shoulders with little puffed sleeves, ample cleavage. I was looking better than I'd ever looked when I was with him. Back then, I'd been a little girl.

"Wait for me. I want to see you. I'll get rid of them," Johnny said urgently.

"I don't think . . . it's been such a long time, Johnny."

"Wait for me."

My heart turned somersaults. "Yes, Johnny."

Marie-Claude and I finished our crêpes Georgette, drank our coffee, indulged in a glass of Grand Marnier. I put mental shutters up across the restaurant, blanking out the region where Johnny was sitting.

"Let's go to our party, Marie-Claude."

"But . . ." She looked over toward Johnny's table.

I didn't. "No, Marie-Claude. *Please!*" And so we left the restaurant.

Outside, walking down the steps in the fresh air, I at last felt freer. Marie-Claude gave my arm a squeeze. She knew all about my feelings for Johnny, about what had happened between Johnny and me. In fact, she knew more about it than Johnny did.

"Solange!"

I turned. Johnny Brandigan rushed down the steps.

"You were bloody well leaving!"

"Yes, Johnny."

"But why?" He was genuinely puzzled and annoyed. He looked so handsome in his dinner jacket, his close-fitting, ruffled silk shirt. "Come on, we must talk."

"No."

"Yes!"

Marie-Claude took my hand, seeing the tears in my eyes. *"Ma chérie,* I will go on. Finish your talking, then join me."

"No, I . . ."

"Go. *Go!*" she whispered as she kissed my cheek. Marie-Claude, expert, knew that I'd never ended this particular relationship. I watched her climb into her taxi.

"Come on." Johnny tugged at my arm.

"Where?"

"To my room."

"Oh, no."

Johnny smiled. "It's a suite. I'm filthy bloody rich now. We can sit in the lounge, as respectable as you like. Come on, Solange, *macushla*."

Of course, I went . . .

We looked at each other, sipping our brandy. Johnny Brandigan, now famous poet and novelist. He'd taken off his jacket and bow tie, unbuttoned his shirt; I could see the lovely sexy black hair on his chest. Sudden panic: I had to get away from him and our past. To me, he was still Johnny Brandigan, love of my life; Johnny Brandigan, the man who'd walked out on me.

"Please, Johnny—I want to go now."

But he pulled me close, and we were unaccountably kissing. I didn't even feel it as Johnny carried me to the bedroom. . . .

After love and sleep I opened my eyes. Johnny was leaning over me, supporting himself on one elbow, watching me as he used to do.

"I'd forgotten how beautiful you look when you're asleep." Then Johnny Brandigan was making love to me again.

The dim bedside lamp was still on. It felt so good, as always, with Johnny, "I thought you wanted to talk."

"We *have* talked, *mucushla machree*." His hands gripped my ass tightly; it felt good.

I raised myself on my elbows, looked into his eyes, and it was at that exact moment that I realized I'd just committed adultery. I looked at Johnny, and knew it wasn't the first time for him.

I sat up, straddled him. I was wet, warm, sticky. His come ran from me onto his stomach. I touched it, tasted it, and he smiled: he'd taught me to do that.

"I loved you!" I suddenly cried out. "And you *left* me."

"Oh, darlin'," he said, cradling me in his arms, "I told you I was leaving, because it was something I *had* to do. It wasn't that I didn't love you. I *told* you."

"You bastard! You didn't *have* to go off like that."

"*You* were the one," he retorted angrily, "who went and got yourself married off as soon as my back was turned."

"Well, what did you expect?" I was still crying.

"I *asked* you to wait!"

"First you left. Then Daddy left." Me, crying as I hadn't cried since Johnny left me and Daddy died.

97

And then, just as suddenly as it had built up, it all dissolved; all the grief and hate. And Johnny was kissing and loving me again.

I spent two days with Johnny. I rang Marie-Claude, of course, and told her everything.

I rang Rand, but told him lies; Marie-Claude wasn't feeling too well. I had to stay and care for her.

The next day, Johnny was leaving for his home and wife, in America.

"I'm divorcing Amy," he said.

"What!" I sat up.

"I'm divorcing her. My lawyer's working on it now. I only stayed because of little Johnno. He's three now." A proud smile from Johnny. "I've got to arrange sharing him. Fifty-fifty. He's my son too. Amy's bein' the fuckin' bitch about it, though."

"Why are you divorcing her?" My heart pounded with exhilaration.

Johnny sat up, lit himself a Gitane, blew smoke forcibly. "It was a bad marriage. We should have stuck at having an affair. And then little Johnno came along. . . .and it's become worse. It's unbearable now." He grinned at me cheerfully. "You *should* have waited, shouldn't you?"

"Shut up!" I hit him.

"And are *you* happy, me little poppet?" He pulled me closer, still puffing at the Gitane.

"No. No, I'm not." I told him candidly about my dying marriage, and about Rand; what a wonderful sweet person he was; how I'd always love him, but as a dear friend, not as a lover.

"That's because you had *me*, me darlin'," Johnny joked.

"Marie-Claude's said for a long time that I should divorce Rand. But I guess I'm scared at the idea of being on my own. I'm very safe in Rand's shadow. I can write when I feel safe."

After that we said no more about relationships; we just fucked. Johnny carried my phone number in his wallet when he left for America.

He rang me from California. He wanted me to come to the States to live. He was unhappy; I was unhappy. He was just getting himself out of his unhappy marriage; I was just wasting away in mine, pretending it was all right. Everyone was accepting each other for what they *pretended* to be. Even Rand was pretending; he must have known that deep down I was intolerably unhappy. Our sex was almost negligible, but

98

he didn't seem to mind. I stayed in my study, writing and working, hardly ever seeing him.

I'd already talked at length to Marie-Claude about divorcing Rand, and after Johnny rang me that night, I decided. I went to Rand's room and woke him up.

"What? What is it, love?"

"I want a divorce." I felt horribly guilty, watching him rub sleep from his eyes.

"What?" Rand, no longer sleepy.

"I can't go on like this any longer."

"Like *what* any longer? What *are* you talking about?"

I realized then that he didn't know. He thought we were happy. I explained my feelings.

"Take a holiday. Think it over before you do anything." Wise words from Rand.

I did exactly that. I went to New York and stayed with Justin and Anna, and then to Los Angeles, where I stayed at the Beverly Wilshire.

Johnny came, and a gentle warmth surrounded us. We were both happy. And I knew with all certainty that even if I never saw Johnny again, even if we couldn't get it toegther, I could never go back to Rand.

Justin and Anna came to California for a week. That was where I first met Solly Steinberg. It all moved so fast, a clockwork whirlwind. Solly mentioned that he was selling his beach house. The person who'd been interested couldn't come up with the money. I went and looked it over: It was a beautiful house, if you could mentally subtract the decor. It had a huge garden, a large pool: enchantment. Justin and Solly fixed up the deal, and my life was changed.

I went back to France and divorced Rand, then Gulley and I moved to Malibu. For the first time. in my life I was on my own.

I went to bed with Phil Westing, who works for Solly. It was fun because I was no longer a little girl. I *knew* all about sex: how to please a man, how to get a man to please me. It was all a delightful prelude to my new life with Johnny.

And then it happened. Johnny rang me. He talked slowly, with long hesitations, telling me that he wouldn't be divorcing. He had to stay, with Amy.

It hurt. Oh, hell, did it hurt! But I was on my own; I was liberated; I could handle it. And I did.

Then, over a year ago, I met Johnny at one of Solly's parties. We slept together that night. For two days we fucked.

Since then, it's been every six or seven weeks. He comes down for three or four days.

How strange, that Johnny and I never really got it together. . . .

. . . "C'mon," says Johnny, "let's go to bed. You know I have to go tomorrow."

And so we do. The fucking is enjoyable. It's always enjoyable.

"I don't know why you bother with me," he says as I'm massaging his back. "You deserve someone better. You richly deserve someone noble and loving, to look after you properly. To faithfully serve you forever."

"I'm not complaining."

He turns over and I straddle him. As he smiles up at me, I ask him the question I haven't yet asked, and I suppose I should have asked before. "How's Amy doing?"

His face hardens. "Bitching, as usual."

Why did I ask the bloody question!

With a hint of cynicism, he adds, "I guess she's got a lot to bitch about." . . .

. . . It had been raining the night Johnny and Amy were returning to Monterey from San Francisco. The divorce *was* at last under way, but she'd been bitchy about the custody of Johnno. She was driving because Johnny had drunk too much. Johnno was jumping about in the back of the car, while his parents argued about him in the front. Amy screamed and shouted at Johnny, then insanely spun the steering wheel hard, sending them crashing through a barrier and down a hillside.

Little Johnno died two days later, without regaining consciousness. Amy lived, but in a wheelchair, never to walk again.

Johnny was riddled with guilt for his beloved son's death; just as he was riddled with guilt over his detested wife's paralysis, even though it was she who had crippled herself.

So Johnny stays with Amy. She continues her painting. Johnny's writing another novel. He can't leave, though they hate each other more and more, for Amy would never let him leave. . . .

. . . I lie along Johnny and kiss his chest, his beautiful dark furry chest. I rub his beard, finger his mustache.

"There's still no . . . ?"

100

"No. Thre's another specialist in Europe—we're seeing him next week."

"Oh." What else is there to say but "oh"?

His eyes are suddenly moist; I hold myself close to him. "Oh, Johnny. . . ."

He falls asleep in my arms. I only wish I could really comfort him, but I don't think anyone can. He wouldn't allow it. It seems to me he *needs* his little walled-in world of hate and pain . . .

I make him a huge breakfast and wonder when I'll see him again. The only two men I've ever *loved* are irrevocably married. Why can't *I* find some happiness?

"You're deep in thought, me little darlin'."

"Yes . . ."

"Darlin' . . . come here, I want to talk to you." I see the seriousness in Johnny's eyes. I go and sit on his lap. He kisses me, carefully. "I've been thinking. For a long time I've been thinking."

"Yes?"

He puts his head to one side as he talks; I stroke his mustache, and he smiles. "I want you to come and live up in Monterey."

"What!"

"Don't you see? With you near, I could see you when I wanted."

Where the anger was hidden, I'll never know. It explodes from me instantly. "When *you* wanted! You fucking bastard!" I'm hitting him, scrambling to get off his lap. "When *you* wanted! And what abou*t me?*"

"It could work, you know."

"Work?"

I didn't really believe he was serious until he said that. Said it with that complacent, self-satisfied smile on his face.

"A fucking mistress? Is that all I'm good enough for?" I slap his face before the infuriating smile has faded from it. With the slap, my anger is exhausted. "I'm sorry, Johnny . . ."

"It's all right. Perhaps I deserved it."

As those ensnaring eyes of his stare at me I know there's only one answer. "I don't think we should see each other any more, Johnny."

"What?"

"I think it's best."

He sulks. "If you'd have waited, there wouldn't be any of this fuckin' mess."

"If *you* hadn't walked out on me," I retorted coldly.

"I told you to *wait!*"

Oh yes, he told me to wait. . . .

. . . I'd graduated, and we were living in our cottage. I was excited about starting my postgraduate work in the autumn.

I'd been writing: my first work on the Pandora stories. Johnny had gone off to Liverpool for a few days: Liam, his friend whom I'd met in Dublin, was there with his ship.

When Johnny returned I met him at the station and drove us home. He was strangely quiet. All through dinner he was quiet. We'd made love before dinner and after, but even that had been unusually subdued.

Finally, in bed, he said, "I need to talk to you, me little darlin'."

I smiled and kissed his nose. "I have something to tell you, too."

He sat us up, the pillows behind him, me in his arms. I remember that his face was against the top of my head; I could feel the warmth of his breath in my hair.

"I've resigned my fellowship."

"What?" I twisted around to look at him.

"Yes, I have. I've done it—I've resigned. At last."

"But why?" I was totally stunned. He was so much, so successfully the Oxford don. *Why* should he throw away such an enjoyable prestigious appointment?

"I've got to write," he said.

"Oh, yes!" So, he'd resigned. Well, he wanted to write, and that was of far greater importance. "Well, you can write, and I can work."

"No. . . . Not *really* . . ." He looked awkwardly about the room.

"Not really? What does that mean? What are you getting at, Johnny? What have you done?" Panic gripped me. Whatever it was he was about to tell me, I knew it was going to be something I didn't want to hear.

"Oh, I know I should have told you before now. I should have talked to you, made you privy to my desires and my vacillations. But I knew you'd be upset, and that was something I didn't want. So—cowardly, perhaps—I waited until the last moment."

"Last moment? How, 'last moment'?" My heart was pounding.

"I'm leaving tomorrow."

Tears welled up in my eyes. "But where are you going?"

102

"I've signed on with Liam." He gave an awkward, distorted smile. "I'm going to be doin' me Joseph Conrad bit—sailin' the world. And betimes, writin' me fuckin' poetry."

I sat back on my heels. My body was shaking visibly; the tears were cascading down my face, a warm waterfall.

"You're *leaving*? Going *away*? Leaving me here? *Leaving* me?"

He drew me closer. "No, it's not that—it's not that I'm *leaving* you, me poppet. It's just that—that I've got to go. I've *got* to do it. For me. For me and me sacred muse." That smile again.

"So you don't love me! All this was only . . . only a diversion. Only getting a good lay."

"Of *course* I fuckin' love you. Not that you're not a good lay." He kissed me and laughed, trying to make it all right. "You have the sweetest little cunt I've ever tasted."

I hit him. "You bastard! You can't leave me. You can't!" I began to sob heavily; Johnny held me, Johnny made love to me . . . and Johnny still left, the next day. Just like that, he left . . .

"Macushla," he said, "try to understand. It's not that I don't love you—I do. But *this* has nothing to do with *that*. So, wait for me. Wait for me faithfully, me little poppet, and just as faithfully I'll be back, bringin' me love back with me, invigorated and enhanced."

He went. Without my telling him what I'd wanted to tell him . . .

. . . I place my hands on Johnny's shoulders. "It's too late for us, Johnny. You know that too, don't you?"

"No. It's only so if we let it be so."

"Do you want me to marry you?" The effect of this barb is predictable: his face clouds over. "I see!" Oh, why do I feel so angry, so bitchy? "You want me for your mistress. But I'm not good enough for a wife."

"You know it's not that."

"Do I? *How* do I know?"

"You would have been my wife."

"Would I?" Disbelief in my voice.

"You know I can't leave Amy now. Not after what happened."

"And what am *I* supposed to do, then?"

"Come to Monterey." He hugs me, kisses me, ignoring my coolness, my mistrust. "I want you to have my baby."

"What?" I stand back from him, shocked.

103

He looks at me gently, so very, very gently, his eyes soft and slightly smiling. "It would be our own work of art, a work of genius, it would nurture the flowering of our twin talents, it would bind us together in love and wisdom. *Us* a child, Solange—just think! It would be so meaningful, so magnificent, you having my baby."

But all I can see is more anguish, amongst his Celtic fantasies. "Get out, Johnny! *Out!*"

"What?" He really doesn't get it.

"I've broken free from you. You can't hurt me anymore. And I'm bloody well not going to let you try, not anymore."

"But I don't *want* to hurt you, poppet." He tightens his arm around my waist. "Please, think of it. It would be good for the both of us." His blue eyes, pleading.

He's lost a son. Amy has no more children for him. And so it follows, by crooked logic, that captive Solange can supply the lack. Except that she is no longer captive. Oh, no, you're not using me any more, Johnny Brandigan!

"Get out, Johnny!" I twist forcibly away from him, point melodramatically to the door.

"But Solange . . . ?"

"Go on. Go away! Please . . . just *go!*"

He stands up, looking pained and obstinate. "It should have been you all along, Solange. I want *you* to have my child."

"You shouldn't have left. Then we *would* have had a child," I reply tartly. "You don't understand, do you, Johnny? Not even now."

"Understand? What is there to understand?"

"Do you remember the night before you left?"

"Well, of course I do. Very heavy going I found it, too. I knew my fuckin' news wouldn't please you at all, and it didn't, did it?" A slight, rueful smile.

"No, it certainly didn't. But I had wanted to speak to you, too."

He looks puzzled. "You didn't though. What was it, me poppet?" He laughs, pulls me to him, cuddles me. He's trying to make everything all right.

"After you told me your news, there was no point in getting into it with you. I'd never have wanted you to stay because you felt you had to. It never works out, not like that."

"*Had* to? Why should I have *had* to stay?"

Oh, hell, I'm sick of these stupid word games! "I was *pregnant!*"

Silence. Total and utter silence. Johnny's face—I've never seen him look so white.

"I'd just missed my second period. You never could keep track of my periods." I trail off.

Johnny storms from the kitchen, into the lounge, out onto the terrace. He stares at the ocean. I come and stand next to him.

"And what happened?" he asks, half over his shoulder.

"I had an abortion . . . Marie-Claude helped me . . ." I see that it's angered him, that he's blaming *me* for the way it turned out. "You'd gone, Johnny. You just up and left. And if you'd stayed, we'd both have been unhappy. I couldn't handle it." I'm crying. . . .

. . . I had been so excited that day. I'd missed two periods. Me, pregnant—Johnny's baby inside me! Such an intimate thing, having the baby of someone you love inside you.

We'd talked about marriage and babies, in a roundabout way; I'd never dared to mention marriage to Johnny, but he'd dropped a few hints. "You just wait until we're married, me little darlin'," he'd said, "and we have dozens of kids." And, "When you've got your D. Litt., me poppet, then Dr. Brandigan and Dr. Osborne can be married in style."

But when he said he wanted to leave how could I tell him? Either, most likely, he'd resentfully depart, rebelliously ignoring his socially-imposed obligations to his nuclear-family-to-be; or, much less likely, he'd resentfully conform, and subdued rebellion would corrode all future relations.

And so I'd lost, because I'd lose either way; and he left. I just watched him walk jauntily down our tiny crazy-paving path and, with a brief wave, disappear into the local taxi. Numb, all I knew was that it was ten-thirty in the evening when Johnny phoned me from Liverpool. I'd been sitting in that chair all day. The ship was leaving on the tide in the early morning. He was a lowly deckhand. He'd write, he loved me, I was to keep the bed warm for him, my little pussy warm for him. Wait for him. He'd send me an epic seafarin' poem.

I sat in that chair nearly every minute of three days, slept in it for three nights too. Too exhausted, physically and emotionally, to think what to do. I was pregnant, yet it didn't *feel* like I was pregnant. What do you do when you're pregnant? I didn't know. I was twenty-one; I didn't know *anything*.

It's strange: Jan-Toby Axelsson's first record was out just

then: *Love Words*. Psychedelic rock, flower power and all that. Sergeant Pepper was playing everywhere.

Four days after Johnny left, I phoned Marie-Claude. It was early morning; I ambled zombielike back to my chintz-covered chair. She arrived the next day, took me straight back to France. I let her make the decisions.

They put me to sleep in the clinic on the outskirts of Nice. When I awoke, my tummy felt slightly sore—that was all. My baby, whose presence I'd never felt, never fully believed in, was gone, dead. Johnny was gone—was dead, departed from my living land. And what did living matter? Nothing mattered anymore. Why couldn't I too depart, be dead?

Marie-Claude's friendship floated me through the next two empty weeks. Then I returned to Oxford. I wanted to be by myself.

There was also a long, long letter from Johnny waiting for me, and a poem, which he later included in one of his books.

I wrote back saying everything was fine, I was fine. It was a strange letter: unemotional, lifeless, no past or future in it, just a dull, listless present.

I sat in my garden for a month, until that party of George and Hilary Mason's where I met Rand.

I wrote to Johnny: that Daddy had been killed in that ghastly air crash. And oh yes, by the way, in case Johnny was interested, I'd married Rand Farraday...

...Johnny holds me protectively as I cry. He picks me up and carries me into the lounge, hugs me to him as he sits us on the sofa. Gradually, many minutes later, I stop, and we both just sit, holding each other at the still, dead center of our lives.

"Why...didn't...you...tell...me?" What an effort it is for him to ask! Doubtless his nimble mind has already computed all the conclusions that for me were a labor of months and, from the masklike look of his face, has come up with the same stony, barren answers.

"I couldn't. I couldn't keep you. Not like that. Not when your whole intention was focused on going."

"But I didn't *know*. If I'd known...dammit, we could have worked something out. It was *my* child, too. Sailors have wives, too." After returning my silent look for long seconds, he suddenly grips my arms and shakes me. "D'you *know* how I felt?, how *I* felt, when you wrote so fuckin' complacently

106

that you'd got yourself married off? I could have *killed* you!" he rants, "I *loved* you!"

"That's why you left me, is it?"

"I didn't leave you. I had to *do* something—that wasn't *leaving* you. I wanted you there for me."

"I know that, Johnny. I know it *now*."

We just sit: me on his lap, him holding me tight. We sit for nearly an hour like that. Just holding each other.

"I have to go." His words break the stillness. "It's a long drive, *macushla*."

"Yes. . . ."

He gets his things and puts them in the car. Gets himself into it. I kiss him.

He grabs my hand. "I can't be doin' anymore talking now, milady. But I'll be ringin' you. And what I was suggesting," he looks at me sharply, "I want it, poppet. I *want* it."

We kiss. Why do our lips feel cold? "Drive carefully, Johnny."

I smile as he drives away. Why does it seem to me that he's leaving in a taxi?

5

It's halfway through February. I'm typing—working on my fifth Pandora book. Miriam's back (she went home to Chicago for a long Christmas vacation), and I'm feeling much, much better; the moody-blues and meany-mean-reds Johnny brought have vanished.

I spent a delightful weekend with Phil Westing. All that fucking and coming cheered me up no end. Dear Phil, I'm very fond of him, and we both enjoy ourselves.

It's a Wednesday. I like Wednesdays. I've just bought myself a strapless button-front dress of baby-pink silk suede —it cost the earth—matching boots, too. And a brown cashmere tee top, and some French jeans, though God knows why, when I can buy French jeans in France.

Miriam bought loads of clothes, too. We're sitting in the

Cafe Rodeo, sipping coffee, giggling together. Miriam saw Burt Reynolds earlier, and it's made her day.

"Solange!" says a voice behind me. Phil Westing, looking, as usual, extremely handsome, in a cream-colored suit. We kiss; he joins us.

"You look *beautiful* . . . but Solly is furious with you."

"Why?"

"Because you won't let him do a deal on film rights."

"I don't *want* Pandora in the movies. They'd fuck it up. Besides which, no one could play her."

"Darling there's always *someone*. And besides which the *money*, darling. Tell her, Miriam."

"The *money*," Miriam says with conviction. They nod to each other, conspiring to humor me.

"No," I reply.

"Come home with me tonight, then?" Phil grins, with a wink. He's got lovely deep-set blue eyes.

"I know—Solly's trying to get you to get around me."

"Not *around* you, *in* you," Miriam giggles gleefully.

"Shut up, Miriam!" I glare, and look around to make sure no one's heard her outburst.

And, of course, I happen to look at a table near us and right into the eyes of Jan-Toby Axelsson. He's sitting with his wife and one of his band and a good-looking man in an expensive blue suit. We just *look* at each other. I become aware that my mouth is open. I feel sick.

I turn my head back, sharply, and stare at Phil and Miriam. My heart's pounding, slamming itself around in the mass of jellyfish flesh I seem to have acquired in lieu of my own sinews and muscles.

"What's the *matter* with *you?*" Miriam demands.

"Nothing. Actually I'm feeling rather peculiar. I want to go home now," I add plaintively.

"Can I come?" Phil grins.

"Why not?" Me, regaining my cool.

"Until tomorrow?" Pressing his advantage.

"Of course." Carelessly thrown away: Ms. Classy-Ass once more.

"You've got yourself a deal." He takes my hand, kisses the palm.

But when we stand up, Phil sees Jan and entourage. Oh, *shit!* Why did I think that could be avoided?

"Jan."

"Phil." Sober nod to Phil; casual, oh-so-casual, glance at me.

Miriam, relishing the obvious, digs me in the ribs, grinning madly as Phil introduces me. I manage to smile and say hello without shouting or whispering. Miriam giggles one of her arpeggio greetings.

"Didn't I introduce you two at Solly's party?" Phil asks, as a sudden afterthought.

"Yes, I believe you did," I answer nonchantly. "But it was such a long time ago"—beatific smile from me—"I shouldn't think Mr. Axelsson remembers."

That lopsided grin appears on Jan's face. I stare at him, poker-faced. Arrogant bastard!

"I was just telling Solange that she must let Solly negotiate the film rights to her book," Phil says to the man in the blue suit, who's introduced to me as Roy Kane, Jan's personal manager.

Roy Kane looks me up and down interestedly, smiles. He reminds me a bit of Justin. I think managers and agents and the like must belong to a well-dressed, well-spoken race someone breeds for the purpose. He's about the same age as Justin, too. He's tall, slim, with rather large hazel eyes in a long, oval, smooth face.

"What does your manager say about it?" he asks me.

"Manager?" I smile, trying to avoid Jan's continued stare. "I don't have a manager, just a literary agent. He and my ex handle all my business affairs."

"But you need a personal manager. Doesn't she?" He looks from Jan to Phil. They both agree so readily that I irritatedly begin to sense a conspiracy.

"I've offered," Phil says. "Lots of things, I've offered." I glare; he laughs.

"Let's go, Jan." Melissa-Sue Axelsson pulls at the sleeve of his suede jacket. "It's so boring, all this business talk." Her voice sounds young and high-pitched, with a strongly Texan accent. She pointedly avoids looking in my direction.

Jan and Roy give each other a look of commiseration, and a little irritation, too, I think.

"We must go." I take Phil's arm, urgent to escape.

"What's your number?" Roy takes a little black notebook from his pocket, sits awaiting my reply. "I'll call you."

"I really don't . . ." I begin indecisively.

"Yes, she does," Phil says. "She's made enough money out of the books already," he grins and winks, "but if you can make her *more.* . . ." He puts his arm around my shoulders and hugs me. Then he gives Roy my number. I feel very annoyed with him, but what can I do?

"Come *on*, Jan. I want to get that jewelry at Edwar's." For the first time his wife gives me a quick glance, apprisingly hostile. I stand waiting for Phil and Roy to finish talking, and notice that Miriam is giving her phone number to Joel, Jan's best friend and lead guitarist. He's very tall and very lean, with long, long golden hair hanging down his back, a golden, fuzzy beard, and a golden earring in his right ear.

"If I'm not *there*," Miriam says with a high-pitched giggle, "Solange will take a *message*." She gives me a cheeky, excited grin.

"Oh, will I?" I smile at Joel. "*She's* supposed to be *my* secretary." Jan's still watching me closely, disregarding his wife's fidgets. "But I *will* take a message."

"Come *on*, Jan." Mrs. Axelsson is getting really annoyed now. She's *beautiful*, I have to admit: tall and thin. She's wearing tight velvet pants, with black boots, and a silk blouse over a sweater, beneath which she's flat. She'd make a great model. Her face is right for it, too, thin, with very large, round eyes, the palest blue, strikingly contrasting with the flame color of her hair, genuine redhead, shoulder-length and swept away from her face. And she's so *young*. Why the hell did Jan bother with me?

"I'll call you," Roy tells me. "We'll have dinner and discuss business."

"We will?" I say, all Ms. Classy-Ass.

"We saw you on the Carson show a while back." He glances at Jan, who nods and smiles. "You *need* someone to handle you properly."

"Do you manage other writers?" I ask. After my first annoyance, I'm pleased at the attention.

"No. But I'm good at anything." He smiles. "I didn't manage anyone or anything until Jan and I got together." He touches my arm. "I'll *call* you."

"Okay." What else can I say? I smile at them all. "Nice meeting you."

"Come on—Edwar's first," I hear *Mrs.* Axelsson tell *Mr.* Axelsson as I grab hold of packages and Phil's arm and we leave for home. Miriam disappears for the day—until tomorrow lunchtime, she says.

Oh, God, I hope Roy Kane *doesn't* ring me. I don't *need* a personal manager, anyway—and particularly not Jan-Toby Axelsson's.

And then Phil's asleep, and I'm eating ice cream and thinking to myself, maybe it *was* good, after all, that I met

Jan again. I mean, I've done it now, and it doesn't hurt all that much. Not anymore . . .

*   *   *

I've been in a mood all day. I don't know why. I got up that way this morning, and it's stayed with me. Cryptically perverse, that's what Johnny would call it. It's his catchall phrase for all my little moods and niggling.

I ignore the doorbell. It buzzes again, and Miriam answers it. Miriam's been in the kitchen all afternoon baking a birthday cake for Howie. Howie is one of her studs and a member of one of those satin-suited, rhinestone-studded, movement-perfect, teeth-flashing, soul-singing black bands. They've been seeing each other—on and off—ever since she came here.

"Someone to see you." A huge smile from Miriam. Roy Kane follows her into the lounge; she winks, smiles, disappears back to her baking.

"Roy." I get up from the sofa, where I was stretched out with Gulley on my tummy, and shake hands. He sits down next to me on the sofa. I'm wondering what this is all about. It's been nearly a month since I met him at the Cafe Rodeo. I'd hoped he'd forgotten all about it.

"What can I do for you? Would you like a drink?"

"Thanks. Scotch." I get him one, and a grapefruit juice for myself. He's very cool and good-looking: immaculate denim jeans suit, cashmere polo-neck sweater. "This is a beautiful place you have here."

"Thank you."

"Have you given any further thought to what we mentioned?" He takes a file from his briefcase. "I drafted a contract." He smiles briskly. "Not a complicated one. I do your deals, get you coverage, get your books sold, get you appearances, lectures, whatever you want."

"And what do you get?" I ask with a grin.

He takes a sip of his Scotch. "A measly ten percent, that's all." He crosses his legs, throws his arm nonchalantly along the back of the sofa.

"I already pay Justin, my agent, ten percent. It's not the money, it's just that I honestly don't see what *you* can do that Justin can't. I mean, it's not as though I'm a rock star or a movie star."

"But you *are* a personality."

"I'm a *writer*."

111

"Yes—a good one. I've just finished reading your three books—I enjoyed them. And Jan says there's some brilliant writing there. He's always liked them."

"Jan . . . said that?" I feel sick.

"Well, he's my expert."

"Is he?"

He looks at me and smiles again. "I asked Solly too. And Phil Westing. And several others I know."

"Oh?" I feel as though I'm being visited by the Gestapo.

"They all think you're great. I wouldn't want to handle you unless you were."

"Oh." What did Jan really say? And how could it ever be an impartial assessment?

"If you were handled properly, we could make you more of a personality. You're beautiful. Intelligent. We could do lots with you. And I needn't tell you, it's names and personalities that sell things now. Books included. Not to mention the film rights. With the extra you'll be making, the ten percent will be nothing, and Justin Markham won't be any worse off. His ten percent will be more, just like *your* eighty percent will be more than your present ninety percent."

"I . . ." I'm still feeling a bit peeved that he went and talked to people behind my back. "Why me? I mean, you only handle rock stars."

"I started out with Jan—and that made me a businessman. A successful one, and rich. Now, he wants to go back to writing. So, why not something different, educated, refined? I'm about due for that now." He smiles complacently.

"Oh. And d'you think it's something you can just move into, like a takeover, like a company merger?" I'm laughing, but it's not *at* him. There's something about him that I like. I'm quite prepared to believe that his enormous self-assurance is justified, that his very belief in himself generates his success. And I know intuitively that he won't do any numbers on me. "Listen," I interrupt just as he's about to reply, "I'm very flattered that you want to bother . . ."

"But . . . ?" He raises an eyebrow.

"Well, quite honestly, I really don't think I need you. I mean. I'm quite happy with what I've got. I'm a little stay-at-home bookworm, really—I just like to be here and write. I don't want to be a *personality*. I'm not into egomania; quite the reverse, I'm far too shy and quiet. And I'm very happy with what I've got."

"Are you?" Enigmatic look, tilt of that long face.

"What?"

"Happy with what you've got?"

"Yes. Yes, of course I am."

"But I think you need more."

"Oh, you do? Why?"

"Well, is it really that you don't want a manager, or is it that you don't want Jan-Toby Axelsson's manager?"

"Pardon?" I feel sick again. Why should he ask that when it's none of his business?

"Look, I know show business, entertainment, promotion, hype. It's all the same thing nowadays. And *I* can see your potential—though I'm not surprised you can't: you're too busy producing the goods to step back and look at the overall picture. But with these Pandora books of yours, you've got a little gold mine going. So, because you're smart enough to see that there's a lot of truth in what I'm saying, there must be another reason for your not being interested in the proposition. And it's not hard to see, it's because I'm *Jan's* manager."

"Why should that matter?" I feel my face growing warm. "I mean, I only met you a few weeks ago . . ."

He looks at me for a moment with a completely neutral expression, finishes his drink. "I'll leave the draft contract and call you in a few days."

He stands, fiddles with his briefcase, takes something else out of it—obviously an album, wrapped in brown paper. He puts his hand on my shoulder. "I'll tell you something, little lady—I may be Jan's manager, but more than that, and better—I'm Jan's *friend.*"

"Oh?"

"Jan talks to me."

"Oh?"

"Yes. He *talks* to me." Again that enigmatic smile.

"Oh!" He knows. I wonder who else does. I was *sure* Joel did. And the rest of Jan's band? What did he tell them—that I was a great lay?

"Think about it." He nods, businesslike. "I think it would be very good for you."

"Okay . . . I'll think about it."

I see him to the door and along the garden path to his car. He turns to me. "You should have an electric gate. I just walked in here."

"I've never thought about it."

"You need one. You're too well known to live so . . . *ex-*

113

posed like this. I'm not trying to throw a scare into you, mind, just to look after you."

"Well . . . I . . ."

He takes my shoulders and kisses my cheek. "I think you need looking after."

"That's what you think, is it?"

"It's what Jan thinks." He looks at me steadily. "And I agree with him."

I turn cold. Watching him drive off, I wonder if he's going to see Jan.

*   *   *

I go and walk on the beach for a while, bumping into Ginnie Seagram's kids. I go back home with them, have a couple of cocktails with Ginnie and Bill. Bill's laughing about a TV film he's doing about a swarm of deadly mutant dragonflies. He says he gets all the roles that Charlton Heston turns down.

As I walk home from the happy Seagrams I suddenly remember the package that Roy Kane left. I run back to the house, eagerly tear away the brown paper. It's Jan's latest album. The cover has a photo of him and his band in a recording studio. Jan's sitting on a speaker, reading a book. And the album's called *The Poet And The Lady*.

It's one of those albums with more photos inside—more of him and the band, and one of him with his son Andrew. Andrew's nearly two and has a mop of his mother's red hair, her big blue eyes, and delightful tiny freckles all over his little kissable button nose.

My hand shakes as I read the song titles. The first number's the album title one and the last two are "Babies Should Be Made In Love" and, lastly, "Literary Lady."

I sit listening to the album. Listen to it again. I cry, throw the album cover across the room, and go to bed.

It's two in the morning when I creep downstairs for the album, take it up with me, and play it while I'm lying in bed.

I like "The Poet And The Lady." It's a bit Cohenesque, quite soft and gentle, not Jan's usual—and sometimes cynical —heavy rock style. The others are good, too—his sardonic poetry—especially "Needy And Greedy," which is funny. But it's the last two that have me crying. "Babies Should Be Made In Love" (I told him that was a good song title), is about how a man needs to give his babies to someone he loves, that they should be made "in a bed full of love."

114

And the last track—I play it again and again. Another soft and gentle one, which to me says so much:

She's a Literary Lady, flashin' words off through the night,
Writin' dreams and hopes for others, bearin' gifts so shinin' bright.
Does she hide behind her own dreams, introspective, soft and free?
She's a Literary Lady, why don't she share some words with me?

From the beauty of her body comes the beauty of her mind.
She surrounded me with softness that I never thought I'd find,
But I've stopped her love from reachin' me, turned mine angrily away
So she's hid herself in her words, a place I'd like to stay.

She's a Literary Lady, prose and poems flow so smooth.
Her world of words, her world of books, is my world— ain't that the truth.
But we're in two separate spaces, holding back the love we feel.
Love my Literary Lady, wish she could share some words with me.

Once again I cry myself to sleep.

* * *

I'm at a party, but I didn't really want to go. It's Solly's party and I've been persuaded to come by both Solly and Sarah, not to mention Phil.

I'm in the dress I went to Matthew's party in, the night we first fucked. Black suede boots, with very high heels, give me an unaccustomed grown-up feeling. I'm wearing the hummingbird squash blossom. I vow to meet someone intriguingly, irresistibly sexy. We'll fall in love immediately, then immerse ourselves in at least a month in bed together.

Sarah's had her baby, a son for Solly—Benjamin. He's beautiful. It's *his* party really: Solly parades around, proudly showing him off.

I have a drink with Phil, who once more starts trying to

115

persuade me to let him move in with me. ("Are you after fifty percent palimony?" I tease him.) I feel an arm around my waist and a kiss on my cheek. It's Roy Kane. Oh no, not *more* talk about my needing a manager.

He smiles at Phil and then at me and kisses my cheek again as though to prove he can do it. "It's been a week, and I haven't heard from you about that contract."

"Oh, Roy . . ." I give a huge artificial sigh, and he grins, then starts talking to Phil. I turn slightly and find myself staring at—inevitably—Jan-Toby Axelsson, with his arm around Mrs. Axelsson's shoulders. She's in a long green dress, sort of formal. Her hair is up, hanging in a mass of curls down her back, very beautiful.

I can stand with a frozen smile on my face to show I haven't a care in the world, don't care a fuck that Jan-Toby Axelsson is standing four feet in front of me with his arm around the youthful shoulders of his slender and beautiful wife.

Solly joins us, laughs and jokes with Roy and Phil. He gives me his usual enormous bear hug and asks, "Haven't you signed with Roy yet?"

"I'm still thinking about it."

"You think altogether too much already." Another bear hug. "Ladies—and beautiful young ladies in particular—shouldn't think too much."

"I've told her," Roy tells us all, "I've laid it on the line. With her talent and my expertise, we can make *millions*."

"And so you should, bless you both," Solly beams. I think he's a little high.

I drift away to the library to look at Solly's beautiful books. I reverently, gently stroke the leather-bound spines.

The door opens and closes. I turn around but I already know who it is. Jan-Toby Axelsson gives me that beautiful lopsided grin, rubs at the side of his nose. "Ma'am." He comes over, perches himself on the back of the chesterfield, stares at me, saying nothing.

I began to feel uncomfortable. *"Don't!"* It comes out raw, edgy.

"Don't *what?"* A ghost of a smile from him.

I'd better end this nonsense. Does it give his precious ego a lift to know someone's in love with him? And he talked to Roy and to *Joel too.* What did he say to them? Hey, she may not be tall and willowy, but man, she was a *great* lay! You wanna try her? I turn away from him and walk slowly

116

towards the door. He's across the room and grabbing my arm before I know what's happening.

"Let go of me!" He does so. "Solange . . ." he begins.

I want to hurt him like he's hurt me. "Shouldn't you be with your *wife?* She wouldn't like it if someone found us in here, would she?" I put on a saccharine smile. "I thought you 'didn't get involved.' I thought you specialized in 'quick name-less fucks.' Like your letter said, you don't want to *compli-cate* things." I give him the sugar smile again as I turn away.

He pulls me sharply around. *"Stop it!"* he growls.

I try to unhook myself from his locked grip. "What's the matter? In need of a chick to *service* you?"

The hard slap across my face startles me. I stand there trembling. It's the first time anyone's ever hit me. We're staring and staring at each other.

The strange thing is that his face is beautifully innocent. His eyes, that gorgeous dark amethyst color, are so big. His hair, that fascinating dark dusty blond color, falls across his forehead where it's cut shorter in the front and hangs untidily almost to his shoulders at the sides. His face *is* deceptively innocent. He's an exceedingly complex man.

He takes my hand very gently, walks me back to the chesterfield, rests himself on the back of it again. He pulls me around so that I stand between his legs. His hands grip my shoulders, move down to my arms. The touch is a caress. He grips me around the waist, presses me closely to him. His hands on me feel so good. They *belong* there, holding me tightly, possessively, so that I won't escape. I *want* it like this, intimate and possessive.

I place my hands flat against his pink silk shirt, and he takes my face in his hands and kisses me with delicate care. For minutes we don't talk, me with my head against his shoulder and my arms around his waist. He kisses the back of my head. Then he slowly releases me, lights a joint, gives it to me to toke, still holding it.

"I'm sorry, Jan." I finally whisper. "I didn't mean to be so bitchy. It's just that . . ." Tears flood my eyes. "I don't know what to do."

He holds me again. "Stop crying." He takes my face in his hands again. "Stop . . . crying," he says, slowly, precisely.

"You sound like Bob Dylan." I laugh as I cry.

"That's what Greil Marcus says." Twisted grin.

"Who?"

117

He laughs and hugs me. I'm *still* crying. He kisses me once more, lovingly.

I let him cuddle me. "We shouldn't be here."

"We are here lady. We're gonna have to face that." He looks solemn.

"I love you," I whisper, "So much . . ."

Between kisses, he replies, "I love you too, lady."

We stare at each other, like two little, lost children not knowing where to go or whom to turn to for help.

I rub my eyes. "Thank you for your beautiful presents."

"You liked them, huh?" he smiles. "I see you liked the squash blossom."

"Yes, I liked them all. The hummingbirds are beautiful. I would have written to thank you, but I didn't know where. And I didn't think you'd want me to, anyway."

"You played the music?"

"Some of it. Most of it, now. And *your* album—it's so *good!*" He smiles broadly. "Is it selling well?"

"Yep. Better than the last fuckin' two!"

"I loved 'The Poet And The Lady.' A bit Cohenesque, I thought."

"Cohenesque?" A teasing, but slightly annoyed, look from Jan.

"Sorry. I really like 'Literary Lady' best."

"You were meant to."

"I was?"

"Sure were, ma'am. . . . I've got a hard-on. Beautiful bitch—just looking at you gives me a hard-on."

"I like the one about babies, too. Really, it made me feel very jealous, though." He looks surprised, puzzled. "Well," I continue, "I guess you got the idea when we were talking?" He nods. "And . . . well . . . I'm glad that put the poem there for you, but . . ."

"But what?"

"Well . . . I guess I was just envious. I mean, Melissa-Sue is the one you love, the one you chose to give your babies to—so it's her poem. *'Made In Love', 'in a bed full of love.'*" There are tears in my eyes again. I feel vulnerable and awkward. "I think we'd better get back to the party." I try to pull away from him, but he won't let me.

"Let's fuck." He winks.

"No." I shake my head slowly.

"No? Why not? I want you." He pulls my hand onto his hard cock, which he pushes at me. I try to pull my hand away, but he holds it there. Besides, who am I kidding?

Nothing would gratify me more than to feel him inside me. But that jagged lump of anger within my middle is growing heavier and spikier.

"No, Jan I mean it. I'm not going to be an easy lay for you."

He's angry too, I can sense it from his eyes. Anger seems to reverberate through the room. My eyes are filling with tears again. "Listen," I tell him, "I love you. Love you very much. But it won't get me anywhere, even if I *do* feel part of you. I want *all* of you. Anything less would be an insult to both of us. So if we can't have what we should have, I don't want anything. I *won't* be treated as some sort of high-class intellectual groupie, just there for you when you need servicing."

I wait for an answer, but he isn't giving one. How can he? He wants me for a mistress, just like Johnny wanted me for a mistress. "Is that where I fit in?" I ask him. "It is, isn't it?"

"I've never had anyone like you to fit in." A ghost of a smile.

"Quick nameless fucks, right?"

"Why are you gettin' so fuckin' *angry?*" he suddenly shouts.

"What do you expect?"

He looks down at me: a self-contained, insolent look, full of an arrogance that seems to claw at me, tear my shaky self-possession to shreds.

I manage to calm myself. "Let's not fight or argue. I don't want it. And I won't have it."

"We could see each other, whenever . . . whenever we can."

His hands on my bare arms feel comfortable, familiar, welcome. I want his touching. But at the same time . . . *"No!"*

"But why not? It's better for us than nothing, isn't it?"

"Is it?"

"Of *course* it fuckin' well is! I *want* you, Solange!"

"Oh, you do, do you? *Want* me? What for?" I say with bitter scorn. "So you can get some head?"

He slaps me, then cries, "Oh, Jesus!" contrite instantly, pulling me into his arms. "I'm sorry. I'm such a fuckin' asshole." I'm crying and he's holding me tightly. "You're the only woman who's ever gotten me angry enough to hit her, you know that? You get *through* to me." He takes my face in his hands, looks at me for a long moment, kisses me. "I wanna get through to *you.*"

"Do you?"

"Sure do, ma'am."

119

"Oh, Jan, you *do*. But it's no good. You love your wife, and I can't be just a quick classy fuck for you. And I *won't* be just a mistress. And I couldn't have some sort of breezy, transient, carefree affair with you. Not with *you*."

He stares at me intently, still with my face in his hands. "I *want* you, Literary Lady."

"And I want you too. But I want us together, loving each other, sharing, doing things together. Helping each other."

He looks away. Yes, as I thought, he wants the best of both worlds: his wife, whom he loves, and me on the side, when he wants to own a Literary Lady.

"Well, why don't we try it?" he persists. "I'd come and see you whenever I could. Please. I've *got* to talk to you about things."

"But I don't want to hear." I turn and walk away. He doesn't stop me.

I find Phil, dance and flirt, share a drink and a joint with him. Of course *he* has to be there with his wife, surrounded by an adoring circle. Roy smiles at me, but there's a puzzled frown on his face. Has Jan talked to him? The thought angers me again.

Jan, of course, pointedly ignores me, his arm protectively around Melissa-Sue. Perfect! He's over there in *his* space, and I'm over here, in *mine*.

"When's the fourth book out?" someone asks me.

"Soon," I reply with my delightful lecture-circuit smile. "Spring."

"More lovely royalties," Solly laughs, rubbing his hands together. It delights him, even though he isn't getting any of it.

"You'd better sign up," Roy says, hugging me. "I need to handle a beautiful literary lady."

I suddenly freeze. I can feel Jan tense, too.

"That's one of the numbers in your new album," a girl says to Jan with a coquettish giggle.

"So it is," he says slowly and dryly. Melissa-Sue looks the girl up and down, then stares at her husband as he sips his drink and gives Roy a complacent, innocent look. Arrogant bastard! I think to myself.

I turn to Roy, feeling mischievously bitchy. "Why, Roy—you can handle me as much as you like." I give him a highly artificial *femme fatale* smile. He looks, for once, disconcerted.

"I'd take her up on that," Solly says.

"Perhaps you're right," I tell Roy, thinking that Jan-Toby
120

Axelsson was probably very relieved to hear I *didn't* want Roy to handle me. "Perhaps you *should* handle me." I hook my arm through his, smile mischievously into his puzzled eyes. "I *need* someone to handle me. . . . Do you get ten percent of *everything?* Perhaps you *had* better handle me."

"Verbal agreements are binding," he smiles, alligator like.

"You'd better just *bind* me, then," I say, all smart-assed and classy.

"I'll be around tomorrow for dinner, with the contract." But his look is still puzzled, like Jan's.

"Good for you," Solly says, always glad to see business going ahead, though he's no idea *what's* going on with me.

Roy and Solly talk. Phil looks at me and winks, ambiguously. Solly's face lights up. I sense a commotion behind us. "Daxos," Solly says.

Daxos Christophidou greets Solly with a warm hug. Solly introduces him to Roy, who's immediately interested. *Everyone's* interested. The girls' attention swings instantaneously from Jan to Daxos. I guess Greek multimillionnaires emit a stronger magnetic field than rock stars.

He turns, incredibly suave and good-looking in an impeccably cut evening suit and frilly silk shirt. I'm suddenly aware that we're staring at each other.

"Solange!" A broad smile from Daxos Christophidou as he leaves Solly and gathers me into his arms. "How beautiful to see you! I was about to ask Solly for your number. I didn't realize you were here." He kisses my cheek, turns to Solly. "Last time I was here, you whisked me away on business, and I lost her." He smiles at me. "This time, I don't lose you. Come on. We go. I'm sure Solly and Sarah will not mind in the least."

"Go?" I laugh. Phil is staring, surprised. Roy is staring, surprised but calculating. And, best of all, *he* is staring, surprised and *irritated.* "Go—where?" I'm enjoying this hugely.

"We have an appointment for dinner. For couscous. You see, I never forget my appointments."

"In Athens, wasn't it?" I say dryly.

"Ah yes, exactly so. And then to Crete. Come." He tugs at my hand. "The last time I lost you, I was told to look in the library. But you weren't there."

"I'd probably gone home."

"Yes—without *me.* It was a great disappointment, I freely admit it." He puts his arm possessively around me.

I look around. Yes, Jan's still looking at me. I turn my

121

head away haughtily, bitchily. "I'm working," I say unconvincingly.

"You could easily take some time off. I have no doubt you richly deserve a vacation—just a short vacation, among the isles of Hellas." Daxos hugs me. "You don't think I'm going to let you go this time, do you?"

He's so very serious, so very sweet, gallant. I think he's just what I need. Definitely what I need.

"Solange, darling, if you don't go," Solly says, "I'll be very annoyed with you. Roy, she can sign your contract when she returns."

"She signs *nothing* without my lawyer looking at it first," Daxos interjects. "Come, we go to Athens."

"*Now?*"

"Come." He pulls, I follow.

I'm aware of a warm glow within me as I leave with Daxos. I attribute it directly to the look, like a stone mask, on Jan-Toby Axelsson's face.

6

How long does it take? That's what Jan asked: How long does it take to know someone? In my case, not very long. But I've decided that it's not going to take me very long to get over him, either. I have to, for my crude, basic survival. Well, perhaps I already have.

For here I am, sitting in an entirely different world, one that I can enjoy without that devastating brand of euphoric anguish I now associate with Jan. This is a world I like. It has calm, stability.

I sit listening to Daxos talk to his father and mother. We're eating dinner. The room is *huge*. We eat by candlelight at the long dining table of dark polished wood.

It's a genteel affair, eating with Daxos's parents. And they're beautifully genteel people. They talk in English, knowing that I speak no Greek.

Spyros Christophidou, at the head of the table, is a handsome man with graying hair; except for this, Daxos resembles him strongly. He's in immaculate evening dress, as is Daxos at the other end of the table. Penelope sits at her husband's right; next to her, Teli (short for Aristotle), Spyros' younger son, who's just turned thirty and is also extremely good-looking. Just got himself engaged. I'm on Daxos' right, opposite Teli, and on my other hand is Violetta, the daughter, a little older than Teli. She's just divorced for the second time.

"We have a lot in common, you and I," Spyros addresses me, with a smile.

"We have?"

"Yes. You went to Oxford, yes?"

"Yes."

"Aha—*lots* in common." He flourishes his hand. "You see—*I* was a Rhodes scholar."

"You were? Daxos never mentioned . . ."

Spyros grins hugely. "That is to say—I was a scholar. From Rhodes. A Rhodes scholar."

We all laugh, and I realize that his joke was solely for the purpose of putting me at my ease.

"I have not read your books, Solange," Penelope says in her quiet, soft voice, hardly a trace of accent. She reminds me of my own mother, not in looks, for Penelope has dark, Mediterranean coloring, with her thick, lustrous black hair rolled into a perfect knot at the base of her slim neck, but in that elegant, classy presence that somehow fills and embellishes the entire room.

"Mother . . ." Daxos gives her a teasing look. "I think you would find them extremely naughty."

"But how divine!" She gives her husband a mischievous glance. "I must read them."

"The day after tomorrow," Daxos says, "we will leave in the *Penelope,* for Crete."

"The *Penelope?*"

"The yacht." Spyros winks at me. "At your disposal. But tomorrow," he says to Daxos, "you will show Solange Athens."

"Of course, father."

"You must show her *everything,*" Spyros says genially.

Daxos does so, the next day. It is beautiful. I haven't been in Athens since I was a child. But now, I'm here standing next to Daxos, with his arm around me. I don't even notice that it's cold. Have I really been here for only a day? Did we really arrive only yesterday afternoon? After the party we went back to my house, where I packed a suitcase and left a message for Miriam. Then we flew to Athens in Daxos's private jet. So simple!

I slept alone last night, in a beautiful pink guest room, full of flowers. I lay in bed and wondered why Daxos hadn't made love to me in the plane, why he hadn't come to me here. Because it's in his father's house? He respects and loves his parents. How sweet—and rather fine, too.

"What are you thinking?" He lifts my chin.

"Don't you think you ought to take me to that marvelous place for couscous? After all, that's what you brought me to Athens for, isn't it?"

"Oh—is *that* what I brought you here for?"

And so we have dinner in an expensive little back street restaurant. Of course *bouzouki* music; and while the little band plays especially for us, and the waiter stands deferentially, Daxos orders the couscous and a beautiful cheesy pie called *tyropita*.

In bed that night I talk to Miriam on the phone for a long time. She is excited and happy, with Howie staying at the house with her for a few days. Roy had called up to see if I'd really gone with Daxos. (I wonder if he reported to Jan?) Justin called to talk business. It seemed that Miriam was thoroughly enjoying herself telling everyone where I was and with whom.

As I drift down into a dream I hear the door open. Daxos is standing there. He walks over to me through the shafts of moonlight streaming through the French windows, sits on the edge of the bed, leans over, and kisses me. I can feel my heart pounding as he pulls the sheet back and admires my naked body before running his hand over it in a gentle caress that ends on my little mound of pussy hair.

"I think you are going to be beautiful to make love to, Solange."

"Do you?" My voice hardly a whisper.

"I think you know much about love."

"Do you?"

"I think you need someone to love—to love you."

"Do you?"

He leans over and kisses my pussy, which is beginning to ache. "You smell beautiful."

"Do I?"

He laughs, pulls me up into his arms, kisses me. It feels so very, very romantic. Just what we little girls all really crave.

"This is my father's house, Solange. In my father's house, I make love only to my wife." Daxos pulls the sheet up over me, kisses me once more. "Sleep well." He smiles in the moonlight. "Tomorrow night, there will be no sleep."

How delightful that prospect is.

* * *

Daxos introduces the yacht's staff to me. I'm enjoying all this, even though I don't quite believe it's real.

"My suite," Daxos announces proudly. It's huge and, of course, luxurious. Extremely modern. Thick beige carpet. A waterbed. It's a masculine suite. The maid, shooed off by Daxos, bobs a curtsy and leaves us; Daxos locks the door.

I watch him pour us champagne. I'm glad I'm looking so beautiful. I'm wearing a dusty-pink tent dress and pink suede boots to match.

"Come." Daxos takes my hand and we go out through French windows onto a kind of terrace, glazed-in to keep the cold out, We stand and watch the coast of Athens grow distant.

He leads me back to the bedroom and unbuttons my dress; it falls around my feet. I'm left standing in my tiny pink silk panties and bra; he reaches around to undo my bra, then looks surprised. I point to the front, with a giggle.

"Ah!" he laughs, "Progress!" He lets the bra fall to the floor, drops to his knees, and gently peels my panties down my legs. He laughs and pushes me slowly backwards, so that I land on the bed, woobling violently up and down. He unzips my boots.

* * *

My life has settled down, it's uncomplicated again. My hurt has been soothed, my pain is being forgotten. No more raw nerve-endings. At last, I'm *over* him.

"She's a strangely wise little thing"—that's what my parents used to say of me. I never mixed much with other children. Luckily, my parents understood that I liked to be alone, immersed in my books. My mother had a passion for literature, my father for music and history. How they understood me! They took me to the Yorkshire Moors so that I could see where Heathcliff had roamed and the Brontes had lived; to Stratford-on-Avon. My father walked with me around the parts of London—now so greatly changed!—where my beloved William Blake had lived.

The only childhood friend I became close to was the boy next door when we were living in Hampstead. I was fourteen, he was fifteen—we're still close friends, family almost. He was tall and skinny, and I adored him. I've always made shiny heroes of the men who have meant something to me. And Lars, the boy next door, certainly qualifies: He was the one who popped my delectable little cherry.

"Strangely wise little thing?" Wise? No, I don't think so. Strangely *unwise*. For instance, to go and fall in love with Jan, a married man who doesn't want me except on his terms. But here, in Crete, on the *Penelope,* my life has taken a turn for the uncomplicated, thank goodness. I'm soothed and made whole again.

Have I really been here for five days? I've been basking in the winter sunshine—cold, yet warming. I've immersed myself in history: Knossos. How I *love* that place! The Minotaur, fantastic monstrous cousin of la Bête. And with Daxos opening doors, we see parts of the ruins that no mere tourist may see.

That night I fantasized, while Daxos was making love to me, that I was lost forever in the labyrinth. I was taken to a secret room lit by a huge log fire, carpeted with fur rugs, to be fucked by the Minotaur.

If not strangely wise, at least I'm strange!

Daxos Christophidou is a wonderful, energetic, demanding lover. For five days and nights we've hardly stopped fucking.

I'm standing by the window looking out into the night. There are only a few lights on the shore. I'm feeling tired and sore. I need to sleep, but for some reason I cannot. I suddenly feel Daxos' arms encircling me, his cock digging into me. He's ready—again. Am I ready, tired and sore as I am? *Of course* I am.

His hands cover my breasts, and my happy cunt's melting again, all sticky and wet. Daxos squeezes my nipples, and I giggle to myself: Me, cunt. You, cock. I can't think. All I can do is feel Daxos battering into me from behind as I'm draped over the pillows on the bed. Every minute seems an hour, and it's at least ten long, wonderful hours before he finally comes. He falls on me and I can't breathe.

"Daxos!" I fight my way out from under him. How unromantically insincere of me, wanting to breathe at a time like this!

Five more days pass, and then I bring up the subject of going home. We've just had dinner on the glassed-in terrace deck, and we're sitting on one of the silk sofas, drinking our brandies.

"You want to leave *me?*" Daxos asks in complete surprise.

It sounds as though we have something permanent that I'm trying to desert.

"I should be working."

"But you can easily work here." He puts his arm around me.

"Daxos . . . I . . ."

"We get along so well together, Solange. Our making love, our talks. There is no need to curtail these pleasures."

"I don't want to overstay my welcome."

"That you could never do."

I don't understand his seriousness. It doesn't *seem* to me that he wants a serious affair between us—a *permanent* affair.

"I don't *want* you to go yet." He holds me tighter.

I wriggle free and go over to the glass screen, watch the lights on the shore. For some reason it suddenly reminds me of Malibu: walking along the sand at dusk and seeing all the lights in the houses. And just as suddenly all my feelings, those I'd *hoped* and *thought* were dead, swirl and overwhelm me. I think of Jan.

I blink back the ready tears. How could I explain them to Daxos? And what's the *matter* with me? All was to be uncomplicated once more. Why should it all return when I'm having a wonderful time with Daxos?

Of course the answer's simple, though I don't want to admit it: I'm in love with Jan. I'm *not* in love with Daxos.

I'm suddenly aware that Daxos is enclosing me in his arms, and it reminds me of Jan doing that, before we made love that first time. Oh, Jesus, why am I crying again!

"Solange . . ." Gentle Daxos. "What's the matter?" He turns me around, holds me to him, gently caresses my hair as I sob.

And suddenly I'm telling him everything.

"You must get over this, Solange. And you will get over it." He leads me back to the sofa, pulls me down onto his lap. I hold onto him fiercely.

"I thought I was. I *am*. But something . . ."

He brushes the tears carefully from my face, and I begin to feel like an idiot. How could I behave like this in front of him?

"You are truly beautiful," he says calmly, taking my chin and kissing me. "You are a complex, emotional, sensitive woman. I like a sensitive woman, a woman with feelings." He kisses me again. "Very few women would have admitted to me what you have just been telling me." He kisses me again, brushes my cheek. "In mourning for a lost love."

"Unrequited love," I correct him.

Another smile from Daxos, another tear brushed away. "Mourning becomes you . . ."

I stare at him, think that was a beautiful thing to say, appealing to my corny little romantic heart. I brave a smile at him. "Yes . . . me and Electra." He laughs, hugs me to him. "I didn't mean to be so stupid, so honest with you," I say. "I hope I haven't annoyed you?"

"No, not at all." He hugs me, kisses me. "Although, actually, between you and me, I think that honesty is a vastly overrated commodity." Suddenly we're both laughing together like crazy.

"I feel better already." And I really do. Jan is forgotten again as Daxos carries me to the bed and makes delightful love to me.

It's the middle of the night. We were both hungry, so we're eating *paklava* and drinking Dom Perignon.

"We could fall in love," he suddenly says.

"What?" I'm disoriented by his remark, find it hard to relate to us. I let the fork with the gorgeously sticky *paklava* fall back onto the plate.

"We could. I'm sure it would be quite easy, if we really decided on it. I think that basically we are each other's type of person, Solange. Whereas, for example, my first wife Aspasia was not my sort of person at all."

"Oh?"

"She was the daughter of Niko Minarchos, as you very likely know. Minarchos and my father wanted a marriage between the two families."

"So you didn't marry for love?"

"Love? She had a mustache."

I'm suddenly giggling, falling onto the bed, sticky paklava and spilt Dom Perignon everywhere, Daxos kissing me.

"And what about your second wife?" We sit up, and I pick the bits of paklava off the bed as he replies.

"Well, Jeanette was a movie star. A *French* movie star, with a little ass and big tits. She fucked like a puppy on heat. I don't remember us talking much at all. Of course, we didn't care. I bought her directors and producers, she became famous and ran off with Antoni Cardinalli." He grins. "He fucked her through two movies, then deserted her. So now she's married to a French lawyer—the F. Lee Bailey of the French courts, you might say. But she is the more powerful personality of the two, she will destroy him. . . . Fortunately, I am no longer implicated in *any* way with that harpy. Fortunately, very fortunately, we are now in the present."

We make love again: Daxos eating bits of paklava from my sticky, contented little cunt; me smearing Hymetttus honey, from a little Greek urn he bought me, over his cock and eating that. Mmm—a taste of honey—the tune keeps swinging around in my brain as I'm eating him.

It's early morning. We've been asleep, but now we both seem to be wide awake again, lying on top of the bed. I wonder what the maid is going to make of it: champagne, honey, paklava, and come. What a gorgeously lovely mess on the sheets!

"Tell me," Daxos says, rolling over and pinning me beneath him.

"What?" I kiss his nose.

"Have you ever let a woman make love to you?"

I giggle. "No."

"It is abhorrent to you?"

What a funny way to put it! "No, not at all. It's just that . . . well, I suppose I just haven't got around to trying it." I suppose I should, really. After all, Pandora has been made love to by Vanessa, the beautiful High Priestess of Lucifer. I had quiet a few ladies write to me offering themselves after they'd read the second book. I smile and kiss his nose again. "But I think I like to be fucked, though, really."

"But you like to be eaten, too."

"Yes. But then those who eat me, fuck me."

"Aha!"

"Have you, with a man?"

"When I was young. What Greek hasn't? Don't you know that all the ancient Greeks were faggots?" he teases as he slips his cock into me. Gay Greeks are forgotten.

"We'll do something very special tomorrow," he says as we move smoothly, perfectly in time.

"What?" I bite at his neck.

"A surprise."

"Daxos . . . ?" I can't say any more because another delightful surprise has caught up with me.

*   *   *

When I woke up this morning Daxos was already talking on the phone. It was my special day. I wondered what the surprise could be. I knew it couldn't be an expensive mink or diamonds. That'd be tacky—and that's one thing Daxos never is.

129

Later, while we were having lunch in Aghios Nikolaos, a reporter managed to sneak himself past Daxos's guards. He asked, very politely, if there was anything of a romantic nature between the two of us. Daxos and I grinned at each other, and I said, with a flutter of eyelashes, "We're just good friends." Daxos talked to him in Greek, producing a surprised expression followed by a broad smile. He took a photograph and left us with a wide, wide grin.

"What on earth did you say to him?" I asked Daxos. "It can't have been rude, anyway."

"Would I ever be rude? Actually"—Daxos gave me the most mischievous smile—"I told him that we were deciding whether to get married."

"What!"

"Well, he would have printed that, anyway. 'Rumor has it that Daxos Christophidou, here seen in Aghios Nikolaos with the beautiful and talented writer Solange delaMer...' and so on. That sort of nonsense. They've been doing it ever since I was eighteen."

"I see that it amuses you to pretend that you would consider marrying me," I said frostily.

He leaned over and kissed me. "Don't worry, Solange. It is *our* joke. You see, I'll tell them the next time—which will assuredly present itself—that *you* turned *me* down."

"Oh, will you?" I began to see the funny side of it too. Then I wondered whether it would get picked up by the French press and the American press. Of course, it obviously would. And then, if it did hit the American press—I couldn't help wondering what *he* would think of it.

"Of course," Daxos said, "we could get married."

"What?"

He nodded, smiling cheekily. "We could."

"But we hardly know each other."

"Not true at all. I know every inch of you, and they all are *very* delectable."

"Daxos! We don't love each other."

"That would be easy."

"Daxos...!" I looked at his lively, handsome face in total amazement. I was totally stunned, and at the same time totally flattered, and totally intrigued. "Better not ask me too persuasively—or too often. I might say yes. What woman in her right mind would turn *you* down, love or no love? Even if it couldn't possibly work."

"But it *could* work, very well it could work. And if not"—he shrugged—"well, we could divorce. I know that you would not . . ." He draws circles in the air. "What is it you say? Do a *number* on me."

"Daxos!" I began to suspect he'd been teasing me. *"You're* doing a number on *me!"*

He laughed loudly. "Come on, let's go back to the yacht."

Nothing more was said about marriage. I was rather glad.

We bathed together, and now we're lying on the huge waterbed. I lever myself up. "Daxos . . ."

"Yes, my darling?" He pulls me closer to him.

"What you said . . . you can't be *serious?"*

"Why can I not be serious?" He frowns.

"But it's stupid. We hardly know each other."

"But we are having a wonderful time *getting* to know each other."

"Yes, we are. But we don't *love* each other. You know that."

"Yet. But you must admit we're falling together."

"Oh, are we?" I laugh. *"Falling* together?"

"Yes!" He kisses me. "Lie back down, on your front."

"That sounds paradoxical."

"I *am* paradoxical."

I follow his orders. "Now what?"

"Do not be so inquisitive. You will see, *now what."* He picks up the phone and says something in Greek.

"What is it?"

"Just wait." He slaps my bottom, then kisses it.

The door opens, and I look up, startled. Four oriental girls enter, wearing tightly tied silk kimonos.

"My surprise," Daxos announces.

"Your . . . ?"

He laughs at my utter astonishment. "A massage."

The girls remove their robes and join us on the bed, two each. They have huge fur mittens on their hands. For the next year or two, it seems, I'm wallowing in luxury. The feel of the soft fur on my body and of the massage (without the gloves) is euphorically soothing. I close my eyes, open my senses to it. Fur. Skin. Tinglings. Eager creamies. I feel like I'm floating.

I'm lying on my back, stretched out, spreadeagled; so is Daxos. The girls are still massaging and gently stroking our skins. They're pretty girls—Japanese girls, with figures like boys.

One of the girls lights a joint for us. Daxos and I share it with some Dom Perignon. He takes my hand tightly. "Close

131

your eyes." I do so. The gloves soothe and caress again. "Don't open your eyes," he warns, pressing my hand; I giggle expectantly. I feel hands on my legs, pushing them upwards while a pillow is slid under my bottom. I open my eyes. "Close them!" Daxos immediately orders.

Then I'm suddenly assailed by new sensations. A mouth on my right nipple. A mouth on my left nipple. A mouth on my wet and so-drippy cunt. The combination is unlike any previous experience. I open my eyes wide, startled by its intensity.

"My surprise. I'm giving you something you never had."

"Oh . . . !"

"Close your eyes!" Before I do, I smile at him. He's smiling too; the fourth girl is giving him head. Number three is chewing away expertly—oh, so *very* expertly—on my sticky little cunt.

"Is it an orgy?"

"It is a present," he laughs.

"Oh . . . Thank you." I manage. "It's a nice one."

The girl sits up from between my legs. The one giving him head moves instead to me, and the girl who was eating me moves over and kisses Daxos.

"You taste so *beautiful*," he smiles.

The two return to nibbling on my nipples. I begin to laugh, quite uncontrollably, as the phrase flashes into my mind: *Nippy nipple nibblers*. Somewhere in the background, Daxos give a long "Ahh . . ." as he comes. And I soon join him, screaming my head off again. I don't believe this much is possible, I really don't *believe* this. . . .

On a word from Daxos, the girls jump down from the bed, bow to him, and very nippily, as nippy nipple nibblers should, leave the bedroom (back to Nippon?).

Daxos throws himself onto me. "I think I love you already," he says to me between kisses as he pulls me into his arms.

"I think I love you too . . ."

I think I'm falling asleep . . .

*   *   *

Two days later. I'm sitting on deck, bundled up in a blanket, wearing a huge floppy-brimmed straw hat and sunglasses. Daxos has been seeing to business all morning. I've been feeling extremely happy and contented. I never saw the four little Japanese girls again. I wonder where he got them from?

132

Now, I realize, is the time for me to go home. I don't want to overstay my welcome. I feel amazingly close to Daxos, and I know that if it weren't for Jan-Toby Axelsson, I'd probably have fallen completely in love with Daxos. I *could* fall completely in love with him. That's why I must go. We have to get some space to ourselves, to see what we really think of this relationship.

We haven't talked of marrying again. The weird thing is, I think that if I had said yes, Daxos *would* have married me. And I think we probably could be happy together.

I can so easily envisage myself here on the yacht or in Athens, writing my books, making love with Daxos, having his babies. What more could I want? Well, for one thing, of course, I could want my freedom. The wife of a Greek millionaire has very little freedom.

Suddenly Daxos is smiling down at me. "You were miles away."

"Hey, don't knock it until you've tried it."

He kisses me, then after a while holds me at arm's length, stares seriously at me for a moment. "My darling one . . . I have to return to Athens."

"Now?"

"Yes, the helicopter is waiting. Important business, it cannot wait."

"Oh . . . You wish me to leave, then?"

He laughs and pulls me close. "No! If you wish, you may accompany me. Or if you wish, you may stay. I will return tomorrow afternoon."

"I'll stay." I smile. "I went up in a helicopter once—never again."

So I stay here on the yacht and catch up with my beauty sleep. I even fall asleep in the bathtub.

Sitting out on the terrace deck, I wonder whether I could really live with Daxos. Is it what I want, what I need? No. I need to get back to my work. That would straighten things out. Putting order into words on a page would also put order back into my life. I must call home.

Miriam! I never realized she could make so much noise over a telephone. She hasn't stopped talking—shouting, I should say—for a whole minute.

"Calm *down*." I finally squeeze in. "What *is* it?"

"Justin's *furious*. Roy's *furious*. Your *mother* called. *Rand* even called. Johnny *Brandigan* even called. And *Matthew* . . ."

". . . Oh." As Miriam goes blabbing on, sounding like an

133

angry bumblebee over the bad line, I realize what's happened. The "news" has made its clever little way across the Atlantic and to the West Coast.

"Are you married yet?" Miriam finally screams. I collapse onto the bed in a fit of giggles.

"We had four Japanese bridesmaids," I say, giggling my head off.

"What!!?"

"It's a joke."

"What was that? I didn't *hear*. A *joke?"*

"Yes—a joke."

Miriam's voice continues yakking, incomprehensibly garbled by the telephone cable, satellite, or whatever.

"Well, *are you?"*

"No." I subdue the giggles.

"But the *press reports* said . . ."

"Fuck the press reports."

"You mean—he hasn't asked you? It's *all untrue?"*

"Yes, he asked."

"But you're not . . . ?"

"Not yet."

"Solange!"

"What?"

"For *fuck's sake! Get him* while you *can!"*

"Thank you, darling."

"When are you *getting married?* I want to *be there.* Call your *mother.* And *what* do I tell *Justin?* And *Roy,* too? And . . ." (actually a pause for an instant.) ". . .*you* know *who*—he was *furious. Roy* said he was so *angry."*

"Roy was angry?"

"Not Roy. *Him!"*

"Oh." How about that, Solange? A lovely little glowworm of sweet revenge is making its way through my body. Well, well, well!

"Why didn't you *tell* me?" Miriam, shouting again.

"Tell you what?" I tease.

"That it was *Jan-Toby Axelsson!"*

"What was?"

"Solange You know *fucking well* what I'm *referring* to— the *man* who brought you *home.* The *man* you had a *few days* with. The *married man.* The *albums.* The *jewelry. Indian* jewelry. *That* one!"

"Oh—*that* Jan-Toby Axelsson."

"Why didn't you *tell* me?"

"I was going to. There was nothing between us, anyway."

134

"*Roy* says *different*."

"Roy doesn't know."

"Then *why* was he *so angry* at the *reports?*"

"Roy, angry? I don't know why."

"Not Roy, *Jan. Solange?*"

"How should I know? The bastard just wants me to hang around and suck if off for him. I won't be *used* like that."

"So you're *marrying Daxos?*"

"I dunno."

"I would. *Jesus*-fucking-*Christ, Solange!*"

"Look . . ." I patiently explain the joke with the reporter, about Daxos asking me later.

"I'm coming home soon."

"*When?*"

"Oh, in a few days."

"*Why?*"

"I need to think. I can't just marry someone cold like that."

"You *could* if you *loved* him. Even if you *don't,* you must *like* each other. Of *course* you must *marry him!*"

"Miriam—not now! Drop it! I'll ring my mother, but *don't* tell anyone *anything*. Oh, except Matthew. Ring *Matthew* and explain what happened, but tell *him* not to tell anyone."

You could if you loved him. Miriam's words echo in my head for the rest of the evening. And Roy said Jan was angry. How *dare* Jan be angry! He's got a wife he fucks. A wife he loves. A wife he gave his baby to. How dare he! I suddenly don't care if I never see the bastard again.

When Daxos returns the next day, I'm feeling just as good about my righteous anger. We go to bed and make love until early evening. But as I lie next to him I know that I have to leave. I have to get back to my own little world for a while. To my house, to my writing, to Gulley—how I miss him. And if I don't leave, how will I feel about Daxos?

"I'm not letting you get away from me, you know. Don't imagine I am," Daxos says as we wait in the VIP lounge at Athens airport for my plane. (I couldn't use the private jet—not for just me—so Daxos bought my ticket. He wouldn't hear of my paying.)

I hold myself close to him. "Dear Daxos. Please understand. I have to be at *home,* doing some *writing* there. It's the *only* way I can sort my feelings out. I know it sounds a round-about way, but . . ."

"I will be ringing you every day," he says softly. "And soon I will be in L.A. again."

As Daxos kisses me good-bye I wonder why the hell I *am* leaving him.

As the plane heads for New York I'm feeling peaceful and looking forward to seeing Miriam and Gulley, to being in my house by the sea, writing my words.

As I'm falling asleep I hear the stewardesses whispering to each other, "She's going to marry Daxos Christophidou."

7

I'm sleepy, but I just want to sit here on the terrace, cuddling Gulley and looking over the ocean. It's good to be home in my own house. I'm a bit cold in my tight jeans and my black tee shirt with a sparkling *Gemini* written across the front, but I don't care. Miriam comes out of the house and sits next to me. Since she picked me up from the airport this afternoon she hasn't stopped her tirade concerning Daxos. I tell her that he's in the middle of some business, so we thought we'd both use the time to see how we felt, away from each other.

"*So,*" Miriam says accusingly, "*why* didn't you *tell* me?"

"Tell you?" I know what's coming, of course.

"About *Jan-Toby Axelsson.*"

"Oh, Miriam—I didn't want to make a big thing out of it. There's nothing between us."

"*Roy's* coming around *tomorrow.* I *told* him that you would be *home today.* He *called,* yesterday."

"Oh." I feel besieged, trapped. Perhaps if I signed his bloody contract, he would leave me alone. Or would that only be the start of his bullying me? Hm, that sounds more likely. More like Roy.

Besides which, I don't want that closeness to Jan. All this is still rattling around in my mind as I sit reading the mail I have to catch up with.

A letter from Johnny. He's heard the rumor, and he's furious. (*He's* furious? So—still thinking of me as his chattel, is he?)

I call up Matthew, explain everything. I tell him I'll be coming to see him soon. He sounds a bit subdued; he's really serious about his chance of having a baby. I cheer him up, for the time being.

Justin and Anna: Anna squeals and gushes over the phone, excited over the idea of me and Daxos. I disillusion them, with long explanations. "Marry him! *Marry* him!" Anna shouts, obviously grabbing the phone away from Justin.

Maman is happy. She understands the situation without explanations. She's leaving for Nice, where she's rented a house for the rest of the year. The divorce from Philippe is going through. I tell her to go and see Marie-Claude and Rand. But only when I've put the phone down do I think of Philippe and me. Oh, shit! I'll tell her when the divorce is through. . . . Well, I will if it's still troubling me then.

All this *explaining* to everyone! I feel as though I've been explaining myself away, leaving only a gray lifeless puppet in my place.

Miriam had the gates fixed. That is, *Roy* made her get electric locks installed on them. She's told me that the cars have some sort of signaling device, so that you just press a button and the gate opens. Dear Miriam, she always gets things done so efficiently. I wish *I* could. There was a reporter waiting at the airport yesterday, but Miriam managed to whisk me right past him with minimum fuss. A few reporters rang today, asking for interviews. All the interest was in Daxos and his rumors, none in my books or my writing, of course!

I sit on the bed and look at the beautiful little solid gold horse that Daxos gave me. Beautiful, gracefully contemporary, it's about nine or ten inches tall. It's called an Elefsis horse. Even though it may look modern, its design has been handed down through the ages, for thousands of years. I pick the horse up and kiss his head. I've called him Achilles.

Daxos has already rung me here, to tell me he has to go to Brazil on business. It would be all so easy to fly to Daxos, shelter in him. But I used *Rand* as a shelter for long enough. I won't do so with Daxos, not with *that* man. If I go to him, and if he wants me, it will be because we *do* want each other.

* * *

I'm up early. I'm still somewhat tired, but I love the sunrise. I sit and drink some grapefruit juice and think about my talk with Roy on the phone last night. He promised me he wouldn't mention Jan to me anymore, and that he could and would keep us quite separate. I believed him. And I'll be glad to have him as my manager.

The room, the whole house, seem strangely quiet in the early morning light, as though waiting for someone, some presence, to wake them up. I rummage among my tapes. Jan's face is on one of them; I throw it down. Another cassette has bits of music I've recorded from various films. I play my favorite piece and set it to keep on repeating. It's a piece of music I play and play while I'm working; I love its haunting, quiet melody. Right now, it fits my misplaced romantic mood.

I get some coffee, settle down to read over the last section of work I did on my new book. But it's no use. I stop and listen to the music, and tears well up in my eyes. How unintelligent of me to go and fall in love with a man I can't have.

As I stare from the huge picture window at the blue, wave-weaving fabric of the sea, Gulley comes to sit by my feet. I stroke him, and he purrs. I'm glad *we* love each other, anyway.

"Ain't you getting dressed, girl? It's past ten," Miriam says, sticking her head in the door. She grins—she knows my huge capacity for daydreaming—and returns to handling the mail.

I read over a chapter and add more corrections. It'll need retyping: so much scribbling in the margin, in between the lines. I only hope Miriam can read it; she usually can.

The door buzzer. I automatically look at my watch: ten-thirty. "Someone to see you," Miriam says, grinning awkwardly.

Roy? I wonder. But it's Jan-Toby Axelsson who walks into the lounge, closes the door. "Ma'am." A slight nod. A slight smile.

How long are we going to stand looking at each other? No good making a scene, protesting his presence. No, I'm going to be the classy Literary Lady: handle him, then send him away. I'm going to *handle* this situation, not be affected by it.

And why is he here, anyway? Fate, again? Kismet, again? Is *he* my Waterloo? (Though, knowing Old Nobodaddy the way I do, I'd say it's more likely to be my personal Armageddon.)

"Come and sit down." Beatific smile. Very classy, Solange.

He smiles his lopsided smile, rubs the side of his nose, slowly crosses the room, steps down into the lower half where I am, and sits next to me. Miriam brings a tray of coffee things, rolls her eyes at me expressively, retreats hastily.

138

"What can I do for you, Mr. Axelsson?"

With a frown, he puts down the cup of coffee I just gave him. "I've got to talk to you. *We've* got to talk."

"*We* have?"

He frowns again, then realizes that perhaps he shouldn't.

"'The Woman that does not love your Frowns,'" I recite to him, "'Will never embrace your smile.'"

He grins. "Readin' my mind, huh?"

I curl myself comfortably in a corner of the sofa. I feel protected here, almost unreachable; even the Lore Blackwine print of my robe seems an elegant talisman against encroachments.

He smiles as I reach for my coffee cup: My robe's loose, he can see a naked boob. I pull back quickly, defensively, in a kind of childish feminine reflex. After all, he's done more to my boobs than just look at them. We each sip our coffee, companionably.

"So, you love my frowns and my smiles, huh?"

What's the answer to that? "Yes."

"I like you quoting things to me." My look asks why. "Ain't had a lady I love do that before."

"Maybe you've been loving the wrong ladies."

"Ain't that the truth! But now I've come up in the world."

"Ah—but are you going to stay here?" I realize I'm actually *enjoying* this. I *can* handle this man, send him away a friend. I feel immensely pleased, and I can't hide from myself that it's so *good* to see him.

I have to move from my safe little nest in the corner, to pour him some more coffee. I lean over and do so. His hand comes up in a flash, inside my kimono, fondling me.

I pull back with a defiant look. At least his hand is out of my robe now, and I can turn my attention back to what we were saying. "I thought you wanted to talk, not to touch."

"I wanna talk and touch," he laughs.

The music tape rewinds. "Let me turn this off, before it repeats."

"What was it? I liked it—it sounded familiar. Leave it until the end again."

"All right. It's called *Sea Dreams.*"

"Nice. Lyrical."

"Mm. It's an interlude. I love it. I guess it touched something inside me. I play it a lot while I'm working. It's from a film I recorded from cable TV. But I wish I had a good stereo recording of it—no one's put it out, that I know of."

139

"Who wrote it?"

"Kris Kristofferson."

"Kris wrote it?"

"Yes, for his Sailor film. It's beautiful, isn't it? It was the favorite part of the movie for me."

"Shit, lady, *you're* beautiful—knowing something I didn't know."

"I know lots of things you don't know. What an arrogant, chauvinist attitude!" I say, smiling.

"I'm sorry, Ma'am. I guess you do, too. Gonna teach me some?" he inquires with a cheeky grin.

"I don't think I could teach you anything."

"That's what you think, huh?"

"Yes."

"You've taught me—you're teaching me—to appreciate classical music. And I like that. But I need to know some more, much more."

Why are we having this beautifully strange conversation? I wonder. He moves closer to me, takes my shoulders. Looks at me. Then my face is in his hands, and he kisses me.

"We'd better talk," he says.

"Yes."

"So—you're going to marry yourself a Greek multimillionaire?"

"That's not mult*eye,* it's mult*ee.*" I tease him.

"Roy said last night that you were thinking of it. *So?*" He's beginning to sound angry.

I explain how it all happened. "But now," I continue, "well . . . I don't know him well enough yet. We're not *in love.* We both agreed, though, that we *could* fall in love."

"So?"

"But then again . . ."

"But what?" he asks impatiently.

I take a deep breath and blurt out, "But I couldn't marry anyone when I'm in love with *you.* I just want to be with *you.* Love *you.* Live with *you.* Marry *you.*"

He looks away irritatedly for a moment. Does my openness and frankness make him angry? Not that I really care, of course. There's not going to be anything between us, so why should he worry? And anyway, if he hadn't come here this morning, he wouldn't have had me telling him I love him. It's all his fault, really. And apart from that, I really feel it'll do me good to get all these bottled up feelings out into the open. If I hold them fixed within me, I'll be holding *him* too, and

I'll never be able to get over him, forget him, fall *out* of love with him.

"I've known you a very long time," I tell him; he rewards me with a puzzled look. "I mean, your words: they've always felt friendly ... familiar. It's like they formed a silver cord between us, even though we hadn't managed to meet. But now, all those dreams and fantasies, all that wishful thinking—they're all valueless, aren't they?"

"Valueless?" He rubs his nose. He's looking interested, intrigued but, at the same time, perplexed.

"Of course—because nothing can come of it. You know, when I met you, when you came and found me in Solly's library, when you came here and said you liked this place and told me how you could just write and write—I knew it was true."

"Knew what was true? Goddam it, woman, you've got me hog-tied in *your* words here."

"That you're the person I've been waiting for—I could be complete with you. We're two halves of the same puzzle."

"That's your belief, is it, Ma'am?"

"Yes. But ... how could something so right be so wrong? How could *I* be so wrong? And I have to be wrong, because you have your wife, your son. You love *them*. The most there could be for us would be an affair—a delectable one, no doubt. but that's not what I want. It's not what's *right* for me. And yet it has to be, because I can't have anything else with you—you don't want anything else. You've asked me to be your mistress—and that's just plain insulting. An insult to me and to you. To *us*." My eyes fill with tears. He's gotten through to me again.

"I love you, so much ..." I whisper. "I lie awake thinking of you. Thinking of us when we made love, and how *good* it was." I sniff back my tears, reach out and touch his face. "You're my *sweet sleep disturber....*" I feel raw and opened up again, but I'm glad I've been able to say these things to him, that he now *knows* how I feel.

"All those things you've been sayin'," he replies slowly, "*I* could have said them to *you*. That's why I want you. To see you when I can."

"When ... you ... can ..." Tears again. "*No!*"

An awkward, tense, silent impasse. How do we extricate ourselves from it? But maybe I really want, deep down, to dissolve the impasse by giving in; maybe I really *want* to see him "whenever *he* can." And maybe ... maybe I should.

He moves closer, takes my face in his hands again, kisses me. "You've *got* to be here if you love me. You've *got* to be here for me. I *need* you here."

"And what about when I need you—and you're at home, making love to your wife?"

He's about to answer when the door flies open and Miriam bounces in. "The phone," she announces. "Justin."

Jan's sitting reading my work when I return. I sit down next to him.

"Jesus, lady, this is so *good!* And funny, too. I love it."

"Really?" All my cares and problems disappear. He's talking about *my* work. He *likes* my work.

He grins. "I kinda recognize this Texas cowboy of a writer."

"You do?"

"There ain't that many Texans who are also Doctors of Literature," he grins wryly.

"Well, what I can't have in reality I can have"—me, being the classy smart-ass again—"in my books. It makes a good *story*."

"It kinda makes me feel sick knowing the way she loves him so much. It's you and it's me, and I feel like a fuckin' asshole."

"You shouldn't have read it. I didn't say you could."

"Why did you make Jon-Bertil Jonsson a writer, not a singer?"

"I didn't want people pointing a finger at you. I mean, you know what people are. In the second book, Pandora fucked with a rock poet, and I had hundreds of letters telling me they *knew* it was Dylan—and was I having an affair with him?" I laugh; he laughs. "And it wasn't, of course. I just needed to use that character—a poet, a rock poet, a living legend—in the plot at that point. I don't even know Dylan," I add, with a wistful smile. "See what I mean? Whatever fiction you write, people *will* assume it's strictly autobiographical. And I don't want anyone thinking it's you, just because the name's similar and he has Swedish ancestry, when it isn't."

"Isn't?" He looks confused.

"No. It's about Pandora—and a writer," I say with my most persuasive smile. "And anyway, you're not the only Swedish-named rock star I know."

"I should be flattered," he says slowly.

"I don't know why I should flatter you, when you insult me." It creates the reaction I expect.

"Insult you?"

"Yes! A mistress! Like, good enough for a quick fuck, but not good enough to live with and love."

He shakes me. "Stop it!"

"Jan, just leave. Please!" I say, simply and definitely, brooking no argument.

"Why can't we try, at least? We can work something out," he says, ignoring my command.

"Oh, *can* we?" I stand up, go over to the window. I feel more in control on my feet.

"We've *got* to try."

I smile ironically, but then the words suddenly seem to pour out. "Okay—let's look at it, me becoming your mistress. Tell me, what does it entail? Do you pay my rent? Buy my clothes? Buy me a car? How about some diamonds, girl's best friend? And what about men—is this exclusive? Do I keep myself just for you? Or am I allowed to fuck other men? Do I have to sit by the phone waiting for your royal command? I mean, just what *is* this being a *mistress?*" My eyes flash at him angrily; I think that at this moment I hate him. "Well, I'm waiting. Is it an exclusive arrangement, this? Do I belong to you? Do you *own* me—you know, like 'O'? How about getting me branded, like 'O' got branded? That should suit you, a Texan—you brand all your cows, right? And why stop there—why not a ring through my cunt, *Property of Jan-Toby Axelsson?*" I stop, trembling.

He gets up, slowly comes over to me. What's coming, the angry outburst I anticipated? I look up; he seems so tall today.

He pulls me into his arms, holds me tight. "I didn't realize I'd hurt you so much, Solange."

I push myself back, stare up at him in amazement. *"Hurt* me? What did you expect? I want to love you. But you just want me for a quick, classy, brainy fuck now and then—*that* shows me what you really think of me."

"I think of you like ... like I've never thought of anyone else. *Ever!"*

"Don't lie to me, Jan!" I shout at him. "What about Melissa? You love *her.* And that's fine if you do—two people happy together. So stay with her, don't come after *me!"*

But, after all that protest, I let myself be led back to the sofa. He sits down, pulls me onto his lap; I can't resist but instead cuddle up to him.

"Now listen to me," he says quietly. *"Listen,* Lady, and understand what I'm sayin'." I stare and listen. "I'll tell you how it is with me and Melissa. Now don't you say anything,

143

just let me talk. It's *my* turn now. You've sure said enough."
He grins. "There's some words, they say exactly how I feel
about me and Melissa:

"When I first married you, I gave you all my whole Soul.
I thought that you would love my loves and joy in my
      delights.
Seeking for pleasures in my pleasures, O daughter of
      Babylon.
Then thou wast lovely, mild, and gentle; now thou art
      terrible
In jealousy and unlovely in my sight, because thou hast
      cruelly
Cut off my loves in fury till I have no love left for thee."

He looks at me. I feel shocked. There are tears in his eyes;
tears in mine.
"I don't understand," I whisper. "What my beloved William said is clear. But how does it apply to you—to *your*
situation?"
"My situation's not what it seems—not what I keep on
making it seem." Jan-Toby Axelsson takes a deep breath
before he continues. "When I first met Meliss', I was so
fuckin' *tired*. I mean, for years—*years*—me, Joel, and the
band had been fuckin' our way around America, Canada, and
twice around the world too. I'd known Meliss' since she was
a kid. Her pa is a business friend of my pa's, in Texas.
They're both ranchers. Well, I met her again. We fucked. She
was young and she wanted me. I was a big hero, a star. She
wanted me—I was the prize she wanted to get her hooks into.
I wanted her too—but just to fuck. She was young, beautiful
—great legs. I stayed home for a month, and we fucked half
a dozen times. I fucked *her*, that is. But then I had to go back
to L.A. for some recording. Before I went she told me she
wanted for us to marry. Marry?—I didn't wanna marry. I'd
never gotten involved—never wanted to. Too many chicks
out there chasin' after us, askin' me to fuck 'em. No need to
get involved. A different night, a different chick. Anyway, she
called me every day, the month I was in L.A. *Every fuckin'
day!* Then one day on the phone, it came—she said she was
pregnant. I said, 'Hey, get an abortion. I'll pay the bill.' Not
that she *couldn't*, of course. But my gentlemanly duty, an' all
that.
"Then the next day, pow!—the fuckin' militia. Her ma and
pa, all the way in his private jet, Melissa in tears. *My* ma and

144

pa—love 'em—wantin' what was best for *me*. Melissa wasn't goin' to have no abortion, her pa shouted at me. I was *gonna* marry her. Do my duty. Support her and my child. Well, I went for a walk to get clear of the lot of 'em for a spell, and I got to thinkin', Well, why not? I mean, the person I had pictured in my mind as My Lady didn't seem to be comin' along. I *needed* to settle down—I was so *tired* of fuckin' around. I'd had the fuckin' clap three times, and it stops bein' funny. So I thought, Hey, why not, Jan-Toby? Might just do you some good to settle down—give it a try. Melissa was religious, I knew that—she got it from her ma—and she was givin' me hell about fuckin' her without us bein' married. And an abortion was unthinkable, sinful. So I did my duty—I felt too guilty, too pressured not to. I mean, she wasn't just 'some chick,' she was the daughter of a real close friend and business associate of Pa's. Christ, let's be honest about it, we've had to pay for a few abortions—band expenses and all that. But ... well, this whole situation, it was different, she wasn't just some dumb little groupie. And Andrew Cantrell is some powerful dude.

"And now there's little Andy. ... I've got to look after him. I *love* that little fucker. He's the one good thing I have in my life with Melissa."

We stare wordlessly at each other. I really didn't expect this. I don't know what I did expect—excuses, perhaps. Nothing so corny as 'my wife doesn't understand me,' not from Jan-Toby Axelsson. Maybe some other kind of evasive persuasiveness. But not this!

"A year ago," he continues, "I asked about a divorce. I mean, I couldn't take any more from her. It was so bad by then, I couldn't take a piss without her wantin' to know where I was goin'. I couldn't write any poetry. If I was in my study for too long, she'd scream that my 'hobbies'—that's what she called my writin'—meant more to me than she did. So I couldn't take any more. I realized, to settle down, you need the *right* person to do it with. We just ain't suited, never were. Of course. I mean, she's a sweet enough girl—but not for *me*. She's just not *my* Lady. I told her she should divorce me, marry a nice, young, clean-shaven, born-again bigot. They'd be *happy* together. I mean, why won't she *let go* of me? She's too young for me, and too fuckin' religious—I ain't into all that, not all that bigoted hypocritical shit she's into. We have nothin' in common. I can't even talk to her, have any kind of a conversation with her, not any intelligent one. We don't even want to do the same things, never mind *have* the same

145

things. To her, money and the power it brings is the only measure of a man. My creativity means fuck-all to her. I mean, she doesn't understand that I *like* to be alone in my study and write poetry or a song. She says I'm *ignoring* her if I do that.

"Shit! I don't like goin' to parties, bein' *seen*—all that fuckin' shit she likes. Our sex is because I have to relieve my feelin's, and bein' a good Christian she has to do her wifely duty. It's wham-bam-straight-missionary-only-man; anything and everythin' else is 'sinful.' She doesn't even come. I told her I could make her come if she let me eat her. She screamed at me that I was tryin' to lead her into Satan's ways by wantin' to do 'unnatural acts,' all that 'abomination' shit. So I don't even fuck her anymore. I'm in my study every night until she's asleep, anyway, then I go and sleep in what used to be Joel's room. I told her: she's got me trapped in the marriage because of Andy—but I don't have to fuck her. So I get chicks to service me. I told her she should get herself a young, clean-livin' little lad, who she could kneel and pray with before they fucked. A good, God-fearin', fundamental Baptist, who wouldn't dream of askin' her to suck it off for him or wantin' to go down on her."

His tone is so bitter, so cynical. But I can feel the hurt within him as he stares at me. He holds my face in his hands, kisses me, tears in his eyes, and I feel so elated that he *can* be honest with me, talk to me so openly about his life and his feelings.

"Anyway," he continues, "when I asked about the divorce, her ma and pa came down on me again like a flock of fuckin' buzzards—of course, she ran to them as soon as I even suggested it. She told me, *they* told me, that if I divorced her I'd never see little Andy again. My parents were on my side, of course. They tried to reason with Charlene and Andrew Cantrell, but those two weren't to be reasoned with. Ma and Charlene don't get on. Charlene's a Fundamental Baptist, and she don't think much of Ma and Pa bein' Lutherans—shit, in Charlene's eyes, that's almost the same as bein' a satanist! Charlene really laid into Ma about me never seein' Andy again unless I stood up to 'my responsibilities as a husband and a father.'"

His eyes have a desperately hurt look. "Andy's my *son*, Solange. I *owe* him. I can't just walk out on *him*. I don't want to, I don't intend to. I've got to look after him. . . . And then one day I went to a party," he shrugs. "Nearly didn't go—but

146

I was feelin' so fuckin' pissed off. And I met a beautiful Literary Lady—a lady whose books I'd read and really dug. A lady I'd wanted to meet. And when I did, I knew she was *my* Lady.... The lady I'd been lookin' for had walked into my life. And I didn't know what to do—how to handle it. Ya know, I'd asked Solly once about meetin' you." He gives me a gentle smile. "Didn't you know that men dream also about their ideal lady? I've fucked my life up, darlin', and I know I've gotta sort it out, somehow. But it's gonna take time; and I need you while I'm doin' it." He kisses me. "I don't want just an affair with you; I want a *life* with you. I *love* you."

"Oh, Jan, I didn't know.... But why didn't you tell me? Why didn't you say something? You knew I was taking it for granted that you loved you wife."

"Yes, I knew—but d'you know, you never gave me a chance to tell you until now? That time in the library, you walked out before I could say anything. And the first time, well, we hadn't really gotten that far then, had we? Though *I* knew, deep down. When I first *saw* you, I wanted to touch you. Jesus fuck, you were so little, so beautiful, and so fuckin' *curvy*. I just wanted to *touch* you. But we've gotten that far now, haven't we?"

"Yes, we have." We just sit there, holding each other, loving each other, wanting each other.

" 'Babies Should Be Made In Love' was your song," he says. "I was so fuckin' *angry* when you didn't realize that."

"What else was I to think?"

"That I love you, that's what you're to think!"

Of course, he knows he's got me now. Knows that I'm unable to run. And I know that, too. I kiss him. He holds me tightly around the waist. Why are we sitting looking at each other with stupid, idiotic smiles on our faces? "I did dream about it, though," I tell him. "That you were saying it to *me*."

"I *was*."

"Yes." Kissing. "I dreamed a lot about you." Lopsided, pleased grin from Jan-Toby Axelsson. "Especially at night, in bed, thinking of how we made love.... You know—a touch of the eager creamies." Another grin. "Thinking about all that delectable eating and fucking." Wider grin. "Me, coming by myself, fantasizing it was with you. ..."

He laughs. "Jesus, Lady, you're beautiful!" He hugs me. "Actually, I know what ya mean."

"You do?"

"Sure do, Ma'am. Except I do it in the shower...." Loud laughter. "Thought of sendin' ya some in a bottle." He winks.

He hugs me, and we kiss and kiss. His hand feels beneath my robe, rubs gently on my pussy hair. Pushes gently into me. Me, creamy, wanting him. He grins.

"What's going to happen?" I suddenly ask him.

He gives me a serious look, removes his fingers. Then he looks at it, smiles, and licks it. I think I'm blushing, and cuddle him so he can't see. But he already has and laughs.

"We're gonna have to take everythin' easy until things get worked out," he says slowly. "We've got *lots* of talkin' to do."

"Yes, we have."

"I've only explained quickly. I want to get into everything with you, some more. Deep, ya know?"

"Yes. Me too—with you."

He sucks on his finger again. "Run out of creamy." It makes me giggle. "Jesus, I'm so fuckin' *horny*."

I feel him. "Mm, you are."

"Let's go and fuck."

"No, I don't want to. Well—I mean, I *want* to, but not now. Not until we've talked some more. I'm not ready...."

He hugs me. "Okay, darlin' whatever you want."

"I want *you*."

We sit in silence for a couple of minutes, just holding each other as tight as we can. Are we both afraid we would disappear if we let go of each other? *Have* we committed ourselves to each other? Are we frightened to say anything because that commitment might spoil, turn sour, become something tediously complex and undesirable?

A secret affair. For a moment, the idea makes me feel frightened. Will this be *all* that we'll ever have—quick, secret fucks?

"Hey—what is it?" He holds me at arm's length. "You're cryin', and you ain't even come yet? It'll be all right. I *promise* you." He holds me to him again, tightly. He's not letting me get away. And I don't want to get away.

There's no escape from this affair, I know that now. For how can you escape from someone you share the same skin with?

"Listen, darlin'...."

"What?" Me, bright and cheerful again, the unsaid doubts and fears thrust aside into some unexamined dimension of space.

"We're rehearsin', for the road. Come with me."

"But how can I?"

"It's at Roy's, in his basement. He's had a studio built. I'm supposed to be there now." He grins. "He's your manager too, now."

"Yes."

"Jesus, I *like* that! I told him to push it until you gave."

"Oh, *did* you?"

"Sure did, Ma'am." He holds me to him again, then takes my face in his hands, looks wonderingly at me, kisses me. "I love you, Literary Lady."

"And I love you too."

"It's gonna work out—you'll see."

"Is it?" He's making it sound so simple, but my doubts and fears are crowding back in on me. Until his kiss makes it all right again.

*　　*　　*

I'm surprised to find that Roy's house is just half a dozen houses away from Solly's. There's a collection of cars in the driveway. Jan pulls up behind Joel's jeep.

We sit in the car looking at each other. I touch his chest, rubbing the palms of my hands on his black tee shirt.

"You know, I can't believe this," he says, smiling.

"*You* can't?"

"Everything you said to me," he says, "the things you did, the things you liked—music, books—I couldn't believe it. Everything, all I wanted in someone I love—in one package."

"Was that why you sometimes looked so puzzled?"

"I *was* puzzled. I couldn't believe it—just looking through all the books and albums you had. But besides that—most of all—our sex, our loving. It's never been like that for me before, lovin' it because I was pleasurin' someone, not just bein' serviced."

I fling my arms around his neck. He's got his hair tied back, so I pull it, making him laugh. "What will everyone *think?*" Suddenly I'm shy and awkward.

"Roy will be pleased. So will Joel and the boys." He holds my hands as we walk towards the house. I'm worried about what I look like, even though my tight jeans, high heels, and silk shirt make a real neat little Ms. Classy-Ass.

It's a beautiful house, one of those huge fake Spanish palaces, fit for megalomaniacs to live in. Roy is delighted to see me. My just appearing with Jan says it all.

149

The basement studio is huge but seems to be full of electronic equipment and band instruments. The band is there, and I feel inanely shy.

Jan introduces me. Joel, George, Wilb, Dan. They're all grinning at Jan and trying not to grin at me too. A huge Irish wolfhound saves me with an effusive, wriggling welcome. I squeal, Roy laughs, and the wolfhound puts his front paws on my shoulders and rasps my face with his tongue.

"Gordon digs chicks," Roy says, rescuing me. "Got him well trained." He winks. "Come and have some coffee with me while these motherfuckers do some work." He takes my hand and leads me back up the thick-carpeted stairs. We talk a little, then he shows me around the house. His bedroom is huge and modern, with an *enormous* round waterbed. I grin; he grins.

"Shame you're already spoken for." Gordon pushes at me, licks my hand. "He sure digs you," Roy nods.

The lounge has Indian rugs on the walls. "I'm glad Jan decided to tell you about the bind he's gotten himself into," Roy says, "and that you've both gotten yourselves together."

"I don't know *what* we've got at the moment. I only know what I want it to be. Jan-Toby Axelsson, seen from afar, always seemed extremely strong, independent, having his own way. And he *still* seems that way. That's why it's hard to understand the whole scene."

"He's wanted out since he was in—and he never wanted in, not really. It was only Andy. Andy, and Melissa's family pressuring him. But they'd have had no effect without Andy. It's his duty to Andy that he feels so keenly."

"I feel awkward talking about it, but it doesn't work, does it, to stay together for the sake of the children?" I say with conviction.

Roy's leaning back in a slub silk chair, looking very handsome. "I know," he agrees. "I've been through the same mill, you know. But my ex is a good girl; I see my two kids twice a month. You know, no hassles."

"Oh, I'm *glad*." And I really am. "If a situation's killing you, how can you be happy in it? I know, I was in one with Rand. Sometimes you just have to do something for yourself, however selfish it might appear to others."

"You don't have to tell me that." Roy's assent makes me feel easier. But I'm still so very unsure, cautious. "You're what he needs," Roy adds. "You understand what he's doing.

His creativity. You understand *him*. I don't think he's ever had that, not from a woman."

"Oh, but . . ."

"It's *true*. You're what he's always needed."

"I'd like to think that. He's certainly what *I* need."

"He's right." Jan's standing behind me, looking very pleased. "Come on—come down and listen." He holds his hand out to me.

I enjoy sharing with him something that he's created—except that it's so *loud*. I'm sitting in one corner of a big old leather chesterfield, my feet tucked up under me. Everyone's eating sandwiches and drinking beer. Gordon's sharing my tuna salad sandwich; I'm happy in his company, while Jan talks to Roy.

Jan watches me, smiles. I wish we were in bed; so does he, I think. I wonder when we *will* go to bed. Today? God, I hope so! But what are the ground rules? Are there lots of them? Devious, complicated, secret ones? I *hate* secrets! I *hate* the idea of all this intrigue. Have I made the wrong decision? I want *everything!*

"How was it?" Jan asks proudly.

"I loved it. It's so good listening to you."

"One more hour, then we'll go home."

"Home?"

"Your home. But it'll be our home." He kisses me.

"Yes."

"I can stay for a few hours."

"Oh?" My eyes fill with tears. "Jan . . . I don't think . . . "

He squats down, takes my face in his hands, kisses me. "Shh!"

"But—" But what? We'll be alone, together, and *soon!*

"You'd better have a key." I sniff, grin at him. "And the electronic card thing for the gate."

They go over another number, argue with Roy, argue among themselves. Gordon and I are cuddling. Well, at least *we've* hit it off perfectly. Whereas this thing with Jan . . . I lose track when I try to consider all the complicated issues involved. But I *must* think them through.

I look up from Gordon and freeze solid in a kind of rigid, panicky horror: Melissa-Sue and another woman have appeared in the room, as though spirited there by a malign deity while my guard was down. I numbly watch little Andrew Axelsson run joyfully across the room to his Daddy. The music stops; everyone else freezes, too. Roy looks furious.

151

Jan's face has a helpless, almost pathetic look; I pretend not to notice it.

"Daddy!" Andrew tugs at Jan's jeans. Jan's face lights up; he throws his small son up in the air, catches him, swings him around.

"Melissa." Roy nods, casually walks over, and sits beside me, gripping my hand tightly. I'm trembling.

"We came," Melissa announces regally. Then she notices I'm here. Looks at me, then back at Jan. "Momma and I have just done with spending lots of Poppa's money on Rodeo."

So that's her mother. Yes, they're alike: tall, so thin, red hair, almost the same shade.

"You've met Solange, haven't you, Meliss'?" Roy asks cheerfully. "I'm handling her now. We came to listen in."

Well, what a marvelous excuse for being here! I guess that's how it's going to be—me being excused away.

Andrew wriggles down, runs and cuddles with Joel, toddles over and gives Gordon a pat. He points to me. "Lady," he says, looking at his daddy.

"Hello." I smile at him—at his blue eyes, his carrot-red hair, the freckles all over his face. He looks much like Melissa, nothing like his daddy. He touches my arm boldly, giggles, runs back to his mummy.

"Can't you come home *now?*" she says to Jan.

I feel confused and hurt. "Excuse me—Roy was just going to run me home," I lie, standing up, giving Melissa and her mother my classiest of Classy-Assed smiles. "Thanks for letting me listen," I tell Jan. His face is an angry mask.

We stare at each other, it seems like for hours, and it feels like we want to touch each other. Why doesn't he come over and touch me? Why can't we have everything out in the open, here and now? We could handle it. Together, we could; we could fight together for him to see his little son. But it's got to be him to start it. The initiative is his; it's his battle. I'm an ally, not a protagonist. He's so close to me here, I want to run to him. But could I? I realize at this precise moment—horrifyingly, emptily—that he isn't close to me at all. Our apparent closeness is only a mockery, an unreal pretense.

Melissa goes over and kisses his cheek. Why can't *I* be the one to do that? "Come on home," she says boredly and picks up their son to cuddle him. Of course, she hasn't a clue what's been going on. Everything here must seem so normal to her; and the way she treats her man, that must be normal for her as well.

"Back soon," Roy says, putting a protective, warm arm

around me, squeezing my shoulder. *"Don't* go, Jan—I want to talk to you."

I give Jan a look that says *it's no good.*

I say nothing to Roy all the way back in the car. When we're at my house, I say, "I don't *ever* want to go through that humiliation again. I don't *ever* want to see him again. I mean it, Roy—*Never!"*

"Solange, how could he know? Solange?"

"No! I *won't* have my life turned into a sordid little secret affair. I've never done that, I'm not going to start now. It's so degrading, so . . . *dirty! No!"*

He squeezes my arm compassionately. "You deserve everything out in the open, darling. I know that."

"But that's just what I'm not going to get, isn't it?"

"Give it time. . . . I'll talk to him. I want to help you both. I don't know what it is about you two, but I just know you belong together."

"I know that. That's why . . . Oh, Roy, it won't work. It *won't."* I scramble from the car and run into the house.

*   *   *

Anna meets me when I get to New York. She knows I'm upset but asks me no questions. She gives me a hot drink, a sleeping pill. I sleep until lunch the next day.

Miriam tells me that both Roy and Jan rang; she told them nothing.

I see Matthew and tell him everything. I have dinner with him and Chris, his new lover. When Matthew invites me to spend the night with them, I nearly do, but I want to be alone. I go home to Justin and Anna, see Justin for the first time, have a drink with them both, and then go to my room.

I lie in bed watching a shit-awful late night movie. After a while I cry myself to sleep.

Anna and I go shopping and spend *lots* of money. Justin's gone off for a few days. How nice—I really don't want a man around the place. *I hate men!!*

How could I have believed all that bullshit Jan-Toby Axelsson gave me? How could I ever have been so *naive?* I'm not going to be made a fool of anymore. I'm not some eager little groupie who can't resist a big shiny poet hero rock star.

Why did I come to New York in the winter? I forgot how cold it can be; it was only by reflex that I brought my arctic fox jacket. I like it because it's the exact color of Pandora's hair: an amazing, delicate shade of silver. Pandora wears her hair parted in the middle, and it reaches down to cover her sexy, curvy, little ass. Perhaps I should let mine grow and grow? But it'll never be that beautiful color. And I'll never have her beautiful bright green eyes, slanted and hypnotic.

I'm just back from Bloomy's and am pulling my boots off when the phone rings; It's Daxos! Miriam gave him this number; he wants to see me. He'll be leaving South America in a few days. We talk for a long time. I tell him I'm in no mood to see anyone, I'd be no good at anything with him. Perhaps I need some more time on the yacht, he says with a laugh. Wonderful Daxos, if only I could; but I tell him truthfully that until I can give him *all* my attention and love, it would be unfair to him.

There's a long pause and then distance, coolness. He tells me to look after myself and that he will call me again. But I know he won't. Women don't turn him down—so why should he bother? Grief overcomes me; I've given away something genuine, worth having, for something I haven't even got.

Bootsie, the basset hound, helps me unwrap my new things, pulling the paper to bits. I put on my new silk blouse—silver —without a bra, to get the feel of silk against my skin. Anna and I cook some dinner. Steak, peppers, *courgettes* (zucchini here, but I can never get used to the Italian name). Bootsie shares with us. He really has it made. No wonder he waddles so beautifully.

Over dinner I find myself telling Anna *everything*, right up to Daxos' phone call. "Stupid bitch!" she laughs. "You should have gone."

"I couldn't. I just couldn't. I hate them *all*."

For consolation we ignore calories and eat a sweet of Anna's own concoction: home-baked spiced fruit and honey cake. "With lots of lovely weed in it," she giggles. We spoon dollops of Louis Sherry rum and raisin ice cream onto it, then take the heaped dishes into the lounge. Anna produces two joints. We pour ourselves huge glasses of apricot brandy.

"Jesus, are we going to get stoned!" I exclaim.

"Super!"

"Let's watch *it*," Anna says.

I, of course, know what *it* is. I have an *it* at home, too. *It* is Anna's videotape of one of our shared favorite movies. It's silly, but we adore it.

So, smoking a joint, eating hash-cake, and drinking apricot brandy, we watch *The Rocky Horror Picture Show*, sing along with all the songs, and dance to the "Time Warp."

Justin watched it once with us. He couldn't believe that two *intelligent*, beautiful, sophisticated, *grown* women could get themselves *enthused* over such *trash!* and, what was even worse, that they could have gone three times to London specifically to see the stage show.

By the end of the movie, we're very giggly and very stoned.

Anna suddenly unbuttons her blouse. "What d'you think, then?" She exhibits her brand-new thirty-four-inchers to me.

"I forgot." I move closer to inspect them. "Wow! They really do look good—It's amazing!"

"It's *astounding!*" she giggles.

"How do they feel? Can you feel anything in there?"

"Here." She grabs my hand and jabs away at her boobs with my fingers. "See? Quite natural. It's not that silicone stuff, it's just water." She sits there with her blouse hanging out, and we continue to eat, smoke and drink. "Are they all that much smaller than yours now?"

Anna reaches over, undoes my shirt and we compare boobs. "Hey, not *too* bad, eh? Yours are still bigger, though. And so lovely and *full*. And still so *pink*. Great to suck on!"

"Oh, really? I've never sucked on them." For some stoned little reason, I find this immensely funny; I can't stop giggling.

"What about someone else's?" she asks. I look blank. "Sucking on someone else's?" she repeats.

"A girl's?"

"Of course! Haven't you ever made it with a girl, then?"

"Not properly . . ." I tell her about Daxos and the Nippy Nippon Nipple Nibblers. We collapse laughing on the carpet, trying to say it over and over. We finish the ice cream and cake, trying to recite, getting ourselves more excited and even more giggly over Peter Piper's pickled pecker . . .

"I'm glad Justin's not home tonight," Anna says as we lie sprawled on the carpet, having finished the joints and drunk all our apricot brandy.

"Mm?"

"We can fuck all night," she says quietly.

"We can?" I sit up.

"Wouldn't you like to?" Anna giggles, sits up, falls back down again, sits up again giggling, then pulls her blouse off with a grand flourish.

"Of course." I agree to the inevitable and pull my blouse off too. We stand up and try to get ourselves out of our

155

jeans. Giggling and stoned, it's an almost impossible task, but eventually I stand there in my scanty, lace-sided panties. Anna stands there in nothing.

"I don't wear panties all the time. If I don't, I can make myself come against the roughness of my jeans."

"Really?" Me, totally impressed. "That's fantastic!"

"It's *astounding*," she sings.

"I'll have to try it."

"While doing the Time Warp," she sings, ending in a stoned giggle.

We sink to the carpet. With sporadic giggles, Anna fondles my nipples, while I fondle hers. It feels so nice: warm and soft and marshmallowy.

"Here . . ." She slips a long finger into me; I notice abstractedly, but without surprise, that I'm wet and sticky. "I'm so ridiculously fucking *horny*," she says.

"Me too, and I've never felt a woman . . . *done* it to a woman."

"It's easy. You just have to do what you know you like yourself."

Of course! I'd never thought of that. I slip a finger into Anna. It feels so good, so warm and soft, so sticky—moist.

"It's *fantastic!*" Anna squeals.

"It's *astounding!*" we both squeal.

We shyly kiss. "You've *never* done it with a woman?" she asks again.

"I've daydreamed about it, while masturbating."

Anna giggles, kisses me, sucks on my nipples. She pushes me back and sucks on my button. Up pops her head as she sings to me: *"Don't dream it—be it."*

"Mmm . . ."

"Don't dream it—be it," she sings again, crawling up to me. We giggle and sing together: *"Don't dream it—be it."*

She pushes me back onto the carpet and dives between my legs. Anna's mouth is on me as I play with my nipples; it's not long before I come, moaning, screaming, wriggling.

Eating pussy, according to some accounts I'd recently read of God-awful first times, needs a cautious approach. But Anna's delectable little cunt doesn't taste fishy or smell yukky. It just tastes sexy, like when I taste me on a man's mouth. It takes Anna all of a minute, too.

How delicious, keeping ourselves stoned and coming all night. *"Don't dream it—be it. . . ."* So soft and sexy, just what I need: an escape from masculine mucho macho. *"It's fan-*

tas-tic!" I shout at one point. "It's as-tound-ing!" Anna shouts in reply.

Us, collapsing in a giggly heap, then reforming into sixty-nines, and thirty-four-and-a-halfs. Mmm . . . perhaps I will go gay, or at least, semeye-gay.

"*Tribadism,*" Anna announces, about three o-clock in the morning. We've slept cuddled up together for an hour or so.

"Tribbles?" I giggle sleepily. "No, not Tribbles. But Spock . . ."

"*What?*"

Our giggling swamps my ears, interferes with reception.

"I said *tribadism,*" she insists.

So we smoke a joint and then we *tribad.* I come to the conclusion that you've got to be stoned and giggling to tribad. We lie sideways like scissors, letting our hard, sticky, excited clits touch, and tribad away in ecstasy . . . .

Hell knows how we manage to come with all our giggling, but we do—*and* together, moaning and screaming, wriggling and giggling.

"It's *astounding!*" Anna declaims.

"*Don't dream it—be it. . . .*" I sing.

We kiss and giggle—giggle and kiss. And as we're still so horny, we smoke a joint and then we tribad again. . . .

We can't stop giggling. And Bootsie leaves the room, disgusted.

8

The beginning of April brings spring and warmth. It's *not* "the cruelest month"—not in California.

I've been working hard since returning from New York, but I'm feeling better, revitalized, soothed, and comforted.

Roy's rung a few times to say Jan wanted to see me: I said No! I told Miriam that if she wanted to keep her job, she'd never let Jan in or even connect him on the phone. But I think it'll be all right between Roy and me; I think it'll work; I hope so. I like him. And besides, he's working hard.

It's my letter-writing day. I have three friends I've always kept in touch with. We have a routine; I write one month, they answer the next. All three do this, so I find myself writing three letters on the same day, at the beginning of the month.

There's my letter to Cynthia, who was at Lady Margaret Hall with me. She was Cynthia Greenham-ffinch then; she's Cynthia Cholmondely now. Married David Cholmondely, younger son of an earl, and they're blissfully happy, up to their eyes in market gardening in Wiltshire. Two kids, too. A *terribly super* life, they tell me. I'm glad they're so happy. It's nice that a couple can fall in love and be happy—even the youngest children of earls!

I've just finished writing to Ben Simmons, who was my Rhodes scholar friend at Oxford. Darling Professor Ben—I always start my letters to him like that. He and Franny, who teaches art, have a daughter, four-year-old Cass, and he has two kids from his first wife as well. I went and saw them all last year. They're so happy, I giggle when I think how terrible Ben and I were at fucking—both so quiet and shy.

My third letter is to the first man in my life: Lars. Dear Lars, we've known each other for such a long time: since I was fourteen and he was fifteen. We always understood each other and liked each other; I had my literature, Lars had his music. When we finished Lynehurst—he was a year before me—I went to Oxford, and he went to the Royal College of Music. Brilliant Lars, famous in Sweden, in fact all over Europe. Unknown over here—as yet, that is.

I first saw Lars over the wooden fence that divided our garden from his. A thin, pale-gold youth, extremely tall, and with the most amazing blue, blue eyes. He had two younger brothers and a sweet, giggly sister of six, all of whom spoke only Swedish. Lars' father is a diplomat; his mother is an actress.

I was surprised when he came over and said hello to me because his English was so perfect. We became friends immediately. Our two families had much in common, both well off, both immersed in the arts. Lars was impressed that my father was Richard Osborne, the well-known cellist. My maman and his mother, Britta, immediately became friends and still are. I think they hoped Lars and I would marry.

My first kiss came *very* late, at my fifteenth birthday party, outside, behind the greenhouse. Lars kissed me, and that started our gentle love affair. Lars would walk me home from school; we'd have tea together; Lars would feel for my pussy

158

and I'd squeal, "No, not *inside!*" I'll never forget that little gasp when Lars finally managed to get his fingers inside my bra and I felt for the first time a man's fingers on my nipples.

And then came my sixteenth birthday. He was so big and manly to me. We were always telling each other how we loved each other. Even saying it in Swedish, after he'd struggled to teach me some.

"I want you," he said, as we lay cuddling and kissing, again behind the greenhouse, with the party in full swing indoors. Me in my first really grown-up, strapless dress. Lars, pulling my hand down onto his hard, throbbing cock. It seemed to have a life of its own. Oh, the feel for the first time of a hard cock bulging beneath tight pants! My mouth open in concentration, I rubbed, Lars pushed. It seemed such a *huge* thing. And then he showed it to me—except that my head was turned away and my eyes were screwed shut. "Look!" he laughed. "No!" I giggled.

It wasn't that I knew nothing about sex; I'd known for years that it was beautiful, loving, something to be shared with someone you loved. Thank goodness for Maman's French practicality and aesthetic good sense! But the actual thing, at sixteen, was something else again.

Lars gently guided my hand—then that actual flesh was against my hand. Me, holding—*it*. Of course, I finally had to peek at that awesome, warm monolith I was holding. "My God!" I squealed, "I never realized it was *that* big!"

"You *know* I love you," Lars said huskily. "Come on, *let* me?"

"No!" Me, giggling, my perceptions and thoughts darting and hovering like hummingbirds. Lars, hot, perspiring, gazing at me fixedly with those blue eyes.

"Please!" Lars, desperate, moving backwards and forwards as I hold it tightly with my little hand . . . a gruff exclamation, Lars coming. Me, looking at Lars' come on my hand, blushing bright red, bursting into tears because of not knowing what to do. Lars kissing me, telling me he'll always love me; wiping my hand with his handkerchief. Pleading with me again after some more kissing and cuddling.

We sneaked up to my bedroom and locked the door. He told me he loved me and that it would be a "proof of our love for each other." As he undressed me there were tears in my eyes and I was trembling. I remember that he gently kissed one nipple and then the other. To me it seemed terribly romantic. My little girly figure was just "filling out," as they say, and

Lars was admiring it. He rested his hand on my pussy hair and I blushed profusely. Then he was on top of me and that great big *it* was digging into me, between my legs. "It won't hurt, will it? Will it?" He kissed me and reassured me, but it *did*, it hurt like hell. It took quite a few pushes before he finally made it all the way and my little cherry popped. It didn't take Lars long to come. Dear gentle Lars, he kissed me and kissed my pussy hair, making me blush again.

"There," he said, "wasn't that good?" "No!" I cried, hurting. "It will be nicer next time," he said. But I wasn't sure I wanted a "next time." "Now," he said as we left the bedroom, "we're special to each other." I was sure that everybody *knew*, when we rejoined my birthday party. Lars's wide smile seemed irrepressibly permanent. I was smiling too, a gentle, pleased, secret smile, because Lars loved me.

I told my mother the next day. She hugged me and smiled and told me I'd better get fitted for a diaphragm or get myself on the pill. I felt *terribly* grown up and important. She said nothing more, except that Lars and I loved each other and weren't using each other, and that was all that mattered; *using* anyone you love, whether for sex or anything else, was very wrong. My sensible, beautiful maman. I even remember how after I first masturbated, at twelve, I said to my maman so innocently: "Maman, I loved myself and it felt so nice." She hugged me, kissed me, and said, "That's very nice, darling. I liked doing it, too. It's a *natural* part of finding out about one's sexuality." I was much older before I found out that people were made to feel or were *supposed* to feel *guilty* about something so natural and enjoyable as "loving themselves."

My letters finished, I joined Gulley on the terrace and sat dreamily listening to my *Sea Dreams* music again. I've *got* to do something, get out of this little rut, I tell myself.

I need someone to make love to me. I feel lonely. But just *who* do you make love to when the person you want isn't available?

* * *

I had dinner with Roy tonight. Jan wants to see me, he said. I told him no, under no circumstances. He said that Jan's been having trouble and really needs to talk to me. What sort of trouble? Roy wouldn't answer me. Do you really care? he accused. After that, we kept our discussion strictly to business.

"You give *far* too much money away."

"No, I don't!" Me, very indignant.

"Whales, for instance. All that money for dolphins, seals, and whales. *Whales,* Solange!" Roy indignant.

"The bastards *murder* them!" I shouted, even more indignant.

"Murder? They're animals—they get *killed.* People get murdered—*murder* is for civilized people."

"They *murder* them," I insisted obstinately.

"You give as much for whales, and other animals as well, as you give for all the kids' charities—and that's a great deal, too." He frowned. "You've adopted more kids than Unicef has!"

"It's the little ones that suffer," I protested.

"You'll be adopting fucking dolphins and whales next."

"Hey—*Adopt-a-Dolphin!* Great idea," I joked, but Roy *wasn't* amused. "They need it, Roy. And it's *my* money, anyway. Jesus, Roy, if you can't share a bit of your own happiness with others ... ! My parents always taught me that."

"And *who* is Raul Sanchez!"

"Oh, Roy ..." Why couldn't he leave things be?

"I *assume,*" he persisted, "that he's something to do with Elena Sanchez?"

"There you are, then. Why ask if you know already?" Me, all little Ms. Smart-Ass. "Raul is Elena's son," I added complacently.

"You pay *her* too much, too. She's only in the house twice a week. *Far* too much!"

"I do not! Listen—is this how you got so rich, being so fucking mean?" I glared, pouting. "I can afford it—and Elena *needs* it. She's been with me ever since I came here. She's a friend, she comes to stay to look after Gulley if I need her. Her sister works for Sarah and Solly."

"So why did you lend her son all that money?"

"He was a farm worker. He had a chance at his *own* little place up near Salinas. The banks wouldn't help him."

"So *you* have to be little Miss Charity?"

"He pays me back what he can, when he can. Every month he pays something. I've been to see them with Elena. It's so nice there—it's not big, but he's making a success of it. It's *his.* He only needed a little help. But no one would help a Chicano, a 'bad risk.'"

"Oh, Solange .... !" Roy shook his head. Then he had the nerve to tell me I paid Miriam far too much, too. I replied that what I paid Miriam was entirely up to me—and it *wasn't* too much, not for what she does. We were both feeling rather niggly at each other. He left early.

I draw myself a bath, sit and soak for ages, thinking about Jan. I'm always thinking about Jan: *Was* I unreasonable about what happened? I want to talk to him. Touch him. Kiss him. Make love to him.

But will I see him? No, I won't. An urge arises to hurt him as much as he's hurt me.

Downstairs, I put a cassette into the video machine and watch Jan singing on the *Midnight Special*. And why the hell do I always seem to be crying, these days? The way I'm feeling now, I think that if I could see him just *once* a month I'd take it! I watch him do a complicated fingering on his guitar, finish, and grin into the camera, introducing the next group. I switch it off and go to bed.

Halfway up the stairs, I hear the gate buzzer. What the hell! It must be well past midnight. It's still buzzing, one wall of sound. I recognize that buzz. No, it can't be, though! I go down and press the OPEN button. *Why,* Solange?

After a moment Jan-Toby Axelsson starts to press the buzzer of the house door.

Should I let him in? The buzzing sounds impatient as he jabs away at the button. Suddenly there's a banging on the door, startling me: He's kicking at it. I'd better stop him making all that noise. I quickly open the door, and Jan-Toby Axelsson almost falls in.

"Took ya fuckin' time, Lady!" Sloppy lopsided grin. He's very, *very* drunk, and a bit the worse for wear: old jeans, dusty boots, the right sleeve of his black tee shirt torn, the left missing, some sort of suede cowboy hat, dark glasses, a half-empty bottle of Stolichnaya vodka in one hand, and a crumpled red rose in the other. Swaying, he presents the rose with an amicable grin. "Ma'am!"

"Thank you. I'd better get you some coffee." I take the bottle from him.

"That's *mine,* Lady!"

"I'm not going to drink it!"

I let him sprawl on one of the lounge sofas, and go make strong espresso coffee. By the time it's made, he's asleep. Why am I smiling? What's the *matter* with me? Look at him, just like a naughty little boy. His hat's pushed forward over his face; I remove it, and take his glasses off. Finally I pull his boots off—he hasn't got any socks on—get a blanket to keep him warm.

For the first time, I notice he's grown his beard and mustache back. They're not really luxuriant yet.

Oh, Jesus, am I never to be rid of this man? But do I want to be rid of him? Why do I lean over and kiss him, caress his face tenderly?

I go up to bed. I guess he'll be all right on the sofa, but I'm going to have to handle him in the morning. Handle *what*, though? Will I be able to send him packing? Oh, Solange, *try* to think straight! Nothing's changed, after all; he'll still want you as a classy fuck. . . .

It's late, and I'm coming up from a deep sleep, with something disturbing and pulling at me. Its Jan!—shaking me, trying to wake me.

"I want you." He covers my body with his.

"What?" I'm in sleepy confusion. I wriggle, push at him, somehow manage to get out from under. I sit up to see his clothes are on the floor.

"*I want you!*" He pulls me roughly to him, too strong for my struggles.

"Jan!" I push and kick futilely; the bed wobbles violently.

Then he suddenly lets go, sits back. "I can't get the fuckin' thing up!" he shouts at me accusingly. "Not since you fuckin' well walked out on me."

"I didn't walk out on you!" I shout back, absolutely furious. "How could I walk out on something that didn't exist?" Then I take in what he said. Can't get it up? He's not quite sober yet, that's what it is. Hell, it's half-past three in the morning. "Jan, you need some sleep."

"I need *you*," he shouts, grabbing for me again.

"Jan!" He still grabs for me, trying to kiss me, pressing himself onto me again. He smells of drink and sweat. "*Jan!*" I can feel his erect cock pushing between my legs (can't get it up?). "Jan!"

"Keep still!" He's trying to hold me with one hand and get it in with the other. Suddenly I'm frightened. But I know Jan would never hurt me . . . . Do I, though? He's drunk, angry, frustrated. God knows what pressures have built up within him. I find myself crying. Oh, Christ! I try to relax, to be able to handle this drunken mess who's trying to rape me. Of course it's rape—any forced, unwanted sex is rape, and this sex is decidedly unwanted, physically *and* mentally.

I panic, cry out in fear. Start to fight and hit at him.

"Keep still!" He stays still a moment himself. Muddled by vodka, he's not sure why I'm fighting him. My arms are free; I try to push away, twist my body from his on the swaying bed.

Roy! I've got to phone Roy! I push and twist more fiercely, but he's too heavy. I can still feel his erection, but at least he hasn't got it in me. His weight is dragging me down helplessly, and I nearly give up, but something in me fights. I reach out and claw at his face.

"Fuckin' hell!" He shifts, and I see the scratch marks I've made; he lets go long enough for me to slip free, off the bed, running towards the door. My only thought is to call Roy, get him to come and take Jan away from me.

I don't make it. Jan has flung himself on me, grabbing. We crash to the floor; my head hits something hard with a dull thump. It all seems to move so slowly, and the thump is so *loud*. I feel sick for a moment, fuzzy; I can't see properly.

"I want you," a deep voice grates in my ear. He presses down, taking my breath away. I want to fight back, but I can't. My head hurts so. I can't lift it. I feel a pain somewhere else now. Jan is cutting right through me: thrusting himself into me. I'm dry, and it hurts. All I can do is lie still and limp; crying, totally unresisting. My head is aching dizzily, my stomach nauseous and my cunt (which I'd willingly give to Jan if he made love to me) is a dry, unwilling piece of flesh, being battered and unlovingly bruised by this crazed barbarian.

I close my eyes. The warmth of my tears somehow feels comforting: the only warmth in this revolting degradation. Jan cries out, somewhere in the remote distance, and flops down even more heavily on top of me.

Everything is so still, so quiet. It seems we've been like this a lifetime, but in fact it can only have been a few minutes. Jan's kissing me, and I start to laugh hysterically, because now his kisses really are tender and caring. Can't he remember what he's just done? Or does he think I *enjoyed* it? Did *he*?

He rolls off me, flops back onto the carpet with a sated grunt and lies there spread-eagled. Another few minutes pass before I can move. I turn my head sideways, painfully. His eyes are closed. Is he asleep? I manage to sit up. He suddenly opens his eyes, stares at me. I have to turn my head away; I can't look at him.

He reaches out for me, grips my hand tightly in his. I'm

164

crying. God, I feel so wretched! I've never felt like this before—so degraded, so used. And so helpless—that's the worst of it. A woman's total vulnerability to any heavily muscled macho male.

I get myself to my feet, and immediately feel nauseous. I just manage to reach the bathroom basin before I throw up. I wash myself in cold water to snap me back and confront what has happened. With a washcloth and warm water, I wash Jan's sex from me. I *want* to wash Jan's sex from me.

He's sitting in the bedroom, leaning back against the bed frame.

"I hate you." My voice is a whisper, a thin, sharp wire of sound.

"I couldn't get it up," he shouts. "Needed you. You walked out on me." He slips down sideways, then drags himself up onto the bed and sprawls across it. I sit on the edge of the bed and reach for the telephone.

He reaches out for me, but I yell, "Don't touch me!" It startles him. He pulls his hand back and flops down onto the bed again.

I stab angrily at the buttons. After long, long seconds, Roy answers sleepily.

"Roy . . . !"

"Solange?" But I can't talk; I can't answer him. "What is it, Solange? Solange . . . ! Are you all right?"

Anger suddenly bursts forth in my throat. "If you're not here—Roy, if you're not here in fifteen minutes, I'm calling the police."

"What?"

"Jan . . . he's just . . . he's . . ."

"Don't do anything," Roy shouts down the phone. "I'm on my way."

I let the phone drop; turn and look at Jan. He's breathing heavily, eyes closed. I think the bastard's asleep again.

I manage to pull on one of my silk robes, wrap it tightly around me. I go downstairs, flop into one of the big chairs and cry until I hear the door opening. Roy has a set of keys now, in case of emergencies. He rushes over to me, takes me in his arms.

"What's the matter? Jan, is he still here? Where is he? Are you all right? Solange, what's happened?" He touches me on the face, gently. "It's bruised," he says. "Solange—what the fuck's *happened?*"

Besides crying. I'm now shaking uncontrollably. Roy holds me tightly. "Jesus! What is it . . . ? What . . . ?"

I feel something at my lips, a sharp smell under my nose. Roy has brought me some brandy. I sip at it, and the bite of it shocks me back again.

I drink some more as Roy looks around, sees Jan's boots and hat on the sofa, grips my shoulders. "What . . . *happened?*"

I'm suddenly coherent, telling him everything, just as it happened, from beginning to end.

"Shit!" Roy pulls me into his arms. "Oh, Jesus! What a mess! I'm so sorry, love. So sorry." He leaves me, and I know he's gone to see Jan. He's back in a few minutes.

"He's asleep." I start to cry once more.

Roy makes strong coffee for us. We sit on the sofa together.

"Do you need to see a doctor?"

"No. No—I mean, I wasn't physically hurt. Well, my head hurts a bit still where I banged it, but I'm all right."

"What are you going to do about it?" he asks. "What are you going to *do?*"

I know perfectly well what I *should* do about it. What every woman should do about rape. But I whisper, "What *can* I do?"

"A lot, lady." He looks concerned.

"Oh yes—go to the police?"

"Every woman who's raped should go to the police," he says authoritatively.

"Yes, I know." But even in this country, with all the equal rights talk, the pressures are immense. A man has a right to rape his wife, and I suppose that attitude goes for lovers, too. In France, of course, nothing has changed. A friend of mine was raped by someone she knew. I went with her to the doctor and then to the police station, but I had to take her back to the doctor. It wasn't that they ill-treated her, not physically. They just smiled, laughed among themselves, hinted she'd deserved it. Asked what she'd done to encourage it. Thinking of it, I'm crying again.

Roy has his arms around me, comfortingly. "It was *really* rape?"

I hit out at him angrily. "You fucking bastard! You fucking men, you're all the same! *Of course* it was! But you really all think we go around asking for it, don't you?"

"Solange!" He grabs my arm.

"Don't touch me! Leave me alone! Don't you understand —he was drunk, and he *forced* himself on me," I shout. "*Forced*—and that's rape!" I start crying again. Roy brings

166

me some more brandy, slowly calms me down. "Oh, Roy
... !" He cuddles me gently.

"You know fucking well I can't go to the police," I groan.
"I don't want to, in any case—I'd never hurt Jan. Besides, I'd
never be *believed*." I look at Roy despairingly. He knows
what I've been thinking. "Just get him out of here, Roy." He
looks at me dubiously. *"Now!"*

Roy goes to the bedroom. He's back in a minute. "I can't
wake him. We're going to have to wait until he's sober ... I'm
sorry." He looks genuinely distressed by the whole scene.

"He said he couldn't get it up," I find myself saying.
"Couldn't get it up!"

"But he *couldn't*, really he couldn't."

"What have I just been through, then?" I ask, furious.

Roy explains to me in detail. Jan-Toby Axelsson *hasn't*
been able to get it up. Not since that God-awful scene when I
walked out. It's not that he's been drinking, until tonight, but
he's been morose and irritable or else wild and capricious.
Last night he and Joel had been at a club earlier and picked
up some chicks, but Jan had left after a while.

"Where's Melissa?" I interrupt.

"Texas, with Andy. With her parents, for the past week.
They'll be there for another week. Jan didn't want to go; the
boys have been working for the tour."

"Oh, hell!" I find myself seeing it from Jan's point of view.
"I thought he didn't drink, though. He was so *drunk*. Why
did he do that?" I ask Roy angrily.

"I dunno. He doesn't usually drink. He doesn't do booze or
pills, never has, thank God. Smokes some weed, has the
occasional snort, that's all."

"A good, clean-living young lad," I comment ironically.

"I told him he had to get this mess with Melissa sorted out.
I've *been* telling him that ever since he married her. In fact, I
told him he *shouldn't* marry her. But he did," Roy says
aggrievedly. "No wonder he can't get the fucking thing up
now. It's psychological—he just doesn't *want* to get it up for
her. Why the fuck should he? He hates her."

"Oh, hell!"

We both sit in silence. I finally say, "I want to take a bath,
then go to sleep. But ..."

"Do you want me to stay here until he's awake?"

I don't know what I want anymore. I just want to scream
and be irrational; but somehow I can't. I just feel an infinitely
weary numbness.

"Um—no, it's all right, Roy. I think he'll be okay when he

167

wakes up. I'll give you a call in the morning. I just want to bathe and sleep."

"I'm sorry for all this, love." He kisses me gently.

"I know." I believe he really is.

"He needs you so much, darling. He really *needs* you."

Needs me? I stare uncomprehendingly at Roy. How can he say that, after what's happened? How *can* he say that? If Jan needed me—*if*—then he forfeited any claims he might have had, once and for all.

"I'll call you, Roy."

"Let me stay in a guest room?"

"You want to? Oh yes, I'd feel safer with you here."

I have a bath, then go to bed in Miriam's room, but I can't sleep, I lie awake, so tired. I start to cry, and that seems to help. So I cry myself to sleep. . . .

* * *

I awake with a start, remembering this is Miriam's room, and then I wish I hadn't remembered. I get into my robe and notice that it's early, only seven-thirty, no wonder I'm still tired.

I find Roy in the kitchen, grinding coffee. I make him some breakfast, and he cuddles me comfortingly, tells me that everything will be all right. Why is it that I almost believe him? I call Miriam, tell her not to come in today. "Got yaself a man there, huh?" Oh yes, I've got myself a man, all right!

"I have to go soon, I'm afraid," Roy says. "I have a business meeting at nine-thirty."

"Oh?" I don't want him to go. I want him here to make me feel safe.

"Look—I'll go and get Jan up. Get him home."

"Yes . . . please."

"Are you all right?" Roy gives me a timid sort of smile, as though he feels guilt for what Jan did.

"Yes." Am I? I don't know.

Roy leaves me sitting in the lounge. I never thought it would end like this: in indifference. An empty nothingness.

"He's getting up. Getting a shower." Roy stares through me. "He's feeling like a fucking asshole."

"Oh?" Empty indifference.

"Why don't you talk to him?"

"Talk to him?"

"Yes."

"We have nothing to talk about." I put on a false bitchiness.

"Oh yes you have."

"It's finished."

"Okay . . . I realize that's probably so. But at least part friends."

"Friends! That's great, Roy. Friends—with my friendly neighborhood rapist."

"Solange! Talk about it, discuss it—but *don't* hate each other. It won't get you anywhere, do you any good, or solve anything."

"He's not drunk now. You're right, Roy. But I can't talk to him with someone else here. D'you understand?"

"Yes . . . yes, I do. You know where I am, if you want me."

He hugs me again, leaves. I know it's awkward for him. Still, it's awkward for me, too. I have to talk to Jan, end it on some sort of amicable terms so neither of us will feel bad.

I go upstairs, hear the shower running. In the bathroom, I take a deep breath. "Roy's gone," I say.

The shower turns off and Jan appears from behind the shower door. His face is so sad. I hand him a towel, and he almost smiles.

"Use my toothbrush," I say. "I'm going to make you some breakfast."

"I don't eat any breakfast."

"You'll eat this," I tell him, watching him dry himself. "You need to eat after all that booze last night."

"Yes, Ma'am."

I turn away and leave him. Now isn't the time to talk.

I make us both scrambled eggs and toast, set places out on the terrace. Gulley comes and sits at my feet, we wait for Jan together.

I feel fidgety, wondering what he's doing up there. I go and put some music on. Jan appears wearing only jeans, bare feet. I bring the eggs and toast, pour grapefruit juice and coffee.

"Eat!"

"Yes, Ma'am."

We eat in silence. For someone who doesn't eat breakfast, he's eating an awful lot. I suppress a smile.

He's combed his hair now, but it's still falling into his eyes. He's had it cut since I last saw him—it no longer reaches his shoulders. I find myself reaching out and touching it. "I'm sorry," I tell him.

"You're sorry! Oh, Jesus, Lady!" His eyes flood with tears.

"It's all right." Why the fuck am I soothing *him?* I gently

169

caress the scratch, then his mustache and beard. "It's growing well." *Why* am I dong this? Why do I *feel* that I need to?

"You like it?" He sniffs hard.

"Yes."

"Then I'll keep it."

"I don't think I scratched you very deeply. It shouldn't scar."

"Serve me fuckin' right if it did."

Silence. Sticky silence.

I pour us some more coffee and clear the things away. When I come back, he's leaning back on the chair, his eyes closed. I stand watching him; he hasn't heard me. I don't think so, anyway. He may even be listening to the music—I hope so.

"What's the music?" he asks. Reading my mind again, knowing that I'm standing next to him.

"Mozart—his twenty-ninth symphony."

"It's so good."

"It's beautiful." I drink some coffee. The sticky silence remains, a kind of persistent fog. Neither of us wants to talk of what happened, yet we both know we have to.

"I guess I should go. I think I've outstayed my welcome," he says with a hint of his sardonic smile. "So we'd better talk first. We *have* to."

"Yes."

He stands in front of me, then sinks to his knees. He looks so tired, unhappy, and lonely, totally uncared for.

"I drank so fuckin' *much* last night." I know it's not meant as an excuse, just as a statement.

"You did. And you shouldn't. You don't drink much, do you? You're not used to it. It's not good for you, Jan."

He takes my face in his hands. "I don't know what to say to you, darlin'. What *can* I say . . . ?"

"Perhaps there *is* nothing to say? Best perhaps if we don't say anything. Just end it off . . ."

"Whatever I say, it won't alter what happened. Jesus, how could I have been such a motherfuckin' asshole! You're the one person I love in this whole fuckin' world." Tears in his eyes again; I feel myself becoming weepy too. I can't handle this, don't know what to say, am afraid I'll shout at him. I want to be angry, to hate him, but at the same time I want to make it all right for him.

"It's all right. Maybe we should just forget it." I caress his scratched face again.

"I can't. Jesus. Solange, I *hurt* you—I fuckin' *forced* it on you, and that's *rape*, lady! How *can* I forget it? How can I *ever* forget it?"

"You were drunk." Why am I excusing him like this? Is it because I ran from him, left him, when I knew I owed him loyalty? I reach out and touch the two silver earrings in his left ear, than rub at the tattoo on his left arm. "You were drunk."

"That's no fuckin' excuse!

"No, it's not. I'm *not* excusing it."

"And now I've lost you. *Really* lost you."

"You should go and get some sleep." I say after a moment's silence.

"Here?"

"Yes—unless you want to go."

He stares at me, sits up straight. "I want to run and hide. I've never felt like this before."

"That makes two of us."

He glances at me uneasily. "You're not . . . hurt, are you?"

"No, not physically. I mean, I'm not a virgin, am I? And you didn't actually beat me up."

"I never meant to hurt you. I just wanted to make love to you. That's all I could focus on, *making love to you.*" We remain silent, but it's a sad, moody silence now. "God, I feel so fuckin' *tired!*"

It seems to me that now he's talking about his life. "Go and get some more sleep."

"I . . ."

"I think you should. I think you need to. Go and sleep all day, then I'll make you a nice dinner this evening. We can talk some more, then you can go. At least that way we won't hate each other."

"I *love* you."

"*Love* me?" Now my anger overwhelms everything. "You can't possibly love me. If you *did* love me in the slightest, you wouldn't have raped me. That was plain physical and mental brutality! So don't come on with that pretense of *loving* me, you bastard! Makes you feel good, does it, all that macho muscle of yours? Just because you're, what?—nearly a foot taller. And you've got to be seventy pounds heavier. You fucking *bastard!*"

I wish I could hurt him. Then, remorsefully, I realize that I have, that my words have cut right through him. "Come on," I say curtly, and lead the way upstairs to the bedroom. I feel so tired. *I* need some more sleep, too.

He looks awkwardly around him. "Can I get undressed?"

171

I can't help smiling. "Of course—get back into bed." I watch him undress and climb into bed. He has a beautiful body, suntanned and muscular; great shoulders and ass. Why am I thinking this now?

He lies there. I feel as though I want to tuck him in and give him a kiss. What's the *matter* with me? Why can't I feel real hate for this man? Is it because he's hurting so much?

"Go to sleep." I go towards the door.

"Solange . . ."

"Yes?"

"I'm . . . I'm sorry, darlin'."

"Oh, I'm *sure* you are!" I turn and hold onto the door-frame. I can't reject that admission of his. I can't go on playing the stupid game of inflicting hurt on him now, in retaliation for the hurt he gave me. An eye for an eye, a vendetta—there's no end to such stupidities. They go on marching in a straight line towards infinity; a straight line marked out by tombstones.

"I won't be able to sleep," he shouts hoarsely. "I can't sleep."

"Of course you can. You haven't tried yet."

"I can't sleep," he repeats in a low voice.

And I know what he means: The hurt he did me is revolving inside his skull. And I can leave him here now, hurting inside his head, and never really forgive him, spite-fully hurt him as he's hurt me. I know I can. If I really turn my hate on him now, it would mean inescapable pain for him.

But if I do that, I'll be the meanest, nastiest kind of bitch. This is it: my Waterloo. Nobodaddy strikes again: my private Armageddon. If I hurt him, I'll be cutting myself off from the one person who understands me through and through, whose thoughts have an uncanny resonance with mine. If I hurt him, I'll be cutting myself off from a part of me, hurting and improverishing myself.

He wasn't *trying* to hurt me. He was *trying* to love me. That was what he said, wasn't it? And I believe him; it's true. What he did, from the moment he started on the first gulp of vodka, was in protest, in reaction against his life with that bitch of a wife. Stupid? Childish? Human? The three adjectives are inseparably combined.

I walk back over to the bed and sit down on the edge to caress his face. My eyes fill with tears. My hand's trembling. "Get some sleep, Jan."

172

"I *can't!*" He abruptly turns himself over and lies face down, sobbing.

No man's ever cried with me before. I realize that to show his vulnerability in this way, he must love me deeply. And I realize that the deeper his love, the fiercer his pain at having done such a hateful thing.

I lean over and kiss the back of his head. His whole body is shaking with his sobs. Watching him, I realize with a detached, clinical accuracy that I love this man at this moment more than I've ever loved him before.

I walk around to the other side of the bed, take off my robe, and climb into bed with him, to pull him into my arms. I gently kiss the back of his head, over and over, as the waterbed rocks us soothingly, rhythmically. "It's all right. It is, it's *all right*, Jan darling." Oh, God, I'm crying as well now.

"What I did . . . I've lost you," he says between sobs.

I kiss his head, stroke it. "How can you lose me—when we're sharing the same skin?"

I hold him until he's quiet, until quietness surrounds us both. I stroke his hair again; he tightly holds my other hand, and with grief in his voice says, "I love you so much."

"I can't help loving you, Jan. You know that."

He grips me tightly around the waist, then touches a nipple with gentle fingers.

"I love your beautiful tits," he whispers. "They're so fuckin' sexy." He's stopped crying. I kiss the back of his head. "They should be full of milk."

I smile. "I guess that only happens on special occasions."

"*I'd* drink it all. Our babies wouldn't get any." His voice is barely a whisper, and his words make me wish everything could stop, freeze, so that this one moment we're sharing would be always with us, always here in bed, with the love we feel for each other completely surrounding us.

"My beautiful sweet delight, I love you," he says joyfully.

"I love you," I reply joyfully.

"I feel like I've come home." He's whispering again.

"You have."

He hugs me tightly. I can hardly breathe, but I don't care. Maybe the hurting is all behind us now, only the loving to come.

He pulls me into his arms, holds my face with his hand, kisses me. "I've got so many things to say to you."

"I have, too."

"I feel so fuckin' *tired*."

I kiss him. "Go to sleep."

"I can, now." He holds me tightly, and I embrace him with my head on his shoulder. "I love you. It's so *easy* to love you."

"I love you." My words a mere annotation to a tangible presence.

"I love *you*." He laughs and hugs me to death.

"Go to sleep."

"After . . ."

9

Solange, the mistress, happier than she's ever been. Solange, in love.

It's the end of May's warm, sunny, slow, lazy days. Solange days.

I haven't seen Jan for two of those days—two whole lifetimes. I feel so lonely without him.

The nights are the worst, though. Janless nights, in bed alone. I feel so painfully incomplete. When we're together we feast on each other. Alone, we feast on our memories. It's a very thin diet in comparison.

I'm lying out on the terrace in the most miniscule of bikinis—four tiny triangles and lots of string. I ought to be writing, but I feel too listless. I was up all night writing, because I couldn't sleep. I slept this morning. I've sent Miriam home—I just had to be by myself.

I sometimes think I can't handle this affair, that it's gotten away from me. It's been seven weeks now, seven weeks of stolen secret minutes of love.

I want Jan, and I don't know what to do about it. Sometimes when he comes here we don't even make love. We just sit, holding each other, looking at each other. Other times, all we do is fuck until it hurts. I think we belong utterly to each other.

I wander upstairs and look around the bedroom. It's not *my* bedroom anymore, I think with a smile, it's ours, Jan's and mine. He's left some of his things here: records, books, two cameras, a tape recorder, and a bunch of clothes: jeans, jackets, socks, and boots. He has so many pairs of boots, which he leaves all over the place. I'm glad he's left things here. It makes him seem not so far away. He's not really far, I guess, half a mile, but with his wife and child. On my bedside table, in a narrow silver frame, is his photo with *I love you* written across it. He loves me, *but . . .*

I put his latest album on and lie down on the bed, tired. I don't feel like listening to *anyone* else when he's not here. I can just see the top of his guitar leaning against a chair . . .

It's after eight that evening when I awake. I take a shower, then slip into a long caftan. I suppose I should eat something, but all I want is Jan.

I sit on the terrace, have a cuddle with Gulley, wonder what Jan's doing now. It makes no sense to get myself depressed thinking about it. How long can I go on like this? In many ways I've never been so happy as I am now, and in many ways I've never been so *un*happy.

Miriam and I argue about it. She says he's *using* me. I say he wouldn't do that. She says I'm *blind.* I say I'm not, I can see perfectly well what's going on. She says I should get myself some *streetwise;* then I'd know when a number was being done on me. Poor Miriam, she does hate men so, and not so very deep down!

It seems such a long time since Jan and I had that first week together. We haven't spent a whole night together since then. We made love for three whole days and nights. We just stayed in bed and even ate in bed. We talked and spent the fourth day at Roy's. Jan had to work with the band. Then for the next three days we listened to music, even watched some TV. All during that time we made love until we were exhausted.

Then Melissa came home from Texas.

I cried myself to sleep that night.

Since then we've seen each other in the mornings, in the afternoons, and in the evenings, sometimes, but *never* during the night. I guess that's all part of being a mistress, but I hate it. I don't know what to do anymore, because I know I can't end it. I love him so utterly, so irrevocably.

Jan has planned out how to handle it. It'll take time, he says, but it's going to happen for us. June, July, and August, he'll be on tour, and he wants no hassles during all that, perfectionist that he is. He wants himself and the band to be the best they've *ever* been. That last album went platinum,

175

and he was immensely pleased, because the others had gone a lot slower. It's at the top of the charts, and a single from it, "Babies Should Be Made In Love," was a number one as well. The platinum record that they presented to him is in the study (*our* study now). He says it's for me, because it was my album. For me.

Anyway, after this tour is over he's going to get into it with Melissa-Sue: divorce, visitation rights with Andy. Roy's getting his lawyers working on it all now so everything will be ready to go. Jan knows there's going to be a fight over Andy. That's why he wants to get clear of the tour first. I guess he's right.

My book, *Magical Secrets,* is out in hardback. It's selling so well. Most of the reviews were good. Jan's so pleased and proud of me, and that means more to me than anything. I've just finished my rounds on the talk shows—Roy got me onto all of them—and I even enjoyed them. But I was nervous because Jan was watching.

I go down to the study to do some work. I had a desk and typewriter put in for Jan. He gave me his poetry to read, and I was utterly impressed. He's working now on something new. He hasn't been able to do that since he's been married to Melissa. I feel immensely pleased that he can write with *me.* "I can write *because* of you," he told me, "you understand about creating—how a poem is waiting there, waiting to be born."

Thinking about Jan's poetry completely distracts me from my own writing. I go to bed and wait for Jan's call. He always goes to his den, late, and calls me. Afterwards I know he goes to bed alone. He doesn't sleep with his wife anymore, not since even before we got together. I lie awake, becoming depressed, weighed down by this expanse of time that has to elapse before he can be here making love to *me,* sleeping next to *me.* Then I cry myself to sleep.

*   *   *

It's almost midnight. I'm massaging Jan's back and kissing that sexy ass of his. I know he has to leave. He's been rehearsing with the band over at Roy's. He rang Melissa and told her . . . something. . . . I try to keep it from touching me, the lying, the secrecy. I *hate* it, but I pretend that it doesn't exist.

We move, and he pins me beneath him. I stare into those beautiful eyes of is, and my own fill with tears.

176

"Hey!" He kisses me. "Stop it. Darlin', it ain't gonna *be* for much longer."

"No?"

"No. Listen darlin' . . . I'll ring you from Portland tomorrow."

"Perhaps it would be easier if you didn't."

I see an angry spark in his eyes. He's not even going to answer me. Silence. Then he says, "I wish you could come with me, darlin'."

"So do I."

But it's Melissa who goes with him. He doesn't want her to, not just because of us, but because the band don't like having her around. Her disapproval of them spreads out like a cold fog.

He kisses me. "I'll call you."

"Yes, please." I cling tightly, my arms around his neck.

"I've got to go, darlin'."

"Yes . . ." All the tears I've held back fill my eyes. "Please don't leave me. Please. *Please* . . . I can't bear it without you anymore. I'm so unhappy without you."

"Oh, Jesus, darlin'!" Jan rolls off me and pulls me into his arms.

What am I *doing*, opening myself up like this? It's the last thing he wants, unbearable pressure from me; he's got enough from *her* without me laying the weepy female bit on him.

"I'm sorry, Jan." Me, frantically trying to calm myself.

Jan, holding me, calming me, kissing me, loving me. "It'll be all right, darlin'."

I let myself be calmed down and kissed. I let myself believe everything he tells me.

* * *

Jan calls me every day and sends me zany cards. The concerts are going well. I stay at home writing, hiding myself and my feelings in my words. I touch the turquoise bear claw that hangs on a silver chain around my neck, just like the one he wears. It was a gift he gave me on the last whole day we spent together. "For you," he said. "Something of me." He put it around my neck. It's on a long chain and nestles down between my boobs. "Just right," Jan said.

This affair of ours intersperses solemnity with surprises. "You only love me because of our sex," I told him once. "It's because you're lonely and unhappy at home. You just think I'm a good lay."

177

He looked hurt, and I was immediately sorry. He shook me, and said, "You just listen to me, Lady! Fuckin' don't need to be lovin', but *our* fuckin' sure is lovin'. Don't you *ever* forget it! I *love you.*"

I could never doubt him. He looked so very solemn, as well as angry, when he said that. I guess our loving *is* a solemn thing that neither of us takes lightly. It means so much. We explore each other as only committed lovers can. He said to me, "You know every bit of me, like a man's woman should know every bit of him." He's right. Not one inch has been left unkissed, unlicked, uncaressed. And he knows every inch of me.

When we're together it's just in the world—*only* us, the last two people left alive. We're removed from space and time, floating in shared, safe, remote dimensions. And oh, how we adore making each other come. Yes, our loving is a joyfully solemn activing, with interspersed surprises.

I came downstairs two mornings ago. Jan had left for Seattle the day before. In the driveway there was a gigantic box with an immense pink ribbon wrapped around it. Miriam and I just stood gaping at it. When ultimately we pulled on the ribbon, the box fell apart and there we unbelievingly saw a white sports Mercedes.

The license plates read JTALL. I giggled. JTALL: Jan-Toby Axelsson's Literary Lady!

Jan came driving up in Roy's Rolls-Royce late one night, and we fucked in it. "This ain't decadence, this is respectability, Ma'am," Jan laughed. "Don't ya know richness equals respectability? I mean," he said, "it can't be *un*respectable to fuck in a Rolls-Royce."

We're having such a beautifully crazy affair!

One morning he came in unexpectedly as I was getting dressed. "What the fuck is *that?*" he asked, looking me up and down as I stood there in my black lace teddy. "Jesus fuck! You look good enough to eat!" And being eaten in a teddy is a very giggly proposition.

I'm slowly but surely learning how to handle this affair of ours. I'm pleased with myself because I'm handling it like Pandora. *Have* I achieved the perfect metamorphosis into her at last?

Little Ms. Classy-Ass is holding her own.

* * *

When he comes into the room, I run to greet him. We make love on the sofa, so impatient to share each other again.

He gets himself into the short, black silk robe I bought him. It just covers his sexy ass. He asks what the music was that I was playing. I tell him, Elizabeth Machonchy's fifth string quartet. He likes it, intrigued by her angular subtleties, but he puts on Prokofiev's first piano concerto, the short one, crammed with fireworks, that Prokofiev wrote at nineteen. "It makes you wanna *come*," he said.

It's still a wonder to us that there are only a few areas where our tastes appreciably diverge. "I never thought I'd find me a lady who loved what I love," Jan said. "I only dreamed about it, thinking I'd have to be content with the second best."

"But I'm first best," I laugh.

"Sure are, Ma'am. And you're the only lady I know with an IQ only two points lower than mine." Lopsided grin. "I may not always use it, but it's there when I need it."

"So I've noticed, cowboy."

"*And*"—he winks—"you're the only lady I know who can recite from the *Four Zoas*."

" 'The Expanding Eyes of Man behold the depths of wondrous worlds,' " I reply on cue, and kiss him.

And so we make love, in this our own little Wondrous World. He's here for the whole glorious day. We kiss; how nice it is to taste yourself on the lips of the man you love!

He's delighted that I like the car, although I was quite happy getting around in my little Volvo.

"I've gotta look after my mistress," he teases with a wink. "Didn't you say jewelry and cars, TVs, and things?" I punch him. "Seein' as there's no rent to pay," he adds, gently pinning me on the floor beneath him, "When we gonna get around to the brandin'? And the ring through your delectable little cunt?" I can feel his hard cock digging in between my legs.

"Fucker!"

"Sure am, ma'am." He proves his point. . . .

"Hey, I've got a surprise for you," he says later.

"You have?" We're cuddled up in one of the armchairs, both naked, enjoying the feel of our touching skin.

"When I go to Frisco tomorrow, you can come." It sounds like a royal command.

"Tomorrow!" I am surprised and happy, then unsure. "Why? How?"

"Meliss' doesn't wanna come. It's her Elizabeth Arden day, or somethin'. She argued with Joel last time. Jee-zus *fuck*, he nearly punched her face in! He did once, too—shit! The band don't like her comin' along, and she knows it. The tour was shit last year with her bitchin' and complainin'. So . . ."

"So what?" I sound slightly bitchy. Actually, I don't know whether I like being snuck in like this.

"I want you to come." Earnest look.

"Yes . . . ?"

"Don't you want to?"

"Yes, you *know* I do." I hug him tightly. "All the time." I feel he knows what I'm feeling.

"I know, darlin'. You will once we're through with all this shit. We'll always be together. I'll always want to take you with me. And the kids, we'll take 'em on *all* the tours."

We kiss, and I straddle him as he sits in the chair, lowering myself onto his erection. He holds me tightly around the waist. I watch him closely as he moves with me, his head thrown back, his neck muscles knotted and straining. He's in his own universe, going for his own orgasm. I touch his neck, running my finger along one of the straining cords. He doesn't seem to notice. Is it only when we're fucking that I really reach him?

His face contorts, and he moans as he comes.

"I didn't come!" I hit his shoulder, kiss him, bite on his beard. He laughs and feels for my sticky little button. I'm going into my own universe now. Is he watching me like I watched him? I cry out as I come, my fingers digging into his shoulders.

"*Why* can't you just stay with me!" I shout out.

He pulls me close to cuddle and kiss, but he doesn't answer me.

* * *

And so we fly together to San Francisco. Me, his little Ms. Classy-Ass, his Literary Lady, the cool, chic, beautiful, calm, loving mistress. Me, the woman he *wants*.

The first class section is crowded with the Texas Rangers, as the band jokingly call themselves. They look it, too: all in jeans and cowboy hats, aviator sunglasses and, of course, the ubiquitous boots. They smoke, drink, talk dirty, chat up stewardesses. But the head stewardess, tall and blonde, has her eye on Mr. Axelsson himself; returning from the john, I find her sitting next to him, laughing with him.

I go and sit next to Billy Wilson, *Rolling Stone* reporter. He's covering the tour, having known Jan since they were in high school together. Jan went on to Berkeley; Billy majored in journalism at T.C.U., then was a reporter on various papers until he hit it big.

180

We talk for a while, and Billy realizes (with a broad grin) that I know extremely little about the rock world. Jan leans over from the seat in front, pushes his hat back on his head, gives us a zany grin.

Billy teases him. "Sure got yourself a beautiful Literary Lady, Jan."

"Ain't that the fuckin' truth!"

Jan deposits me in our room at the hotel, then disappears for an hour of business. I shower and dress—we're all going to Chinatown. I'm wearing the pink suede dress I bought those many months ago on the day I bumped into Jan and Roy at the Cafe Rodeo. The front buttons are undone to above my knees. My high-heeled boots are the exact same shade of pink. I open the door to Jan.

"Jesus, you look beautiful."

"Thank you." Classy-Assed smile.

I look up into Jan's eyes. He's looking incredibly handsome and sexy this evening. His hair is brushed tidily, and his slightly darker mustache and beard are very neat and trim. He has on tight black pants and a cream-colored, tailored silk shirt under a natural-colored suede jacket. I smile seductively, put my hands inside his jacket, hug him around the waist. I kiss the blond fuzzy fur on his chest, where his turquoise bear claw rests. "Mr. Jan-Toby Axelsson, superstar, himself, in person!" I lift my face for an onslaught of kisses as he presses himself against me. I feel loved, secure, whole, sharing his life with him at last. It's something I'll always want.

We all have dinner around a huge table. A few times, Jan has to sign autographs; he handles it with panache, winking at the girls, joking with them, along with Joel and the rest of the band. "It's all a load of bullshit," he tells me. "As long as you realize that, it's all right, ya keep ya head on straight. As long as ya don't start in to believin' it." Smiling, I watch my beloved Jan-Toby Axelsson. Obviously, the dreaded rock star disease of terminal egomania is something he's never suffered from.

We go back to the hotel and sit in Joel's room. There's a lot of little girls there. Where do they come from? Jan sits next to me on a sofa, finishes off my Scotch, tokes on his joint, and leers at the little girls, who excitedly twitter and flutter amongst themselves at his attention.

We sit and whisper, cuddle and drink, share another joint. It's strong; I sleepily sit enthralled, listening to all their tall stories about the previous escapades. Billy Watson fondles

181

some girl. Roy grins around him as a girl climbs from between his legs while he zips his pants up. There's a noise from between the beds—Joel and one of the other groupies. Before long they'll probably be playing their favorite game, which Joel and Wilb invented years ago to combat boredom on the road. Having previously chosen and suitably noted a girl, they take turns being blindfolded and trying to guess which is theirs. They call it "Match the Snatch."

"I think I'd better go," I tell Jan, "I'm not into orgies."

"But I want you to stay. We're enjoying ourselves."

"I'd rather go." I smile and kiss him.

"One of the chicks'll blow me, then." He glares at me belligerently.

"I'm sure they'll stand in line for the honor." I giggle at the mental picture.

He pouts—that arrogant, wide sexy mouth of his. "You'll be jealous." He rubs one of my boobs defiantly.

"I will, will I? Jealous of a little girl who 'doesn't mean anything?' " I'm reminding him of what he told me when he first met me. "Darling—even if we were married, I wouldn't be jealous of that. A pretty little toy to suck it off for you, a threat to our relationship? That's hardly an emotional involvement, nothing to get uptight about." We're kissing, and he pulls my hand down over his cock. He grins broadly, swings me up into his arms, makes for the door. "Jesus, I love you, Lady."

"I love you, cowboy." I nuzzle his neck.

We spend the night in delightful, frantic fucking. We wake up just after six, after a few hours' sleep, and make soft, gentle love to each other.

Jan, an excited little boy, is showing me a part of his world. He and the band are setting up for the concert.

"What are those little speakers for?" I ask Jan.

"Monitor speakers, darlin'. Without them, we couldn't hear ourselves."

"Which ain't such a bad idea at times," laughs Joel.

I stare out at the huge empty auditorium, the endless stretch of seats, and visualize them full of screaming fans. "My God, I'd be *petrified!*"

"So are we, Ma'am." Jan winks.

In the evening, the concert goes well, packed full of excitement. When he comes off the stage I'm amazed: His shirt drips with sweat, his hair is soaking wet, his mustache and beard and chest hair glisten. My shiny, wet angel cuddles me, and I don't mind getting wet too.

"We're miles ahead of last year's tour," he tells me proudly. "That's havin' you with me."

I'm with him, part of his world at last.

10

I put the phone down and smile to myself. Marie-Claude will be here next month. I'm looking forward to introducing her to Jan and Roy, to Joel and the rest of the band. I'm sure they'll all love her. I wonder what she'll make of Texans.

I climb out of my swimming pool, lay my naked body next to Gulley on the terrace, and doze off . . . .

A little later I come up from a dream I've already forgotten. Three little faces are staring at me, Jody, Tim, and Suki, three of the Seagram kids.

"Hello, fellas," I grin at them, and one by one they kiss my cheek. All have big hazel eyes and long brown hair. Their huge Old English Sheepdog, Colonel Blimp, tries to sit on my lap. Gulley spits at him and runs for cover.

We're all nude, but it's totally unimportant and totally familiar, both in my place and at their home. Ginnie and Bill are always wandering around "natural and beautiful," as Ginnie says, and the kids have never known anything else. That's how I want it with *our* kids, when Jan and I have them. Why have hang-ups about something as commonplace as a body?

"I cut my arm," Jody says. "Look!"

There's a large Band-Aid on it. *"Very* impressive." That pleases him.

"We've come for ice cream," Suki says.

"Be quiet, Suki," Jody tells her.

"Don't be so rude," Tim says, patting her on the head.

"Come on, then," I say, and they all jump up and down, squeal, hug me. Colonel Blimp woofs and licks my legs. We troop into the house and I give them ice cream. Colonel Blimp has his in a dish on the floor.

"Mummy's pregnant," Tim announces importantly, cheerfully.

"*That's* having a *baby*," Suki giggles.

"She told us yesterday," Tim adds, observing his empty dish and then scrutinizing Suki's half-empty one.

"It's all Daddy's fault," Jody informs me.

"Well, I should hope it is," I say.

He smiles. "We know all about *babies*."

"Very good. And so you should."

"Babies grow in Mommy's tummy," Suki says solemnly. "Daddy puts them there." She looks at my tummy, touches it, then looks closely at her own. Then she pats my springy pussy hair, pats her own smooth little pussy.

"Did you know that?" Jody asks me.

"Yes, I did."

"Have you had a baby?" Tim asks.

"No, not yet."

"You want one?"

"Yes."

"You don't have a Daddy," Jody says.

"But I have someone I love."

"Are you married?" Tim asks.

"Not yet."

"Babies come when you're married." says Jody.

"Yes, but not always," I say ambiguously.

"Can we have some more ice cream?" Tim asks.

I give them some more. They're beautiful. Talking with kids for a while brings me back to reality. They see things in simple terms. Ginnie and Bill Seagram treat their kids marvelously. I've never repaired the hole in the fence between our houses. I don't want it repaired; it's the kids' private gateway to come and see me. There's part of me that's never grown up, that *will* never grow up: I'm going to keep it that way.

* * *

So here I am sitting at home thinking about my birthday tomorrow. Miriam has gone, leaving a huge package for me, wrapped in pink and silver. I told her not to come in tomorrow.

I'm feeling a bit sad, because I haven't seen Jan since we returned from San Francisco three days ago.

He rang me this morning, but didn't seem to have much to say, except that he's seeing me after lunch tomorrow, to wear something pretty for him, and he's got a lovely present for me.

I shower and put on a strapless silk dress, but who the hell am I dressing up for—Gulley?

At the moment Gulley's sleeping among the presents I've stacked on a leather chair in my bedroom. There's Miriam's present and Maman's. Rand's sent a present. Roy has. So have Justin and Anna. Solly, Phil, Johnny, even Matthew. I'm going to have a great time opening them all by myself.

I guess Jan would spend all my birhday with me if he could. And his birthday, ten days after mine, will I see him then? I suppose he'll be expected to spend it with Melissa. Mistresses are out in the cold when it comes to holidays, birthdays, Christmas, excluded from sharing them. And as a mistress, what do you have for an anniversary? The day you first fucked?

I put on one of his albums. Is this all I'm every really going to have? And yet, in San Francisco he was so caring and considerate.

The buzzer goes. That's funny—how could someone. have got in through the gate? I hear a key in the lock, the door opening, and I feel frightened.

"Solange!" It's Jan's voice. "Darlin' . . ."

I run down the stairs and unchain the door. He has red roses, an armful of presents, and a big smile.

"Jan!" I'm suddenly crying, so pleased to see him.

"My beautiful sweet delight!"

We go in; he puts the presents down and swings me around.

"Listen," he says, "a surprise. I didn't wanna tell you on the phone. I saw Meliss and Andy off to Texas earlier. They're gonna spend the rest of the summer there, while we're tourin'."

"You mean you can stay tonight?" I ask incredulously.

"I'm staying, *period*." He hugs me close.

I make him something to eat, and I'm thinking how strange it is that underneath the happiness of having Jan here unexpectedly now, and the joy of knowing that we'll be together for the next six weeks, there's a tinge of sadness, almost regret. *Will* it one day be forever? Why is there a part of me that can't fully accept that it *will* happen for us?

It's three in the morning when I awake. Fast asleep, he looks all golden and blond.

185

I get my presents and open them with a pleasant, childish excitement. The noise of the paper rustling wakes Jan; he smiles with sleepy love, looks at the complete leather-bound set of Colette that Maman has sent me. He notices that I haven't opened his presents. I always save my special things for last. He hands me the small package.

"To match your beautiful eyes." He grins. "They're gold and green, like the eyes of a Sun-Angel of the Sea should be."

In the package are emeralds. Studs for my ears and a beautiful square-cut emerald on a short golden chain.

"They're so beautiful!" I quickly take the diamonds out of my ears and put the emeralds in. Jan puts the chain around my neck, so that the emerald rests in the hollow of my throat. I admire them in the dessing-table mirror: they *do* bring out the green in my eyes.

"Oh, *Jan!*"

He breaks away from our kiss to hand me a big box. He grins: cowboy boots for me, and a cowboy hat. I giggle and hug him again.

"That's gettin' you in practice for bein' a Texan."

"I'll have to learn to be a simple little cowgirl, won't I? Liking what? Cows? And ... grits, isn't it?" He grins and pulls me on top of him.

"It ain't *grits*. It's bacon cheeseburgers." He kisses me. "And burnt steaks. And bourbon and branch water—that's what ya'd better like, Ma'am."

"Oh, yes." I caress his erection. "And cowboys with hard-ons."

I crawl down him, looking into his smiling face. And then give him the greatest head he's ever had.

Afterwards he says, absurdly exaggerating his Texan drawl, "Ma'am, I'm delighted to inform you that you've just passed the test—you can now be accepted as a Lifetime Member of the Texas Rangers." His warm mouth on my sticky little button. And we've six whole weeks together....

Breakfast. I'm the birthday girl, and I'm loving it. Rand, Marie-Claude, and Maman call me. Oh ... isn't it nice, being loved!

Of course the only thing I really care about is that Jan is with me.

"I've got something else for you," he says with a mysterious smile. He stands up, naked, looking suntanned and gorgeous. His chest hair, his beard and mustache are all slightly darker

186

than the sun-bleached hair on his head. Looking at his muscular shoulders, his slim hips, his great ass turns me on.

He bends and stretches. "Jesus, all this fuckin' ain't too good on the old legs."

"Are you complaining?"

"No way, Ma'am." He stands grinning at me for a moment, then leaves the kitchen, to return with a tiny black velvet box. He sits down, pulls me onto his lap, and says, "It's not really a birthday present." He gently touches my nipples, so that they stand up.

"No? What is it, then?"

"Open it and you'll see."

I open it. "Oh, hell!" My eyes fill with tears. I'm staring at a huge emerald-cut diamond solitaire.

"Here." He slips the ring onto my wedding finger. "It's our engagement ring."

"Engagement ring?"

"Sure is, Ma'am." He kisses me with suitable ceremony.

"Can you be engaged if you're married?"

"You ain't married." It makes me smile. "And since when have *I* ever cared about convention? It's ours. Because we belong together. And I want you wearing it."

"Oh, Jan!" Me, the tears streaming from my eyes. "It's . . . so . . . beautiful. And it's so big. I've never had . . ."

"Eight point two carats. It's called a radiant cut, or something."

Oh, God, here I go again, crying my eyes out.

Jan-Toby Axelsson carries me upstairs and makes love to me.

It's late in the afternoon when we emerge from the bedroom. Jan's padding around in his bare feet and a pair of cutoffs. Me in my black silk strapless dress, looking my most beautiful for him.

"You have a gorgeous body," I tell him.

"Very athletic, that's me." He smiles at me, sidelong. "Play a lot of video-pong." I go into giggles. He *is* athletic, though. He always jogs, and exercises with his weights. He's bought a set to leave here.

I examine the boots he left beside the sofa where he took them off last night. They're incredible: tan leather, with fancy stitching all over. *"They* are some boots," I say in awe.

"Lucchese—Sundance. All us genuine cowboys wear them there boots, Ma'am."

187

Cuddling. Quiet intimacy. *Our* intimacy. Lying on the sofa, telling each other things. Laughing about our disastrous sex lives as teenagers.

"I bet you were a *gorgeous* little teenager," I tease him.

"Very clean, with short hair," he admits, with an embarrassed laugh. "Jesus fuck!"

"Class president, no doubt. Honor student too, I bet."

"*You* are gonna get your ass spanked, lady."

"Mm . . . all the little girls must have been dying to get you alone in a corner."

"Me? I was studious and clean-livin'. Always home readin'."

"So was I." Kiss. "I'm glad I went to the school I did. We didn't have all that class president stuff, senior proms, queen of the ball or whatever. Are you *sure* you weren't voted the boy most likely to?"

"Lady! Watch it!" He interrupts me with a kiss.

"I'm glad I went to Oxford, too. No fraternities and sororities, all that social stuff. All that barbaric and childish pledging shit." I giggle. "Oops, so sorry, Mr. Phi Beta Kappa. Mind you, we did have the Boat Race and Rag Weeks."

"Jesus, I bet you were a cute little bitch. I wish I could've popped ya little cherry."

"It wasn't much fun, not for me. It *hurt*. Anyway, I'm sure you popped your share."

"Me? I was quiet and shy, Ma'am."

"Hm! I never came. I don't think girls did very often then. Not with boys, fucking." I giggle. "That came after, at home in my bed, thinking deliciously naughty thoughts. Romantic dreams."

"What kind of dreams?" He kisses me, his tongue finding its way around inside my mouth, his hands firm on my ass. We both know we'll be fucking again very soon.

I tell him about La Bête and how much in love with him I was. I tell him about the silk scarves tied to the bedposts. "Every lady wants to be tied down with silk scarves and fucked until it hurts."

"Oh, really?" He laughs. "Silk scarves, huh? We *are* suited —matching masturbatory fantasies."

"Oh, really? That's *handy*."

"Sure is, Ma'am," he laughs.

I tell him about Lars and Ben, all about Johnny and how embarrassed I felt the first time he ate me and I came.

"How many men have you had, then?" he asks suspiciously, with narrowed, eyes.

I tell him—name them all, in order.

"Ain't many, is it? Jesus, you can name them!" He laughs and holds my ass tightly as he pulls me on top of him.

"It's enough for me. Listen, Mister Jan-Toby Axelsson, I don't *want* to fuck anyone else." I kiss him tenderly. "Not now, not anymore. I want to be with you. I want you to be with me. Forever."

"We will be."

"Will we?"

"What the fuck does that mean?" he asks, irritated.

"Look, let's face it," I say, sitting up and straddling him, "there's no way Melissa is going to let you go." We've talked about this so much: why does it feel like we haven't?

"I told you. After the tour I'll get into all that," he replies defensively.

"She's not going to just say 'Of course you can go,' is she?"

"Then I'll leave."

"Without being able to see Andy? No, you won't."

He gives me an angry look, because he knows I'm right. "It's my duty to look after him. I have a commitment to him. That's the only reason I've stayed. It hasn't been for *me*, lady. Jesus fuck, I've told you that so often!"

"I know you have. You know I agree with it. But Melissa knows that's how you feel, and she'll go on using it, as long as you let her."

"I'll handle it," he says, with that stubborn but defeated expression he always gets.

"Look, I don't want you to lose Andy. But it's time you realized you have a commitment to *yourself* too. You can't live your whole life for someone else."

He pulls me down onto him again. "I'll *handle* it, darlin'." He holds me tight.

"Of course you will," I murmur in his ear, but I know Melissa will go on using Andy in order to keep Jan as her property. And I know, too, that I love him. I love him so much that I'll always be there for him, whatever happens. Solange, the eternal mistress. . . . We lie silently for a while. "Jan," I whisper.

"What, darlin'?"

At that moment I realize what it is I want. "I want your baby. Make me pregnant."

Silence. Utter silence.

"I want to have part of you inside me. When you're not around, I want to have part of you with me. You see, Jan, I know you have your commitment to Andy—a commitment

189

that might even keep you in a marriage you don't want. I want you and your love. It wouldn't matter in the least to me that we weren't married, you know that. Commitment and sharing aren't a piece of paper. He'd be *your* baby. We'd always be here for you."

I look into Jan's eyes. They're swimming with tears. Mind you, mine are too.

"Why"—I try to sound flippant—"you could bring Andy to visit all his little brothers and sisters."

He pulls me down onto him, holds me tightly. "I love you, lady," he whispers. "My beautiful, sweet delight. But listen," he says with a very serious face, "I want *our* son being born with *my* name. *Our* son ain't gonna be born a bastard, ain't goin' to be labeled illegitimate."

"Illegitimate!" I say with mock sternness. *"That's* just a medieval, male chauvinist bias."

"Yeah? Well, *this* chauvinistic cowboy wants *you* to have my name too."

"Want to make an honest woman of me, huh?"

"All the way, Ma'am." He kisses me; then he changes the subject. "You know, I still can't get it up with her. I tried it once, a while back, after you walked out at Roy's. I guess I thought I should. I was so pissed-off when you went. But I couldn't manage it." He gives an abrupt, bitter laugh. "She wasn't even worried. I'm sure she just thought to herself, 'At least he ain't fuckin' around if he can get it up.' "

Within every woman there's a touch of cat. I feel a feline pleasure: I don't want him to fuck Melissa. But even so, I don't want him worrying about it. "Hey," I say brightly, "what d'you expect, with all the gorgeous fucking *we* do?" It doesn't work; he doesn't respond. "Darling, you're not a machine, a sort of sex robot. Why should you get it up for someone you detest?" I caress his face. "It'll be all right, darling. It *will*." Why is it me that's reassuring *him*, when I'm the one who needs reassurance?

"It was very good this morning, wasn't it?" I say with a sated, lazy smile. "And last night."

"Sure was, Ma'am."

"I was good, wasn't I?"

"Very."

"You were good, weren't you?"

"Exceptionally!" He laughs.

I hit his chest. "I'm good for you."

"Unquestionably." His look is soft and gentle as he strokes

my face tenderly. I laugh, and rub myself on him as I begin to burn.

"I want to make love with you," I tell him as his hands cover my breasts, "in all the beautiful places of the world. You know—Paris, Kashmir, on the banks of the Avon, the Summer Palace in Peking, and in a vast desert, someplace—everywhere. There's a hotel in Dijon—"

"Mustard," he interrupts.

"Right." I kiss him. "Well, the bathtubs have four faucets."

"Four?"

"Yes. Hot and cold, and the other two are for red and white wine."

"What!"

"Honestly, there are four rooms like that. The wine all comes from vats in the cellars, so there's no way of telling how much each room uses."

"Handy." Lopsided grin. "We'll have to visit there, Ma'am."

"Mmm." Lovely sexy thoughts. "It's real French wine, of course."

He's lying there, all blond and golden, looking like a mischievous angel. I sit back as I move myself on him, my breasts swaying. He touches them, then holds my waist, keeping me pulled down onto him. Jan and Solange are making love. . . .

* * *

It's past midnight. He's at his desk, working on his poetry. We both worked all day together. He's been at it solidly for four days, ever since my birthday. Seeing him so obviously pleased and excited turns me on. I go up behind him and enclose him in my arms; he kisses my cheek and stretches.

"I think I'm too tired to do anymore," he says.

"You've been working so hard, darling." I kiss the back of his neck. "Can I get you anything?" Oh, this domesticated bliss! But he seems worried. Something's up—what can it be? I know I'll find out. I can always tell when there's something he just *has* to tell me.

"I have to go to Texas the day after tomorrow," he suddenly says.

"Oh?" Why hasn't he told me before this? I look at him in anxious inquiry.

He brushes some long hair out of his eyes, rubs the side of his nose. "It's . . . Oh, shit, lady, I *hate* this!"

191

I go over and kneel between his legs and he leans forward on the sofa. "Calm down," I tell him. "What's going on? Why do you have to go? Your Dallas concert isn't for ten days, is it?"

"Yeah, I know. But . . ."

"But what?" He's too embarrassed to tell me. As though he considers it wrong to go. A betrayal? I smile reassuringly. "What, darling? *Tell* me, for fuck's sake."

"It's my birthday."

"I know. You're thirty-nine. Wow!" I roll my eyes upwards and giggle. "Wait 'til you see what I've got for you, besides me, that is."

He holds my shoulders. "My Ma always gives a party for me. At home, on the ranch."

Ah! Now I understand. A party I'm not invited to. Well, what did I expect? After all, I'm only a mistress!

"My folks . . . My elder brother and his wife and kids will be there. My younger brother. And my sister comes from Houston with her husband and kids." He paused, staring at me. "And the Cantrells—them too, now, of course. The band, and all the roadies, and Roy too. And Jed and my other friends from around those parts. Everybody."

I stand up, take a step backwards. I suddenly feel totally excluded from him and his life. His real life, that is—I'm just his *secret* life.

"Everybody except *me*, you mean! Everybody *else!*" My anger won't stay hidden anymore. *"I hate you!"* My eyes fill with tears and I turn and run from the room.

It's obvious he's always going to be with Melissa. She's *never* going to let him go. She's got her claws in, and she's going to *keep* him. She'll always use Andy against him. So why doesn't he just up and leave her and fight her for Andy? Because he doesn't really want to, that's why—not while I'm always willing to fuck him when he wants. Why should he disrupt his pleasant little life for *me?*

"Solange . . ."

"Go away!"

He comes and holds me. "Solange . . . Darlin', I . . ."

"Go away. I hate you. Go away. To your wife. To your home and family. Go anywhere, except where I am!"

"Solange, darlin' . . ."

"Go away. Go away. I *hate* you! Don't *touch* me." I try to shake myself free from his hands, but he's too strong and pulls me into his arms. "Let me go! Don't *touch* me!" I beat at his shoulders with my fists.

"Stop it!" he insists as I still struggle. *"Stop* it!" He points a finger at me in emphasis; his grip on my arm is agonizing. *"Stop . . . it . . . !"*

"I just want you to *go."* I pout. "This is my house you're in. *Go away!"*

"Just calm down, Solange." He hugs me tightly to him. I struggle, but I can't get away. "Just keep it cool, babe."

"Don't you patronize me, you bastard!"

He laughs, kissing my face.

"Stop it, you goddam chauvinist cowboy! Go away, I don't want you here!"

He gives me a push, and I land back on the bed; he throws himself on top of me, crushes me beneath him, kisses me. I can't move. I'm crying again. I don't *want* this.

"Jan!" I try to free myself. We're still fighting and struggling. "What are you going to do? *Rape* me again?"

Shocked, he suddenly stops, sits up, and looks at me. "I don't want to rape you. Jesus fucking Christ! Just what the fuck d'you think I am?"

I sit myself up, sobbing. "I think that you're a fucking prick bastard, that's what I think you are."

"Well, considering I love you so very much, thanks for that, lady!" He glares at me, so very angry.

I want to hurt him because he's hurting me and he doesn't seem to care. I'm not thinking rationally, I just want to strike out at him, wound him. "Oh, it's obvious you love me, isn't it? Very!" I retort ironically. "Well, I'm fed up with being your secret little fuck." I hit out at him, over and over, trying to rid myself of the frustrated anger I'm feeling. "And you *did* rape me, you fucking pig bastard!" Tears are streaming down my face. "Fucking prick! Fucking asshole!" I slap him hard across the face, then get myself off the bed and into the bathroom, to wash my face. I can feel him standing behind me. Me, my eyes red and swollen, my hair all over the place.

"You never let me finish what I had to say," he says. I swing around to face him belligerently. "I was going to suggest," he goes on, "that you come too. We're all flying down together—me, Roy, and the band. You could come too." He smiles softly, gently, as though nothing is wrong. "You know I want you to meet *Mor* and *Far."*

"Great!" I laugh bitterly and go back downstairs; he follows me. I pour myself a rather large Scotch and see a ghost of a smile on his face as I sip at it with distaste.

"Well?"

"You *are* a fucking bastard!" I say, gulping at the same

193

time and almost choking myself. "What do you plan to do? Sneak me in with Roy? Introduce me as the band's groupie? Fuck you! I can imagine you introducing me to your parents as your *mistress!*"

"It wouldn't be like that," he says quietly, getting himself a drink. "You know I hate all this as much as you do."

"Do you?" I scoff. "Do you really?" I feel thoroughly bitchy. "Well, I'll tell you what. I'll come with *you*. If you get it handled with Melissa. *And,* if I can be there with you. Not secretly, but with *you!*"

I watch him finish his drink and pour himself another. I nearly tell him not to drink so much; but instead I pout and take a drink from my own glass. How come he's not answering?

Jan paces up and down in front of me like an irritated, stalking tiger, restless and tense. His eyes flash fire; tyger tyger burning bright . . .

"Oh, don't worry," I tell him. "I didn't expect you'd be turned on by that idea." I smile sweetly. "No, Solange the mistress is a much better proposition for you, isn't she? No difficulties that way. So much easier for your uncomplicated little life. No loss of equilibrium!"

"I thought you loved me," he says quietly.

"I thought that you loved *me!*" I fling at him.

We glare at each other, and he takes my drink from me, grips my shoulders. "I don't wanna argue with you, Solange."

"Don't, then. Just go!"

"Jesus *fuck!* You're all a bunch of bitching cunts! All of you!" He turns and storms across the room.

"You haven't got your boots on."

"Lady," he turns around and points a finger at me—"If I want bitching shit laid on me, I'll go to my wife."

"Well, you'd better just go to her, hadn't you? All I'm good enough for is *fucking!*"

He faces me, his anger somehow held in check as he stands with clenched fists. "Lady, you're always eager to spread those lovely little legs of yours!" He flashes me an unpleasant, ironic smile. "Your delectable little cunt's always—what is it?—eager and creamy!" He turns and strides from the room. I can hear him thumping around upstairs.

I stand frozen, feeling as though he'd actually slapped me. Is that really all he sees me as—a voracious cunt?

He comes furiously down the stairs with his suede jacket and his boots on, impatiently jingling his car keys in his hand. "I thought you were my beautiful, sweet delight," he says bitterly, "my darlin' little Literary Lady. But I should've known; it's always the same with chicks: Every one of them always ends up as a *bitchin' cunt!*" The last is delivered in a shout, over his shoulder, as he slams the front door. I hear his car start up, drive away.

Running to the front door, I lock it and put the two chains on. "Fucking bastard!" I call out, kicking at the door, over and over, like a spoilt brat. "Bastard!" I kick and pound at the door again. Irrationally irate, I go upstairs and cry myself into a numb, restless, unsleeping state.

*　*　*

I sit silently drinking the orange juice Miriam has poured for me. "You look *awful!*" she brightly informs me.

I make a kind of squeaky noise in my throat, to signify agreement. I guess I *must* look awful; I was up half the night, crying and moping.

"I *told* you, girl! I told you he was *using* you! Those Goddam fucking *assholes* will *always* walk all *over* you!" She gives me the few letters she's brought for me to deal with and leaves.

Johnny wants to see me. I sit and answer that. I'll always see him as a friend, but that I just don't think we could have the same sort of relationship, not again. And I tell him I'm in love with someone. Strange, how I feel so disconnected from Johnny now. I wish I felt the same way about Jan-Toby Axelsson.

Alone in the house, I go up to the bedroom and lie down. I'm feeling weirdly paranoid. I can't help but think about Jan and me: the last few happy days. It made me feel so good to see him working on his poetry, even asking my advice in a few places. "I've grown up some since I first started writing it," he admitted. He played his guitar and showed me how to play a few simple chords, but I couldn't do it very well; I don't have very strong fingers, and I found it hard to keep the strings pressed down. He kissed my grooved and painful fingertips, showed me how his own were calloused. He even wrote a song—"Lover Lady"—for his next album.

"Oh, Jan . . ." I turn over and cuddle the pillow. Gulley comes to me and slumps himself down with his furry little bottom up against my back. His purring feels warm and comforting, I can feel it right through me. Gulley, my little tyger, my little protector and comforter. . . .

I wake up again, hungry, but I can't be bothered to move. I'll have to, though, because Gulley will want his supper.

What on earth am I going to do with myself *now*, I wonder. I've shut myself into a trap again. Where have all those carefree, happy love affairs gone? The trouble is that it's *Jan* I want, only Jan.

I think of him: how he looks when he concentrates and when he's writing. I hear again that low moan when he comes. Sometimes it's almost an agonized shout—that's when we've fucked a lot. I *love* it like that (what lady doesn't?).

I sit up; the bed wobbles. Shit, it's not fair! We're so damn good in and out of bed together.

"I'm sorry, Jan . . ."

He can't hear you, you know, Solange. He's probably picked up some tall, long-legged, sylphlike little chick. A sixteen year old who gives great head. Bastard! Bet she wasn't as good as me, anyway. *I* know *exactly* what you like, Jan-Toby Axelsson. *Exactly!* Every soft spot. Every sexy spot. *Everything.*

Maybe he's sleeping with her now? All cuddled up together like we do. Lying on him. We went to sleep like that and woke up like that. Sometimes I'd wake up and he'd be in me, making love to me. But wait—he told me he didn't like sleeping with chicks that serviced him, that he hardly ever did that, unless he had to. He hated strange chicks in strange hotels, in strange towns, on strange mornings. He hated to have to be polite and talk to chicks he'd just fucked. Most of them couldn't talk anyway. "We don't want them for their conversation," Joel told me when we were in San Francisco. "They all end up asking you whether you can introduce them to Rod Stewart or Kris Kristofferson or Paul Stanley. And they'd do *anything*—and they would—if you'd take them to a party where simply *everyone* was going to be."

I wish I were lying in Jan's arms right now. I feel for the emerald around my neck, touch the studs in my ears. Jan . . . I want you. I'm so sorry.

During that first week we spent together, after we had made love one time, I lay here in his arms and he told me the whole story about his family. . . .

"Ya see, *Far*—that's Swedish for Pa—well, he came over here to settle in Texas when he was just ten. That was with *his* ma and pa, of course." Jan, with a warm reminiscing smile, evidently recalling times when his father imparted to him the family history. Me, with my head on his shoulder, my hand on his fucked-out, limp little cock.

"They came from Malmo. My pa, Axel, and his pa, also

196

Axel, and my grandma Ingrid. They were quite well off, but they wanted to make themselves a new life. *Farfar*—that's my grandpa—wanted something better for them all, so they came to Texas, where some distant relatives of ours had already been living for ten years. Anyway, they all took to it. *Farfar* was successful at ranching, made a pot of money.

"Then when my pa was twenty-one, he wanted to visit all the relatives back in Sweden, so he went for a few months. That's when he met *Mor*—that's Swedish for Ma, of course." Jan laughed and hugged me tighter again. "Her name was Kirsten Jansson. She married my pa after only a few weeks, and he took her back to Texas with him; and a year later Axel, my elder brother, was born. Then two years later I came, and I was named Jan-Tobias after Morfar, that's my ma's pa, Jan-Tobias Jansson. Then after me come Nils, and after him my younger sister Ulla." I climbed on top of him, and he held my ass in both hands. "And that's the Axelsson history."

"Very impressive."

"Axel, my big brother, he married Susan, who's our second cousin, daughter of the relatives who'd been here longer. Axel and Sue have a place quite near *Far* and *Mor*—Axel does all the Axelsson wheelin' and dealin'. Enjoys being' a *Mogul*, Axel does. And Ulla, she married some damn rich Texan lawyer, Bernard Hastings the fuckin' Third, moved to Houston and had four kids already. Lives it up at the fuckin' golf and tennis club."

"And you—you've had a good life." I kissed his nose.

"Yep. Never had to sweat. Far and Mor gave us everything, though we were never selfish brats; Far made us earn it. But we never had to call him *sir*, that fuckin' shit. Always *Far*. Shit, they love us so. And I don't think I need tell ya just how much we love them. Never wanted for nothin', we didn't."

"Like me."

"Suited, ain't we?"

"Immensely." Kissing. "What does Nils do?"

"Nils . . ." I saw a sadness come into Jan's eyes. "Nils always wanted to fly. He did. We learned to fly the plane together. But after college, he joined the army. He was a chopper pilot in Nam."

"Was? You mean he was killed?"

"No, he didn't quite manage to get sent home in a fuckin' plastic body bag." Bitter irony in Jan's face. "He was 'lucky' —he only lost his fuckin' legs." Bitter, unhappy, contorted

197

smile. "He helps *Far* run the ranch. Jesus, he's got some guts in him."

"Why don't we have him here for a while? D'you think he'd like that?"

'He'd love that, darlin', I know he would. And he's gonna love *you*. Melissa's always ignored him—I mean literally. Pretends he ain't there. Never talks to him, the fuckin' bitch!"

I held him tight for a while, feeling the pain and hurt inside him, feeling so helpless. Finally I said, "Jan-Tobias—that sounds very classy."

"My ma always calls me Jan-Toby." He said it with a Swedish accent: *Yahn-Toby*. "Everyone else calls me Jan with a J, of course."

"It's a lovely name. I like Swedish names."

"Had a lot of Swedes then, have you?"

"Had my share." He raised an eyebrow as I giggled. "Lars, for one. The only one, actually—before you, that is. The boy next door I told you all about—the one who popped my cherry. I told you I was still friends with him."

"He's Swedish?"

"Lars Larsson," I said, "comes from Stockholm."

"Lars *Larsson?*" Jan laughed, teasing me.

"Listen you, with a name like *Yahn*-Tobias Axelsson and a *Farfar* and a *Far* and a *broder* called Axel Axelsson, don't knock it, cowboy!" I got my ass pinched for that. "Lars's father's name is Lars too—what else?—and he's a diplomat. Lars' mother is an actress. Anyway, the last time I was in Sweden was the winter before last. I spent a few months with Lars. I loved it, I always do. He wanted me to stay, he always does."

"Glad ya didn't. But at least ya had the sense to get ya little cherry popped by a Swede—next best thing to a Texan."

We laughed and cuddled, and then I *really* surprised him: "He's a rock star, too."

"Lars Larsson is?" Jan looked thoroughly disbelieving.

"I told you a while back that you weren't the only Swedish-named rock star I knew and had fucked." Then I quickly retrieved a couple of Swedish albums. Jan read the covers quickly.

"Shit, I *know* these dudes!"

"I know, and well you should. They're Sweden's top heavy-rock group. They're classical influenced, from their early training. A sort of Swedish Pink Floyd. See, that's Lars." I pointed him out on the cover, tall and thin. "And that's his twin brothers Kris and Sven, they're younger. And Bo, their cousin, there on drums."

"Jesus, they came and saw us when we were in Sweden a few years back. They're good."

"Of course they are," I said. "Didn't you know I only like Scandinavian-type rock guys?" Jan looked at me suspiciously. "You know," I said, "Jan Axelsson, I think he's my favorite." Kiss. "Lars Larsson . . ." Another kiss. "Kris Kristofferson. Nilsson Schmilsson." Giggle. "And my very, very favorite, of course—Bob *Dylansson?*" At that point Jan jumped me and punched me and of course fucked me.

And how could I have been so stupid as to blow something I want so very much? How could I have been so stupid as to turn him away from me?

I've sent him away thinking I'm a bitching cunt. He said, "If I want bitching I'll go home to my wife." That is what he gets from her, and now I've cast myself in the same role.

Solange, you're going to have to do something, and quick, if you want to keep him. You're the one who's going to have to apologize, make things all right, mend the hurt you've caused.

I ring Roy, but he tells me Jan is at home. Well, at least I know where he is. I shower, rub cream and perfume into my body. There, my hair's nearly dry. I'll wear a beautiful dress—yes, and go to him. I want Jan to fuck me and fuck me and . . .

I rush into the bedroom, and stop, startled, but then filled with exhilaration. I'm looking at a smiling Jan-Toby Axelsson: a Jan-Toby Axelsson with an armful of roses.

"Ma'am . . ." He winks. He looks me up and down as I stand naked, staring at him. "That sure does look mighty temptin', Ma'am," he says in an outrageous Texas accent, offering me the roses. Why can't I answer? Why can't I move?

"And I'm reckonin' I'm gonna be givin' in to all this sinful temptation, Ma'am," he says with another deliberate wink.

"Promises, promises." I place the roses on a chair and fling myself into his arms. "I was just going to . . ."

"I'm so sorry, little darlin'," he interrupts, whispering into my hair.

"I'm sorry, Jan darling. Oh, I love you. Forgive me. I love you." And I'm thrown on the bed.

"Sure glad I got tempted," Jan says after we've made love.

"Was just thinking that myself, *Yahn*-Tobias."

199

"I've got something for you," he announces and goes over to his suede jacket, thrown down on the floor. He brings a velvet-covered box, and takes out two pendants on chains—beautiful shiny gold, glinting under the lights.

"I had them made. I want your opinion."

"Oh?" I look at the one he puts in my hand. Stare at it for a long, long moment. Look at him, look back at it again. Feel tears in my eyes.

"See what it is?"

"Oh, yes . . ." On the chain hangs a small golden sun. In the center of the sun is engraved a small angel, just like Blake's engraving of the angel coming out of the egg.

He takes the pendant and shows me what's written on the back: *I LOVE YOU—JAN.* He hangs it around my neck.

"You wear this one all the time." He shows me his pendant and puts it on. He gives me a calm, direct look, taking hold of my shoulders very gently. "I'm so *sorry*, darlin'." He pulls me into his arms. "I was an asshole, sayin' those things to you."

"Don't let's hurt each other anymore," I whisper between kisses. "I can't stand it. I've been so unhappy."

"So have I, darlin'." He takes my face in his hands and kisses me.

I go and make a huge mushroom and cheese omelette: He'd forgotten to eat today, and he's ravenous. "You need looking after," I tell him, and kiss the top of his head.

"You offerin'?"

"Oh yes!"

"Good—I'm acceptin'."

11

Janless nights and Janless days. I miss him so much. His "I'll call you once a day" turned into twice a day, night and morning, and how I love him for it! And we've written to each other, too: beautifully exquisite love letters.

It's his thirty-ninth birthday today. "Jesus, I'm nearly grown up," he said to me before he went.

I touch the little sun-angel he gave me. I wonder how he'll like the present I've had made for him; what he'll think of it.

I lie soaking in the bath. My mind, this evening, is a whirl of jumbled thoughts. Jan. Me. Us. Babies, Books. Marie-Claude will be here soon. I must call my mother. When will Jan call me?

I think of us laughing and playing in the shower the morning he left. I still wonder at us being so close, so intimate. I had a closeness with Johnny, but it was never like this. I was always in total awe of him, for one thing; with Jan, we're totally equal.

I know all about his previous relationships. We've talked for hours about them—every detail. His only serious one was Jennie, and she was uneasy about Jan being a rock singer; when he went on the road doing gigs she was upset about it. After a year they'd more or less drifted apart. Jan didn't want to settle down. He didn't know what love was and had begun to suspect that it didn't really exist. So Jennie departed and the band went on tour. Jan met her a few years later; she was happily married to a teacher, and they had three kids.

After that there were too many chicks out there waiting to be fucked. Until, that is, he met Melissa-Sue Cantrell and got himself hooked. And until he met Solange delaMer . . .

The phone rings. My hand's trembling as I pick up the receiver, like an excited teenager when the handsomest boy in the class calls her for a date.

"Hello. Solange delaMer."

"Is that so?" That beautiful deep sexy voice of his, that lazy drawl; they make me feel horny: creamy and dreamy.

"Happy birthday, darling. I love you."

"Well, thank you, Ma'am."

"Are you having a nice birthday, darling?" Me, sounding breathless, happy, and excited for him.

"Sure am, Ma'am."

"Oh, I wish I was with you."

Silence. Another five seconds of silence. "I wanna fuck you."

"I want you to fuck me, too."

"I've thought of two things I'm gonna do to you that no one's *ever* done to you."

Me, pulse racing, heart beating fast. Pussy eagerly creaming. *"What?"* a breathless whisper.

"I ain't gonna tell you."

"Jan?"

"Nope! I'm gonna let you get yaself all horny thinkin'

about it. Then I'll get horny thinkin' of you gettin' all horny . . ." Laugh. "What are you wearin'?"

"Nothing. I've just got out of the bath." Me, dripping bathwater over the bed.

"I've got a hard-on."

"Poor baby." Giggles from me.

"Darlin' . . ."

"What?"

"Your gifts—they're beautiful. Thank you, darlin'. I'm amazed at the coincidence, that you thought of that and I thought of the sun-angels. . . . Jesus, I love you, lady."

I go and lie in the sun, think of Jan. I'm still feeling so very pleased with myself for choosing the right gifts for him: a gold-embossed, leather-bound copy of Blake, and a platinum identity bracelet. I bought the Blake years ago in Oxford: a special printing of his collected works, bound in smooth morocco leather. There were only two left in the bookshop, and I bought them both. I used one; the other I kept, because I knew that some day it would make a present for someone I loved.

Johnny worships Blake, yet I never gave it to him.

Rand admires Blake too, yet I never gave it to him, either.

"To Jan," I wrote on the flyleaf, "With all my love, Solange."

And on the identity bracelet, the kind with huge flat links, I had the jeweler do some engraving. First a sun shape, and then:

to J-T A

with all my love

J-T A L L

and then the baby angel copies from the Blake engraving. How beautiful, that we should both think of using the same symbols!

I think we really do need each other, just as much as we want each other, just as much as we love each other. I lie awake thinking about it. It was only a short year ago that I admired him, his words and his music, but I didn't know him. Even so, I felt close to him; there was only the trivial detail that we hadn't yet met.

I'm lying on my tummy, watching my cassette. Jan looks good on the big screen of the TV he bought me. I'm smoking a joint and occasionally sipping at a glass of champagne. I haven't eaten today, and I'm feeling light-headed and rather delicious. On the screen, he's beardless. It seems all wrong now that he has his beard and mustache again. He occasionally shaves them off and for a few weeks can go around unrecognized, particularly with a hat and dark glasses. Don't they recognize his boots, though? I giggle, and lie in a dreamy state, fingering my creamy little cunt, almost succeeding in persuading myself it's Jan.

*　　*　　*

I've just finished an interview for *Cosmopolitan.* Normally I don't like interviews all that much—who does?—but this one was enjoyable. Interviewers always ask why I write so freely about s-e-x, when it was Literature (with a capital L) that I studied. My clipping service always sends me copies, which I have Miriam file away, usually unread.

But Judy, who interviewed me for *Cosmo,* was a delight. We giggled together over all sorts of things. She wanted to know whether I received alimony from Rand. I told her I didn't believe in it, apart from money to help with the kids, if any. She wanted to know about my sex life. I told her it was great. Was I multiorgasmic? Yes, especially when I'm working at my typewriter. Who is my man? Someone I love, I smart-ass answered. Am I *wholly* for ERA? Even unholy, I'd be for it, I told her with a grin.

I'm talking to Jan. It's after two in the morning. He tells me that he, Nils, Joel, Billy, and the rest are at his friend's ranch. His friend is Jed Brackett. I've heard all about Bullhead Brackett before. Four years older than Jan, he taught him the ropes—i.e., how to fuck women—and then introduced Jan and Joel, at the tender age of sixteen, to "the raunchiest little whorehouse in Dallas." Jan, Joel, and Jed own a ranch together, equal shares; Jed runs it.

Jed, according to Jan, "can't wait to meet this great little piece of tits an' ass" that Jan's found for himself. And I can't wait to meet bullhead Brackett. "Ya ain't seen nuttin'," Jan seriously told me, "until ya've seen a Texan wheelin' an' dealin'." I believe him.

"Hey," Jan says on the phone, "Someone wants to say hello to you."

"Well, howdy, Ma'am." A deep, *deep* voice comes on the line.

"Bullhead Brackett, no less," I say dryly.

"Sure is, Ma'am." I giggle. "I've been hearin' some mighty purdy things about you, Ma'am."

"Really? I've been hearing a few, um, *interesting* things about you too."

"Whoo-whee! I'm sure you have, Ma'am. And ya sure do speak all purdy and classy, like ole Jan here says ya do."

"Well, thank you, Mister Brackett." I wonder what else he's told him I do all purdy and classy?

"Guess where we've been?" Jan back on the line, sounding more than somewhat smashed.

"I can't."

"The Dallas concert's tomorrow."

"Yes."

"We like our Texas concerts best."

"I'm sure you do, cowboy."

"We ain't Country Outlaws, but we sure is *Texans.*"

"Is that so?"

"And they *love* us."

"I should hope they do."

"So—guess!"

"Guess what?"

Pause. Heavy breathing. Is he thinking I'm a bit slow?

"Where we've been celebratin'."

I suddenly get it! "The raunchiest little whorehouse in Dallas, I bet."

"Aw, shit, ya looked!" Jan laughs. "I tell ya, there's one hot mama there, one suck and ya comin' all over the fuckin' place."

"Really? How interesting." I try to suppress my giggles. "So, *she* sucked, and *you* fucked, huh?"

"Jesus, lady, you're too much." He's laughing again. I hear him repeating what I said to Bullhead, and then all the rest of them are laughing. "Ya didn't mind, didya?" He sounds smashed again; I hear him swigging at something—bourbon and branch water, no doubt.

"Darling, I don't think your having it sucked off by some kindhearted hooker can be what you'd call an *emotional* involvement. No threat to *us.*"

"It sure ain't, Ma'am. And you don't have to worry none, either. She's warranteed clean, they all are." Slurp.

"And you enjoyed it?"

"Enjoyed it!" Another slurp of drink. "Darlin', it was *first aid.*" Slurp. "I mean, I was wearin' my hand out." Me giggling, Jan slurping. "Me and Jed like to share."

"Share?"

"Yeah . . . You know, two girls, one bed."

"Oh. You mean you leave Joel out of this?"

"Joel does all right with his own two chicks."

"Well, I'm glad about that. So . . . you and Jed *share?*" Suppressed giggles from me.

"Sure do, Ma'am. It's kinda tradition. Pardners, like."

"Pardners. Well, I can understand that . . ."

"Jesus, I love you, Literary Lady. And I *miss* you."

He misses me! "I love *you*, darling. And I certainly miss *you*." All this *missing* each other—so why the hell aren't we *together?* "So, tell me about this . . . tradition."

"Well . . . ya see . . ."—slurp—"we get blown—together, that is. Then the chicks perform—that gets us horny again, of course."

"Of course."

"Then we fuck 'em, and Jed pisses on 'em."

"Oh . . . Sounds really . . . *delightful*, darling."

"It's good for ya cock when ya haven't got ya old lady around."

"I'm sure it is. Rests your hand, too." Giggle. "But tell me, how much does this all cost?"

"We got an account."

"An *account*. I bet you have, cowboy!"

Slurp. "Jesus, I *love* you, lady."

"I love you too, cowboy."

"Jesus! I wanna fuck your ass off"—slurp—"till it hurts."

"Well, I'd like that too, darling."

"Shit! I've got a fuckin' hard-on."

"You want me to talk dirty?"

"You beautiful bitch!"

Contented smile. "Ain't that the truth."

*   *   *

I'm too excited to sleep. I feel like it's Christmas Eve.

Jan's home tomorrow. We'll have nearly two whole weeks together before his next few concerts. And even then, we won't be separated—because *I'll be going with him.*

I lie in bed feeling pleased with my life. My writing is going well, and Marie-Claude will be here in a few weeks. Johnny and I are friends—no hard feelings, no angry recriminations. Rand seems fine, too. He sounded a little distant on the phone the other day, but he said everything was going well for him and that there was a lady in his life. I feel immensely pleased about this—there must have been some buried guilt hidden somewhere in my subconscious about having deserted him the way I did. Now that he's started a new scene, it seems to make it all right. And besides Rand, there's Maman. She's settled in her house in Nice. There's even a man in *her* life, she tells me, and she's looking forward to meeting Jan. I feel like it's some kind of personal reward, knowing that the people who mean the most to me are happy. Well, nearly all of them: Matthew was rather grumpy, slightly bitchy when I called him yesterday. He *still* wants me to have his baby. I must have a serious talk with him about it when I'm in New York next; I don't want to lose his friendship.

Lars is happy, too. He has a new lady in his life now; a Norweigan girl named Hjördis. And Kris, his younger brother, wrote me a long letter. Kris is almost as close to me as Lars, though we haven't fucked. I love all my Larssons. I wrote them a long letter to tell them Jan and I will come and see them soon. Jan and I have it planned: I'll take him to Stockholm to stay with the Larssons; he'll take me to Malmo to stay with the Axelssons. "See, we really are meant for each other," he said, "having Sweden in common too." Yes, I feel immensely pleased with myself—almost as if I'd personally brought all this happiness about.

Reward for me: my own little bit of personal happiness will be with me tomorrow. I fall asleep aching for him; I dream about our making love, and sleepily wonder what those two things are that no one's ever done to me. I'll be so eagerly creamy by the time he arrives, one look from him and I'll come.

That feels so good. What is it? A dream? It feels like lips, kissing me, kissing my pussy hair, my nipples. It's such a beautiful dream, this ... Sucking, beautiful sucking on my nipples. It's so real—so real—so ...

"Mmm ..." I open my eyes. I *am* being kissed: a tongue searching around inside my mouth. And hands on me ... an erect cock trying to get into me. "Mmm ... ?"

"Mornin', Ma'am."

"Jan?" My hands reach out. "Jan ... !"

Slippery, slidy, sexy motion. Together. Jan and Solange.

"Thought I'd surprise you ..." Whispered voice against my mouth.

"Oh, yes ..."

"Pull your legs up." Order from my lord and master.

"Mmm . . ." Dreamily answered. Why am I still so sleepy? Perhaps it *is* a dream . . . ?

Sudden thrust. Sharp, hurting. Another!

"Jan!" Eyes wide, startled; I'm suddenly awake, filled up by cock.

And I'm looking into the sardonically smiling eyes of Jan-Toby Axelsson. . . .

"You should have told me," I say excitedly as we sit in bed eating breakfast.

"Surprise for you."

"Oh, yes." I cuddle him. "And it's for nearly two weeks. Oh, Jan." I cuddle and kiss him, excited as a child. "The concerts went so well for you, and your birthday was good for you. And the raunchiest little whorehouse in Dallas—that was *obviously* good for you." I giggle, watching him chew on his toast, his eyes on me. "Oh, I love you so much, darling." My love for him's spilling over. My coffee spills, too—over the sheet. I nonchalantly push the wet sheet aside. "We'll make love all day."

"*Nearly* all day," Jan corrects with a wink.

"*All* day's better."

He moves his breakfast things off the bed, sits back on his heels, pulls me to him. "Darlin' . . ." He frowns. I know that look: Something is up.

"What? You have to go away somewhere?"

"Not exactly."

"*What* exactly? What d'you mean?" I say agitatedly.

"Melissa-Sue came back with me." He looks embarrassed; it shows in his funny little smile, in the way he looks away from me. "Listen—she decided to come back until the next concert. Jesus, there's no way I can stop her. It's her home too."

"Oh, yes. She *is* your wife. I mustn't forget *that!*" Me, slightly bitchy.

"I couldn't argue with her." He holds me, kisses me. "She would have become suspicious. She was angry enough with me for spending hardly any time with her in Dallas. She knows I fuck chicks when we're tourin', and she knows I visit Rosie's with the guys."

How can I be angry. I cuddle him around the neck, resolving not to turn into the Bitching Cunt again, resolving to be his contented little Literary Lady. "It's all right, darling," I tell him.

"Roy's gonna be givin' a party."

"That's if I go, isn't it?"

"You're goin'."

"Is that an order?"

"You bet the fuck it is."

"And will I be there in secret, at the party? I assume you'll be taking your wife. Do I get myself a date? Can I pick someone up there, have a nice little party fuck?"

Jan frowns at me.

He pulls me up into his arms. "Come and fuck," he invites with a groad grin.

"Don't you mean fuck and come?"

"Fuckin' cute, ain't ya!"

He deposits me front down over two of the pillows, pushes into me from behind. Me, masochistically his—loving it, biting on my arm as he batters angrily into me. He feels around me, touches, just touches, my magic button, and I scream. How long does this go on for? I don't know, I don't care. All I do care about it that he's back with me.

*   *   *

I rather enjoyed Roy's party. Me, wearing my golden silk dress I look so good in. My emerald studs, the emerald at my throat, and Jan's ring. It seemed bizarre. He took his wife to the party; she was wearing his wedding ring. His mistress was also at the party, wearing his engagement ring. She'd driven there in the car he'd bought for her. For an instant, I felt as though he'd bought *me*.

Perhaps no one else saw me and Jan staring at each other, gazing into each other's eyes. I felt so naked and raw as I stood there, peeled bare of everything but my love for him. I automatically clutched at my little sun-angel and was rewarded by a smile in those beautiful amethyst eyes of his, a loving, caring smile. Even Melissa being there didn't bother me because I knew something she didn't: Jan and I would be together soon for she was returning to Texas.

The party shuffled its people, dealt a few interesting hands, danced them around a little in advances and retreats. I wandered, got myself chatted up, danced with a few unattached males, and turned down a few interesting invitations.

I went home alone, a bit peeved because Jan had to go home with Melissa. But the next morning I awoke to find his cock digging into me from behind. I didn't even bother to wake up properly but just let him make love to me in that deliciously sleepy state. And when Jan had seen Melissa and

Andy onto the plane back to Dallas, it was as if we'd stepped into another, weightless, carefree dimension.

We settled back into our delightfully domesticated routine again; working, making love, and, simply, just playing together.

He took me to Berkeley, proudly showed me around. And we went to see Raul and Rita Sanchez, spent two delightful days with them on their farm.

Trading new experiences is fun, but being the honest little Literary Lady that I am, I have to admit that there have been times I felt slightly awkward. For example, when Jan has taken me into his world, to meet his friends and fellow musicians, who are used to his being with Melissa-Sue and not with Solange delaMer.

And the silly, crazy surprises: We went to an "adult" motel—round waterbeds and sexy movies. We also had an extremely giggly and exceedingly messy half hour with two packets of Pop Rocks.

Once we went to the supermarket—Jan wanted a Roman orgy of a feast in bed. We were nearly finished, our cart full of things we both knew we'd never get through, when we noticed a middle-aged lady with blue hair looking at us suspiciously. She bore down on us, her eyes glinting as much as her diamanté glasses. "Jesus fuck!" exclaimed Mister Axelsson, "can't even go to the fuckin' market without someone jumpin' me." I laughed and hugged him. "You shouldn't be so gorgeous. But isn't she a bit old for you?" He pinched my ass as the now squealing lady got within a few feet of us. "She'll say it's just for her daughter," Jan said out of the corner of his mouth as she was upon us. A few people had begun to be aware that they had a *star* in their midst. Jan stood looking embarrassed, hiding behind his sunglasses, as the lady planted her peach-colored, polyester-pantsuited two hundred and something pounds in front of us. Jan gave me a resigned look just as she gave him an expertly executed elbow in the ribs. *"Get out* of my way, young man!" Her voice echoed like a King Kong roar around the supermarket. She pushed him again, and the breath was audibly forced from his lungs. "Miss Delmar," she addressed me effusively, "can I *please* have your autograph?" She looked around at the little crowd, and it was my turn for embarrassment. *"Angela Delmar!"* she clucked, thrusting a pen and large box of Fruit Loops (I felt like one) under my nose. "I recognized you from my daughter's paperbacks. 'To Hazel'—that's my daughter.

I've read all your books; I do so like to keep up with my reading. 'To my good friend Hazel.' ''

Needless to say, Jan-Toby Axelsson was hanging over the frozen food counter, doubled up with laughter.

And Jan took me to meet a really close friend of his, T.G., who lives a few houses away from him. Tom G. Watson is a fellow Texan and famous country singer. T.G. has recorded a few of Jan's more famous numbers, country style of course. He also had a big country hit with a song Jan wrote for him. Teasing me, Jan told T.G. that his Literary Lady liked classical music best—"a beautiful little highbrow, I've gotten me"—and that the only country singers I knew of were Waylon and Willy, whose albums *he'd* given me.

"You mean she don't even know who . . . ?" T.G., laughing, listed off a roster of names that all sounded totally interchangeable to me: Willy T., Billy J., Jimmy-Bob, Billy-Jack, Flap-Jack, Jam-Roll, Odd-Job. "You mean," T.G. winked at Jan, "she don't even know who Hank Williams is?"

"She don't even know who Jerry Lee Lewis is," Jan laughed.

I *still* don't know why that struck them both so funny! But it was a nice visit. It made me feel a part of Jan and his life.

12

Marie-Claude's plane is going to be about half an hour late. I'm sitting drinking coffee, paying no attention to the airport crowds, mostly thinking of Jan. I'm always thinking of Jan. I think my whole life has become Jan.

He's in Chicago. Before that he was in Washington, D.C. before that, Cleveland. I was there with him. It was fun, and the concerts went well. But now Jan's alone in Chicago because I wanted some time with Marie-Claude, just by ourselves.

I talked with Jan for an hour on the phone this morning. He sounded a bit hung over. He said he missed me, wanted me. "What a coincidence," I said.

"Abstinence isn't too good on the old creativity," he laughed.

"*No* little girls?" I joked.

"Nope. *Honestly*. I want *you!*"

"How gratifying. But I'm sorry about all that abstinence I'm enforcing on you."

"I should hope so, Ma'am. It ain't good for me." And then he quoted:

> Abstinence sows sand all over
> The ruddy limbs and flaming hair,
> But Desire Gratified
> Plants fruits of life and beauty there.

"You sure have a way with my William's words, cowboy."

"Ain't that the truth. Your William said everythin' first."

*   *   *

"Are you *sure* you won't mind flying to New York?" I ask Marie-Claude. We're lying in the sun, naked, drying off after splashing about in the pool.

"Not at all, *ma chèrie.*"

"But you've only been here for four days. This interview, you see—I did have it booked a while back, Roy did that is, when I knew Jan would be in New York."

"We go. There is always so much in New York. Lots of shopping."

We fly to New York, and I have my interview with a short, quiet, astute, personable young man for *Book Digest*.

And then we do some very giggly shopping.

How strange, watching Jan-Toby Axelsson on stage, as though I'm reliving last year's concert. But the big shiny hero is no longer seen from afar. He's a big shiny hero of a lover. And I love him and want him and need him . . .

Marie-Claude touches my arm. I think she knows how excited I am at the prospect of seeing Jan—after all, it's been all of a week. She smiles. *"Tu es prêt?"*

Am I ready? *"Oui, bien sûr, je suis tout prêt."*

I open the dressing room door and we go in.

Smoke filled, noisy room, crowded with girls who stare at Marie-Claude and me.

"Solange darling!" Roy comes over to us, hugs me, gives me a peck on the cheek. Meanwhile I've quickly scanned the room: no Jan-Toby Axelsson.

211

"He's in the shower," Roy says.

"Roy, this is Marie-Claude, I've told you about her." Marie-Claude smiles, offers her hand. Roy smiles, looks her up and down, takes her hand and shakes it.

"I've heard all about you from Solange." Sexy, come-on voice from Roy.

"Oo là là..." Marie-Claude smiles shyly, and Roy grins broadly.

I compliment the band on their performance, and they all say their hellos to me. Joel has his arm around the same gnggly, curly-headed blonde he was with at Roy's party—must be serious.

I grin at Billy Wilson, who's sharing a joint with the girl on his lap, but my attention is caught by two men whom I don't know. I think I recognize one of them. He stands there holding a drink, smoking a cigar. He's tall (a bit taller than Jan, I think), lean, *good-looking*, with golden-brown hair down to his collar, deep set, light blue eyes, and a graying, tidy mustache and beard. He's *got* to be a great lay! He's wearing jeans, a tight shirt beneath a tan leather jacket, and a cowboy hat. There's a thick silver chain around his neck, and I can see a chest full of sexy golden-brown hair peeping through the top of his open shirt. And there're those boots. Sundance boots. I try very hard to hide a smile.

Someone hands us drinks. The tall, good-looking stranger, and the other stranger as well, are still staring at Marie-Claude and me. The other one, in a jeans suit, is also quite good-looking; he has dark eyes and dark curly hair.

"You know everyone here, don't you, Solange?" Roy says.

"Well..." I smile in turn at the two strangers. Just then, Jan walks in, wearing only a pair of jeans. He stands still and looks at me. He has a joint in his mouth, and he screws up his eyes against the smoke that wafts around him.

I nod to the tall stranger. "Bullhead Brackett, no doubt."

"Delighted to meet you, Ma'am." He takes my hand, smiles.

"And I'm delighted to meet *you*, Jed." Sexy smile. "Jed, meet Marie-Claude, a close and dear friend from France; she's staying with me for a while."

She shakes hands with Jed, who leers at her undisguisedly. In fact, I'd say I've never seen a more leerful leer. Well, I guess he and Roy are going to have to battle it out, unless Marie-Claude's already decided. Actually, I can guess *how* she's decided.

"Hello," Marie-Claude says pertly.

"Ma'am" Jed replies, undressing her with his eyes. "Marie-Claude sure is some cute and purdy name, Ma'am."

Marie-Claude smiles up at him from under her blonde fringe. I know that come-on smile. She's already daydreaming about the way he fucks. "I like 'Zhed,' too."

"Zhed?" Jed laughs. "Shit, if that ain't the fuckin' cutest thing I've heard!—beggin' ya pardon, Ma'am," he says respectfully, then winks at Jan.

I take Marie-Claude's hand and she comes over with me to meet Jan. We kiss tenderly. "Jan darling, this is Marie-Claude."

"Ma'am."

"Hello, Zhan," Marie-Claude offers Jan her hand, and he smiles.

"Now, Ma'am," Jed says to Marie-Claude, taking her arm and leading her to a chair, "whereabouts in France are you from?" I watch as she and Jed begin a conversation.

Jan and I both smile, and he gathers me up into his arms and kisses me. "Come and meet Wes Carter." He leads me over to say hello to the dark-haired guy. "Wes writes for *Playboy*. He's following me around for a while, for one of the interviews."

Wes Carter looks me up and down—I think he approves. And well he should: I'm looking good, with tight black silk pants, high-heeled sandals, a natural-colored silk blouse tied tight with a silken sash. "I've read your books. They're very good. I think we should do an interview with you, too."

"I'm a very dull person," I tell him, suddenly defensive. "And I'm not famous enough."

"I can't believe that," he says, with another inspection of my body, "not that you're *dull*. Not with the way you write, and your background and education. Not to mention"—wry grin—"the way you look."

"Which d'you want," I retort dryly, "an interview with a writer or centerfold photos?" He smiles, and I continue with a pet peeve, "How come you don't put any beautiful over-thirties in the centerfold?"

"Are you offering?"

"Me—with *my* figure!" I think of some photos Jan took of me one day—in all my beautiful and naked glory—in silly, sexy, *Playboy*-type poses. Jesus, he'd better not show them to anyone!

Wes Carter looks me up and down. "*Especially* with your figure."

213

Jan puts an arm around me. "She thinks she's too fat," he informs Wes.

"I think I've missed you," I say, desperate to change the subject.

"You have, huh?" Jan-Toby Axelsson stands looking at me, hands on hips, the joint in his mouth again, eyes screwed up and smoke enveloping him like a kind of smoky halo.

I can hear Marie-Claude giggling with Jed. I'd wondered what Marie-Claude would make of Texans. Love at first sight? "A fuck as soon as we can get into bed" at first sight!

Jan places his hands on my shoulders, rubs his hands up and down my arms. He holds me around the waist, then moves his hands up so that he's feeling the sides of my boobs. For me, everyone in the room disappears, and everything goes into slow motion. I'm burning as he grabs my hand to pull me along into the bathroom. I hear the door slam, and Jan presses me against the wall and grinds himself into me.

"Jesus, I've missed you, lady!" There are warm hands inside my blouse and on my bare breasts. Me, burning—burning and creamy.

Solange—little Ms. Contented-Ass!

*   *   *

We've been home from New York for a week, and Jan's stayed with me for every minute. And most minutes have been spent in bed.

My life doesn't seem to be fragmented any longer; I feel secure and whole, and I'm enjoying the feeling. There's the temptation to worry about whether it will last, but then I feel guilty for having such a disloyal thought.

Jan and the band have four more concerts before their tour's finished for the year, but all in California and Arizona, so he'll be here most of the time. Anyway, he wants me to go to the concerts, so we won't be apart.

But after this precious time together, his tour will be over, and he'll be going to Texas to handle everything with Melissa. *That's* where my doubts begin. I know she's going to keep using Andy against him, and Jan's feeling of duty towards Andy is so strong that I know he won't just walk out on him (and I don't want him to). All the same, Melissa's power to hold him, using Andy, makes me jealous and angry, because it seems stronger than the love Jan and I feel for each other.

I cut short these negative thoughts to get on with making up a batch of yoghurt in the kitchen. Jan's in the study, working on his poetry. I haven't seen Jed and Marie-Claude at all today.

What will happen if she won't let him go, if she denies him visitation rights? Jan says her father is rich and influential enough to find some way, legally, of stopping him seeing Andy, if that's what Melissa wants.

I plug in the yoghurt maker, pour Jan some coffee, and take it to him. He has the back off the typewriter; the ink cartridge and erasing ribbon are lying on the desk with the type ball next to them, and he's attacking the machine's interior with a screwdriver.

"It's stopped underlining," he says exasperatedly.

"I'll ring my repairman. Use my typewriter."

"No. I'm good with fuckin' machinery."

"These correcting ones are a bit delicate, darling," I say dubiously. "Let me call Mr. Rubicoff. I have a service contract."

"*I'm* doin' it," he insists, irritatedly. I guess there are times when men love to be little boys again, playing with their mechanical toys. I give him a hug and a kiss on the back of his head and leave him to it. It's so good to see him happy, working on his book, writing some new material for his next album, and ruining the typewriter. I want it to be like this always. It will be, as long as we're together.

I cried yesterday because I'd started my period. Maybe next time I'll fall pregnant; I set my calculator so that I know my fertile days. How would it work, I wonder—my having Jan's baby, if Melissa won't let him go? I don't care; he knows I'd always be here—for him. Sometimes I feel as though I'm throwing all my liberation away. Maybe I don't really want to be independent?

I'm surprised to find Jed in the kitchen, standing there in a pair of old jeans, talking on the phone (in Spanish), and drinking coffee. Graying, golden-brown fuzz on his chest; wide shoulders.

He puts the phone down and smiles at me. "Ma'am." I smile—always "Ma'am." How genteel these Texas cowboys are!

"Hello, Jed. You speak Spanish well."

"Ain't pure Castilian, but I get along." He gives me a sexy wink.

"Can I get you anything? Where's Marie-Claude?"

"She's still asleep." Grin. "Plumb tuckered out." Another grin. "Me, I can just about take this here coffee, never mind anythin' else, thank you, little lady."

215

"Busy night, huh?" I giggle, and Jed beams. I pour myself some coffee and sit at the table in the bay window. Jed sits down opposite me, obviously intending to talk. About what?

"You and Jan . . ." His voice is drawly, much more so than Jan's.

"Yes?"

"It's so nice seein' you so happy together. I've never seen Jan so happy."

"You haven't?" Me, elated, ecstatic.

"Nope." Grin. "You're *good* for him, Ma'am. You understand him. And I reckon that means a lot to a man." Thoughtful nod. "Sure does, Ma'am." Jed lights up a cigarette, swigs at some more coffee, glances at me. I'm in cutoffs and a bikini top. "He said you was the purdiest little thing he's seen in some time. A classy lady. Intelligent—ole Jan likes that." He looks at me with his head on one side, the cigarette still in his mouth. "Says you're the sweetest-tastin' little lady, too."

Oh shit, I think I'm blushing. I smile, hide in my coffee cup. "I have your approval, then."

"You bet your beautiful little pussy you do, Ma'am."

I'm enjoying this conversation, but then, I like this man—not only his great body and eyes, but *him*. It's obvious why he and Jan are good, close friends.

"Jed?"

"What, sweetheart?"

"D'you think Jan will have much trouble with Melissa? With the divorce? D'you think she can really make trouble about the visitation rights?" The questions tumble out of me and my eyes fill with tears. Jed takes my hands between his large ones, give me a fatherly smile.

"Listen, little lady, I won't give ya no owlshit. That bitch has her hooks in. Yep, I think there's gonna be a whole mess of bad-mouthin' goin' on. Ya see . . . Jan, well, he's different than me, he's more kinda *sensitive*. Now me, I wouldn't let no blue-ball bitch blackmail me, no way. My first wife, Emmy-Lou, she tried that on with my two daughters. But I fought—and I see 'em, support 'em. They're cute little fuckers, too. Now if it was me, well I'd jus' tell than ornery bitch to shove her visitation rights. I'd walk out and fight like hell. But he ain't like that."

"She could make him *stay*?"

"Well, little lady—not if I have anythin' to do with it. I'm *talkin'* to him. I don't like that bitch anyhows, she's more fuckin' ornery than a hen with a month's worth of backed-up eggs." Jed grins. "Don't you get all worried, now. Don't you look so sad, neither."

"Sad? Do I?" Sighing.

"Sadder'n a pig at a barbecue."

"What?" I start laughing.

"There ya go." Jed beams. "That's better."

I pour some more coffee. "What did you want to talk to me about? Jan and me?"

"Nope."

"What then?"

"Marie-Claude." He gives me a wry look with half-closed eyes; with that expression, he looks a bit like Clint Eastwood.

"Marie-Claude? You mean something's wrong between you?"

"No, Ma'am." He fingers his mustache.

"What, then?" Is he wondering how to say good-bye to her? I hope not—I know Marie-Claude, and I think she loves him.

"I think . . . wait, correction, I *know* that I'm in love with that little lady. I wanna marry her."

"*Marry* her?" I look incredulously into Jed's solemn face.

"Yep."

"Oh, Jed, that's great! Marie-Claude hasn't said anything to me about marriage. When did all this happen?"

Jed rearranges his solemn look into a broad smile, scratches the side of his beard. "Well, I ain't asked her."

"Oh. Have you talked about being together? Staying together, I mean?"

"Yep." He stares past me at something, blinks slowly, looks back at me, smiles again.

"I know it's serious with her," I tell him.

"Oh? Has she talked to you about us, then?"

"No—but I know Marie-Claude, just as she knows me. We're like sisters. I knew how she was feeling. In fact, I was going to ask her about it. Of course," I say with a smile, "she's said how lovely you are, and how she enjoys bed with you." I think my smile is a little shy.

Broad grin from Jed; his gaze wanders past me, then back again.

"Why don't you ask her, Jed?"

"That's just what I want to talk to you about, little lady." Jed lights up another cigarette and I pour him some more coffee. "I guess . . . I guess I don't want her to turn me down. I don't know whether she'd give up the way she lives now. She's so uppity and independent—like you, Ma'am."

217

I realize what it is. I reach out and touch his hand. "Listen... what's bothering you, is her *men*. Right?" Jed nods. "Mm. Listen, Marie-Claude's men are a sort of refuge from the world, a refuge from being hurt after Étienne died. He was her husband and they were very much in love. They only had a couple of years together; she nursed him through his last illness, cancer."

"She told me. Plus the fact that she'd never want to marry again."

"I don't believe that. That she wouldn't remarry, I mean. It's just that she's never fallen in love to remarry."

"We're from different worlds."

"Yes, you are. But then, so are Jan and I. Lots of people are; it doesn't affect the things you *really* feel about each other."

"You and Jan share your writing, though."

"Yes... but I know Marie-Claude. And if it's really there between you both... Do you want me to talk to her?"

Jed looks solemn for an instant, then there's another transition to a grin. "I can do my own talkin', thank you, Ma'am."

"I'm sure you can." We both smile soppily at each other. "Jed, if you love her, don't let go. Us ladies like that. I know for a fact that she'd like little ones."

"I don't want her goin' home and fuckin' with those other men!" Jed bursts out.

"So that's it. Have you told her that?"

"No."

"Well, you better had, and tell her that you love her. If you don't tell her, she won't know, will she? Not for sure, she won't. Why don't you take her back to Texas for a while, and then go and stay with her for a while. Get used to each other's worlds."

"You think she'd like Texas?"

"Jed, she loves you. She will. I know Marie-Claude. And besides, she's my best friend, and you're Jan's best friend, it's like we'd all be family."

"We would be, wouldn't we, little darlin'?"

"Sure would, Jed." I giggle, but then it's my turn to look solemn. "Oh, I wish it were that simple for Jan and me. He may never be willing to leave Melissa, because of Andy. He may never be able to marry me, because of that."

"That would just about break you in two, wouldn't it, little lady?" With his head on one side, Jed looks past me, but I'm

218

concentrating on my feelings for Jan, not on Jed's wandering gaze.

"I've never loved anyone like I love Jan. It frightens me sometimes. I don't mind not being married because I'm not trying to trap him. But I do want us to be together."

"Jan would never let you go, little lady. I know Jan just like you know Marie-Claude, and he's never been this way with a woman before."

I smile at this. "It would be nice, Marie-Claude and me becoming Texans."

"Now ya talkin' Ma'am!" Huge laugh from Jed.

"I think, Jed, that if you ask her, you'll find she'll say yes."

"Jesus fuckin' Christ. I surely hope so. I want *her*. Jan and I would be some kinda stupid, dumb assholes not to want to love and look after your two little ladies."

"Jed, about her men: she's French; such relationships are purely a matter of convenience, nothing else. They mean no more to her than that. There wouldn't be any second thoughts about giving them up. When you're going *to* something, you're not giving anything up, anyway."

"That's a mighty purdy way with words, Ma'am."

"Sure is."

I turn on hearing Jan's deep voice behind me. He's standing in the doorway, leaning on the door frame.

"How long have you been standing there?" I put my hand to my mouth as I realize he's what Jed was looking at. Jan comes over and sits next to me, squeezes me, kisses me. He must have heard all our conversation!

"I'm thinkin' I'd better jus' be gettin' along and proposin' to my little darlin', then." Jed stands up, leans over and kisses me, winks at Jan, leaves. Jan pulls me onto his lap.

"Looks like there's gonna be a weddin'." He grins.

"Yes . . . I wish it could be ours." Solange delaMer Axelsson—how nice!

"It will be."

"Will it?"

"Are you all right today?"

"Yes—why?"

"You cried so much yesterday."

"Yes." When I started my period. "I'm sorry . . ."

"We'll just have to try harder." Cheerful, sexy grin.

"Oh, will we!"

"Yep," Jan says as he picks me up. "Oh, yeah, and by the way . . . perhaps you'd better call that typewriter guy. . . ."

Who cares that I've got a period? We go and try harder. Not the best time, perhaps, but you never know. . . .

* * *

Candlelight. Perfumed candles; musk and patchouli.

Marie-Claude and I wearing strapless, clingy silk dresses. Me in pale pink, Marie-Claude in baby blue. Our ears full of gold filigree hoops and diamond studs. Me with my baby sun-angel around my neck. Marie-Claude with a gold necklace Jed bought for her. Isn't it us?—two beautiful French *filles!*

The whole atmosphere of the evening feels exquisitely, deliciously sexy.

I smile at Marie-Claude. We're both watching Jan and Jed enthusiastically eating the superb meal we've prepared for them. Jan asked for steaks with Bearnaise sauce, so that's what we're having.

"I tell you somethin', Ma'am," Jed smiles at me, waving his knife in one hand and picking up his glass of Médoc with the other, "this sure does beat barbecue sauce."

"I should hope so, Jed."

"D'you think you two little darlin's could be cookin' up some of this delicious fixin's when we give our Come And Meet Our Womenfolk barbecue back home?"

Jan's smiling at me as he sips his Médoc. Marie-Claude's looking a bit mystified as she stares adoringly at Jed.

"And how much of this, um, *delicious* fixin's are we supposed to make?" Me. Innocently. "I mean, how many people will be at this barbecue to meet your *womenfolk?*"

"Whaddya reckon, Jan?" He glances speculatively at Jan, who bursts out laughing. "Won't be too big. Mayhaps a couple of hundred."

"Sounds 'bout right to me," Jan agrees.

"Oo là là," says Marie-Claude.

"Jed, I really think you'd better stick to barbecue sauce. Bearnaise sauce for two hundred Texans, the mind boggles."

"I'm sure you two little ladies could make this delicious, outa-this-world fixin's in sufficient quantity. Jus' a matter of boostin' up the scale of production a mite, ain't it? I'm tellin' ya, Jan boy, these two pretty little Frenchy womenfolk of ours are sure gonna stand the folks back home on their heads."

"My sentiments exactly, Jed," Jan says, starting to laugh again.

"We are, are we?" I still have a straight face. (He really *was* serious about the sauce.)

"Can't go wrong. What with all ya Frenchy cookin' *and* ya bouncy titties, you've got it made, little darlin's."

"We've sure gotten ourselves some classy-ass, Jed," Jan chimes in.

"Whoo-whee! The ole Triple-J ain't gonna be the same again with you two little darlin's around the place."

"It has lots of bulls?" asks Marie-Claude. "The farm, there is lots of bulls and cows for the cowboys?" Jan and Jed fall about, laughing. Marie-Claude looks slightly taken aback, but after all, she never was a country girl. "You do not have cows and bulls for the cowboys? To round up on the prairies?"

Jan and Jed are still helplessly laughing. *"Ignore* them, Marie-Claude," I tell her.

"Whoo-whee! If that ain't the cutest thing I've heard all day!" Jed manages to say.

"It is?" Marie-Claude's still puzzled. "I thought you had cows on your farm? The cowboys milk them?"

"We eat 'em, darlin'!" Jed reaches out and strokes Marie-Claude's arm, her throat, one of her bouncy little titties. Jan's still laughing; he slices off another huge slab of steak.

"It's a *ranch,* darlin'," Jed "Bullhead" Brackett painstakingly explains.

"Is same," Marie-Claude says with finality. *"Rahnsh."*

"D'ya hear that? Ain't that the cutest?" Jed laughs. *"Rahnsh*—shit, I *love* it! I can't wait to take these two home."

"What is wrong with *ranch?"* I say in my best British accent.

"Ranch—ain't that class?" Jan says.

"Well, I'm dying to see the *rahnch,* cows and all," I tell him with a straight face, teasing.

"We go to get Chou-chou first," Marie-Claude insists.

"Sure thing, little darlin', we'll go and collect ya little old pooch for ya. Then ya can get yaself married to me in Dallas with nothin' to fret ya mind over."

I'm quite amazed that Marie-Claude has fallen in love like this, and it *is* love; it radiates from her and warms me with an empathetic glow. I'm wondering what she'll make of Jan, Jed, and Joel's Triple-J. I feel an instant's sadness, even a jealous twinge, because she can go there *now,* and I have to wait until Jan has everything settled.

Jan pours wine from a fresh bottle, winks at me blithely.

"I'm assumin' you two little ladies know how to sit a

221

saddle?" Jed asks. "Whoo-whee! I can't wait to see you two on horseback with ya titties bouncin' all over the fuckin' place."

"You two!" I glare at them in mock indignation. "You really are a pair of chauvinistic cowboy motherfuckers!"

"Aw, shit," Jan laughs, "we've been found out, Jedediah, ole buddy." He reaches out and, taking me by surprise, caresses one of my boobs. *"Some* bouncy titty!" I punch him.

"Don't you mean *lungs?* Isn't that the accepted Texas term?"

"Lungs?" Jed scoffs.

Jan points at me and grins. "Jed, ole buddy, little Ms. Bouncy-Titties here has read *Semi-Tough,* and that's the nearest she's been to Texas so far. Mayhaps apart from eatin' the occasional steak—some good red Texas meat."

I suddenly reach out and in retaliation grab a handful of Jan—a very special handful, which begins to become hard. "You've got a great piece of Texas meat yourself, cowboy!"

"Beautiful bitch!" And we're all laughing.

Joviality and frivolity continue throughout the dinner. Marie-Claude and I have made *pêche flambé* for dessert. Jan and Jed devour it hungrily. I thought they'd like it, so I made extra; they devour the second helping even more greedily.

"An important point has just occurred to me, Jan ole buddy," Jed says seriously.

"Important point? What's ya *important point,* Jed?"

"Football season's 'bout due." They simultaneously acquire a manic look in their eyes. "We've gotta be takin' our little darlin's to see the cowboys play." Gleeful grins from them both.

"Your cowboys, they play football too?" Marie-Claude asks, even more bewildered.

Jed eventually manages to suppress his laughter long enough to be able to pull Marie-Claude onto his lap. "The *Dallas* Cowboys, little darlin'. They're a football team."

"It's just American football, Marie-Claude," I say innocently. "It's not proper rugby, just the American version." I gradually realize that the two men have become quiet.

Jan deliberately finishes his glass of wine and places the empty glass on the table, keeping his fingers on the stem and jiggling it back and forth.

"Jan, ole buddy . . ."

"Yes, Jed, ole buddy?" Teasing glint in Jan's eyes, dry irony in his tone.

222

"Now, I know that little Ms. Bouncy-Titties is your own special little darlin' an' all."

"Sure is, Jed."

"And I know she has a way with words."

"Sure has, Jed."

"Probably got herself A's in penmanship, too."

"Could be right there too, Jed."

"And I know she's one of these all-fired-up-an-liberated little ladies the world has been thrustin' on us."

"*That* sure is true, Jed."

"And you know I'd never put a lady down, except mayhaps your Ma-in-Law, Charlene Cantrell, but then that Baptist blue-ball bitch ain't no lady."

"Exactly my thoughts, Jed."

"But takin' all that into account ... d'you think I heard it say what I *think* I heard it say?"

"I *think* you did, Jed."

They both have a sardonic smile in their eyes.

"*It*" I say. "What's this *it?*" I glance from Jan to Jed. Both are looking incredibly handsome tonight, with their shirts unbuttoned down the front. Jed's chest hair is darker and slightly thicker than Jan's.

I realize, of course, that I've let myself in for a lot of teasing, and they're not about to let me escape any of it. Texas cowboy teasing, laid on thick and with a heavy hand.

"Not *proper* football, huh?" Jed says. "Sumbitch!"

"Sumbitch"—I translate for Marie-Claude—"that's the same as son of a bitch."

Jan and Jed burst out laughing uproariously again. Marie-Claude squeaks and escapes from Jed's lap.

I stand up. "Shall we go into the lounge and have some brandy?" I ask the still-laughing men, with just the right degree of affront. "Really! Come on, Marie-Claude."

Marie-Claude and I walk towards the door.

"Ow!" That's me, being scooped up by Jan-Toby Axelsson. "You bastard!" Me, trying to escape as my arms are held tightly. "That *hurt!*"

"That was an intercept, Ma'am. An *unproper*, America one."

"It was?"

"Sure was, Ma'am. I played myself a lot of football at school and college." Lopsided grin. "Now we're gonna stay right here where we are, until a certain little lady explains that profoundly disturbin', not to mention a mite insultin', statement of hers."

"Let me *go!*"

"No ways, Ma'am."

"*Let me go!!*" If he does, I'll kill him.

"Ain't you heard a word I said?"

A squeal reminds me of Marie-Claude. I turn my head to see her being carried from the room.

"Jan . . ." We're kissing and laughing and cuddling.

"You wanna fuck?" he whispers.

"Don't you dare!" I hit him.

At last he puts me down, only to pull me into his arms. Still laughing, he takes me into the lounge, where Marie-Claude is getting Jed a brandy, while he lights one of his huge cigars. I get Jan a brandy too, while he helps himself to one of Jed's cigars. I hand him the glass with a sugary smile, then sit with Marie-Claude on the other sofa: Us against Them.

"Did little Ms. Bouncy-Titties explain that fearful derogatory statement of hers, Jan?" Jed asks with a grin.

"She did not, Jed. Just beat up on me, that's all."

"I'll get us a brandy, Marie-Claude," I say, standing up and pointedly ignoring them.

As I pick up the decanter, Jed asks with a horrified look, "You ain't gonna drink that, are you, Ma'am?"

"Of course. Why not?"

"A good brandy is completely wasted on a woman, that's why not. That's what I always say. Ain't that right, Jan-Toby?"

"Sure is, Jedediah."

Of course, I realize that Jed Brackett is joking, but also that not far beneath all this teasing he really *means* it.

"Why don't you drink some of that sweet, sticky stuff you ladies like so much?" Jed and Jan laugh.

I pour *large* portions of brandy for Marie-Claude and myself, smile sweetly again at our male chauvinist Texas cowboy menfolk. I happen to know Marie-Claude would have much preferred a Grand Marnier or a Cointreau, just as I would, but we smile sweetly at each other as we sit demurely and sip the brandy. She's adamantly determined not to let these Texas cowboys of ours have any more of a winning teasing hand than they have already.

"You won't have much trainin' to do, Jan, ole buddy—at least she knows how to choose a good brandy."

"Even chose a good wine."

"That she did, Jan. Probably knows all them Frenchy wines."

"I sure hope so, Jed."

224

"Bastard pricks!" Me, indignantly.

"*Cochons chauvinistes!*" Marie-Claude, with even more indignation.

We sip and giggle and keep our eyes on the two of them, waiting for another onslaught of teasing.

"We're gonna have to watch them with that Frenchy talk, Jan. Who knows what they're gonna be plannin' up against us if we can't understand 'em?"

"Sound point, Jed." They laugh cozily, companionably.

"I suppose you'd never think of learning French?" I ask with a sweet, sweet smile.

"We sure will," Jan says, "when you two learn Texan."

I look evenly at both of them. They continue to laugh. "You know the things they put on number plates for each state?" I continue. "Like, Hawaii has 'Aloha State.' Arkansas has 'Land of Opportunity.' "

"Yeah, and Idaho has 'Famous Potatoes,' " Jed says, with a roll of his eyes.

"Yes. Well, Texas has 'Lone Star State,' but I think it should be something else."

"Ya thought of an improvement?" Jan asks with a grin.

"Yes, I have. I mean, I saw something about Texas a while ago now. About a barbecue party. They had armadillo races and chili pepper eating contests and beer can rolling contests —even a chicken-imitating contest. *'Des grands enfants,'* as we French say—but *worse*. So . . . you know what I think Texas plates should say? They ought to say, 'Kindergarten State,' that's what."

I watch Jan and Jed stare at each other through their state of shock. I'm enjoying teasing *them* for a change, but I have a horrible feeling I'm going to get beaten up on at any moment.

Marie-Claude is still giggling uncontrollably. Jan looks at me through narrowed eyes.

"Are you goin' to thump little Ms. Bouncy-Titties or shall I?" Jed asks Jan belligerently. He comes over to me but takes hold of Marie-Claude, lifts her bodily, and removes her to the other sofa, where she snuggles up to him; Jan, meanwhile, joins me and pulls me onto his lap.

"So?" he says.

"So—what?" I look innocently up at him.

"That's two derogatory statements you've made, Ma'am. Not to mention derisive, to boot." He gives me a teasing grin. I take a sip of my brandy before answering.

"I don't recall making any *derisive* statement," I say with a smile of sweet innocence.

225

"Is that a fact? Well, unless you're wantin' Jed and me to beat up on you. I'm reckonin' you'd better just explain yourself. And quick too, Lady."

"I had, huh?"

"Sure had better, Ma'am," Jed says, very politely. "Ole Jan an' me don't wanna get tough."

"You don't?"

"Sure don't, Ma'am," agrees Jan-Toby Axelsson.

I unbutton Jan's last two shirt buttons, slip my arms around him. "I *love* it when you get tough!" I kiss his chest, then I look from Jan to Jed. Both have teasing, self-satisfied smiles on their furry faces. "American football was based on Rugby, wasn't it?" I ask sweetly.

I look for some sign of agreement but see none. The smiles are a trifle more laden with irony, if possible. "Except," I continue, "you Americans couldn't have been very good at it. You had to change it to your own stupid dumb rules."

The same indulgent smiles are still on their handsome faces. Oh, well, if they can tease, so can I. "I mean, well, there's dozens of men on a team," I press on boldly. "You change them every few minutes. Of course, in *proper* rugby you have fifteen men and *one* reserve in case someone gets injured. *And* they don't wear all that dumb shoulder guard stuff, those helmets. What's more, in rugby you can only pass *backwards*, not forwards. Forward passing would make the game far too *easy*. And not only do you have forward passing but you use a smaller ball that's easier to hold, too. *And* it's continuous play in rugby, no standing around discussing what to do next. Mind you, your guys do wear those sexy tight pants—all that great ass!"

Marie-Claude is giggling and clapping her hands in agreement. The indulgent, tolerant smiles have subtly changed: The men's faces are still smiling, but barely.

"I mean," I continue, again taking my life in my hands, fully expecting to be jumped on at any moment, "you don't even have a *scrum*, do you?" I pull boldly at Jan's beard. "Um . . . you do know what a scrum is, don't you, cowboy?" I dissolve into fits of giggles.

I think that's finally done it. Yes, that's done it. I'm suddenly on the floor with Jan on top of me, pinning my hands above my head. I lie still: who wants to struggle? He sits up, straddles me, sits back, and supports himself on his heels.

"She sure told us about football, Jed." Jan winks at his friend.

"She sure did, Jan."

"I'm *right!*" I insist.

"Is that so?" Jan leans forward and kisses me tenderly.

"How come you know so much about all of this, little Miss?" Jed asks me.

"Marie-Claude and I are very fond of rugby—real rugby."

"*Mais oui, c'est vrai, ça,*" Marie-Claude agrees between giggles.

"Is that so?"

"*Véritablement!*" Giggle. "*Zhed!*" She hits Jed's shoulder as he tries to get into her panties.

"Jan! Let me up"

Laughing, he helps me to my feet, and we go over and sit next to Jed and Marie-Claude.

"So, you two little ladies—you know all about rugby, huh?" Jed asks. Marie-Claude and I look at each other: I know we're both wondering how we can tease them some more.

"*Mais oui.* Jean-Claude, 'e play for France."

"Who's that?" Jan asks.

"Marie-Claude's younger brother. He's an International."

Slight disbelief has given way to the beginnings of respect. One up for us! Female classy-ass holds its own!

"That's Rugby Union," I say. "Not the same as Rugby League, of course." I can't resist adding, with a grin, "I don't suppose you cowboys from the Kindergarten State would know about that, though."

"You're gonna get your ass spanked, lady!"

I cuddle and giggle. "Promises, promises . . ."

"Stop all this huggin' and stuff," Jed commands. "We've a mite serious conversation goin' on here."

"Sure do, Jedediah," I say in the deepest, Americanest voice I can muster.

"You little ladies ain't puttin us on, now?" Earnest Jed.

"Would we do that?" Un-earnest Solange. "It's *true*, you know," I tell them. "Jean-Claude plays for France. He's a forward."

"*Mais oui,* Zhed, *mon chéri.* We do not kid you."

"We've jus' gotta take 'em to see the Cowboys play, Jan, ole buddy," Jed continues.

"Show 'em some *real* football, Jed."

"Real football!" Me, opening my big mouth again. "Listen, cowboys—we'll take you to see Jean-Claude play, *then* you'll see some *real* football."

"Are you going to thump little Ms. Bouncy-Titties or am I?"

227

"Think I'll just fuck her ass off, Jed, works just as well."

"Sure does," I giggle.

"Me too, Zhed, *mon cher*," says Marie-Claude, rubbing her hands up and down on him.

I think rugby and football are forgotten. There's an awful lot of cuddling and kissing going on.

"I think we're gonna have to retire soon, little darlin'," Jed says. "Unless we're gonna make a foursome out of it, that is. Seein' as we're family."

I see a glint in their eyes, and they're fingering their mustaches in unison, stroking the little patches of beard just below their lower lips.

"Perverts!" I give Jan's neck a lick, which makes him laugh.

"Aw, shit, they found out, Jan," Jed laughs.

"I forgot you two like to share. Is that what you've got in mind?" I feel a touch of the eager creamies. . . . "Well, if you two think you're sharing *us*, you can just think again, cowboys."

"Ma'am!" Jed looks affronted, but then smiles. "We'd never *swap*. Just . . . all together, like." Leer from Jed 'Bullhead' Brackett.

"All *together!* Oh—well, thanks for letting us know."

"Sure thing, Ma'am," Jed winks, looking sidelong at Jan.

"Ain't that the truth!" Jan winks, looking sidelong at Jed.

All Marie-Claude and I can do is to look at each other and giggle.

"It's not the sharing that worries me," I say cheekily. "It's Jed's predilection for Golden Rain afterwards." Jan laughs.

"What's she talkin' about?" Jed asks Jan, puzzled.

"*Pissin'*, Jed. *Pissin'*."

"Whoo-wee!"

"So you two cowboys think you're turning this pleasant evening into an orgy, do you?"

"Beats jerkin'—beggin' ya pardon, Ma'am," Jed says.

"*Qu'est-ce que c'est, le* zhairking?" asks Marie-Claude.

Jan and Jed stop laughing, look at Marie-Claude. "What was that she said?" Jed asks me.

"*Qu'est-ce que c'est, le* zhairking?" I repeat very precisely.

"Cute, ain't ya, Ma'am?" Jan comments.

"*Zhair*-king!" Jed laughs. "If that ain't the fuckin' cutest thing I've heard since . . . since she last said somethin' fuckin' cute!"

"What is it, the *zhair*-king?" Marie-Claude asks earnestly, pulling at Jed's beard in exasperation. "Solange?"

"Tirer son coup."

"O*o là là!*" she giggles.

"What's that mean?" Jed asks.

"Tirer son coup? Well, quite literally, it's 'firing one's shot.' But you could also say," I giggle, *"polir le chinoiserie*—literally, 'polishing the *chinoiserie.'* "

"The *what?*"

"You know, *chinoiserie*—Chinese antiquities. Something special you'd polish carefully, with a lot of love."

Jan and Jed continue to explore, with great interest, these unexpected avenues of French culture. They think the French very funny. But then, Marie-Claude and I think *they*—Texans, that is—are very funny.

"Ma'am," Jan says, placing my hand over his hard cock, "you can polish my *chinoiserie* any time."

"Jee-zus! We gotta take these two little darlin's home!" Jed winks at Jan.

"Will be nice," Marie-Claude smiles. "To Dahl-lahs."

Our two menfolk stare, teasingly, at Marie-Claude. "Where we goin'?" Jed asks her with a grin.

"To Dahl-lahs," says Marie-Claude.

"Dahl-lahs?" Jed laughs. "Shit!"

"Dahl-lahs," Marie-Claude reiterates, immune to their teasing, "in Tex-ahs."

"Dar*lin'*," exclaims Jed Brackett, "I think I'll just fuck your little ass off right here and *now*."

Seems the evening *is* turning into an orgy. Before we know where we are, Jed and Jan *do* have our dresses and panties off. And before we know where *they* are—they're inside us. . . . I think it takes all of three minutes before we have what can only be called the Amazing Quadruple Come.

And a little later, we're still here. Me lying in Jan's arms; Marie-Claude lying in Jed's arms; the four of us, all lying naked and glorious next to each other on the carpet.

"I'm sure glad we're family, Jedediah."

"Was jus' thinkin' the same thing myself, Jan-Toby."

"You two sound insufferably pleased with yourselves." Me feeling just as insufferably pleased.

Jan and Jed laugh. Jan kisses me. "Ain't that the fuckin' truth!"

13

I finish Xeroxing all Jan's poetry, and put it in a large looseleaf folder. I label it JAN, and put it away with the folders of my own work.

I once lost a manuscript, my second Pandora one. We were burgled (Rand and I); the thief took some jewelry, the TV and the stereo, our two typewriters and my manuscript. He left Rand's manuscript, though. That upset Rand. He kept on wondering what was wrong with it.

Jan's L.A. concert is tonight. He's with Joel and the band, doing their sound checks. He wouldn't let me come with him, said I had to stay home and rest. I think I frightened him a little this morning.

I awoke with a pain in my right side. I went and got myself some orange juice and a couple of codeine tablets.

"What are you taking?" Jan's question made me jump—I thought he was still asleep. I told him. "Why?" He rubbed his beard and ran his fingers through his hair, pushing it out of his eyes.

"It's for my *mittelschmerz*."

"Your what?" Jan sat up and took the tablets from my hand, inspecting them. "What the fuck's that? It sounds like a German airplane."

"My *mittelschmerz*." I reached for the pills, but he closed his fist around them. "It means 'middle pain.' It *is* German—there's no English equivalent that I know of."

"You hurt in the middle?" He gently touched my tummy. "It's not your appendix, is it?" A look of alarm in his eyes.

"No. It means the middle of the monthly cycle. Not the same as menstrual cramps—it's when I ovulate, actually. On the right side—not on the left, though—I get this lousy pain until all the jellylike guk comes away."

"*What?*" Total incredulity.

"Sorry to be so clinical. I just take a couple of pills and go to bed until it's all over. It's all right, it's always like this." I popped my pills and lay down.

Jan leaned over me. "Darlin', pain isn't *all right*. There's somethin' *wrong*. Have you seen a doctor? I've never even heard of the thing before."

I explained I'd seen several, and they'd all said nothing could be done—apart from a hysterectomy, of course, which seemed rather drastic. "It's the same thing with menstrual cramps, I still get them sometimes. But there's a good remedy for them." I grinned at him. "A few orgasms relaxes them marvelously."

"You're seein' my doctor, right away," Jan said seriously.

"No, Jan. I mean . . ."

We argued. He rang Roy. So I'm going for a complete checkup tomorrow.

I go and sit in the hot tub and daydream. The pain's nearly gone, just a vague ache in my side. I like the hot tub. Jan got it for me. You've *gotta* have a Jacuzzi in a hot tub if you're living in California, he said; besides, we can do all kinds of sexy things in it. He was right about that.

I smile to myself, thinking of the four of us—Jan and me, Marie-Claude and Jed—in the hot tub the morning after our little dinner party. I thought I'd have been shy, but I wasn't. It just seemed so nice, so loving and natural, all of us together. We laughed, smoked pot, and fucked in the hot tub.

Today's Jan's last concert. In two weeks he'll be leaving for Texas. I can't believe that everything's getting straightened out; that we'll be together properly at last, not secretly anymore. We were talking about it last night. I guess I won't feel *totally* settled until Jan has everything totally settled.

I still miss Marie-Claude and Jed. I even miss the Texan teasing. They've been gone a week now; they're returning from France to Texas tomorrow. I still can't believe how Marie-Claude is totally in love with her "Zhed." She's rung me up every day. She told me she's written to all her men, thanked them for their friendship and their love. And yet she always seemed so happy with her relationships, not wanting to get involved any more than that. I guess she just needed her special person. I always suspected she really did.

Marie-Claude wants to wait until Jan gets his divorce, so that the four of us can get married together, at the ranch. Not a religious wedding, but a simple ceremony, promising to love and cherish, understand and commit ourselves to each other. All four of us really want it.

I hear a meow. There beside the tub is Gulley, my fat cat, telling me it's time I stopped lazing and gave him his dinner.

* * *

I sit on the sofa and write my letter to Lars and Kris, now and then looking at Jan as he writes. I love to watch him.

"I can't get this fuckin' verse right!" he expostulates, swinging around to look at me. He's been irritable all day; I think it's the situation with Melissa and Andy. He was talking to them both on the phone today. He's soon going to be in the thick of handling it, and he knows it's going to be a fight to the death over Andy. I feel so helpless, so inadequate because there's nothing I can do to help. I think of Johnny and Amy and how they lost little Johnno.

"Do you want to go there earlier, to Texas?" I go and sit on his lap, caress his face.

"I dunno. I . . . I can't, anyway, because of that special we're recording next week." He still looks irritated, and I don't know how to help him when he's in this mood. "I wanna go to bed."

. . . I lie holding him in my arms. "The concert was so good last night, Jan." I feel him smile. "You must be pleased, having all that touring over."

"I'm pleased because I'm here with you. *That* makes me happy. Hey, you've got to come with me while we're workin' on the album. I'd like that. Are you sure the doctor told you everything was all right? You're not handin' me down no fuckin' owlshit?"

"I wouldn't." I wouldn't. "Of course, he doesn't have all the results of the tests yet, but he's sure I'm all right."

"All that fuckin' pain *can't* be all right."

"It's the curse old Nobodaddy handed down to Eve," I grin, and he hugs me closer. "Didn't you know that old Nobodaddy was a male chauvinist?"

"I believe I read that somewhere."

We're kissing and fondling. We love just cuddling. I don't think people do it enough.

"Mmm . . ." I'm feeling hot and excited. Eager and dreamy. Creamy and flushed. I think I'm feeling everything that Jan-Toby Axelsson always makes me feel.

The phone rings. "What the fuck?" Jan picks it up, barks "Hello!" into it. "Nisselill!" Broad grin. "It's Nils." Jan rolls off me completely, sits up, and talks to his brother in Swedish. After a while, he says to me, "Nils wants to come for a few days, with Jimmy-Joe Freedman. Can we put 'em up?"

232

"Of course."

"Come *on* then, Nisselill," Jan shouts down the phone. It's good to see him happy, out of the mood he's been getting himself into all day. He hangs up the phone, beckons. "Come here." He pulls me close. "I want to fuck your ass off."

"Mmm..." I snuggle up to him, and he pushes at me, turning me over, pulling my ass up, kissing it. *"Oh!"* It seems he means it, quite literally.

* * *

"Hello," I say as Nils Axelsson comes into the room in his wheelchair, with Jan and another man behind him. I'm nervous. I kiss Nils, and he smiles at me, his smile the same as Jan's. "It's nice to meet you at last," I tell him.

Nils looks like a slightly younger version of Jan, but perhaps with a touch of the hippie in him. He too has long hair, but much longer than Jan's and a beard and mustache. His eyes, though, are bright blue. Around his neck, a string of turquoise and, also, an animal fetish. In his right ear, a small silver hoop.

"Ma'am." (What else did I expect from a Texan?) "It sure is good to meet you too." His voice is as deep as Jan's, but it has a slightly graty, scratchy quality to it. I watch him as he wheels his chair into the middle of the room. I feel a lump in my throat for a moment. What if I say or do anything wrong?

"Ain't she beautiful, Nils?" Nils nods and I feel stupidly shy. "Darlin',"—Jan catches me around the waist—"meet Jimmy-Joe Freedman."

Jimmy-Joe Freedman looks me up and down, and smiles at Jan to convey his approval of me. *"De-*lah-ted, Ma'am." Jimmy-Joe owns the ranch next to the Triple-J. He's older than Jan, early fifties, I'd say. He's wearing one of those cream-colored suits with piping around the edges and has a string necktie, a bola. A Stetson and, of course, Texan boots complete the outfit. He and Jan share a private jet; he flew Nils here in it.

It's early afternoon. I get the three of them beer and sandwiches. Miriam comes in, and I introduce her, then go off to her office to sign some letters.

I always knew that Miriam was a wonder, but these past few days have proved it once again. When Jan knew Nils would be coming in a few days, we both worried about his getting around the house. Miriam had one of those little seats that go up and down the stairs installed.

"Jesus!" Miriam exclaims, giving me a hug. "He sure is *good*-looking, like Jan is."

233

"Mm."

"Bet he fucks *great*."

"Oh, Miriam!"

"How long's he *staying* for?"

"Three or four days."

"*Fantastic!*" Miriam giggles and claps her hands together. She must be in one of her "I like men today" moods. "*That's if he fancies me, of course.*"

*   *   *

The next afternoon, after four hours hard but enjoyable work, I go and find Jan and Nils by the pool. Jimmy-Joe Freedman is off doing some wheelin' and dealin' for himself and Jed. I settle on the chair Jan's stretched out on. They both look so much alike, sunning themselves in their faded cutoffs.

"*Hur mars ni?*" I ask them, immensely pleased with my Swedish. I receive broad grins from the Axelsson brothers.

"*Tack, bra,*" Nils replies. "And how d'you come to know Swedish, Ma'am? Jan been teachin' ya?"

"No . . ."

I sit and listen to Jan explaining in Swedish how I know their second language. They laugh, and I hear the name "Lars Larsson." I notice that Nils has the same Aztec eagle tattooed on the top of his left arm that Jan has. "You match," I comment.

They laugh as Jan explains: "When we was just teenagers, Jed introduced Nils to Rosie's. That's the raunchiest little whorehouse in Dallas. Well, afterwards to celebrate Nils's deflowering by the delectable Maggie, we went to Jim-Bob's bar to get pissed. Ricardo, who worked for Pa, was with us too, and he had tattoos all over him. We both like the eagle one, so along we goes, pissed out of our gourds, and Cesar, Ricardo's friend, he tattoos us."

"*Mor* cried," Nils joins in. "And *Far*—"

"*Far!*" Jan interrupts. "Jesus *fuck!* He bawled us out, but *good!* Never touched us, never laid a hand on us—he never did, not once, *ever*. But shit, we had chores all fuckin' month. Grounded, too. Jed got a going-over, too—*Far* knew he'd taken us to Rosie's, but he didn't mind that part of it, of course."

I smile in delight as I watch the Axelsson brothers hug each other and laugh together over shared times; I touch Jan's eagle and then Nils's; smile broadly at them.

234

"I hope you don't mind me layin' around like this?" Nils asks seriously.

"No, of course not." Then it dawns me that he means he has nothing covering his legs—or lack of legs; they're both amputated just above the knee. "It's quite all right, Nils. Really it is." I feel uncomfortable now it's been mentioned. I really don't want him to feel I'm being condescending or patronizing. "As long as you're comfortable and feel at home, Nils."

"Sure do, Ma'am," he grins. "It feels so calm and friendly here." He looks around the garden, approvingly. "Do you like livin' here in California? You'll *love* Texas."

"I'm sure I will. I can't wait for Jan to take me there." Jan gently caresses my face. "Actually, Nils, I don't get around all that much. I like staying right here, in my own little kingdom." I smile in anticipation of what I'm about to say. "But as for liking California, well, it's so very different from England or France. The way it seems to me, California, well . . . it's like living in a kind of cross between the *Gong Show* and the *Twilight Zone*."

Eventually, Nils points across the garden and asks, "What's that cabin thing over there?"

"It used to be a guest bungalow. It has a lounge and a bathroom and a bedroom. But I've never had a use for it. You know," I say to Jan, "you might want to use it for something. You need some space for yourself." Jan grins and hugs me. "It could be made into one big room, if you want."

"Could make it into a practice studio."

"Let's go and look," Nils says and gets himself into his chair. They both go off to investigate.

I sit thinking about how it must be for Nils. I wonder if he's lonely for a personal and loving relationship with someone. He was engaged when he went off to Vietnam, Jan told me. But when she heard about the accident and that his legs were gone, she went off and married someone else. Candy, she was called—Candy Cantrell, Melissa-Sue's older cousin. Maybe that's one reason why Melissa just ignores him. Candy wouldn't even come and see him when he returned. That's something I really can't understand. Nils is such a quiet, sincere kind of person. He's intelligent and educated, and he's handled the whole situation so amazingly well.

They return, talking excitedly about how easy it would be to knock down the wall between the lounge and the bedroom. Jan asks me for beer.

"Jesus, Lady!" he says as the froth cascades from the glass and over my hand. "You still ain't got no idea how to pour one. There's too much fuckin' head."

I look at him and can't resist the reply: "I thought you couldn't get enough of that."

"Fuckin' cute, ain't ya?" They're both laughing.

"Immensely."

Jan once more shows me how to pour beer, explaining in great detail how to hold the glass at the correct angle. Sends me in for another one so that I can practice. I think I'm being subtly bullied. And I think I'm loving it.

*　　*　　*

It's just past midnight, and I'm sitting up in bed doing some editing. I hear loud guffaws, laughter from downstairs. The bedroom windows are open and so are the French windows of the lounge below, where Jan and Nils are having their party. He has the band over and the roadies, Wes Carter (still doing the *Playboy* interview), Tom G. Watson (who brought me a couple of Hank Williams albums and patted my ass), and Roy too. Jimmy-Joe Freedman is there, of course, and two other Texans whose names sounded to me the same as Jimmy-Joe's.

A truck came and delivered cases and cases of Coors beer and food, so much that I don't believe even *that* crew can get through it all, but by the sounds of them, they're succeeding. Roy brought some dirty movies, too. And I overheard Jimmy-Joe suggesting that maybe they should invest in some kind-hearted hookers. I left them all to it.

I drink the last of my champagne and cuddle myself down to sleep. As I drift into a dream about Jan and me on the beach, I seem to hear high-pitched giggling. The dream—I'm sinking into it again, floating, letting it wash over me. Jan and me on the beach, and the white, white surf warmly washing over me—no, it's Jan's come . . .

What's that? A hand on my face. The bedside light's on. I open my eyes sleepily as the hand caresses my face.

"Jan . . ." I grip him around the neck and he pulls me up to him. But I'm still so sleepy. Laughter's still coming from downstairs. "What . . . ?"

"Everyone's fuckin'. There's a great *live* show goin' on down there."

Jan rolls himself into bed, pulls me onto him. His body's so strong and hard. I love falling asleep on him. I kiss his chest.

"I love you, Jan."

"I love you, baby. It's so good with you, darlin'. Have I mentioned that I want to marry you, Lady?"

"You do, huh, cowboy?"

"Sure do, Ma'am—you're the only lady I've ever asked."

I melt. "Mmm . . . You think I'd make a good wife, then?"

"Oh, Lady . . ."

"Why? Because I'm good in bed?"

"Aw, ya guessed." We laugh and cuddle. "Listen—you know what old William said:

> In a wife I would desire
> What in whores is always found—
> The lineaments of Gratified desire.

"So he did. And he should know. I mean, he thought very highly of sex."

"So do I. *Very* highly."

"Got something in common with my beloved William, then?"

"Yeah, Lady, I do—a lady we *love*."

I can't let such a boost to my ego go unrewarded. "What do you want?" I whisper into his neck, with a kiss. "Anything . . ."

"*Anything?*" Gentle laugh.

"Got yourself all horny watching Roy's dirty movies, huh?"

"Aw, ya guessed!"

"Sure did, cowboy."

"Actually"—he rolls us over slightly, so that he's half leaning over me, looking at me, caressing my face—"The first one, all chicks, was kinda sexy. But the second . . ." He shakes his head, with a shudder. "That's when I left. That sort of thing *don't* turn me on."

"What sort of thing?" I'm intrigued.

"Fucking' *snuff* movies."

"*What?*" The look of disgust on my face prompts him to cuddle me reassuringly. "You mean it was *real?*"

"Supposed to be."

My mouth's open. "But that—that's not sex. It's just plain *violence*." My thoughts seem fuzzy, perhaps because I'm still half asleep. "You mean they actually . . .?"

"Fucked her, then knifed her. Yeah."

"Oh!" It makes me feel physically sick. I really don't understand how men can get turned on by such violence. I suddenly recall Philippe, saying he'd like to hurt me; I bet he'd love snuff movies. Ugh!

I sit up. Jan sits up and looks at me. "Films like that, they fuckin' scare me," he says. "That people can . . . I mean, well, I guess it's probably faked. Wes says they've faked 'em good, even though they spread the tale that they're real. But all the same, he says there *are* real snuff movies around. And Roy says this one is real. His tastes are totally fuckin' bizarre, anyway. Shit, it fuckin' scares me. I mean, what if that one *was* real . . . !"

Jan's eyes are full of confusion and sadness. His face looks pale. I lie down again and pull him into my arms. He's trembling slightly. It really did upset him. I caress and kiss him. He loves me holding and touching him. He's so shy and quiet, so beautiful: Jan, the man in my life, my gentle, caring poet. So different from that laughing, sardonic, extrovert rock star people see from a distance. They think that's the real him. . . . But I know so much better.

I kiss the top of his head, but he's fallen asleep.

*　　*　　*

Jan's away all day. He and the band are recording a few numbers for a TV special they're guesting on.

Elena, who comes twice a week, has been helping me and Miriam clear up after the party, having told me all the latest about Raul's farm while we had coffee and some of the cake she brought with her. Nils hasn't yet put in an appearance; Miriam told me she spent most of the night with him. He left the party when Jan did, and she was waiting for him, asleep in his room.

I'm still typing when Nils eventually comes into the study. He looks at a few pages of Jan's poetry. He smiles at my poster of R2D2 and C3PO on the wall.

"Miriam told me how much you both enjoyed yourselves last night," I say cheekily.

"She's some *very* sexy lady," he says with great satisfaction.

"I reckon she is."

"I'm hungry." Before I can turn around, he's wheeled himself from the study.

A couple of hours later, I go out into the garden to get myself some sunshine. Nils is there, smoking a joint, reading Jan's latest *Atlantic Monthly*, and sunbathing. I'm aware of him scrutinizing my bikini-clad figure; for a second, I feel inanely shy. I calmly sit down next to him.

"You read a lot?"

"Jan's gotten me into it."

238

"You and Jan, you're very close, aren't you?"

"Yes, we are. He's just a year older than me. Axel's always been our big brother. Total straight arrow, Axel is—should have been a CPA." A smile. "Jan and I, we're always together. When I came back from Nam, well, Jan, he canceled his tour so he could be with me. That was a lot of years ago. He saw me through it all, and I gave him a rough time of it, too. I don't think I'd have made it if it hadn't been for Jan. Gettin' through all that shit I had to get through, gettin' to accept what had happened to me . . . Well . . ." He smiled that lovely Axelsson smile.

"I can't imagine you as an army captain," I say. "The short hair, I mean—I can see you handling responsibility." How can I comfort him, with all he's been through? I just hold his hand. "I guess it must have been very hard for you," I say, feeling supremely awkward. "I'm sure I couldn't confront anything like that happening to me."

He takes my hand between his two large ones. "Yeah, well . . . I couldn't either, as it turned out. I told the surgeon, if you can't save my legs, well, don't bother tryin' to save me."

We stare at each other. "But he did. Save *you.*"

"Yes. He did."

"And you're glad?"

"Yes. Very."

My eyes fill with tears, and I lean forward to kiss him gently. "I'm glad, too. It's always nice to make another friend. I mean, a *real* friend." Nils kisses the back of my hand, so gallantly I can't help smiling.

We look into each other's eyes understanding each other's silent feelings.

"I'm glad he's got you now," Nils finally says. "He's needed someone for a long time."

"I think *you* need someone, too, Nils." I put out my hand and caress his beard; he smiles.

"Yeah, well . . . It's difficult, for obvious reasons." He stares down at the legs he does have left, so brown against his short, faded cutoffs. His body, like Jan's, is beautiful, muscular. "Women don't fall for you when you've only got half your legs." He states it as a truism, without bitterness.

"You haven't got half a cock, though, have you?"

He looks at me, surprised, then bursts out laughing. "Oh, Jesus—I don't think it'd matter with you, would it?"

"Not the legs, no. But I'm not too sure about half a cock,

though." We're both laughing. "Have you tried walking with artificial legs? Can you get them to fit you?"

"I can't get on with the fuckers. I guess I should try some more. It *hurts*, so I give up. I guess I shouldn't. I could get back to flyin' the fuckin' plane again."

"You obviously like flying."

"*Love* it."

"You flew helicopters?"

"Yeah . . ." Grin. "You been up in one?"

I blush. Oh, hell. "I . . . um . . . Oh, God, it's *embarrassing!*"

"You're afraid of flying?"

"I'm afraid of *crashing!*" He laughs, and I continue, "It's true! People aren't afraid of *flying*—they're afraid of crashing." Nils shakes his head as he laughs. "I went up in a helicopter just once. A friend in Cannes has one. I was *petrified*. I mean, it's not the same as a plane, is it, and I hate *them*. I feel so stupid telling you this. Anyway, I started to panic. I was so *frightened*. I kept on screaming until Jules took it down."

Nils is laughing. "*I'll* take you up, little lady." He winks. "You can sit between me and Jan."

"Oh, no. Not even for you and Jan." I touch his tattoo, bat at his earring, making him laugh again.

"I don't believe that. You love Jan a great deal."

"Yes, but a lady could love *you* a lot, too."

"He told me so much about you when he was home. You both have so much in common. He's never had that before."

"It's extremely easy to love him."

"That's what he says about you."

We play a game of chess. Nils is *very* good. He beats me. Jan and I play a lot of chess; we're pretty evenly matched, but nowhere near Nils' standard. "It's just a natural part of my devious mind," he says. We play a game of *Go*, and of course he beats me—Jan always beats me at *Go*, too. Jan and I enjoy being Scrabble addicts, too: loser does whatever the winner wants.

It's a few hours later, and I'm working again, when Nils comes back into the study. "Can I stay?" he asks.

"Of course, love."

I see a tray on his lap, with plastic pieces on it—a model kit. "What have you got there?"

"It's for you. I'm making you a present."

"For me?" I get a little automatic thrill of delight.

"Yes, Miriam got it for me. I like making things." He wheels himself over and shows me the box.

"Oh, I love you," I say with a laugh. I go and hug him, kiss him.

He's making me a little model R2D2.

* * *

I take one last glance at myself in the mirror before hurrying from the bedroom.

"Now, listen!" I tell Gulley, "I've put your dinner out, and we'll be back later." He looks up at me indignantly.

Jan's been gone all afternoon, at Roy's for some business meetings. He rang me to say that Roy wants us to go out to dinner with someone; he told me to wear the white silk dress he likes so much, and to meet him at Roy's.

Roy meets me at his front door, leads me into one of his huge lounges, and pours me a dry martini. He disappears for about five minutes, and I sit thinking about the past few days. It feels lonely without Nils around: after so little time, he's already a close friend. He and Jimmy-Joe Freedman left for Texas yesterday, he said he was looking forward to showing me around the ranch, and I guess that'll be soon. Jan's leaving for Texas the day after tomorrow, to get everything ended and sorted out with Melissa-Sue, and he wants me to go with him, to stay with his parents and also, of course, at the Triple-J with Jed and Marie-Claude. I think I will. Marie-Claude told me she loves "Dahl-lahs," especially Nieman Marcus. She was even talking about babies. . . .

Roy pops his head around the door. "Listen, love, I'm just off to pick the guy up." I wonder why there's a huge, amused grin on his face. Before I can ask anything, he's gone. Where's Jan, I wonder?

I go into the hall, can't find a light switch. I begin to feel that I've wandered into one of those Spanish horror movies where it's all creaking doors and flickering shadows. There's a light showing dimly at the end of the hall where the stairs are. When I get there I stand quite still and gape. The light is coming from candelabras, all the way up the huge winding, ornate staircase.

I suddenly feel chilled with a ghostly fear, imagining the reverberating echoes of offbeat crimes. Not long ago, there were those sex murders, the "Movie Star Murders" the press called them, in Bel Air and Holmby Hills. Shit, this *is* Holmby Hills!

Candelabras? I stare at them, puzzled. What's Roy doing

with candelabras? I try to bring some rationality back to the situation. The candelabra remind me of something, but for the moment I can't place it. "Jan . . . ?" My voice is a whisper. *"Jan . . . ?"*

Standing at the bottom of the stairs, I still stare at the candelabras. I find myself expecting them to move. Move? How stupid! Then I recall that it's not stupid at all: I remember where candelabras did move—in Cocteau's *Beauty and the Beast.* The candelabras there were held by arms, and zombie figures beckoned la Belle on.

Suddenly something moves at the top of the stairs, in the deep shadows there.

"Oh!"

"Belle!"

"What?" I whisper. It was a deep, muffled voice, somehow sad and desperate.

"Belle!"

The candles flicker around me in the darkness. I'm aware of an indistinct form moving slowly into my line of vision.

"Belle!" the voice calls again.

I look at the form at the top of the stairs: a tall, well-built man in tight, tight trousers, black boots up to his knees, and a white silk shirt with wide, floppy sleeves. One hand holds a candelabra, the other beckons to me. My mouth is open; I can't move; I just stare at the strange face of the muscular form that stands there beckoning me. I'm looking into the animal face of la Bête.

"Oh . . . Oh . . ." I'm trembling. I watch ma Bête place the candelabra carefully on the floor and start slowly down the stairs towards me.

"Oh!" I say in a high-pitched squeak as I retreat a step downwards. "Oh!" I feel as if I'm going to faint.

La Bête has reached my step. He laughs—oh, that sardonic, gruff laugh! Grabs for me, picks me up in his arms. He's carrying me up the stairs, to a room lit only with candelabras. In the center of the room is a brass bed. I'm placed on it so gently. It's a waterbed. Why can't I say anything? I lie staring at La Bête as he stands handsomely, sensuously with his hands on his hips, his legs apart, staring down at me.

No longer fantasy. No longer dreams, unreality—this *is* reality, at long last. Ma Bête is going to ravish me.

He leans over and takes my left hand, presses it to his lips, then suddenly pulls it above me. I look along my outstretched arm and notice something white tied around the brass bedpost. Now he's tying it around my wrist—a white scarf. I feel totally and overwhelmingly excited. My body feels like it's going to melt away to nothing as ma Bête goes around the bed and ties my other wrist with another white silk scarf.

Good-bye, masturbatory fantasies! This is *real*. My eager creamies were never so eagerly creamy.

Leather-gloved hands at my breasts, gently fondling them, untying the bow holding up my strapless dress, pulling my dress from me. I'm laughing and *loving* it.

"Quiet!" orders the rough, resonant voice of ma Bête, and I obey so willingly....

My tiny lace-sided panties are peeled down my legs, a pillow is pushed beneath my bottom, and then my ankles are tied with white silk scarves to the other bedposts.

Ma Bête kneels between my legs and I see a bulge—a beautiful Bête bulge—beneath the black pants he's wearing. I close my eyes, but then the quick, abrupt noise of a zipper makes me open them again. I smile, slowly, as I'm confronted with a beautiful, familiar Bête cock.

A hand is placed at one side of my head; I stare into the face of ma Bête—close, so close. "Ah!" He thrusts himself into me. And on outstretched arms, hands either side of my head, ma Bête fucks me. I can't move, tied spreadeagled with silken scarves. What is this? I think it must be heaven. But I don't believe in heaven! No matter, I believe in this.

I close my eyes. I think I'm laughing. How could my dream have come so completely true? I'm aware of a coolness; ma Bête has left me. I open my eyes and I can't see him any longer.

My fantasy, ma Bête. Silk scarves. How beautiful of him to make them come true for me. His words echo in my mind: "I'm gonna do two things to you that no one's *ever* done to you."

Love is a lived-out fantasy....

But now I want Jan—my beautiful, gentle lover who's given me all this.

"Jan. Jan . . . I want *you*."

I hear a laugh to my right, behind the bed where I can't see.

"Close your eyes." Voice no longer muffled; just Jan's voice now.

I close my eyes. I feel a mouth on me: Jan's mouth on me, tasting me, kissing me, licking me—eating me.

"Jan . . ."

x

243

Naked now, he crawls up my body, flinging himself onto me, kissing me.

How many hours do we spend in loving? I don't know, I don't care. We're lost in a maze of fevered loving. I tie him with the silk scarves (he laughs hugely) and eat him.

"Untie me!" he orders, laughing, trying to raise himself.

"No."

"Solange!" He's still laughing.

"No!" I laugh, and bite the inside of his thighs, his cock—very gently, of course. His arms, his neck. Kisses and licks everywhere along his hard, tanned, muscular body.

I untie him and we collapse into a heap, laughing and kissing until we lie close in each others' arms: wet, sticky, sated. We doze for an hour or so until Jan wakes and tells me he's hungry. "Wait," he says, jumping out of bed and leaving me. A few minutes later he's back in the bedroom, pushing a trolley loaded with food.

"Had it all prepared. Everything you like best."

"Oh, Jan . . ."

We feast on cold fresh salmon poached in wine, with freshly-made mayonnaise and salad. There's one of those *huge* bottles of champagne—a jeroboam or a methuselah, I think. After we've greedily demolished the salmon, Jan pours champagne over me and licks me.

"Strawberries and cream," he announces, and begins spooning whipped cream onto me: on my nipples and at intervals down by body. He puts a strawberry onto each dollop of cream, then begins to eat it all. When he's finished all those strawberries, he puts more cream on my magic button of happiness and eats the cream and me until I'm coming.

Amidst cream, champagne, and come, we cuddle up and fall asleep again.

I return from the bathroom and smile at Jan's sleeping form on the bed. I feel so sticky: the flat of my stomach is sticky when I rub it. Champagne, licked-off cream, come.

The head mask of La Bête is mixed up with the pile of Jan's clothes on the floor. I wonder where he got it—it's such an exact copy. I remember that I couldn't find my Cocteau film the other evening; he must have borrowed it. Such a lover I have!

I caress the face of an empty mask and whisper, *"Où es tu,*

244

ma Bête?" But this time I know exactly where he is: I turn my head and look at Jan-Toby Axelsson, lying there with his head propped up on his hand, looking at me with a smile on his face.

"You liked that, huh?"

I can only stare, tears brimming in my eyes. Finally I manage to say, "Thank ... you ... It was ... beautiful."

"I *love* you, Solange."

The tears roll slowly down my cheeks. "I love you, too. . . ."

We're looking at each other, just looking at each other.

He suddenly grins his sunny bright Axelsson smile. "I don't mind dressin' up as your Bête—but *no way* do you get me dressin' up as your Frank N. Furter. Come here," he says, beckoning, "come here!" I go to him and he pulls me down, so that I'm lying along him. "I don't ever want anyone else fuckin' you." He grips my ass tightly.

I smile and kiss his chest.

"I *mean* it. If you ever fucked anyone else, I'd kill you."

"You don't have to worry about me fucking someone else." I mean it.

"You're the only woman who's ever made me feel *vulnerable.*"

"I'm not going to leave you. We're engaged, remember?"

"Beautiful bitch!"

It's still the middle of the night when we drive sleepily back to my house. We sleep in each other's arms until late morning.

I go and splash cold water on my face, scrub my teeth, give my hair a brush. My tender pussy is sore; there are slight bruises and love bites on my thighs and at the top of my arms where Jan held me so tightly. I really need a shower, I'm so sticky. And even my throat feels slightly bruised. Sore throat from deep throat. I feel so raw, so sore, so *used,* and so *perfect!*

I get myself some coffee. All is quiet. No, there's rock music coming from somewhere, from around the front of the house—the driveway. From Jan's car radio.

He's fiddling with something under the hood. Unnoticed, I stand and watch him; in his short, faded cutoffs he looks so golden and muscular like an erotic angel.

"Shit!" He throws a spanner down onto the driveway. Sees me, smiles, winks.

I throw myself into his arms and let myself be kissed over

and over again. He sinks to his knees, holds me tight around the waist, pushes my robe aside and buries his face in my pussy hair. "My beautiful sweet delight . . ."

I kiss the top of his head. He kisses my little pussy.

"You smell so good and I'm hungry," he said. "Make me an omelette thing."

"Yes, O lord and master."

He hugs me, looks up at me, and says, "I'm glad you realize that."

* * *

I awake and lie in a dreamy reverie. Perhaps I'm not really awake; perhaps it isn't morning. I try to move, but I can't: I'm held tightly in Jan's arms. I feel completely safe, inviolably secure—as long as he never lets go.

Today . . . Oh, God, we're going to Texas today. I'm suddenly wide awake and feeling very, very frightened because I know Melissa-Sue won't let go. She'll go on using Andy, and Jan will go on caving in; he doesn't have any new answers to that one.

Stop it, Solange! No negative thoughts, not today!

From downstairs, Miriam's high-pitched laugh floats up through the open window. She must be on the phone to someone.

Jan's arm grips me tightly. I look up at his face; he smiles sleepily. "Mornin', Ma'am." He kisses me; we doze and cuddle. We're always loving, like two warm and sleepy children, in the morning. Waking up together in the morning is such a loving experience.

It suddenly feels to me as though I *am* Pandora, with La Bête in his Chateau, the mists swirl around outside, enclosing the two lovers in safety, keeping the wicked world from touching them.

I kiss Jan's beautiful, sun-tanned body, decide to have myself some liquid protein for breakfast. I look up for a moment and see a contented smile on his face as he lies with arms outstretched: effete Bête!

My concentration is disturbed slightly by Miriam's shouting. "Jesus!" Jan says as his langorous servicing is interrupted.

"Ignore it," I whisper. I return to eating him. I've grown very fond of that thick blue vein that stands out; I kiss it.

"Jesus fuck!" A shout from Jan as he abruptly sits up, a split second after the bedroom door is flung open. Instant floppy cock in my mouth.

"You bastard!" screams a voice behind me.

I turn and see Melissa-Sue glaring at him from the doorway.

Oh my God!

Frozen tableau: Jan leaning up on his elbows. Me kneeling between his spread legs. Melissa-Sue, rigid. Miriam anguished behind her.

"I knew you were with this little whore!" Melissa screams in rage.

"I couldn't *stop her*," Miriam explains uselessly.

"Jesus Christ, Melissa, what the *fuck* d'you think you're playin' at? Jesus fuckin' *Christ!*" Jan's furious.

"Don't you take the Lord's name in vain!" she retorts with the invincible scorn of the self-righteous.

"What the fuck you *doin'* here, woman?"

I watch, numb and shocked, as Jan scrambles off the bed, strides furiously across the floor to the chair where he'd flung his jeans, and manages to continue looking angry while climbing into them. I observe it all, but I can't move.

"What are you *doin'* here?" Rage makes his voice indistinct. His fists are clenched.

"I knew—I just *knew*—that you were having an affair with that little slut!"

"Melissa . . . I . . ." Jan's rage quickly collapses into a pool of hopelessness. He wearily lifts his fist—still clenched—to his forehead. *"Jesus fuck!"*

"Stop that filthy blaspheming!"

"Melissa, I . . ."

"What do you *see* in that . . . that *whore?*" Melissa's face has now gone bright red. "She's not even as pretty as me. And she's *twelve years* older than me—she's *old!*"

Jan looks frustratedly at me. Why doesn't he *say* something? Miriam comes over to me, protectively kneels on the bed and puts an arm about me.

"That filthy, degrading act she was performing when I came in . . . !" Melissa shudders theatrically. "You filthy little whore!"

Oh shit, I'm going to cry. No, don't cry, Solange! *Whatever* you do, don't cry!

Jan grabs her shoulders, shakes her roughly. "Don't you dare call Solange that! I *love* her." At last, at long last! Jan coming to my rescue. Jan standing up to Melissa!

"Love her? That adulterous little bitch?" She shakes him off, pushes him away. *"I'm* your wife. It's *me* you should love. It's your duty, your *duty* to love me. Your *wife.* Not that little *whore* there."

247

"My *duty* is to Andy," Jan replies, suddenly serious, suddenly deadly calm. "Not to love somebody I've never loved." They stare at each other silently for the longest of pregnant pauses. "I've got to speak to you. I was coming today to speak to you." Jan's voice, when he finally speaks, is just about a whisper.

"I bet you were. About leaving *me* for that whoring slut!"

"Stop it, Melissa!" Jan shakes her again.

She ignores him, shouts at me again. "You're lower than one of those perverted faggots—doing one of those filthy, abominable acts *they* do!"

"Stop it, Melissa! I tell you . . ."

"I'm telling you now, Jan. I'm telling you—if you ever want to see your son again, you'll leave with me *now*, right now. And don't you think, if you ever saw that whore again, that I'd ever let you see Andy again. If you go with her, you'll never see him again. *Never!* Not when my Daddy has finished with you. No law-abiding Christian judge is going to let you visit a son and influence him into Satan's ways, doing those things you do. All those filthy little groupies on tour, don't think I don't know what they do, too, doing those disgusting things to you all. And her!"—she points scornfully at me— "A judge would only have to read the perverted, filthy pornography that slut writes, and he'd never let Andy be exposed to you ever again—and not to *her* filthy influence either!"

I sit there naked, paralyzed, not even trembling anymore.

Jan looks at me blankly, hopelessly. I can see that his eyes are swimming with tears. He's in an unbearable position, unavoidably trapped, and there's no obvious way out for him, except . . .

"This is it, Jan. If you *ever* want to see your son again, you come now. It's either that whore, that slut, or your own flesh and blood!"

Silence.

A frozen tableau: the four of us: figurines of ice.

"Now, Jan!"

The figurines split and crack, the ice shatters as Melissa turns and flaunts from the room.

Jan looks at me. Just stands and looks at me, opaquely.

"Solange . . . I'm sorry." His voice is a husky whisper. *"Melissa!"* A cry of wounded agony. He rushes after her.

Miriam, with an angular, brittle, exasperated gesture of her arms, runs to the bedroom door. *"Bastard!"* she shouts after him.

One little ice figurine remains unshattered: me. I hear the front door close, a car start up and drive away.

The little ice figurine doesn't crack or splinter; it just melts. I crumple into a little ball on the bed and cry and cry . . .

14

I'm sitting like a wrung-out dishcloth. Even now, four days later, I cannot accept what has happened. How can I ever compete with "his own flesh and blood?" I can compete with Melissa easily—but compete with his own little son?

Our whole affair was riddled with lies and illusions. Jan knew Melissa would never let him go; he knew there was no way in which he would handle it. I too knew that she would use her son, I knew it was a delusion, a triumph of hope over reality, to think anything else.

It's my own fault, I know that—it's because I was a dreamer, because I allowed myself to dream a dream I was dumb enough to get myself enmeshed in. And now I'm left feeling tragically incomplete, sitting in the middle of a dark, ferocious misery.

"Do you *want* me to *stay?*" Miriam startles me, coming into the study where I'm curled up on the chesterfield. "*Shall* I stay?" she repeats.

"No . . ." My eyes flood with tears. "No . . . You go. I just want to . . . to sit."

"You've been *sitting* for *four days!*"

"Just go, Miriam . . . *Please!*"

"Okay, baby." She comes and gives me a comforting hug, telling me that her friendship will always be here for me.

"Are there any of your pills, Miriam? In case I can't sleep."

"*Nembutals?*" I nod. "In my *desk,* baby."

"Thank you." We kiss and hug again, and Miriam leaves me.

I can't even write. Can't even edit anything. My precious writing rituals have been alienated from me. What *have* I done to myself?

Maybe a drink would help. I go and pour myself a whiskey—a large whiskey. Sit and drink it; it doesn't take long. It doesn't seem to have helped much, either. Perhaps a brandy would be better?

Why the fuck am I crying? The brandy has made me feel sorry for myself, that's why. Sorry and sad—and it's making the room move, too.

Actually, I feel quite warm now. I don't think it hurts so much, either. Hurting? Why was I hurting? "Jan!" I shout.

Why doesn't he answer me? It's late, that's why. Too late. Perhaps I should go to sleep. But I feel dizzy, not sleepy. A couple of Miriam's pills, they'll help me sleep. Maybe some music would help too. Jan's music, that is.

There, that's nice. Jan's voice—it sounds so good. Not loud enough, though. Full volume! Who says Jan-Toby Axelsson's walked out on me!

What was it . . . ? Oh, yes. Pills—to sleep. I wish the floor didn't move when I did.

Frantic, giggly search through the drawers in Miriam's room. One brown plastic bottle. Oh fuck, why won't the top come off? Oh yes . . . need a drink to take the pills with.

The lounge. Was I in the lounge? Oh dear, the music, it's coming from the study. Never mind, put some on here, too. There we are. Up loud. Oh, yes—the drink. Let's make a cocktail. Some Cointreau. Apricot brandy. A little crème de menthe. Oh, yes, and some crème de cacao too, I love that. And some Stil . . . Stillich . . . the vodka that Jan likes. There! A fantastic tumbler of cocktails. Cocktail de tumbler . . . What a lovely, weird, gucky color!

Take my drink upstairs. Oh dear, why are they going *down* when I want to go up? They're the wrong way. Nils left his machine. Wheeee! It's like a ski lift.

No music in the bedroom. The other music's nice, though.

This cocktail doesn't *taste* very nice. Must have mixed it wrong. Oh well, it's half gone. Oh yes, got to save some for the pills. The pills. There . . . put the glass down. Open the bottle—twist, turn, push. No, push, turn, twist. No. I know, smash it. Throw it at the wall. Oh, where's it gone? Oh . . .

"*Solange!* Jesus fucking *Kerist!*"

"Mmm . . . ?" Who's that swaying around over there? Miriam?

"Solange!"

"The bottle—couldn't open . . ." I'm falling. Bouncing up and down. "Waterbeds are lovely!"

250

"Jesus *Christ!* I was *halfway home* and thought of the fucking *pills* and that you might *take* them. Jesus! You're *pissed* out of your little *gourd!*"

"Hey . . ." I wave a finger at Miriam and giggle.

Why has the music stopped? Was there music? Was there Jan? It feels like a dark, dark cave. *The blind cave of eternal night.* Is *that* where I am? Is that where I'm going to stay?

Is that why I feel so tired? I think I'm falling asleep.

*   *   *

"Oh . . . !" I try to sit up, but quit halfway. "Oh . . . !" My head hurts.

"You're awake, are you?" Miriam's voice comes from somewhere distant.

"My head hurts. Oh . . . !"

"*Fuck* it, girl, you were *bombed* out of your *head!* Just how *much* did you *drink?* You *know* you don't *do* drink!"

"What . . . ?"

"Of *course* your head *hurts!* God *knows* how much *booze* you did!"

"I feel sick. Oh . . . I'm . . . Oh, Miriam . . ." I struggle to get up; Miriam helps me to the bathroom. "What's that— rain?" No, it's the shower; Miriam's pushing me under it. It's cold!

*   *   *

I've just finished talking to Marie-Claude. Miriam told her all about me getting drunk, and that I'm still feeling rather fragile. Marie-Claude's upset about what happened. So is Jed. I talked to him too. He was so gentle, so concerned. I hope it doesn't influence his friendship with Jan just because Marie-Claude is my best friend.

"I'm *staying* tonight," Miriam tells me flatly, bringing more coffee.

"Miriam, I can't possibly drink any more coffee. I'm peeing all the time. And I've had so much caffeine I'll *never* sleep tonight."

"Then we'll sit and *talk*. But I'm *staying*."

"Thank you, love." I smile at Miriam.

The buzzer goes. For a moment I have a wild, euphoric wave of expectancy flow over me, until I realize how stupid I am, and that if it were Jan he'd have used his key.

I'm aware of Roy standing in front of me. "I'm so sorry, Solange."

"Listen," I tell him, "I mean, there was always a chance that this would happen. I even thought it might. I should have realized . . ."

"It's not the way I want it," Roy says.

"What a coincidence! It's not the way I wanted it, either," I explain. "Have you . . . seen him?"

"No." I watch him light a cigar. "He went straight to Texas with Melissa. But I've talked to him on the phone."

"Oh?"

"He asked me to come over and see that you were all right."

"Oh, very *decent* of him, Roy!" I sneer. What exquisite consideration! "He could have talked to me *himself*."

"I don't think he was able to do that."

"You mean, he might get into trouble with Melissa? Of course, he couldn't risk that, could he?" I'm angry. But at least it feels a lot better than feeling sorry for myself.

"The Cantrells have got him by the short hairs now, and they're gonna make sure they pull." Roy looks cynical, but that's okay—it matches the way I'm feeling. "He's talked to me a lot about it. He's torn in two. It's made him incapable of thinking straight about this shit-awful situation. That's why he's not getting anywhere with it. Well, I'm flying down there tonight. Last night he was so drunk he couldn't talk. Jed did the talking."

"Roy, please just go."

"Where's his Gibson?"

"What's that?"

"His acoustic guitar."

"Oh. It's, um . . . oh, it's upstairs." Now I *know* it's really over.

"And . . . Oh, Jesus, darling, I hate this!" Roy hugs me to him. "And his folder of poetry. He's staying down in Texas for a while. The band are all joining him down there. They're going to work on their new album material there."

"Tell him to be happy, Roy." I don't even notice that he's left.

* * *

"Are you just going to *sit* there?" Miriam asks me angrily. "It's been *over* a *week* now. A *week*, Solange! The fucking bastard *isn't worth* it."

"Oh, Miriam, it's not his fault. I mean, he couldn't give his son up."

252

"*Bull . . . shit!*"

We're sitting out in the garden, sunning ourselves in bikinis. She hasn't left my side.

"It's not."

"*Yes* it *is.*" She swings herself around and sits up. "Now you just *listen* to me, girl. And listen good! No *way* does Mister Jan-Toby Axelsson take *any* bullshit, *any* blackmailing by that *blue-ball* bitch of a wife. No *way* is Mister Jan-Toby Axelsson, *su—per—star,* going to *allow* himself to be *caught* in a relationship with someone he doesn't *want* to be caught in one with! No *way,* is Mister Jan-Toby Axelsson, su—per—stud, going to *stay with,* stay and *fuck,* a chick he doesn't *want* to! Haven't you *gotten* that yet, *girl?* Don't you *understand* that *yet,* girl? Can't you *see* that? He's staying with her *because* he wants to *stay* with her. No one makes Mister *su—per—star—su—per—stud* do what he *doesn't want to!* Haven't you *figured* that out yet, girl? You *still* don't get it, *do* you girl? He was *using* you, just *using* you. That's *all* he was doing, *using* you."

"No—he wouldn't! Not Jan!" I recoil violently from the suggestion.

"*Yes!* You were a great fuck, darling. I mean, you're *beautiful.* And you *know* what to *do* to a man. Can't you get *that* through your beautiful little *head?* Jesus Christ, you *should* be able to, you're *intelligent* enough. But force *him* to make a *choice,* and he's *chosen* the woman he *wants* to be with!"

"No! That's not the reason. It's not like that!"

"*Yes!* It *is* like that, baby. *Look* at it, girl. He's *chosen.* He *is* with her!"

Oh, God . . . !

"I'm right, baby. While you were a great little secret *fuck,* everything's *fantastic.* But comes the *choice* and *you're* out in the fucking *cold,* baby."

I stare at Miriam, my mouth open. Her words, her forcefulness, seem to hammer at me. God, she's right . . . because he's not here. He *did* have a choice, for that long, long instant in the bedroom, and he *did* choose. He chose Melissa . . .

Miriam leans forward and grips my shoulders, shakes me. "Don't you *see*—all this shit about *Andy* is just *that* and no more. Of *course* he'd be able to get *visitation* rights. He *could* fight in *court.* But he's *not* fighting, and it's *not* because that *bitch* is *blackmailing* him. It's because he *doesn't want* to leave her, he has *no intention* of leaving her *and* his *kid!*

253

But that means he was lying to me. "Jan wouldn't lie to me. He loves me!"

"He's never *loved* you. If he'd *loved* you, he wouldn't have *left*. You don't *leave* someone you *love.*"

"But what we shared. I couldn't have been so wrong. It *can't* all have been blatant lies—that's totally impossible!"

"It *was*, baby. You were *taken in*. And you're gonna have to *face up* to that. He *did* lie. He *did* use you. He's a fucking *asshole*, the *biggest*, and you couldn't *see* it. You *refused* to see it. Jesus, *you* thought the sun shined out of his *cock!* Him and his fucking *words!* I *told* you, baby!"

"Oh, Miriam." I'm crying, helplessly and hopelessly. Miriam's words have taken away everything that I had, leaving only a raw, painful vacuum.

At least I had the loving memories of us together, but now I'm left with nothing.

"Lady! You should *pull* yourself *together* and *do* something." She shakes me hard. "Take a *vacation*. Get yourself some *fucking* with a *good man*. *Forget* that bastard. I *told* you he was an *asshole!*"

"Is that what I need? Do you think so, Miriam?" Why can't I think for myself?

"Yes! *We* were all *right*, working here together, *before* that fucking *asshole* came and *spoilt* it. Just *look* how he's *hurt* you! *Hate* him, baby, *hate* him!"

*　　*　　*

I'm doing what's known as indulging myself. All I can keep my attention on is my memories of us together. Slushy emotion—that's what I'm indulging myself in, even though I know it's doing me no good and I should stop it.

But I'm sure Rand would say, "Serves you right. I *told* you. You're so *childish*, Solange! Falling in love with a . . . with a *rock* star! What did you expect?"

I've been wandering around the bedroom, picking up Jan's things. I've put them all together; he'll probably send Roy for them sometime. He's got ten pairs of boots here. Him and his bloody size 12D boots! Also a couple of hats, his weights, his cameras. He's left me here, too.

I'm standing naked in the bedroom, just about to get into bed, when Miriam bursts in on me. "Are you all *right?*"

She sounds impatient, but so am I. I'm just slightly beginning to resent feeling like a baby chick tucked under mother hen's wing.

"I'm fine, Miriam. Just getting into bed."

"Go *on*, then." She looks me up and down. Her interest in my body irritates me. *"We're* going to *Vidal's* tomorrow."

"What? Are we?" Surprised, I sit up again, uncharacteristically pulling the sheet up over my boobs.

"Yes, *Vidal's*. Tomorrow."

I assume she's talking about Vidal Sassoon's. She makes it sound so personal, as though Vidal himself were going to do my head of silky hair.

"Thought it would *do you good*. Then I thought you could *perhaps* pop *off* somewhere."

I realize Miriam's heavy-handedly trying to get me out from under all these regrets I've been wallowing in.

She picks up a couple of leather-bound books from the floor, looks at them closely, frowns, hands them to me. I recognized them already: Yeats and Keats.

"Poets!" Poet is a four-letter word to Miriam. *"Yeets* and *Keets*—hm!"

I can't resist telling her: "You mean Yates and Kates."

"You know what you need, girl?"

"What's that?" She comes and sits cross-legged on the waterbed, bounces up and down. "Miriam, I'm getting seasick!" She stops. "What do I *need*, Miriam?"

"You *need* a man that doesn't know *anything* about fucking *words!* About fucking *lit-e-ra-ture!*

"Oh, do I?" Why is this antogonism suddenly springing forth?

"Yes, you fucking well *do!*" she snaps. "Someone who doesn't *know* about *verbs* and *conjugating*, *adjectives* and *onomato* . . ."

". . . poeia," I help her out automatically.

"Someone who just knows how to *fuck!* I mean, all you've *ever* had is *literature* dudes, and what *good* has it done you? *Zilch! Zip!"*

I can feel my face going blotchy with anger. She's downing Jan again, that's what she's doing.

"I like men to have something in common with me. I need that in a relationship. I *want* that in a relationship. I like gentle, quiet men. Sensitive men," I tell Miriam.

"Sensitive! Shit, Jan-Toby-fucking-*Axelsson* was sure fucking sensitive! He *used* you. Tromped all *over* you. *That's* sensitive?"

I can't even answer her; I want to scream and shout at her, telling her she's wrong, that she's never liked Jan. At this instant, I realize she *never* has. I want to tell her peremptorily to go away, leave me alone, never come back. *'Miriam, you're fired!'* But I know that I can't, that I won't.

"I'll get his *things* out of here *tomorrow!*" she decrees with an expansive wave of her hand.

"Don't you touch anything!" I screech at the top of my voice. I couldn't bear not to have his things around. Not yet, anyway.

"Get some *sleep*, baby." She climbs off the bed and stands looking down at me. "We don't *need* fucking *men*, anyway." She abruptly leaves the bedroom, leaving me rocking up and down on the waterbed.

What's that? It takes me quite a time to realize that the phone's ringing. I put the bedside light on. Hell, it's after four o'clock!

"Hello . . . ?"

"Solange . . ."

Suddenly I'm awake, very, very wide awake.

"Solange?" asks Jan-Toby Axelsson again.

"What do *you* want?" Bitchy.

"I . . . I had to see that you were all right."

"All right?"

"I've been sitting drinking with Nils. He got me to call."

That angers me even more. "Didn't want to yourself, huh?"

"No, I . . . I just *couldn't.*" His voice sounds hoarse.

Silence.

"Are you all right, Lady?"

"I am fine. I mean, the man I love and wanted to be with, share with, do things with, have his babies—he's walked out on me. *Of course I'm all right!*" I shout ironically, scornfully.

"Jesus fuck!" he mutters. I think that's a sob I hear.

"Melissa let you off the leash, then? Got away so you could *secretly* phone your *ex-secret-fuck?*"

"Solange!"

"How *dare* you ring me up at four o'clock in the morning —or any other time—to see if I'm *all right!* How *dare* you, you bastard! Jesus Christ, Jan, what d'you think I am?"

"I just want you to know: I'm sorry. And that . . . that I love you." His voice cracks.

"Love me? Don't lie to me, Jan."

"It's just . . . I don't want to have anyone pointing the finger at me and saying I couldn't be responsible for my own son."

"What am I supposed to say to *that?* 'Well done, Jan'?"

"I've got to get this handled," he says exasperatedly. "I don't know what to do. Andy's part of me—I *can't* desert him. Without me, he'll only have . . . Solange, please—I *need* you, Solange."

"Need me! What for? More secret fucks? Keep me in my secret mistress place? I hate you, you bastard!" I shout, tears streaming down my face. "*No,* you know I don't *hate* you. I *want* you. I *love* you. Jan, *please* come home, I need you so much."

No answer. Of course there's no answer. I *know* the answer to that, don't I!

"Please don't cry, darlin'."

"I love you, Jan. I mean, I hate you to hell. And yet I love you."

"And I love you, darlin'," he says very quietly. "I want you, but we've just got to . . . What I've done, what I'm having to do, isn't because I don't love you. It doesn't *mean* that I don't love you."

"I know," I whisper, emptily. "It just means that you don't love me . . . *enough.*" I look at the phone in my hand, then drop it back onto its cradle, lean over and pull the phone jack out of the wall, realize that Miriam is standing there, watching me.

"He wanted to make sure . . . that I was *all right!*"

* * *

The anger I felt after the phone call jolted me out of feeling so damn sorry for myself. Miriam and I went to the hairdressers the next day. I had my hair done. The bottom layer still reaches to my shoulders, but that smooth sleekness has gone. A new me has emerged. It's a mass of silken curls now. It's made me look even younger, feel bouncy and bright.

A new Solange delaMer got onto the plane for New York.

Matthew didn't even recognize me at first. "It's beautiful!" he said, hugging me, then pulling gingerly at a springy curl. "We're going to my beach house. It's the last week of the season," he told me.

And so here I am, sitting in the sand. Sunning, resting, remembering . . . trying not to brood.

Matthew's building a sand castle with Chris, Norman, and William, while I lie and think and not-think, my mind blinking on and off like a traffic signal. If only I could hold everything in amber—a blissful state in between.

All the same, I'm glad I came. I think it's helping. Matthew is so gentle, so considerate. "We've all been through emotional letdowns," he said, with a hug and a kiss. He hasn't even mentioned babies.

"Come and help us, Solange." I shade my eyes as I recognize Chris's voice; it still sounds so very young.

I stare at them all for a moment. "Maybe soon," I say, lying down again, turning over onto my front. I have only the tiniest of bikini bottoms. My bikini top is covering two little mounds of sand—sand-boobs—that Chris made for it.

Malibu seems thousands of miles away from here. What an asinine thought!—I smile. It *is* thousands of miles from here.

We came here yesterday, the day after I arrived in New York. Chris, whom I'd met before, was waiting at the Cherry Grove dock with Norman and William; Matthew and I were kissed, quite indiscriminately.

Matthew's house is on the Bay side of Fire Island, on Bayside Walk. As soon as I saw Cherry Grove, I knew it was my kind of place, with its little wooden houses, and little wooden boardwalks—enchanting. The house had belonged to Matthew's parents; he'd spent every summer in it since childhood. His parents were killed in an air crash when he was eighteen—maybe knowing how that feels is one of the bonds between us. Of course, it's only over the past few years that Cherry Grove has become really very popular; Matthew has twice had enormous offers for his house, but he says he'll never sell.

It's a nice old comfortable house, well-worn—leather chesterfields, Indian rugs, a Persian carpet on the lounge floor—two bedrooms, and another one converted from a tiny storeroom. The house is called "Moby Dick." A few summers back, someone painted 'S after *MOBY;* that summer, every visitor asked Matthew, "Well, *where* is it, darling?"

Matthew always spends the last week of the season here, and the following week too. And weekends too, of course.

Chris has been here for three weeks already. He's living with Matthew now. He's also an artist. I think they go well together. Matthew's helping him with his art work; they've formed a little company. They're a "couple" now.

William and Norman come from Nashville, Tennessee. They always spend the last month of the season here; they've been coming to Matthew's, renting their room, for the past four years. They have to be over fifty; they're both very gentle and friendly. Apparently Norman insists on doing all the cooking.

Needless to say, I'm in the tiny storeroom-bedroom.

Something is tickling my back; it takes me a few moments to realize that it's sand being trickled onto me. I turn over and look at Chris, tall and lanky, blond and blue eyed. He left home two years ago, to the relief of his father—who was embarrassed by Chris's interest in drawing and painting in preference to manly sports—and to his own relief at not having to live the life his parents prescribed for him.

We all build a sand castle. Norman and William are in matching technicolor swim trunks—tiny ones. They both have brown fuzz covering their chests, and the same tidy hairstyles too, except that Norman wears his parted on the left and William on the right. Matching neck chains and wrist chains—they match in every way.

Chris and Matthew are naked, as are quite a few other men on the beach. My God, Solange—all this fantastic, freelance cock, all totally inaccessible to you! But there's only one cock I really want, anyway.

"Let's swim!" Chris suggests exuberantly. They all gang up on me in the water, and Matthew steals my bikini bottoms. I really know I'm on Fire Island when I walk up from the water, passing numerous naked, glorious, sexy cocks, and not one male takes any notice of my naked, suntanned, ample-boobed little body. Except that I hear someone say, "Nice ass," as I pass.

* * *

I need these days on the beach, swimming, sunning, building sand castles. Chris built what he affectionately called a "sand cock." Mm—it was rather delicious, *very* artistic. We ate out a few nights, the five of us, at local nightspots. A couple of nights, Norman cooked: curry one night, and a succulent *coq-au-vin* another. Norman and I spent delightful hours discussing recipes and Nashville. He and William like living in Nashville. William has a construction company; Norman is a "homemaker." "You *must* come and visit with us, darling. We'll show you *everything*. Take you to the Exit In, it's *super* there. And the Grand Old Opry, of course."

"Prefer the Met or Covent Garden."

Norman laughed uproariously at my weak joke. "Oh, you *must* come."

We made an enormous fruit cake—a hash cake, actually.

259

Norman was giggling all the time—we smoked the hash we didn't actually put in the cake. Norman has a terrific throaty giggle—worse than mine.

Afterwards, I joined Chris on the beach. Norman and William had disappeared for their "little afternoon snoozles," as Norman puts it. We haven't seen Matthew since the morning; so Chris and I sat on the beach, drinking Tab and eating hash cake, both naked. Chris lacquered my toenails while I buffed my fingernails.

Two naked little boys trailing two naked little girls passed by. They all shouted "Hi" and waved; we waved back and grinned like idiots. It settled me, seeing these happy children in this safe place.

Matthew disappeared again halfway through Friday, "to see a friend," he said with a wink.

Norman and William got themselves excited, getting dressed up for an outrageous fancy-dress party. They went as little brown mice—except that their tails were at the front . . . .

It's Monday morning, the last day of the season, Labor Day, when we see Matthew again. "Where have you been?" I ask him as he kneels in the sand next to us all: me, William, Norman, and two of their friends, John and John. Matthew has two men with him. One, called Simon, is small, effeminate, all smiles and teeth. (I immediately christen him the Tooth Fairy). Guido, the other, is obviously Italian, huge and *good-looking*: but his body is covered in thick black fuzz, and his arms are long, too. Too long. Guido, a good-looking gorilla; actually, he looks like a reject from the Mafia. I smile at Chris, who's staring disbelievingly at this great big chunk of hunk.

"Such a *truck driver*," he whispers in awed reverence.

Matthew sits next to me and gives me a kiss and a hug. But he has me worried; I noticed as he sat down that there were red welts across his bottom. I stare at him with my mouth open.

"It's all right," he whispers. But I'm still alarmed.

Everyone sits and talks. We pass a joint around. But I keep on looking at Matthew, worried about what he's been up to (though that's obvious). It reminds me of Philippe. *He* wanted to hurt me, but Jan didn't. He just tied me gently with silk scarves, became ma Bête for me . . .

I suddenly realize I'm being stared at. A little boy of about ten or eleven is standing near me, staring at all of us. His little, skinny body is tanned very brown. He has untidy black hair and big brown eyes, round and staring, and carries a little black cardboard box in his hand.

"Hello." I smile at him.

"*You're* not a faggot." He rubs his hand up and down the side of his cutoffs. The talking stops and the men all look at him. "Why are you with a load of faggots?" he asks me with a sniff. "Everyone's a faggot who lives up here at the Grove and the Pines. New York businessmen faggots, that's what my pop says. Faggots!" He disregards the uncomfortable fidgets and animosity of my friends and concentrates on looking into the open end of his little box.

"That's not a very nice word," I tell him. "We're all friends."

He rubs his nose. "Faggots aren't friends. My mom told me to keep away from faggots, they try and get your dicky-doo."

"Oh. That's not true, you know. It's a lie, told by people who don't want to face their own feelings—ignorant people."

"My mom won't let me run around with no clothes on like some of the kids. *You've* got no clothes on. That's 'cos you're *cheap*." He looks around the group. "*They're* not getting at my dicky-doo," he tells me.

"They wouldn't want to," I say. "You're only a little boy."

"Faggots like little boys."

"I told you, that's not true. It's a stupid, ignorant lie."

He stares at me blankly. I don't seem to have any hope of deprogramming Mom's indoctrination. He peers into his little box again.

"What's that?" I ask.

"Look." He comes closer, forgetting my cheapness and all the depraved faggots sitting around, and shows me the box. It's open at both ends. "See—for the roaches. See!" He thrusts it in front of my face. "They all stick to the glue stuff; they can't move. They kick and wiggle until they die in *agony!*" He smirks at me triumphantly, then gives a sly look at my boobs and my patch of pussy hair. "See!" He pushes the box closer. I can't help looking inside.

"See! Got them! They're dying—it's *torture!*" He looks down at my pussy hair again, with a sly grin. Then he looks at all the cocks around him.

"I've got four boxfuls," he proudly informs me, prodding at my shoulder with the box.

"That's disgusting." I wiggle aside, then prod his shoulder gently in return.

261

"They're only roaches," he sneers. "Vermin! Like *faggoty fairies!* If you catch a roach you can stick a pin through him. He takes a long time to die that way." He looks at us all, suddenly loudly yells, "Faggots!", pokes his tongue out as he runs off.

"Come back in ten years, darling," shouts one of the Johns after him. "He'll make a terrific master then," he comments. Everyone laughs.

"I think he would *now*," I say, still watching the running boy. "Little monster! And his mom sounds like a real bigoted monster, too."

"I've seen him before," Matthew says. "I think he lives along at Sea View."

"Little bastard!" I exclaim.

"Not everyone understands us, let alone accepts us, Solange dearest," Norman says with a small sigh of resignation.

"I've come to the conclusion," I say, "that anyone who thinks gay sex is dirty, thinks *sex* is dirty, period." They nod. "Sex is sex, and should be enjoyed. It's something beautiful that you want to *share* with someone." I stand up, and they all look at my shapely little body. "But sorry, boys," I add with an outrageous wink, blowing them a kiss, "I'm closed for business today." I run down for a swim, leaving them laughing.

* * *

I'm liking it even more here now the season's over. Without so many people around, the calm impermanence of these little rows of matchbox houses along the ocean's edge blends with the unhurried season's march towards winter. It will take a little while, but it will all change, in the end; meanwhile, take it easy.

Norman and William left us, after we'd swapped addresses and telephone numbers. I hope they get in touch with me. I must get in touch with them, such a nice couple; been twenty years together. Even Guido gave me his number—he told me he comes from Noo Joisee . . .

We go for a picnic, crossing sand dunes to reach the Sunken Forest. I love it. Pandora must come here, I tell Matthew and Chris, who sit on either side of me while we eat shrimp and cold chicken, salad and melon. A nude picnic, how divine! Matthew sketches me all afternoon. I've never been sketched in the nude before. He says he's going to do a painting from the sketches.

The forest is sheer enchantment. I daydream of making love to Jan here. The forest is primeval, mossy and musty, with twisted branches and grapevine trails. We eat blueberries from the bushes, and Chris does a blueberry painting on my tummy and boobs. I sit on a moss-covered log and gaze quietly at the hollies, maples, pines, cherry trees. Each is different, each has its own individuality. Enchantment! I want to love *here*, in this late summer paradise forever. Pandora *is* going to visit here!

"Let's not go home for Sunday," Matthew says, catching the same mood. "Let's stay here forever, in a little vacuum of time that never changes."

Matthew and Chris came and sit next to me on the log, on either side of me. We put our arms around each others' waists.

I look from one to the other. And I know what I have to do. What I need to do. "Listen," I say, "while I've been here, I've been sheltered. You've both kept me from feeling any pain. I've tried not to think about anything, about Jan. I've pretended that it wasn't there, but it *is*. I've *got* to get over it. I've got to be able to think about him, about *us*, without hurting. I've got to be able to *handle* it.... And then there's Marie-Claude and Jed. I've got to be able to see them without any ..." I stop; I don't know what to say—what I want to say. "I think what I need to do is to see Maman now."

15

The Mediterranean winks blue beneath a beautiful burning sun. Welcome home, Solange.

I feel so weary. I hate flying. It's so *good* to be here in this house. I guess it's Rand's house now. Where is he, though? I feel disgruntled, lonely; why is there no one here, when I need them?

From the airport I went straight to Maman's house, but the housekeeper told me that she was in Paris, had left yesterday, and would be there a week or so. So I ran to Rand—what else? But the house is silent.

I go to my room, soak in the tub for half an hour. Almost falling asleep. Oh, *yes*, I just want to sleep ... and sleep ...

I dress, go and get myself a chunk of *pain restaurant* with too much butter, some grapes, a glass of wine, and sit on the terrace. The sun on my back warms and heals me.

Why don't I come back here to live? But Maman isn't here; Rand isn't here: my shelters from the storm. And now, too, I have no Marie-Claude here. Oh, Marie-Claude ... I can't even see you, talk to you, because you're part of Jed's life now, and he's a part of Jan's life.

"You bastard!" I shout my anger out towards Jan, those thousands of miles away around the curve of the earth. "You've even taken Marie-Claude away from me."

Oh God, Solange, don't cry! For God's sake don't cry! God? Old Nobodaddy, hiding himself in his Clouds, taking his spiteful judgment out on me again. Nobodaddy's revenge! "You bastard! What have I ever done to you? Fucker!" (Oh, stop crying, Solange!) "You were quite right, William. You understood what a smug old fucker Nobodaddy was. *You* always put him in his proper place!"

"What the hell are *you* doing here?"

I turn at Rand's angry voice. "Rand, I ..."

"What are you *doing* here? I don't recall inviting you to my home."

He stands there looking furious. What the hell have I done to him, that he should greet me like this?

"I ..." Hell, is that all I can say? "I came to see Maman, but she's away."

"Okay, but what are you doing *here*? It's not your house anymore." He comes and stands opposite me. I've never seen him look so dark and furious.

"I had nowhere else to go."

"I see. So you just thought that you would make use of me, as usual."

"No! Anyway ... half my money bought this house. It's still half *mine*."

"Get out, Solange! I don't want you here."

"*What?*"

"You walked out on me. So for God's sake *stay* out! I don't want you turning up whenever *you* feel like it. How dare you!"

"Rand, I ..." I burst into tears. "I ... I just can't take any more, from anyone. I wanted Maman."

"Oh, you stupid bitch! I *told* you what to expect. So your

rock star walked out on you, did he?" I stare at him through my tears, feeling myself tremble. "Doesn't feel very nice, does it? But don't come crying to me. I don't want you here. Now just get *out!*"

I can't even cry, just sit and tremble. Rand's rage has totally overwhelmed me. His fury and hostility are something new. I can't begin to comprehend them. Was all this anger lurking there all the time when I was with him?

"How do you know about Jan?"

"Your mother rang Miriam, she wanted to talk to you. Miriam told her everything. I saw . . . I saw Véronique the other day." Rand just *stares* at me, stonily. And besides the cold, the lack of any welcome, there's something else . . . but I can't tell what. "Just go. Go to a hotel."

"Rand, I need . . ."

"You *always* need! You, you, *you!* Well, isn't that too bad!" He folds his arms and smirks at me. We're just staring at each other. I don't understand his hostility; I have no means of resisting it.

"Look," he says, with a wave of his hand, brushing away his abruptness, "I'm sorry, but I think it'd be best if you go."

I suddenly recall what he told me on the phone—that he has someone he sees. That must be it. She's here, and he doesn't want us to meet.

"It's your lady?"

He doesn't answer, just glares, his eyes still cold.

"You don't wish me to meet her?"

"I *wish* you to *go*." Yes, he means it. But why is he so *angry?*

"Rand, if you have someone you love I'm pleased for you. You know our marriage was dead. You *know* that. So why so angry?"

"Solange, just go!" He looks down at me as if at a tiresome, spoilt child who's being unusually obnoxious, but isn't that how he always looked at me?

What else can I do? I pack my things and leave, without saying good-bye.

*　　*　　*

Sleep. At last I can sleep.

I sleep through the night. Through most of the day. Have dinner in my room: an omelette, ice cream, and a bottle of champagne. It's only then, when I'm feeling slightly high, sleepy, and relaxed, that I can think.

What am I doing in London?

When I got to the airport yesterday the flight to London was the next flight out, so I took it.

I slept through most of the taxi ride from Heathrow. The taxi driver, one of those cheerful little cockneys, whistled and winked as he carried my two cases to the hotel entrance for me. I always stay at the Ritz when I'm in London. I like it; it's old-fashioned and courteous. My suite overlooks Green Park.

I look out into the night: a sprinkling of lights among the wet blackness of the trees. It's raining; the empty footpaths glisten. It looks sadly lonely. I escape to the TV. At least the BBC knows how to present the news concisely, informatively. And the weatherman from the Meteorological Office has proper weather maps, not like that dumb map I see at home sometimes, with little faces drawn on chubby little clouds.

Oh God, I need some more sleep; I still can't think straight. Why can't I make peace with myself? At least there's no sharp, jagged pain any longer, just a dull, continuous ache.

Be thankful, Solange, for that. You can't win them all.

What have I got myself into now? I who lived in that shiny creative land of Golgonooza, now wallowing in depression; I've managed to sink myself into the depths, to become a denizen of Ulro ...

* * *

After three days here, I decide I'd better ring Miriam. She tells me everything's all right. Marie-Claude rang, wanted me to ring her. No, Miriam says, I won't tell *anyone* where you are. (And she won't—she'll enjoy *not* telling anyone.)

I give Matthew and Chris a call. They both sound so cheerful. It's so good to hear them; I almost wish I were back with them.

I ring Lars, talk to him and Kris. I say nothing about Jan, don't even tell them I'm in London; it's just good to talk to them for a while.

I ring Marie-Claude. She's very happy, bubbling and laughing. She's become a Tex-ahn ...

"Ma chérie, but where are you?"

"Rome," I say. Why did I do that—lie to Marie-Claude? The Jan connection, that's why.

"Darling, you come to us," she pleads.

"No. Not just now."

"Are you all right?"

"I'm fine. Fucking my way around the world. Ten men in two weeks," I lie again, but now it's because I have the idea that she'll tell Jed, and Jed will tell Jan.

"*Solange!* That's not like you, *ma chérie*."

"It's the *new* me," I lie. But why lie? Why not make it a reality? Perhaps I should? Why *shouldn't* Solange fuck her way around the world, if she feels like it?

"Ma'am." That's Jed, suddenly on the line.

"Hello, Jed."

"Now you jus' listen to me, little lady. Me and Marie, well, we want to come and get you, bring you back here with us. I want to get you and Jan together immediately, where you should be."

"Oh, Jed, that's very sweet of you. But he walked out on me. He obviously doesn't want me, except to wait around in case he can sneak away from Melissa and keep on with our clandestine little affair."

"And what are you doin' in Rome, lady?" Jed says "Rome" as if it were a Martian colony. Perhaps it is, to a Texan.

"I'm fucking my way around the world. I told Marie-Claude, ten men in two weeks. I'm gonna keep on fucking my way around the world, too. That *bastard's* not going to get me down or make me cry."

"Darling. *Ma chérie*," Marie-Claude says. "Zhed and I want to marry ourselves next week. I want that you should be there. Please come, darling. *Please*."

"Oh, Marie-Claude! It would be too awkward. Jan is Jed's best friend; he's bound to be there. And . . . I wouldn't want to come between them. I can't, Marie-Claude. I couldn't just *see* Jan and not . . ." My voice breaks. "I don't *want* to see him!"

"Stop crying, *ma chérie*."

"Now listen here, little lady, we *want* you to come," Jed barks at me.

"No, Jed. I wouldn't want to cause any bad feelings. Of course I'll be wishing you a happy marriage. Marie-Claude and I are friends, we always will be. Sometime in the future when I'm over all this, you can come and see me, and I'll come and see you too. But I just *can't*, not now. Not *now!*"

"Sweetheart . . . Look, I *wanna* help."

"I know that, Jed. I appreciate it, really I do."

"Then *let* me."

There's a pause. Then I find myself asking the question that I've been trying to avoid: that I've been pretending I didn't want to ask. "Have you ... seen ... ?" I can't even finish it.

"Yeah, I have, little darlin'."

"How ... ?"

"He was jus' about as happy as you are, darlin'. Maybe a mite less so, even."

"Oh, Jed, why did he walk out on me like that? Why? We could have fought, together, so that he could see Andy. I want him to have Andy."

"I know, darlin'. That's what I'm tryin' to get him to do. But for some reason his head's completely fucked up over this. He don't even know which end up his ass is."

"I think I hate him, Jed," I say in a small voice.

"No you don't. You love him, lady, that's the plumb fact and matter of it."

"Yes, it is. I do. But ... I mustn't. I won't let myself be used like that. I respect myself too much." I sniff hard. "Jed, please put Marie-Claude back on the line." He does so, and Marie-Claude and I talk, quite uselessly, for another ten minutes or so. "Marie-Claude, be happy, darling. I'll call you again soon. Oh, and listen ... there haven't been ten men—*any* men."

"I knew that, *ma chérie.*"

"I'm so *glad* you and Jed have each other. Be happy, darling ..."

Could I really have been crying the whole night away? Oh, yes, quite easily. Now it's dawn, and I'm wide awake. I turn the bedside lamp on and sit looking at my photo of Jan in its silver frame. Why did I bring it? Because I need to see his face, that's why. I finger my bear claw and my sun-angel.

"Oh God, I *hate* this!" I shout out.

But how the fuck do you stop loving someone you love so very much and *don't want* to stop loving? The answer, of course, is simple: You don't.

I touch my ring, look again at Jan's photo, caress the mustache. "I suppose this means we're not engaged?"

"Ain't that the truth!" the photo seems to answer back.

"I suppose I should return the ring to you?" I ask the photo.

"Now that ain't necessary, Ma'am," Jan answers. "Just look on it as a nice little thank-you present for bein' such a great mistress, Ma'am."

Oh, I was a great mistress, all right. *"That* I'm good at—being a *mistress."*

"Sure are, Ma'am!" The photo seems to give me a lopsided grin. *"Ain't that the fuckin' truth!"*

* * *

Solange, out and about, walking down Bond Street on a gray but unrainy day, not allowing thoughts or emotions to reach her. No more engagement ring. No more sun-angel. No more bear claw. No more emeralds. No more photo. Those are all buried at the bottom of her expensive leather case.

Little Ms. Diamond-Hard-Classy-Ass is going to use men for a change. No man is going to get to her like Jan-Toby Axelsson has. Not ever again!

I go and visit two of my favorite shops on Bond Street. They're at the bottom end, near Picadilly, opposite each other: a jade shop and an amber shop. Marie-Claude collects amber, so I go and buy her an amber necklace and some earrings. Then I go and buy Miriam some jade jewelry.

I decide to be brave and investigate a nearby pub. It's quite all right for young ladies to have a drink in an English pub; it's not like sitting in a singles bar. Not quite, anyway; at least, there's more subtlety about it.

It's cold and damp as I walk down St. James's until I find myself a little pub called the Admiral Nelson. It's quiet, warm, inviting. I order myself a dry sherry, take it and sit on one of the padded benches at one of the little round tables.

It sounds funny, hearing English—cockney English— voices again. Two men are chatting and laughing next to the glass partition that divides the saloon bar from the public bar. The one with his back to me has a voice that reminds me of someone, but I can't place who. It's very London, a kind of refined cockney. I sip at my sherry, than take off my fur jacket; it's warm in here. I'm in a cashmere sweater, with jeans rolled up to my knees to show off the black suede boots I bought at Fortnum's.

The cockney man's voice seems to echo around the bar: "Do you know—a man's 'ead weighs fourteen pands."

I can't help smiling. I wish I could see his face. He's quite tall, anyway. And why does his voice intrigue me so?

I quickly finish my drink, decide to get another. I leave my handbag on top of my fur jacket and go over to a space at the bar (near the two men) where I can get the barman's attention.

"An 'ead can't weigh fourteen pands, Reg." The small, ginger-haired little man is still arguing with the tall one. "Stands to reason, don't it? Fourteen pands—that's an 'ole *stone*, Reg."

"Oh yes it do. Fourteen *pands*," That's my man, still with his back to me. All I can see is that he's dressed in a well-cut dark blue suit and is tall, with light brown hair. " 'Ere, tell you what, though," he goes on to say, "do you now, a man ate twenty-five yards of spaghetti in forty seconds. Wait, tell a lie—forty-two seconds."

I laugh as the barman takes my order. "Whiskey sour, please."

"American, then?" he asks, professionally friendly.

"Half," I reply with a polite smile.

"Over 'ere on yer 'olidays, then?"

"Yes." He finishes making the drink, gives me change from a pound note. I go back to my bench.

"On ya own then, darlin'?"

I turn on hearing the voice of "my man," and it suddenly dawns on me who it is his voice reminds me of. I turn and smile back.

"Yes." I look up into an extremely handsome face—sort of craggy, brown eyes. He looks like Michael Caine with a Genghis Khan mustache.

" 'Ow about joinin' us, then?"

His voice! He even *sounds* like Michael Caine with a Genghis Khan mustache.

"Well, I . . ."

"Don't ya leave yer bleedin' fings over there then, girl. Someone'll nick 'em."

Who *is* this man who's taking charge of everything, when we don't even know each other? I think I like it.

"Come on then, girl." He gives a broad smile and shoos me with his hand. I meekly get my things and put them on a bar stool near to "my" man.

"That's better, girl. Can I buy you a drink?" He looks at the barman before I reply. "Give the lady anovver one, George."

"Oh, thank you."

He gives me his hand. "Reg Reynolds," he says with a little nod of his head.

"Hello. Solange delaMer."

"Oh, are ya? Bleedin' funny name that, ain't it? You a froggy, then?"

I can't help laughing. "I'm half French. My father was American."

"This 'ere's Dusty. Dusty Miller." The small, ginger-haired man offers his hand.

"Evenin'."

"You work around 'ere, then?" The Genghis Khan mustache seems to smile of its own accord.

"No, I'm just on vacation, on holiday. Just thought I'd come and investigate a pub."

"Well, ya sound classy to me. You *sure* you ain't English?" He looks at me a bit suspiciously as he sips his drink. Does he think I'm doing a number on him?

"We lived in England for a while. I finished my schooling here, went to college here."

"Oh." He takes another sip, looks me up and down. " 'Ad a bird went to 'Ornsey Art College once."

What do I answer to that? I think I'd better be polite, drink his drink, then make a tactful exit.

"*You* look like an arty bird," he says, looking me up and down again. "*You* didn't go to 'Ornsey, did ya?" he asks me, a lazy smile on his face.

"No, I went to Lady Margaret Hall."

"Where's that, then? Ain't never 'eard of that one." He turns to his friend. "*You* 'eard of that one, Dust?"

"No, mate, I ain't never 'eard of it."

"It's one of the Oxford colleges," I explain.

"Went to bleedin' Oxford!" He looks slightly taken aback. "Gawd!" He smiles at Dusty. "Got a bleedin' brainy bird 'ere, Dust."

"Thank you." I try not to let my smile break out into a laugh; finish my drink, then start on the one he bought me. God, I'm feeling slightly smashed. I haven't eaten anything.

" 'Ere, 'ere's a good one for you. Do you know that a 'uman brain can feel no pain?"

I burst out laughing.

He smiles and takes a swig of his drink, then looks me up and down appraisingly. "I like ya barnet."

"My *what?*"

"Barnet fair—hair, of course. All ya bleedin' curls like that, all over the place. It *do* look pretty on ya."

"Oh, thanks."

"See ya like earrings, then."

"Yes, I do."

"Gawd, ain't seen that before—*three*. 'Ere . . ." He touches my left ear, closely inspects my earmongery. "Not *real*, are they?"

"Real?"

"Diamonds."

"Yes."

"Bleedin' big, ain't they?"

"A quarter karat."

"Cor, me wife's engagement ring didn't 'ave that much diamond in it." He laughs with Dusty.

"Oh, you're married, then?"

"No. Not *now*. Divorced, ain't I?"

"Well, it's been nice talking to you both. But I really must get back to my hotel. I'm expecting a phone call from home."

"Where ya stayin' then?"

"The Ritz." It's out before I realize I may have let myself in for a lot more of this. Still—why not? He seems a nice man, interesting, certainly. Different, to say the least.

"Gawd! Must be doin' all right ta stay there, girl."

"I manage," I say dryly.

"I bet ya do, girl." He winks at me; we exchange conspiratorial smiles. "Where's home, then?"

"In California."

"Cailifornia! Gawd. Whereabouts? 'Ollywood?"

"No, Malibu. It's by the sea."

"Fink I've heard of it. Ain't it the place all them stars live, then?" A definite gleam of interest in his eyes.

"Yes, a few do live out at Malibu."

"What d'ya do for a livin', then?"

"I'm a writer."

"Famous?"

"Well, I'm . . . um, quite popular. I write about a witch called Pandora."

" *'Ere!*" He turns to Dusty, greatly amused. "She's that sexy bird. Ya write all that sexy stuff, do ya?" He winks and nudges me.

"I really must be going. As I said, I have a call coming in."

Reg Reynolds shifts on his stool, finishes his drink, digs his hands in his pockets. "Wouldn't like me to walk ya 'ome, would ya, darlin'?"

"It's not very far, I can manage all right. But thank you." I put on my coat. "And thank you for the drink, Mr. Reynolds." I give him my "lazy, amused" smile. "Nice to have met you both." I give Dusty a nod; he grins broadly.

Reg Reynolds, huh? I smile to myself as I walk back up St.

James's. Why did I leave, I suddenly wonder. Perhaps someone like Reg Reynolds is just what I need.

* * *

I'm wondering whether I should get myself out and about again. Meeting Mister Reg Reynolds on Friday perked me up some. But what did I do with all that perk? Nothing. Just sat around all weekend. Still, I did do the Tate Gallery and the British Museum today. Staring for hours at the works of my beloved William cheered me up.

What I *actually* want to do is to go home. I want to write and write. But I'm frightened to go home. I'm frightened of being in the house without Jan: all those memories. I *try* to con myself into pretending that it doesn't matter anymore; but it *does*.

I went to Foyle's and bought all the books I could find on ending relationships. I've been reading and reading. But none of them have helped much. One of them told me to list all the positive points about breaking up. All the things you can now do on your own. And another: List all those irritating habits your man had. But I couldn't find any positive points about breaking up, and the only habits I listed were the endearing ones: his lopsided smile; the way he rubs the side of his nose, chews on his knuckle, rubs at that little patch of beard under his lower lips; his bark—"Jesus fuck!"; and the way he incessantly crunches on ice cubes when he has a drink—even *that* I loved. I remember how he took one crunch, and a piece of filling fell out. He hates dentists; he would only go if I went with him, so I did. Even the boots he left all over the house seemed quaintly endearing.

Solange! Polish up your diamond hardness. Get up off your little dumb ass. Why eat your heart out over someone who doesn't want you? That's an exceedingly foolish thing to do. Start, instead, wiggling that classy ass of yours.

William Blake, as usual, had the right idea, and expressed it with sublime simplicity:

> He who binds to himself a joy
> Does the winged life destroy;
> But he who kisses the joy as it flies
> Lives in eternity's sunrise.

Solange, a sun-angel, should always live in eternity's sunrise. I feel suddenly at peace: my William always makes me feel peaceful.

Solange *is* Ms. Classy-Ass once more.

The phone rings. I bet it's Miriam. I must go and eat; I'm hungry. I answer the phone.

"Miss delaMer, there's a Mr. Reynolds here to see you. He *says* you're expecting him."

What! I don't believe it! Reg Reynolds?

"Shall I send him to your suite, Madam?"

"Tell him I'm on my way down, please."

Reg Reynolds: standing there looking impeccable, and so good-looking. Solange, if you don't take advantage of this unexpected situation, this different and interesting man, you'll be letting womanhood down. And let's face it, he's *got* to be a great fuck!

I go and stand myself in front of him.

"Fought I'd come and chat ya up, like."

"Did you now, Mr. Reynolds?"

" 'Ow about dinner, then?" He looks me up and down; I think he approves.

He's in a beige-colored vested suit, together with a floppy bow tie. Exceedingly handsome. "I'm expensive, Mr. Reynolds."

"I bet you are, darlin'."

"Where do you suggest we eat?"

"Anywhere you want, darlin'." Smile from behind narrowed eyes.

"Actually, I was teasing. I'm not expensive. I mean, I don't particularly like expensive, posh restaurants. I'd prefer somewhere smallish and quiet."

"Fought ya would." Laugh.

We go to a small but expensive restaurant in Soho. The headwaiter treats him like a prince. Reg orders, I let him. I think he *uses* that cockney act of his, just as certain Texans I know use that Texan act of theirs. The wine he orders is perfect. Expensive, but perfect.

"Why, Mr Reynolds, you are deep, aren't you?"

"Deep as they come, darlin'." We smile knowingly at each other. "So, 'ow long are ya stayin' 'ere for, then?"

"I don't know."

"Why not?" I watch him sip his wine. "Bleedin' good stuff, this."

"Because . . ." What can I tell him? I notice that his eyes are fixed on my silk shirt. "Actually, I'm getting over a rather disastrous affair. I needed to get away."

" 'Onest, ain't ya?"

"Immensely," I answer dryly.

"Was it a long one?"

"No . . . six months, is that long? But I thought it would . . . I don't really wish to discuss it. It's over."

"All right." He looks at me, fingers his mustache. "Enjoyin' ya dinner?"

"Yes, it's very nice."

"Charlie always knows 'ow to cook a good steak."

"Charlie?"

"The chef. Mon-sieur Charles, really."

"You come here a lot, then?"

"Quite a lot." Smile. "Me and me friend Harry Landers, well, we own it."

"Oh!" I'm taken aback. Well, it explains the wonderful service.

" 'Course, it's only a partnership thing. I mean, I don't run it. Just invested in it; Charlie runs it."

"What do you do, then?"

"Lorries."

"Pardon?"

"Lorries. I'm in lorries. Among other fings, that is."

"Oh—you mean you're a *trucker?*"

"Don't *drive* 'em girl." He rolls his eyes at my imprecision. "Reynolds and Landers, that's us."

"Your friend again?"

"Yeah. Met 'im in the Scrubs. We both 'ad a bit of money put by, so we fought we'd better do somefing wiv it. Better than meetin' every few years in the bleedin' Scrubs."

"The Scrubs? Where's that?"

"Wormwood bleedin' Scrubs." He can see I still don't know what he's talking about. "Wormwood Scrubs—you know, like Brixton, Pentonville."

It suddenly dawns on me. *"Prison?"* Solange, what *have* you gotten yourself into now?

"Yeah." He laughs, knowing that I'm somewhat over-whelmed. "Did porridge together, me and "Arry."

"Porridge?"

"Bird. A stretch. In stir. *Time."*

"But why *porridge?"*

"Haute cuisine, weren't it? That's what they used to feed ya on, in the old days, porridge. Listen, girl, I'm *straight* now. Honest. Straight up." He grins me an honest grin. "Listen, darlin', ya don't *never* 'ave to worry if ya wiv me."

"I don't?" What else can I say? Oh, well. I've never been

275

out with an ex-con before. "So—are your lorries successful?"

"Gawd, yes, girl. Da a *big* business, me and 'Arry do. Even got a coupla juggers."

"Juggers?"

"Juggernauts. S'what they call 'em 'ere. Big long lorries. Bleedin' gov'ment won't let 'em run in this country—say the roads are too bad. Why don't they build better bleedin' roads, then, that's what I say."

"What do your lorries carry?"

"Anyfink, darlin'." He winks. "Includin' maybe a few fings what falls off the back of other lorries."

"Oh." I can't help laughing.

" 'Course, now I'm forty, I'm finking about 'avin' a straight business. Got fed up, I did, poppin' in an' out all the bleedin' time."

"I bet you did."

" 'Course, got a few friends on the force. They always find the odd twenty nicker comes in 'andy."

"Oh."

He smiles at me. "Like ya blouse, girl."

"You do?"

"Like ya bristols, too."

"My *what?*" I put my fork down and stare at him.

Reg Reynolds laughs. "Cor, don't ya know nuffink? Rhymin' slang, ain't it? Bristols. Gawd, girl, ya did live in England, didn't ya? Mind you, bleedin' *Oxford* . . . !" He rolls his eyes upwards.

"Cockney rhyming slang? I've heard of it, of course."

"Yerse. You know: up the apples. Apples and pears—stairs."

"Oh, yes. Trouble and strife—wife. That's a famous one."

"There ya go, girl."

"So . . . ?"

"Oh, yeah—bristols. From Bristol *City*, ain't it?" I look blank. "Rhymes with *city*, girl. What ya've got there tucked in behind ya blouse."

"Oh!" I laugh and look down. "A pair of bristols. I've heard that before, but I never realized . . ." I'm laughing. "*You* are cheeky!"

"Oh Gawd, ain't I, girl?"

"Tell me, Mr. Reynolds . . ." I look at him; I've decided. I've never met anyone like Reg Reynolds before, and I'd be an imbecile to let a chance like this slip by.

"What?" Slight smile on that handsome face.

276

I lean over and ask, "Tell me—do you fuck on the first date?"

16

I stand by the window, looking out into the cold damp night of a London square. I'm aware that I'm waiting to hear that metallic click of Reg's key in the front door.

Reg Reynolds' apartment is beautiful. It surprised me. Perhaps there's a touch of the snob in me. I didn't expect Reg Reynolds to have such an unpretentiously luxurious, tasteful apartment. It totally surprised me. But then, Reg Reynolds totally surprised me.

It's modern. The floor throughout is covered with thick white carpet; in the lounge a huge Persian rug sits in the middle of the room. The furniture's in a beige slub silk, with a chrome and glass coffee table. On the wall is a Picasso. I mean, a real *Picasso*. "I always liked women wiv three tits," Reg commented.

There's a master bedroom, a smaller guest room, and a modern dining room—"Me Danish room," Reg quipped. And the kitchen's got every gadget you could imagine. "Got this poofy French geezer to do it, didn't I?" Reg said when he first, proudly, showed me around. The apartment is on Grosvenor Square, in one of those expensive apartment blocks that surround the gardens, next to the American Embassy.

"You must be rich, Reg."

"Got a bit tucked away," he admitted.

So after spending three nights with Reg at my hotel I moved into his apartment.

Miriam knows where I am, of course, and, of course, is telling no one; just passing on the message that Solange delaMer is alive and well and living in London.

I *must* go and buy some records. Reg has a marvelous sound system and an unmarvelous taste in music. His music collection consists of albums of Shirley Bassey, Matt Munro,

Lulu, and opera favorites sung by Harry Secombe. Plus his classical selection: an album of Tchaikovsky's "Greatest Hits"; Beethoven's "Fabulous Fifth" and "Glorious Ninth." Reg *likes* the *1812 Overture*. Last Sunday he took me to the Albert Hall for its Tchaikovsky night, which always ends with the *1812* (we'd sat through the *Marche Slav* and the *Swan Lake Suite*). The cannon and mortar fire crash and echo around the hall, and you sit there thinking that the glass roof is going to come splintering around your ears at any moment. You come out of the hall with your ears buzzing worse than from a rock concert.

As we walked to the car, Reg commented, "Bleedin' good composer, 'e were."

"I prefer Mozart, Reg," I said. "How about I find us a nice Mozart concert to go to?"

"Mozart? Mozart! Gawd, girl, 'e wrote all that bleedin' fiddly poofy stuff, didn'e? Gawd, Mozart never wrote anyfink like the *1812*. *You* should know that."

"Oh, I know, Reg. Wolfgang Amadeus would *never* have written anything in such exceedingly bad taste."

"Gawd, give over, girl!"

I giggled at Reg's shocked expression. He thought I was teasing him, but in fact I was never more serious.

Reg Reynolds is a delight to me. At least I'm keeping myself entertained and happy.

I hear the key go in the lock. " 'Ello, then, me little darlin'."

I can't help smiling. He's brought me flowers. I put the roses in a silver vase, then give him another kiss. "Such a gentleman I've found me."

"A gentleman takes 'alf the weight on 'is elbows," he tells me, straight-faced.

"What?" I giggle. "What does that mean?"

"Come to bed and I'll show ya."

"You will, will you! I *have* found me a gentleman."

"Course I am. You know what a gentleman is, don't ya?"

"No . . . *tell* me, Reg," I insist as he stays silent.

"Well, a gentleman . . . 'e's someone who gets outa the bath to take a piss."

"Gawd, girl. That was good, weren't it?"

We're lying in the dark, in Reg's platform bed, with the slippery satin sheet just managing to keep itself over us.

"I'm good, ain't I?"

"Yes, Reg, terrific."

"Was it good for you too, weren't it?"

I decipher his cockney. "Yes, Reg—fantastic," I say dryly.

Reg fucks like there's no tomorrow. It's always the same. Reg is your actual English lord-of-the-manor M.C.P. Reg believes that a woman gets her enjoyment by having her man fuck her until she's exhausted. Never mind all this messing about with the magic button of happiness; *fucking* is where it's at. Reg's belief goes: Keep your woman fucked and you keep her happy. He's fucking me, therefore I'm satisfied. Sometimes I am, of course.

"Eat me, Reg," I asked him once.

"Gawd, girl, give over," he replied. "Don't ya feel fucked enough, then?" Whereupon he fucked me some more. But one little sore pussy doesn't equal one contented little cunt.

"Reg," I pleaded, frustrated and exasperated, "orgasms *don't* come from the vagina; they're *clitoral*."

"Don't bust ya bleedin' rivets, girl! I dunno what you're on about. All this bleedin' feminist female stuff ain't doin' ya's any good. Gawd, I can't fuck ya any more than what I'm doin', ya know."

"Reg—that's what I'm saying. It's not just *fucking* that makes women come."

"Gawd, girl, I don't know where ya get it all from, reely I don't."

Thank God I *can* come with me on top. And thank God Reg likes it that way, too. I explained about the pressure being different in the right places, but I don't think he believed me.

"Gawd, I dunno . . ."

"Let me give you head."

"Give over, girl!"

"Don't you like head, Reg?"

" 'Course I does. But I go to Rita in Shepherds Market for that. Once a month. I mean, Gawd, ya don't expect ya lady to do *that*. You ain't a scrubber, are ya! It ain't proper, not for ya *lady* to do it, is it?"

I go to get out of bed, but he pulls me back and kisses me so very tenderly.

"I likes doin' it wiv you, girl."

"That's nice. I like doing it with you, Reg." Solange not actually lying. I don't think I've ever had so much sex with so few comes. Maybe I'm greedy. Jan just had to look at me, touch me, to make me come. And, I must say, I do miss all the nuptial cannibalism.

"I fought ya'd be good to sleep wiv when I first saw ya," Reg says, sitting up and turning the bedside light on. That's another thing: it's always done in the dark.

"Did you now . . . ?" I kiss him gently. I love him for being Reg; and because he doesn't realize how much he's helping me to get through everything.

"Wanted to sleep wiv ya."

"Did you now . . ."

"Wanted to do it wiv ya."

"Fond of euphemisms, aren't you?"

" 'Ere, give over, girl. I ain't a bleedin' pervert!"

* * *

I'm listening to music and reading my beloved William. I couldn't sleep. Reg and I made love, but afterwards I couldn't sleep—especially with the sound of Reg's gentle snoring.

I'm trying to work out how to tell Reg that I *have* to leave. I want to go and see my mother. And I want to go back home and write. But how do I tell Reg? He's been so sweet and caring, so loving. He actually wants us to marry.

Oh, Solange, what have you got yourself into now? *Why* do you do it?

I've played Jan's music, thinking that might help. There were tears on my face as I listened to "Babies Should Be Made In Love." I wanted part of Jan inside of me so much. A dream, Solange—a lovers' dream you'd better awaken from.

I put *The Poet And The Lady* on again and take up my book of William's words.

"What you doin', girl?" I look up at a sleepy-eyed Reg. He comes over and sits by me on the sofa. "Why aren't you in bed asleep?"

"I couldn't."

"It's 'im, ain't it?" He nods to the albums, all Jan's, that I've surrounded myself with.

"What d'you mean?"

"You know bleedin' well what I mean, girl."

"Yes." But am I *that* open and obvious? Well, Reg had it figured out.

"Let's get married, girl. I'll get a special license tomorrow." He pulls me into his arms and kisses me. "I fink that if we got ourselves spliced, you'd get over 'im proper, like."

"Do you?"

"Yes, I bleedin' well do. Get a new perspective, like. After all, there's three hundred and sixty ways to look at an elephant."

"But I *can't*, Reg. It really wouldn't be fair to you. An affair, a relationship like we're having is fine. But marriage is a big step. We don't know each other well enough, you don't love me enough, Reg. Not for marriage."

"Yes I do!" He grabs my shoulders, shakes me, quite gently. "I do, girl. I *am* in love wiv ya."

"No, you're not. Not really. It's just a sort of crazy infatuation."

"Is that all you fink it is, then?" he asks huffily.

"Reg, it's that with most people, to start with. It's just sexual attraction at first and for quite a time after. Until you really get to know someone. It's only then that the deep love comes, the sharing and the commitment."

"Dunno what you're on about, girl. Gawd, you do come out wiv some bleedin' awful rubbish, ya do. That's bleedin' Oxford for ya, that is. All that bloody learnin'! Gawd, I dunno why they *let* girls in there; you girls don't need none of that bleedin' stuff, gettin' ya ideas all mixed up."

"Oh, Reg!"

He ignores me, pours himself a Scotch and lights a cigar. "What ya readin,' then?"

The subject of love must be closed! "It's William Blake."

"We used to sing 'is song at school sometimes, at mornin' assembly. You know—'And Did Those Feet.' "

I giggle. "It's called 'Jerusalem,' Reg."

"Bleedin' good song, that were. Written some more stuff, then?"

"Oh, quite a bit, Reg."

"Where d'ya go this afternoon, then?" he abruptly changes the subject.

"To a bookstore. I bought some books—you know, first editions. Rare books. And then I went to the British Museum, to the Reading Room. And also, the Rosetti Notebook is there, among other things."

"'I ain't never 'eard of that. Like them Eyetalian painters, then, do ya?"

"Well . . ." I realize it might take me several hours to get across to Reg some glimmering of the significance of the Rosetti notebook; and somehow, I don't want to have to explain *anything* about my beloved William. Certainly not to Reg, the arch philistine. And then I realize, yearningly and poignantly, that my needs *can* only be fulfilled by someone who knows all about my loves, like my beloved William and all my other literary heroes. I know that I *have* to tell Reg—right *now*—that I can stay no longer.

"Didn't 'e just write 'ymns, then?" he asks.

"Pardon?"

"That Blake geezer. Religious, were 'e?"

I smile. "Well, he wasn't religious in the accepted sense of the word. The Spanish Inquisition would have taken a very dim view of him; he'd have been burnt at the stake as a heretic." I take a long look at Reg—so suave, sitting back with his long, dark blue silk robe wrapped tightly about him, a glass of Scotch in one hand and a cigar in the other.

"Go on, girl. Ya know I likes to learn new, interesting fings."

"Yes, Reg." I lean forward and kiss his cheek.

"Didn'e believe in God, then? But everyone 'ad to, then, didn' they, girl? By law."

I smile. "William didn't. William was one smart little cookie. He was a neglected genius, poor all his life. He persisted in an art form, an original art form, with almost no support. But he was doing what he wanted to do. He was a visionary. He hated churches. He thought that to obey a bigoted moral code was against the spirit of life itself. The accepted Christian ideal was to mortify the flesh, to deny oneself, to sacrifice, to submit to authority. He was against all that. To William, God was the outcome of Man's fallen perception. He didn't believe God really existed, only as a myth that he called 'Old Nobodaddy'—by which he meant, Big Daddy who's really Nobody. Nobody's Daddy—see?" Reg is looking perplexed. "But Jesus—well, Jesus was dear to William. Not because of any divinity, but because he was a revolutionary, a rebel against dogmatism, against blind vengefulness, against 'an eye for an eye' and all that Jehovah stuff. Christ was a hippie who said we should help and love one another, and *that* was what William found a joy. Oh, there's so much, Reg."

"You know a lot about 'im, don't ya, girl?" Reg sounds quite impressed. He gives me a strange look. He can't fathom me—but that's all right, because I know I haven't fully fathomed him yet.

"You know, Reg—William, well he didn't believe in *sin*. He said there was only 'intellectual error.'" I grin, but Reg looks like he doesn't dig it at all.

"What—did 'e want to free the criminals and such, then?"

"Oh, Reg . . ."

Reg stubs out his cigar. "Ain't you a Christian, then, girl?" He pulls me onto his lap.

"No, Reg, I'm not. I'm a Blakean." I grin again, but he's still serious. "I believe Christ was just a gentle hippie who didn't wear shoes and who had a lot of funky friends." Reg is looking really perplexed now, and for a fleeting instant I wonder whether I have any right to fling such bizarre speculations into his highly conventional belief patterns. "That's what Kris Kristofferson sings, that he had a lot of funky friends," I go on. "You know?—'Jesus was a Capricorn.'" But of course Reg doesn't know. "Of course, Kris forgot about his snubby nose." Reg is really puzzled now. "William says he hopes Jesus had a snubby nose. William liked snubby noses.

"Me Grannie finks she's going to 'eaven. Do you believe in 'eaven?"

"No, I don't."

"Where ya goin', then? The other place?" Reg laughs.

"This *is* the other place," I smile. "But actually, I'm coming back, Reg. I believe we come back—again and again and again. Maybe," I laugh, "until we get it right."

"You're a funny girl, ya know. Rum. I ain't never met the likes of you before, I ain't."

"Well, Reg, the feeling is mutual. I've certainly *never* met anyone like you."

"I fink I love you, girl. That's what I fink."

"Reg . . . I . . ."

"Let's get married, girl?"

"Reg . . . I . . ."

"I'll look after ya, Solange. I'd never let anyone 'urt ya."

"Reg . . . I . . ." What can I say or do?

"You wants to go though, girl, don't ya?"

"Reg . . . I . . ."

"I guess I'm gonna 'ave to let you . . . for the time bein', that is."

I cuddle myself closer to him. "You've been so good . . . so kind. And I *have* enjoyed it, loved it. But I've . . . I've got to see my mother. I've *got* to go home and write. I can't write here, you know I can't."

"Maybe when you've been at 'ome writin' for a bit . . . Maybe then . . ."

"Yes, Reg. Maybe . . ."

But of course we both know that 'maybe' is like tomorrow —it never comes.

17

I give Maman a hug as warm contentment runs through me. She looks beautiful, but then, I always find Maman beautiful. She has a scarf tied around her head, the same exact shade of sea green as her silk blouse. Her sunglasses are huge; she takes them off, and I see her smiling eyes.

"Oh Maman, thank God I'm here."

She kisses my cheek, hooks her arm through mine as we walk to the baggage claim area. A porter almost runs us down with his trolley. He grins and winks, asks us if we need assistance. How nice to hear the Midi accent again! He chats on: Are we on holiday? No. He smiles, compliments us on looking beautiful. Now I *know* I'm home in France.

He packs my suitcases into Maman's car. I started out with two when I left Malibu, but I bought so many clothes in London that I had to buy another two. Driving to Cap d'Antibes, I feel cheerful and excited.

"You've come home for the *vendange*," Maman smiles.

When I was young, Marie-Claude and I loved the *vendange* —the grape harvest. Her uncle Auguste owns a vineyard near the tiny village of Pourrières, near Aix-en-Provence, and we used to love to help. Raul, Elena Sanchez' son, the farmer, wouldn't believe me at first when I told him I used to pick grapes with the other workers. "Ah—now I know who to call when I need an extra pair of hands," he teased me.

"Solange?"

"Maman . . . I was miles away, thinking of Marie-Claude and me picking grapes together."

"And now she is married," She laughs. "To a Texan!"

I tell Maman all about Jed and Marie-Claude. And then, of course, I tell her all about Jan. "But what is your news, Maman?" I finally ask her.

"It is a surprise," she says, with a mysterious smile. Knowing Maman, I don't waste time trying to wrestle it out of her; it'll remain a surprise until we reach home.

We pull into a long, winding driveway.

"My new home."

"New? Why?"

"I have bought it. The other, it was only rented."

"It is beautiful, Maman." And so it is: huge and white, with archways, balconies, and wide patios. There are French windows around the ground floor.

Maman shows me to my room. It's big, with a balcony overlooking the Mediterranean. Tall cypresses, pine trees, and the bright sun upon the glinting ocean. Oh, *why* did I *ever* leave *La Belle France?*

I shower and change, then meet my mother on the patio.

She hugs me. "Solange." She turns me around, pulls gently at a curl. *"Très belle."*

"You really approve?"

"Of course."

Squinting in the sun, I lean on the patio rail and look down the sloping rocky cliff to the narrow beach below.

"Solange . . ."

"Yes, Maman?" Now the surprise! I turn expectantly.

She comes over to me slowly, holds my shoulders.

"Solange, I am married."

"What!"

"I told you, when you rang from London, that there were things I had to discuss with you."

"But . . . Who to? Do I know him?"

"Oh yes, you know him."

I jump up and down excitedly, hug her, kiss her. *"Tell me!"* Over her shoulder, I see Rand walking across the patio to join us.

"Rand!" I run over and hug him too, feeling that I must make up for that awful last time we met, when he got so angry with me. "How nice! Oh, Maman, you should have told me that you were asking Rand over." I hug him again. "Please forgive me for turning up like that, before. But I *did* feel so wretched."

He smiles, a funny, embarrassed sort of smile and plants a kiss on my curls. *"I'm* sorry I got so angry. I shouldn't have." His smile doesn't survive the apology.

"Maman just told me she's married again. Oh, Maman, who . . .?"

Rand places his arm, with self-conscious possessiveness, about Maman's waist. I find myself computing and recomputing the situation, disbelieving the answer.

"Oh, my God . . . !" I find myself shouting indignantly. "You married my *mother?* You married my *husband?*

Ohh . . . !" I wail, collapsing into a little heap on the patio and starting to bawl. "You bastards!"

They both kneel down and cuddle me.

"There . . . there . . . it's all right," they say, almost in unison, Rand in English and Maman in French. It's a few minutes before I get myself together and Rand helps me to my feet and over to one of the huge, shaded garden tables, where he pours us some wine.

"Why? Why didn't you tell me?" I scream at them both.

"Darling . . ." Maman kisses me again; I shrug her off. "I tried to. I asked you to come as soon as you could. And you did."

"I don't want to hear!" I scream.

"Solange!" Rand says strictly; I feel it, like a whiplash.

"Jesus *fuck!*" I stand up. "You really are a pair of fuckers! How *could* you do that?" I hit out at my mother. "Marry *him!*"

"You *did* divorce me," Rand says dryly.

"That's nothing to do with it!" I snap, sitting down again.

"Solange . . . darling . . ." My mother touches me soothingly. "We fell in love. We go very well together."

"I bet you do."

"At least I waited until you were divorced before I slept with your husband," she tells me, calmly.

I stare at her, aghast. She knows I fucked Philippe.

"Oh, God . . ." I feel on the point of collapsing again.

"It is all right, *ma chérie.*" She cuddles me to her.

"He told you . . ." I whisper.

"Yes. After the divorce. He was trying to hurt me."

"I thought that's *why* you wanted to divorce!" I snap ironically.

"Solange . . ." She looks at me reproachfully, my beautiful mother, to whom I've never been spiteful in my life.

My eyes fill with tears. "I'm *sorry.*" I look from her to Rand, brave a smile. "Listen . . . it was such a shock. Of course you must love each other, or you wouldn't have married. It's just . . . oh, that's not what I'm upset about. Not *that* . . ."

My Maman hugs me from one side, Rand from the other. And I cry, sobbing, like I've never cried since Jan left me . . .

*   *   *

The next two weeks I spend with Maman and Rand is the best time I've had for a long time. I call Miriam to get up-to-date with the news. Marie-Claude and Jed are still away on their honeymoon; there's a postcard from Tahiti. Miriam's sent on the rest of my mail, including a letter from Justin and one from Roy, both wanting to know when I'm returning and what's happening about my next book. Roy wants to schedule me for a promotion tour. I tell Miriam to tell them I may never be back; that I'll let them have the manuscript of the fifth Pandora book as soon as it's completed. And I emphasize to Miriam: *Please* don't tell anyone where I am.

Rand and I have found our perfect relationship. He should always have been my stepfather, anyway. I always suspected that was the reason I married him.

Watching Maman and Rand together, I can't deny that they're happy and genuinely in love. They work well together. Rand's latest manuscript is nearly complete. This one's very technical. "Sheer brilliance, of course," Rand said. Maman too is halfway through her next novel; that too is exquisite as always.

Rand wanted to sell our house, as he and Maman had bought this one. But I pointed out to him that it was still half mine; I promptly paid him for his half. So now I have a house here as well as in Malibu, a residence in *La Belle France*. I've been thinking that perhaps Miriam and I should come back here to live.

"I must go home," I announce at dinner.

"Mais non, ma chérie!" Maman says emphatically.

"I have to. I need to write. And I want to see how I feel when I'm back there. I think I might just move back here."

"Don't do anything rash," Rand counsels. "Véronique and I are always here for you."

"Yes, Papa," I giggle, causing Rand to raise an eyebrow. He smiles gently.

"I really *am* glad you're both so happy," I tell them honestly. "You've helped me over Jan ... well, somewhat. Oh, I did so want you to meet him."

"Darling ..." Maman pats one of my hands while Rand pats the other. "You must stay as long as you want with us. Or, you must return to us. We are here for you. We understand what it is you have been going through."

"Well ..." I've suddenly realized what it is I must do next. "I've got myself some parents. So what I need now is to see my gorgeous adopted brothers."

Maman smiles. "You will go and see Lars and Kris in Sweden?"

"Yes!—Well, they always were like brothers. Sort of." I

smile. "I guess that makes it incest, all the fucking Lars and I did. But then, that's okay, isn't it?" I look cheekily at Rand, pat his face. "After all, I fucked my stepfather too, didn't I?"

"Both of them!" Maman laughs, sending me off again in a chain reaction.

I kiss them both tenderly. "I think I'll leave *tomorrow*."

* * *

Before me, two tall and smiling Larssons. Lars, just over six feet six; Kris, just under. Both in fur jackets, jeans, boots to their knees. And they've brought the children with them, their blond, excited, shining little faces bobbing around me.

"Lars!"

"Solange, *älskling!*"

Lars lifts me up and swings me around in a warm, loving hug. I swear he gets taller every time I see him. "It is so beautiful to see you," he says, kissing me.

The children hug me around the waist, tug at my arms. "You've all grown so *big*," I tell them, giving each a kiss.

"Solange"—Lars put his arm around my shoulders—"this is Hjördis." I'm face to face with a very beautiful girl. Hjördis is Norwegian, in her late twenties. She and Lars have been together for over a year now. Hjördis is very pregnant. A faint smile crosses her face, hardly reaches her huge, round, blue eyes. She has that Scandinavian china-doll kind of beauty. Her long platinum hair is plaited around the back of her head.

"Hello." I hug and kiss her. "It's good to meet you at last."

"Hello, Solange," she replies, shyly.

"Let us get *out* of here." Lars has spoken. He drives us to the Larsson home, in the country quite a way from Stockholm. I sit in the back with the twins and Kris, who keeps his arm protectively around me; Hjördis sits with Lars in the front, with the other children.

"You have got curls now," Lars remarks. "And why did you not bring Jan Axelsson?" He glances at me in the driving mirror. But I don't say anything.

We drive westward from Stockholm, through Vastera, until we reach the tiny village of Kolshammer, on the other side of which is the huge Larsson estate. It's dark already, though it's only early afternoon. Sverige—images of snow and silent forests. Fir trees, birch trees, larch trees, tiny lakes.

The wrought iron gates swing open and the big Mercedes limousine cruises up the long, winding driveway to the house.

The Larsson clan all live here together: Lars, twins Kris and Sven, and Bo, their cousin, who's also a member of their group. It's two years since I was last here, when I spent two months with Lars. Our loving at that time was so different from the awkward gaucheneses of teenagers. Lars wanted me to stay ... I wonder why I didn't?

We're greeted at the huge chateau of a house by Sven and his wife Anni. Oh, I love it here! The house is so big, and yet so warm. The lounge, huge, overlooks an enormous garden flanked by a wood on one side and a tiny lake on the other. Perhaps in this studied landscape simplified by snow, I can find myself.

"So . . ." says Lars, "why do you not stay with us? You are unhappy, *älskling*."

"Not now, I'm not."

"Come . . ." he says, striding across the lounge and grabbing my hand. "We go and talk."

We talk, and I tell him about what's been happening.

Over dinner that evening we're all still discussing the situation with Jan.

"It is no good," Lars says. "Why did you leave? Don't you know that the situation of Jan and his wife will never work? No one could go on like that, least of all Jan Axelsson. Why did you not wait, *insist* that you be together?"

"It's easy enough to say that," I tell him, "but it's *over*."

"And you make sure it is, huh?" Lars retorts impatiently.

"Oh, Lars!" I flash him a halfhearted smile.

"I know you, Solange, love. You cannot pretend with me."

"I don't want to pretend with you. I want to get over everything with you all here. That's why I came. It always feels so good here."

"Then you should stay," Kris says. "You should have come here instead of going off to America. Didn't we all tell you that at the time?"

"Yes, and perhaps you were right. I don't know. Perhaps I will, now. But I don't know that, yet."

* * *

My room is warm and comforting: whitewood furniture; a lovely king-size bed. From the window I can see the forest; but everything's so dark. I think I'll finally get over Jan-Toby Axelsson here, finally be made whole again on this warm island of friends amid the gloomy northern snows.

And I think Jan would have loved it here too. I think that he would have loved my Larsson clan. Dear Lars—I always feel so close to him. He's definitely the brother I never had. And Kris, too; in fact, they're all brothers I never had. Lars is just over one year older than me, and the twins Kris and Sven are just ten months younger. All of them look so much alike—so tall and thin, and all with pale blue, deep-set eyes, and that long, long hair, pale yellow, hanging down their backs, worn tied back or plaited. They've always had long hair, ever since I've known them.

I look at Jan's photo, stroke its mustache. Oh Jan, why aren't *you* there with me?—you should be.

The Larsson clan are working on an album down in the basement studio. I listen to the music. It's very good: heavily classical-influenced, spacey at times. "My Swedish Pink Floyd," I tease Lars. "Why don't you come to America?"

"With all that competition?" Kris laughs. "We couldn't take it."

"Too many rock groups there already, without us," Lars says, with a hug for me.

I grin at them all: my long, blond, lanky Larsons. "Don't you believe it. Jan . . ." I stop for a moment. "Jan likes you. He was looking forward to meeting you again. *Really* getting to know you."

"We like being kings of the mountain here," Lars says. "In America, they don't even know us. And Sweden's already exported Abba. We're a national treasure, aren't we?" He winks.

"But they're only a pop group, not a heavy rock group. And besides, you'd pay less tax there."

"We have all we could possibly want here."

"Roy would soon get you into the top ten," I tease.

"Thanks, but no thanks. We prefer the *civilized* Europe."

"There I find it hard to disagree with you," I admit. "Now I have to collect the children from school. I've put myself on the rota to do things."

"Domesticated already, are you?" he laughs. "You need someone to be domesticated *with*."

"*That* is a good idea," Kris says, striking a chord on his guitar.

"I think I will have to watch these two," Lars says to the rest of the band, striking an answering chord on the piano.

"You leave us alone," I tell him. "You have Hjördis to watch."

"There's hope for me yet, then," Kris smiles, taking a toke

at his joint. He stares at me intensely for a second or two, then winks and smiles.

"I should be so lucky!" I say, with the sudden thought that it *would* be nice to fuck Kris.

I go and collect the kids from their school. It feels nice to drive the Saab station wagon with all the kids jumping around and shouting with excitement. I know I need to be a mama, with my own kids jumping around in the back of the car.

*   *   *

"Come up *here*, Solange." Krista's voice echoes down from above me.

"It's too hot up there."

We're all together in the sauna: a huge sauna full of naked, pink bodies. Everybody's on the top shelves except me. Maybe I should brave it, too, melt away some of my unwanted inches.

"Come and *try*," somebody shouts.

I stand up, climb up onto one of the top shelves. "Oh my God, it's too hot!" I climb down again.

"You come out now!" The children jump down, pull at my hands and feet. "We go out in the snow now."

"NO!!" I sit up, cling to the shelf. "Oh, no! Last time I was here, Lars threw me into the snow and I caught pneumonia."

"Oh, such an exaggeration, Solange!" Lars protests.

"It was awful; so *cold!*"

"You are spoilt. Thoroughly spoilt," Lars says. "It is through living in the south of France and in California."

"They are at least *warm*," I say heatedly.

"You do not know what is good for you." Everybody gets up to go.

"I am *not* going out in the snow. Don't you dare!" I pout.

Lars laughs. "You are a coward."

"I'm not in training to be a Spartan, so I'll be a coward, with pleasure. And with *warmth*." I lie back and close my eyes. The heat's making me daydreamy. I think I'll get a sauna built at home.

"Why don't you come up here with me?"

I open my eyes. I didn't think anyone was left, but I should have guessed!

"Come on . . . !" Kris's voice echoes down.

"It's too hot up there. I've tried it once."

"Hot? It is not, not at all. Come on up; you will like it."

I go and sit next to Kris, lie down next to him, and he leans over me and kisses me. My arms go around his neck and I smile. I think Lars was right. Some loving *is* what I need.

"You want to fuck in the sauna?" I ask Kris.

"Is impossible," he laughs.

"It is?"

"Totally."

"I'm getting too hot up here."

"Come." Kris jumps down and pulls me into his arms, into a long kiss. . . . "We go cool off," he says at last.

"But not in the snow?" I panic.

"Of course."

"No! It's too cold!"

"Then after, we go to bed and warm up."

"We do?"

"We *do!*"

And that's just what we do, of course.

* * *

"Why did Greta go?" I ask Kris. We're sitting up in bed, eating, in the middle of the night.

"It did not work out."

"But you were together for three years."

"We grew apart during three years."

"How long has it been since she went?"

"Two months. But I am not upset about it now. Well," he adds with a gentle smile, "not much, now."

"Do you still see . . . what's her name? The one you used to see on Wednesdays?"

"Ingrid? Yes, I still do."

"Oh yes," I tease. "And tomorrow is Wednesday, isn't it?"

"Yes." Kris pulls me closer. He's sitting up against a pile of pillows; I straddle him, and he holds onto my bottom. "I will not go."

"Why not? You must. You mustn't disrupt your routine for me. I'll only be here for a few more weeks; it wouldn't be fair. You go."

"Are you sure?" He looks uncertain for once.

"Of course I'm sure." I kiss him to show it's all right.

"You know, she is thinking of divorcing Erik."

"And then, will you get married?" I feel happy at the idea of Kris being settled and happy at last.

"I don't know. . . . Our relationship has not been on that

level. Just once a week, for five years. But I think we might try living together. We are good friends. And of course, we enjoy our fucking together."

"Like us?" I ask happily.

"You I definitely enjoy fucking."

"So I gathered." We kiss. "I'm glad. It brings us even closer."

"I like that too, *älskling.*"

I hug myself to Kris, and he grips my ass firmly in his large hands. "I've been thinking about staying," I tell him, "or about coming back, I should say. I really have to go home first, but I think I've almost decided to move back to France, and to here as well. I can commute."

"You would like that?"

"Mm. Start a new life. I'm lucky that I can do that. How many other people can? Or have the resources to do it?"

"Yes, you can write your books here just as well. Why not?"

"Yes, I think so. The Nordic muse may not be quite the same as the Californian one, but it should be an interesting mixture, don't you think?"

"Yes. . . . Well, I would be very pleased." He holds me tightly around the waist.

I lean back, looking into those pale blue eyes of his. "Would you, really? And what about Ingrid, then? You said you might marry Ingrid."

"I might. If she gets a divorce and puts our relationship on a different level. But *we* would still be friends."

"Yes, please." I hug him tightly around the neck. "You know, I'm glad we're having this little affair." I sit myself back and look at him again; he stares intently back at me. "I'm very lucky, Kris. I've known some beautiful men. And even Jan . . . I mean, though it has hurt me, I'm glad I had it. I'd never have *not* had it—the experience of it. And the love."

He pulls me closer to him, and we dissolve into a prolonged kiss.

He puts the rest of the white wine into the glass we've been sharing. We drink a little of it, and then he pushes me back onto the bed, pours the rest of the wine onto my pussy, and begins to eat me.

"It is nice, yes?" He licks at the wine.

"It is nice—oh, yes . . ."

Wednesday afternoon I stood in the doorway and waved to

293

Kris and he left for Stockholm, and Ingrid. The car disappeared from sight, and I felt a slight twinge of something I don't often feel—jealousy. Maybe that's good for me.

Now I'm in bed, reading and thinking. I talked to Miriam for hours on the phone today, as I did with Maman. I phoned Reg, too. I felt I had to. I feel it's not fair just to never get in touch with him again. All the same, nothing could ever come of our relationship, I'm sure both of us know that. Our differences are too great.

Kris returns. He seems to be in a bit of a temper. I'm curious, but I don't feel I have the right to ask why.

The week goes quickly. We take the children for walks in the woods, play snowballs, make a snowman. For the first time since Jan left me, I actually wake up without mentally hurting, get through the day without remembering and without the pain those memories still bring. And how could I *not* be happy here with my Larsson clan?

It's Wednesday again, and again I wave Kris off to Stockholm. And again he returns in a temper the next day. And again I wonder why.

I go for a walk with Lars. We talk and laugh—my beloved Lars, who always makes me feel so happy. He is pleased that Kris and I are finding this little patch of happiness together. I ask him about Kris, and he tells me that Kris *always* returns from Ingrid's in a bad temper. Why? "I don't know," Lars laughs. "Evidently, he should not go, don't you think?"

After the third Wednesday, and the third time Kris returns in a temper, I think that maybe I *should* say something, but again decide not to. Me, the coward: after all, I tell myself, I don't have the right. We make love; his temper isn't directed at me, and it soon evaporates.

Lars and Britta Larsson arrive to spend the weekend with us all. It's so good to see them both again; to me, they seem as much my parents as my own do. The weekend goes pleasantly, too quickly, like a heady glass of champagne.

Monday evening: After the children are in bed, we're all sitting in the lounge, talking and laughing. The phone rings. It's Marie-Claude, home from her stunning Tahitian honeymoon, and back in Dahl-lahs. Miriam told her where to find me. Jed comes on the line; they both talk at once.

"How do you *do* that, both talking to me? Is it an extension?" I ask.

"An amplifier," Jed answers. "Are you all right? What in tarnation are you doin' in *Sweden?* You sound a mite bit peaky to me, Ma'am."

"A mite bit peaky?" I burst out laughing.

"*Es-tu chez Lars?*" Marie-Claude asks.

I reply in English, "Lars is about to become a daddy, with Hjördis." I smile at Lars. I'm sitting on Kris' lap, sharing a joint with him. "I'm with Kris. I'm going home to California at the end of the week, though. But it won't be home much longer. I'm going to sell the Malibu house and come back here. I have the house in France now, and I'll be here too, some of the time. A new life, you know."

"What d'you mean by that, Ma'am?" Jed barks. "Whaddya mean, you're leavin' Malibu?"

"What I said, Jed. There's nothing there for me anymore."

"But why don't you come to us?" he asks. "Me and Marie-Claude . . ."

"I don't want to," I reply, a little abruptly.

Marie-Claude talks in French, fast and excitedly, upset. I try to answer her questions.

"And how come you don't want to be comin' and visitin' with me and Marie, Ma'am?" Jed demands affrontedly.

"It's just that I don't want to be in Texas—anywhere *near* Texas. But I'd love it if you came and visited me."

"Lady . . . I don't think you know what you're doin'."

"I *do*, Jed. Really I do. Listen here, you Texan cowboy, I've had to start a new life. It's not something I wanted, but it's something I've *got*. And I'm *doing* it, I'm getting on with it. Jan-Toby Axelsson isn't the only man in the world. And *he* walked out on me, remember." My hand is shaking, and my eyes flood with tears, but I battle on. "I'm not letting that bastard get to me again. Not anymore. I'm stronger than that, I'm getting myself over it. But he's *not* strong. He obviously *needs* that little blackmailing prison Melissa keeps him in. He's not tearing *my* life in two, though. Not anymore!" God, I feel so angry! "Miriam was absolutely right. She tried and tried to get me to see the truth, and she was right. You *don't* walk out on someone you really *love*. It's so obvious to me now, but I couldn't see it then. I'd have done anything for him, Jed, I loved him so much. But I was put in my little mistress place. He sure showed me how much he loved me!" I say scornfully. "Miriam was right; he didn't *want* to work the situation out so that we could be together. And I'm damn fuckin' sure we could have. *If* he'd wanted to, that is."

I'm still shaking at the end of this tirade. Solange—little Ms. Feisty-Ass for the first time! And it's about time, too!

"I don't wish to discuss it anymore," I say into the dead silence from the other end. "I don't wish to hear that name anymore. It's over, finally, absolutely. *Over*." I calm myself down with a deliberate effort. "But I don't see why it should affect *our* friendship, though. I hope it doesn't. As soon as I'm settled, I want you both to come and stay with me for a while."

Still silence in return. Why don't they answer, say something? "How is Nils?" I ask. "Give him my love, when you see him. And tell him he's to come and see me too." Listening to the faint crackle of the phone line, I realize for the first time that everyone's eyes are on me. I smile nervously, feel Kris's arm tighten about my waist, kiss the side of his head. "How *is* Mister Jan-Toby Axelsson, super-star-and-super-stud, anyway? Back to his sixteen-year-old groupies who give great head? Visiting the raunchiest little whorehouse in Dallas?"

"I reckon that's about the size of it, Ma'am," Jed answers dryly. "But you forgot to mention the booze." I can't make out what he's trying to say. "That's on the itinerary as well, these days," he adds.

"I don't understand." I don't. Jan doesn't drink. I feel concerned now, though. "What d'you mean? Jan doesn't drink."

"I mean he's got it down to a whole quart of Scotch and a six-pack. Unless of course it's a quart of vodka and a six-pack." Jed sounds cynical. Why? He's Jan's best friend. What's been going on? But maybe I don't want to know.

"You mean Jan-Toby is drinking a whole bottleful of whiskey a *day*? But why? What's got into him to make him do that? What's wrong with him? Can't you stop him, Jed? No, I don't suppose . . . *Why* is he drinking, Jed? I don't understand. I mean, he ought to be happy now, he's got his son with him, and that's the most important thing in his life, isn't it? Nothing else is as important as that." I feel stupid, as though I'd had no sleep for a week.

I look around my Larsson clan, all watching me intently. "Jed, he's your friend, your best friend. You've got to stop him. *Talk* to him, get him to stop."

"Why don't *you* talk to him, Ma'am?" Jed says quietly.

"*Me?*"

"He's here listening. So's Nils and Joel."

"*What!*" My hand shakes. I hold the phone away from me, nearly put it down.

Okay, Solange, get yourself together. After all, Jan doesn't want you any more, but that doesn't mean you have to be petty, spiteful, revengeful over it. It's a blow to your ego, sure. But you wouldn't want anything to happen to Jan.

And this may be a good time to show him how well you're managing without him. Show him how magnanimous you are; show him you can still be "friends."

"Solange." Jan's deep voice comes over the phone, sounding huskier than usual for some reason, like he had a sore throat. Why can't I answer?"

"Solange?"

"Jan?" My voice shakes.

"You're in Sverige?"

"Yes, I'm in Sverige."

"I'm in Dallas."

"I gathered you're in Dallas."

Some great conversation! But what else have we to say to each other? That's all we're left with these days. Perhaps I should discuss the weather next!

"How is your wife?" No answer to my bitchy question. "And how is Andy?"

"Talkin' a lot more than he was, last time I saw him."

Last time he ... ? "That's good," I say automatically. I hear him slurping away. It reminds me of that crazy conversation we had before, such a long time ago now, when we were lovers. "Are you working on your book? On your album?"

Why doesn't he answer?

"Are you all right, Lady?" he finally barks at me.

"*I* am fine, Jan. But you sound so ... *Why are you drinking?*" I sound angry. Suddenly, I *am* very angry with him.

I hear him drink some more. He sniffs hard. "Don't knock it, Lady! I mean ... it gets me through the day, through the night. Through my fuckin' life."

"But why do you *need* to drink, Jan? You never did before." Such an irate tone in my voice. "Seems to me, if you need booze to get you through something, then the something you're doing is *wrong*." I hear him slurping his drink again. "Jan, are you working?"

"Ain't done any work on my book, not since ... Can't seem to concentrate. Done a song, though—'Mad Man.' But that was easy—'cause that's how I'm feelin'.'"

"Are you recording?"

"When I get back to L.A." Slurp.

I don't know what to say next. I have to try to care for him, even if it seems hopeless from this distance. "Jan, please don't drink. You can't work well that way. Your work, your creativity, they're most important to you. Don't throw them away, darling. They're so good. You're so good." I'm surprised at how *gently* I'm speaking to him. "What's the matter? Why are you unhappy? I thought you'd be happy, with Andy. After all, it's why you ended our relationship, isn't it? I guess it's nothing to do with me anymore, but . . . you *must* take care of yourself, Jan." He takes another gulp of drink; it's amazing how the amplifier picks the sound up. "Well, I'm glad we could talk, anyway. Take care of Andy. And of yourself, too. Jan? *Jan . . . ?*" He doesn't answer. "Jan—put Marie-Claude on."

"Solange?" Marie-Claude's voice sounds so warm and friendly and welcoming after that weird, empty talk with Jan.

"Darling, listen—I've got to go. I'll call you from home. My love to you both, to you all."

I put the phone down slowly. Stare at it.

"Jan doesn't drink," I say to Lars and Kris. "I don't understand that . . ."

"It sounds as if he is not happy," Lars says.

"But why not? He left me so that he could *be* happy—with Andy. There's nothing else meant anything to him. So now . . . I just don't understand . . ." I stare at Lars, at Kris. "Why can't he be happy when he's doing something he *wants?* Something he *chose* to do? I don't understand that at all."

Lars comes and squats in front of me as I sit on Kris's knee. "Are you all right, *älskling?*"

"Yes . . . It just . . . it just shook me up a bit. But at least we've talked as friends now."

Lars caresses my face. "It sounds as though Jan is a very disturbed man."

"But his son was the only important thing to him," I say once again. More important than what we had together—than the babies we could have had together. So why . . . ?" I brave a smile. "I don't think I understand men at all."

I cuddle myself close to Kris. I feel strange, but relieved: I've talked to Jan, and I didn't cave in. Maybe now I can accept the fact that he doesn't want me, doesn't need me, doesn't even love me anymore. Yes . . . I think it's good that we talked. I think I *have* proved to myself that I'm getting over him at last.

*   *   *

Kris and I make love for a long time. It's almost dawn when we finally cuddle up to sleep. Kris *enjoys* making love so. He makes me feel so female. It's just what I need. And I

298

think it's just what he needs, too. At least he's not bad-tempered the next morning.

I feel warm and safe, cuddling up to him with my head on his shoulder, falling asleep with his arm tightly around me.

When I wake up, I'm confused for a moment, then I suddenly remember. Everything comes back to me, all in one condensed but orderly sequence. The phone call and then Kris and me, making love.

I sit up, see it's nearly noon. Noon? I couldn't have slept that long!

I'm by myself in the bedroom. I kneel up on the bed, looking down at the blue sheet, crumpled and stained. My body smells sexy. Kris' sex. But all I can think about is poor Jan. You'd better just get your act together, *Ma'am!*

I go down to the kitchen and have some coffee and one of the delicious freshly-baked rolls Anni has just taken from the oven. My Larsson clan are rehearsing in their studio; I slip in quietly and wait until they finish the number. Lars and Kris notice me and beckon to come and see them. They cuddle me in turn and ask if I'm all right. Kris leans over and kisses me. They're so tall, it makes me giggle—I have to lean my head back to see them properly.

"Skall vi gå ut och gå?" Kris asks me, smiling teasingly as he watches me translating what he said. Even after all this time, my Swedish isn't good. I can get by with it, but I wish I were as fluent as the children are with their English.

"Ja?" he prods me.

"Ja." I go on tiptoe to kiss him. "We will go for a walk."

Our long walk in the woods does me good. He's concerned about last night; I feel fine, I reassure him. If only I could reassure myself that I were really fine!

Next day is Wednesday, and I wave Kris off to see Ingrid again. In the night I wake up. It feels strange sleeping by myself. I don't think I like sleeping by myself. It's an extremely lonely proposition, sleeping by oneself.

It's afternoon when Kris returns, again in a temper. He lights up a joint and gulps at his hot coffee. His temper this week is decidedly fiercer than the three previous times.

I kneel in front of him. *"Vlad står på?"* I ask.

"Nothing is the matter," he replies in English, still fiercely. He stands up. "Come," he says, holding out his hand. "We go to bed."

"We do?"

"Ja!"

I have to run to keep up with his gigantic strides. In the bedroom he pulls off his black velvet jacket, sits on the bed, pulls off his boots and throws them across the room.

"Kris, what is it?"

"I do not wish to discuss it."

"Then I do not wish to be fucked!" I walk away.

"Solange!" I turn back. "I'm sorry..." He holds out his arms to me. "Solange?" he says, standing up. He's in tight brown cords and has a pink shirt over a black polo-neck sweater; his long hair is loose, falling limply around him. He looks rather delicious. I smile, walk over, hug him around the waist, press myself against him. My long, lean Larsson.

"It fits in my tummy-button," I say, pressing against him.

He laughs. "There are other places I prefer it to fit."

"I know. It has—all three!" I giggle.

We're soon in bed. He fucks me angrily, and it reminds me of Jan, a thought I angrily turn away.

We sleep for an hour, and when we awake his temper is gone. I enjoy myself with him, massaging his back, licking and kissing him, giving him another beautiful erection. I sit up and straddle him, lower myself onto him; he holds my waist as we move together slowly, sensuously. We're gazing at each other, concentrating on each other's sensations.

Kris comes, and we stay quiet, just looking at each other, still smiling at each other. Straddling him there, it feels good, warm and loving, sticky and nice. Kris pulls me down onto him, and we kiss and cuddle for a long time.

"I wish I didn't have to go," I whisper. "I'm going to miss you."

"We'll miss you, too."

"Tell me, Kris—why are you always in a temper when you come back from seeing Ingrid?" There, I've asked it at last.

"She annoys me so," he says immediately. "She annoys me, not getting the situation with Erik resolved. She wants to leave him, yet..."

"And you—you want her to? You want to see what you both really have, together?"

"I think so. Yes, I think so."

We sit up. I pile pillows behind him to make him more comfortable. And I straddle him again, so that he's holding my ass in his hands as we sit up against the pillows. "Do you think you could be happy with her in a permanent relationship?"

"We would have to try...." He sounds defensive.

"Yes, one can only try." I hug myself close to him, kiss him. "I hope you'll be happy, Kris. I *want* you to be happy. You've given me so much happiness, happiness I didn't think I could have, after Jan."

He kisses me tenderly. "You are beautiful, *älskling*."

"*You* are beautiful, Kristoffer Larsson. I've always thought that." We kiss some more. "I don't know how to thank you, you've helped me so much," I tell him. "I feel . . . I feel *whole* again. I know that's an awful cliché, but it's true. I feel I have a life to look forward to again, a life of my own. I was just running away from my memories of Jan. I can accept them now. Now, I feel like if I had a relationship, I'd be going to that person, not just running away from Jan." I hug and kiss Kris over and over again, making him laugh. "Dear, darling Kris. *Älskling* Kris. I do so want you to be happy. You *must* be happy with Ingrid, if you want her."

"I hope that you will come back again soon. You stayed away from us for too long." Kris holds me to him, smiles softly, kisses me.

"Our little affair has been nice," I tell him, with kisses. "And if you ever want someone . . . need someone . . . I mean, if it doesn't work out with Ingrid . . . well, you know where I'll be."

Kris glances at me, then looks away, smiling. "It has been so good with you, *älskling*. We would easily fall in love with each other, I know, if you did not have Jan—but he is still there for you. And if I did not have Ingrid, and the thought of what she and I could have. Maybe after it is all over we shall say we should have taken what we had and made a good deep love from it. It would be so easy to do that. But now you *have* to go back and get you and Jan sorted out, and I must be here and get me and Ingrid sorted out. We have helped each other, *älskling*, to reach this point of departure. It was help that we both of us needed." He kisses me. "But perhaps even now, I should not let you depart." He winks.

"Oh, Kris . . . let's make love *all* day and night."

"That is a good idea, *älskling*."

"Let's do everything to each other, for each other. It will be something to remember, something nice."

"*That* is a very good idea, too."

He kisses me. But we don't say anything more; we don't need to.

18

"What are you *taking?*"

Miriam looks at me suspiciously as I clutch the four tablets in my hand.

"Two Pamprin for my period, and two Bufferin for my cold."

"It's nearly Christmas, too." She leaves my bedroom, and I'm left wondering what the connection's supposed to be. I pop my pills with the Perrier water I got from the fridge.

Miriam comes back with a glass of bright green liquid, which she swirls around over ice cubes. "For your *cold,*" she informs me brightly.

"Miriam, crème de menthe won't help a cold. Or will it?"

"It's not crème de *menthe.* It's *Nyquil*—on the *rocks.* A *double.* It's *great.* It'll knock you *out* for the *night.*" She hands me the glass. "Come on, *drink* it."

I drink a little. "Oh God, it's strong, Miriam!"

"*Drink it!*" I drink it. "Now, settle *down.*" I do, and Miriam sits on the edge of the bed. "Well, you're certainly looking *better* these days." She leans over and kisses me gently on the cheek, stands up. "Well, I'll *see* you in the *morning.* Now, go to *sleep.*"

I close my eyes and listen to her leave the room, open them as soon as she's gone. I'm beginning to feel a little drowsy already.

I've been home from Sweden for nearly a month now, and I've been working very hard. At least twelve hours a day on my book. Hiding myself in my words allows me to become whole again.

* * *

Miriam's fussing around me as I drink my morning coffee. "Are you *sure* you don't want to *come* with me?"

She looks annoyed. I refused to go with her to Chicago for Christmas with her parents. But I really do just want to stay at home. Just me and Gulley.

Maman and Rand also wanted me for Christmas, and Marie-Claude and Jed wanted me to go there. Then there was my Larsson clan, but I just wanted to be by myself.

So, with Gulley, I spend Christmas Day writing.

Maman and Rand call. It's good to hear their voices, and they're glad I'm happy once again. Marie-Claude calls too, excited and happy with all the things Jed has bought her.

My presents: I'd been so busy, I'd forgotten to open them. Gulley and I sit excitedly among the wrappings. Such nice presents. Books and a beautiful lace nightdress. A gold Peretti heart-shaped compact from Marie-Claude and Jed.

Two more packages. The larger one contains earrings— large hoops and two smaller ones—and a pendant, all of beaten silver. The pendant, on a silver chain, is a small, stylized Aztec eagle—like the tattoos Nils and Jan have. The note with the package is from Nils. He *made* all the jewelry.

And lastly, a small package. Inside it, a huge square-cut emerald ring. And a note, from Jan of course: *"Saw this and thought it would go well with your pendant and earrings. All my love to you, Literary Lady. I love you. Jan."*

Why did he do that? You don't send presents to ex-mistresses. Guilt—that's why. Perhaps he thinks he's buying me off? Why, yes—a nice *expensive* emerald ring should do it!

But he really didn't *have* to send me a present. I wish he hadn't. Now I have to thank him. What sort of a thank-you letter do you send to an ex-lover? Why the hell are you worrying anyway, Solange? After all, you sent *him* a present, didn't you?

When I was in London, at a favorite little bookstore that specialized in rare books and special editions, I saw a new edition of Joseph Conrad. Each book was exquisitely bound in leather. I knew Jan would like them. It really didn't matter that we weren't lovers anymore; I'd always want him as a friend.

And for Nils—I saw in Bond Street an antique chess set of Chinese jade. I sent it and Jan's books enclosed with my parcel of Christmas presents for Marie-Claude and Jed. I hope they liked them.

It's late. The phone rings again. Miriam? Marie-Claude? No, I've talked to them already.

"Hello?"

"Solange?" A deep voice. Deep Texan. Jan! I put the

receiver down hurriedly and leave it off so that it can't ring again. But then I realize it was Nils, not Jan at all. They sound so much alike, especially on the phone, but I can always hear that distinctively gratey quality in Nils' voice. Oh, hell! I feel so foolish.

He was ringing to thank me for his present, and to see what I thought of his. I guess I'd better call him back. But I can't, can I?

I'd have to call the Axelsson ranch, and what if Jan's there? No, he probably isn't though. He's probably with his wife and her family over Christmas. And anyway, Nils wouldn't have called me in front of Jan, would he? Nils is sensitive and understanding. He'd know how I feel.

I find the number and punch it out. The phone rings. My hand's actually shaking, in the brief space before I hear a voice.

"Hello. Kirsten Axelsson."

I manage to stammer, "Could ... could I speak to Nils, please?"

"Who is this, please?" Kirsten Axelsson, Jan's mother. Even after forty years in the U.S.A., her voice has a Swedish accent.

"Could I speak to Nils, please?" I repeat, then realize that I pronounced his name "Neels," not with a short "i" as people do here. "He called me a little while ago. . . . I . . ."

"Is that Solange?" she asks, her voice soft and gentle.

"Yes ... yes, it is." I'm trembling again because it's Jan's mother I'm talking to, and she must know all about us. "I'm sorry to disturb you," I say as coolly as I can manage. "I put the phone down on Nils, stupidly. I thought it was ... Oh, I'm sorry ..." Stop talking! You don't have to let everyone know what an absolute imbecile you are!

"It is nice to speak to you, Solange. Axel and I have wanted to meet you for a long time."

"I'd have liked to have met you, too."

"Nils tells me that you have recently been in Sverige?"

"Yes, I have some family there. Well, they seem like family."

"Are you having a nice *Jul?*"

"Oh yes, thank you. Quiet." I feel easier, and the trembling stops. "Marie-Claude and Jed wanted me to come to them, but . . . I just couldn't."

"Solange, we have been quite concerned . . ." Her voice trails off.

"Oh?"

"It is a bad situation. Sometimes . . . sometimes it is very hard for us women to understand why a man acts the way he does. Axel and I . . . we are very unhappy about this whole situation. It is not good to see one's son . . . I think you understand?"

"Yes . . . Yes, I do understand. And thank you for talking to me, Mrs Axelsson."

"It would have been nice to . . . I have never heard Jan speak of anyone, the way he speaks about you."

"Yes, well . . ." Why don't I feel upset or embarrassed anymore? We're just speaking woman to woman, I think that's why. "I loved your son very much." Silence. "I . . . I still do. I guess there's no point in denying that. If I *didn't* still love him, the love we had then couldn't have been very strong. But I'm learning that I *have* to manage. I understand what Jan's doing, what he's going through. Andrew is his son—he means a lot to him. And so he should . . ."

Silence. I think—I hope—we both understand each other. Women can hate each other in an instant for unknown reasons, but they can also understand each other.

"I will get Nils for you. He will be on the other line."

I listen for a while, hear voices faintly; hear another extension phone being picked up.

"Solange." Nils' voice, deep and gratey.

"I'm sorry, Nils. I thought . . . and I put the phone down without thinking. If you see what I mean. I'm sorry."

"Hey, it's all right, honey, I understand."

"How are you, Nils?"

"Fine, thank you, Ma'am. But how are you?"

"I'm fine, too. I've been watching my two favorite Franks on my video cassettes." He makes a puzzled noise. "Frank Langella as Dracula, and Tim Curry as Frank N. Furter." Nils laughs. "Your present, Nils—it was beautiful. And you *made* it! I'm wearing it now. I'll cherish it, always."

"I thought that making you a little silver tattoo would remind you . . . It'll look prettier than an actual tattoo, on you." He laughs. "And the chess set, it's beautiful. But you shouldn't have. I think it cost you a great deal of money."

"Oh Nils, that's got nothing to do with it. We're *friends*."

"We surely are, Ma'am."

"It's so good to hear you, Nils. Are you really all right?"

"Yes. But why didn't you call me before? You've been back home a whole *month*."

"I've been writing. Working. Actually . . . it's been good to be by myself. No *man*, I mean."

305

"Had a lot of men, then, have you?" he laughs. His laugh reminds me of Jan, filling my eyes with tears.

"No, not a lot."

"Solange—why don't you come here? Come to Marie-Claude and Jed's. We could talk. You need someone. You shouldn't be all by yourself, Ma'am."

"That's sweet of you, Nils. But, well . . . my writing is going well. And I'm thinking of selling this house. In fact, I *will* be selling it, after New Year's. Then I'll be moving back to France. Probably go between there and my Larsson clan in Sverige."

Silence.

"I've decided I'm not going to think about a man in my life until I've finished this book."

"Well, my brother may be an asshole—I've told him so, to his face—but I'm not. If he doesn't want you, well, I'm certainly interested, Ma'am. Now, how ya doin', lady? No owlshit, now."

"No owlshit, huh?" I laugh. "I'm *managing,* even though I still love him. The fact of his walking out on me doesn't stop me loving him. I don't know *how* to stop loving him, Nils, and I don't want to anyway. I think it will be easier when I'm living in France again. When I came back here and saw all the things around the house, I sort of . . . caved in again. It's all those *boots* he's left!" I sniff hard, but I know Nils knows I'm crying. "Why did he do it, Nils? Why did he throw away what we had? Jed says he's drinking. When he talked to me on the phone, he was smashed. He sounded so . . . Is he all right? It worries me so. It's so unlike him. It scares me. Nils, I . . . I think I'm beginning to *hate* him for what he's done to us. Oh, Nils, I feel so empty without him . . . and I love him so very much. And I find that so confusing. That I should still love him, when it's over."

Nils and I finish talking. It would be nice to see him, and to see Marie-Claude and Jed, too. I *need* to see Marie-Claude. Perhaps I could pump up my courage and go visit them all.

I tell Nils to thank Jan for me, for the beautiful ring. Jan was pleased with the books, he tells me. More than pleased; in fact, it shook him up a bit to receive them so unexpectedly.

When Miriam returns a few days later, I'm still considering whether I should go to Texas, whether I *can* go.

* * *

"Happy New Year, Gulley."

Purr and a squinge of eyes, from Gulley.

We're in bed, reading. What better way to see the New Year in? I stare at the Bête mask hanging on the wall—strangely empty now, like my relationship with Jan.

Miriam tried to persuade me to go to that party with her and Howie, but I didn't want to. Seeing the New Year in with my beloved Gulley, reading, suits me fine. I'd rather shut myself off in a warm, orderly, safe cocoon, than feel myself alone amid a raucously rejoicing crowd.

New Year's Day. I receive phone calls from all my friends, and even Johnny Brandigan. Nils rings too. It's a nice feeling to have so many people thinking of me. I go to bed early.

The day after New Year's sees me arguing with Miriam about another party she wants me to go to this evening.

"Look," she says, despairingly holding out her hands to me, "I think you *should*. You can always *leave*, if you really *want*."

"I won't like it. You know I don't like parties much."

"You *can't* stay at *home* all the time, just *writing* and *reading!*"

"Why not?"

"It's *not good* for you!"

"Of course it's good for me, Miriam. It's what I like to do. It's what I enjoy doing!"

"Please! Just this *once."* She changes to cajolery from argument, comes up behind me as I sit at my desk in the study, encloses me in her arms, kisses the side of my cheek. *"Just* this *once.* You *know* I worry. *Please,* Solange. *Please!"*

Of course, she knows she has won. Maybe a party will do me some good, at that . . . .

It didn't. I stood around and watched starlets chase biggies who couldn't care less. Phil was there, and in exchange for a dinner date, I talked him into leaving early and driving me home.

I watch Phil drive off, then unlock the gate, stroll up my short driveway. The house lights are on: I always leave them on if I go out. But they show that there's a car in the driveway. Mine are in the garage—so . . . ? I cautiously walk closer, recognize the car: a black, dusty, beat-up old Porsche.

Oh God—Jan Toby Axelsson, what are *you* doing here?

I rush up to the front door. I want to scream: "Get out of my house immediately!"

But he'd expect that; he'd know he'd really got me uptight then. No, Solange darling, you are going to have to play this one coolly. Little Ms. Sophisticated-Ass *has* to reign supreme: "Why, Jan, what a lovely surprise! How delightful to see you!"

I open the door, hear some music playing. He's in the study. The nerve! The audacity! To just come into my house like this! Who does he think he is!

Cool down, baby. I stand by the study door, listen to the music. Oh yes, César Franck's "D Minor Symphony." Well, at least I taught him to appreciate good music, if nothing else. At least he got that out of our disastrous little affair.

I'm shaking—hell! I nervously rub my hands together. I turn the knob, open the door. Step through the doorway. He's sitting at my desk, reading a book. I slam the door behind me.

Jan-Toby Axelsson turns quickly and does a sort of double take. He stares at me. Perhaps he *is* drunk. But *I* look all right, don't I? Of course I do—tight black velvet pants, pink silk shirt. What's wrong with curvy and little, anyway? Some men love curvy and little. Doesn't he recognize me? Or, after all those tall, leggy, little-titted, willowy chicks he's been having, perhaps he just can't believe how short-legged and bouncy-boobed I really am?

"How are you, Jan?" I ask, quite naturally and with polished detachment. I stare at him with a look of indifference, and I step into the room, smile beautifully.

"You've got curls!"

"Great opening line!" I kick off my wooden sandals, stroll over to him, stand close by him.

I've never seen him looking quite like this. Even that night when he came here drunk, he didn't look like *this*, like a rumpled, crumpled disaster area. His face is drawn; there are dark circles beneath his eyes. He's lost weight. His hair is so much longer, down past his shoulders again, which I like; but it's untidy and looks as though it would do with a wash. His beard and mustache need trimming. He's wearing a dirty pair of jeans and an old tee shirt. I notice (pleased) that he's got his sun-angel on. And the identity bracelet I bought him. The same two tiny silver hoops in his left ear.

But in spite of the jewelry, Jan-Toby Axelsson looks a drunken mess.

I notice that there's an empty bottle of Chivas Regal on my desk and a half-empty bottle of vodka. Jan's holding a nearly empty glass in his hand. He finishes it and refills it with vodka and immediately gulps some down.

"*Do* help yourself," I say sarcastically.

"You've got curls!" he barks at me again.

308

"Very observant, Herr Axelsson."

He cocks his head to one side, looks me up and down. "Where've you been?" he snaps.

"You're asking *me* where I've been?" I don't believe this! He stands up, towering above me; sways. I look down at his feet: high-heeled boots. His chest is a few inches from my face, and I have an almost irresistible urge to kiss it (I used to do that once). I step back. "Jan ... I don't want to sound rude, or belligerent even, but ... What the fuck are you doing in my house? It's breaking and entering, you know. I mean, stop me if I'm wrong, but wasn't it *you* who walked out?"

"Where've you been?" He pointedly ignores what I said, takes his glass, and retires to the chesterfield.

Okay, Solange. Answer his dumb question. Perhaps you can get rid of him then. ... Get rid of him? He looks as though he could do with a good meal and a long sleep; no wonder his mother was so worried. What's the *matter* with him? Why is he doing this to himself?

"I went to a party with Miriam and Howie, only it was *awful*, so I got a lift home with Phil."

"Party?"

"Yes ... Well, it was imbecilic! It was like a damn goldfish bowl full of obnoxious, narcissistic peacocks, floating about in all this *disco* noise." Jan laughs and takes another swig. "Mind you, it seems to me that here in California atrophy of the brain is considered to be a desirable state."

Jan laughs again. "You're right, lady."

I watch him finish his drink, place the glass by the side of the sofa, stare up at me. Jan-Toby Axelsson—my golden angel with his golden aura. Jan-Toby Axelsson—who totally absorbed me in his charisma. Jan-Toby Axelsson: his pallid, empty face seems almost featureless.

"What are you doing here, Jan?

"I flew in this afternoon from Texas. Went home for Christmas and New Years."

"I talked to Nils the other evening."

"I know, I was listening on the other line."

"I hope you enjoyed our conversation!" I say angrily.

"Nils didn't know, till after. He's already bawled me out." He stands up, swaying slightly, comes over and stands in front of me, grips my arms. "I just *had* to see you."

"Oh, did you? Well, *I* don't want to see *you*."

"Hm" He stares at the carpet, kicks his boot against it.

"Jan! *What* are you doing here? How *dare* you just come into my house like this!"

He lets go of my arms and just stares down at me. He smells strongly of drink. God, this is awful!

He touches me once again. I want to cry, cry for all I suddenly feel I've lost, including a healthily sober Jan. No, I should scream; that's what I should do: scream out in frustrated anger at him. But . . . his hands feel so good on my arms. Oh God, I *hate* him! My mind is conditioned for hate, but my body is still conditioned for love. Where is my armor plating?

Be bitchy. Yes, be smart-assed, Classy-Assed bitchy. Get him *out* of here.

"Jan—what *are* you doing here?" I repeat, shaking myself from his grip, taking a step backwards, staring up at him. "Well?" I smile sweetly. "Don't tell me—you came for your clothes? For your cameras, for your weights?" I clap my hands together: "Of course!" (Bitchiest smile I ever smiled.) "Your boots. It must be the boots. I mean, ten pairs at four hundred bucks a pop!"

He stares at me: a cold, undaunted stare. I go on regardless.

"Wait! I know. What else," I say in mock realization. "Only one other thing—right? The only thing you really ever came here for—*you want me to suck your cock.*"

The slap across my face sends me flying across the room, to land in a crumpled mess of my own. Undignified, very undignified, but for God's sake don't cry, Solange. Don't give him the satisfaction of letting him make you cry.

I'm dragged to my feet, held tightly in Jan-Toby Axelsson's arms. "I'm sorry, darlin' . . . I didn't mean . . . Oh, shit, I'm so sorry."

"Let go of me!" I push myself away from him, hit out at his chest. "Don't you ever touch me again, you sadistic bastard! Hitting me really turns you on, doesn't it? Get out of here!" I turn away from him and try to calm myself. It doesn't work, so I turn back to him and say, "Jan, please . . . I don't want to argue or be angry. Please, just go. If you wanted to see that I was all right, well, you've seen. I *am.* Now please go. Just go."

"Did I hurt you?" He touches my left cheek, where it's stinging from his slap. Pulls me into his arms again. "I'm sorry, darlin'."

I push myself away from him. "No . . . please go." Is that all I can say? Yes—that's all I *want* to say.

"I was readin' your stuff when you came in," he says.

"I gathered that."

He waves his hand towards the desk. "Not the Pandora stuff, the other—it's so *good*. What are you doing with it?"

Solange and Jan, immediate friends: talking about writing, as one craftsman to another.

"It's a project I'm working on. I do it in between my work on Pandora."

He's staring at me, that lost, puzzled stare he has at times. The same stare as when we first met. Why does he have to use *that* stare? He knows I love *that* stare. The bastard! He's doing it on purpose, that's what he's doing!

"Are you gonna publish it?"

"I don't know if anyone would be interested."

"Of course they would! But how do you know so much about her? There wasn't all that much written about Catherine Blake and her private life with William."

"I know. But what I do know . . . well, I'm a writer. It's fiction. But I've always known what she was like. Identified with her, known her feelings and her love for her man." I smile smugly, "I know all about loving a creative writer."

"You do, huh?"

"Yes," I say dryly, "I was married to Rand for a good many years."

Jan flashes me an Axelsson frown, then rubs the side of his nose. "I liked it. I more than liked it. And Pandora too—she's pregnant."

"Yes, by Jon-Bertil Jonsson, her Texas writer. Of course, she loves Jon. Only he doesn't know; he already has a wife and child." I flash him a delaMer frown, watch him retrieve his glass from the floor and go over to pour himself another drink.

"Don't!" I cry out. "Please don't! You've drunk enough. It frightens me to see you drinking so much."

He looks at the empty glass, fidgets from one foot to the other. Then he goes to his desk (well, it *is* his desk. I haven't moved or changed anything). He has some grass in the top drawer. I watch him roll a joint.

"Have myself some happy tobacco, if ya won't let me have my booze." He goes and sits down again, and again I'm wondering how I can get him out of here. Do I *want* him out of here? Of course I don't—I want him to stay. Forever. But he won't, so I want him gone.

"Tell me . . ."—Solange being polite and carefree, keeping our relationship on friendly terms so as to be able to broach the subject of his leaving—"how's your book of poetry coming along?"

"Told ya—wasn't doin' any. . . . I can't concentrate. It's not the same as workin' here with you." He frowns at me again, as though it was *I* who sent him away. "Been workin' on some songs, though. We've gotta start recordin'. I looked at the poetry manuscript only yesterday. That's when I realized I *had* to see you."

"Oh . . ." I go and sit in the corner of the sofa, curl my feet under me. "You've got all the songs you need?"

"Got a couple more to do. Been workin' 'em out with Joel. But I wish I could do somethin' on the book, though."

"Well, why don't you? You can take the typewriter and the desk and put them in your den."

"I ain't got a den." He frowns again, looks irritated, rubs the side of his nose. Brushes some greasy hair out of his eyes. "I've sold the house!" he barks. "Melissa-Sue didn't want to live there anymore."

"What? But you *liked* your house. It was so nice! You liked being by the sea. Have you bought another?"

"Nope! She wants to keep based in Texas. They've decided that Andy should go to the local Baptist kindergarten and school that she went to."

"They? Who's this *they've* decided? He's your son, remember? You gave up *our* relationship so that you could have him. That's all that *matters* to you."

"I don't want to discuss it, Lady!" he says fiercely, and tokes deeply on his joint.

"All right."

"The house was never the same, anyway," he proceeds to discuss it. "I liked it how Joel and me had it. The waterbeds and the pool table. I never felt right with that pink velvet shit."

"I know."

"Jesus fuck! He ain't even three yet, and the other night when I went upstairs at the Cantrells', there were Melissa and Charlene both kneelin', and with him kneelin' between them —*prayin'!*"

I see that there are tears in his eyes. I don't know what to do; I feel helpless, inadequate. Whatever I did would be wrong. He doesn't want me to help him, be with him, love him.

"*Prayin'*, for fuck's sake! He's not even three, and they're startin' in on that bigoted, hypocritical *shit* already."

"He's *your* son, Jan. *Tell* them. Tell them you don't want him brought up that way." He glares at me, miserably. "He's your son, Jan—why should he have his head filled with weird

312

foreign doctrines that were written in the Bronze Age by a load of bigoted, ignorant, uneducated, *superstitious* old men?"

I watch his mouth tremble, watch him close his eyes, squeezing the tears from them. I want to hold him, comfort him, but I don't think he'd let me. He doesn't need me anymore; he just needs his son, and it looks to me as if he hasn't even got him, now.

He goes and pours himself a drink, and I don't protest. In the state he's in, he doesn't need me getting at him anymore. But then I suddenly can't control myself anymore, I just can't. I go over and stand in front of him as he guzzles the vodka.

"Look at you! Why isn't someone taking care of you? *Look* at you!" Of course, what I mean is: Why don't you let *me* take care of you? "You can't go on like this, Jan. It frightens me. Stop it, please *stop it!*"

I kneel down between his legs as he sits perched on the edge of the sofa, and hit out at his shoulder. Uncontrollable rage spills from me, but it's really my love for him.

"You bastard! What have you done to yourself? What have you done to *us?* I hate you for what you've done. *I hate you!*"

I slap him hard across the face. Hit him again, accidentally scratching his face with my fingernails. I can't stop myself, I'm so *angry* with him. All my bottled-up feelings are no longer under restraint. It drives me to keep hitting out at him, over and over. I stop, suddenly spent, burnt out; I realize now that it's totally useless to try to get through to this man.

He sits looking at me, with his face bleeding slightly from the scratch, crying.

"I always thought you were so much in control of yourself and your life," I say quietly, "I admired you and respected you. You always seemed so much in control. But I was wrong. Do you really *enjoy* being a puppet? Is there some sort of sadomasochistic streak running through you? Melissa-Sue is *using* you, trampling over you, keeping you chained to her hate. And you're just *taking* it. Maybe you're even *enjoying it?*"

Jan-Toby Axelsson gulps at his drink. Stares at me.

I continue, "Well, you can live out *your* life in some sort of weird masochistically-shadowed twilight zone. But that's not how I'm going to live *mine*. I was so proud of you and your love, but you managed to turn it into some kind of sordid, dirty little affair! Do you have *any* idea of how I felt when you walked out on me like that? You made me feel cheap and dirty. I've never felt like that before. And you are *never* going to do that to me or my life again!" With the rage I've built up again I reach out and slap him again around the face; but he just sits there immobile. "Do you realize," I continue, "I kept on asking myself for days—no, weeks—after you walked out on me. Asking myself what it was that *I'd* done. I thought we had so much together, in and out of bed. Our creativity meant so much to me. And then ... I thought *I* was lacking in something. And I thought: Well, he's only gone because of his son. He *would* be with you if it weren't for that.

"But you know, Miriam's right. She got me to see that no one stays in a situation they don't want to stay in. Not even because of 'their son.' Of course you could have fought to see Andy. Miriam got me to see that you're not with me because you *don't want* to be with me. There's nothing wrong with me at all—it's *you*. I mean, what you're doing is senseless, because all Andy can be to you is a son, nothing else. He can't supply *all* your emotional needs; he can only be your son. He can't be your lover, your mistress, your wife. He can't be your *life!* All a son can ever be is a son. And to give up your life ..."

I can't say any more. I sit back on my heels and watch him drink the last of his drink. He stares at me; I can feel an anger within him. What's he going to do? Hit me again? But I don't care if I'm making him angry; I've *got* to say these things, or they'll turn inward and stifle me.

"You know something?" I continue. "One day you'll wake up and you'll realize what you've thrown away. Look at you! What do you have? A wife you haven't got, never had, never wanted. A son you haven't really got, either. He's not your *son*. He's never been your *son*. You're just his biological father, that's all. He's not *your* son, an Axelsson, he's a *Cantrell*. He'll never be *your* son.

"And your mistress—the woman you *supposedly* loved more than you'd loved any other woman—you haven't got her either. Not anymore. And *you*—you haven't really got *you* any more, have you?"

I stand up and go to the window. I don't want him to see that I'm trembling. I've hurt him, but I'm glad I have. Maybe I can have some peace of mind now. Yes, I'm glad he came tonight; he's done me a favor. Maybe I *will* be able to get over him at last. Little Ms. Classy-Ass fighting her way to the top again, and she's going to stay there!

"Have you *finished*, Lady?"

"Yes, I have. So would you kindly leave."

He doesn't.

"Shouldn't you be going home to your son? To your beautiful, sylphlike wife who loves you so very much? You're in your little trap, on your little leash—or I should say, wearing your slave collar?—doing your husbandly and fatherly duty! I'm sure it's time you were reporting in." I flash him an unpleasant smile. "Melissa certainly *owns* you, doesn't she? Has she branded that sexy ass of yours with her mark? Maybe it's *you* who should have a ring—through your *cock!*

"I ain't even touched Melissa," he tells me impulsively.

"Sounds like a great relationship, Jan. So tell me, who's *servicing* you these days? Back to all those sixteen-year-old groupies who give great head? Visiting the raunchiest little whorehouse in Dallas? Well, I guess that's what you've been used to all these years. . . . What's the matter with you? Are you *afraid* to have a decent, loving relationship with someone who loves you?"

He gives me the Axelsson frown. A glare—so cold. "Yeah, I've been gettin' serviced," he snaps at me. "Fuckin' someone to get my rocks off. Fuckin' someone that'd maybe remind me of *you*. Even in the dark, though her tits were nice, they still weren't yours. They didn't feel like yours, and the rest of her just didn't feel like you either. She didn't smell like you or taste like you. Every little thing you do, it's in my mind, photographed and printed there—I'm forever thinking about it. All the little noises you make when you're comin', the way you always blush so pink—it's so beautiful. I can feel you coming. And then, afterwards, sometimes you cry; but you *always* melt right into me . . ."

He pauses, stands up, comes over to me. He holds my shoulders. "You're the only woman I've said 'I love you' to—*ever*. And I *do*. You're the only woman I *make love* to, not just fuck to get my rocks off. You're the only woman I want to be tender and caring with. The only woman I can have a conversation with." He stares at me with that helpless little-boy-lost look of his.

"Yes. I know all that means such a lot to you, Jan. That's why you *threw it all away*, isn't it?" The look I give him is one of pure, cynical hate. "Now I think you should leave, Jan. *Now!* We've said enough to each other."

Why doesn't he let go of my shoulders? I try to shrug myself loose from his strong grip. "Please go, Jan."

315

He releases his tight grip, and my shoulders stop aching. He looks uncertain, trying to find words for what he wants to say.

"I . . . I just *had* to see you. I was thinkin' at home this mornin'. Decidin' . . . I dunno, I can't talk about it. I can't *talk* about anythin' these days. I just *had* to see you."

"Well, you have. So *go!*" I reply harshly.

But why am I feeling sick? Why am I suddenly searching for words that will enable me to legitimately and convincingly detain him? Face it, Solange: even now, you still want him, need him. And you love him so much; you'll always love him. You're sharing the same skin; you always were and you always will.

"Jesus fuck! I need a wash," he says gruffly, and rubs at a smudge of dirt on his arm: it makes me smile.

I wet my finger and rub at the smudge until it's clean, look up and say with a smile, *"Mr. Axelsson's skin don't dirt."* My eyes fill with tears. Is that a lopsided, pulled-out-of-shape smile I see on his face? Do I see tears in his eyes? "Listen . . ." —me, finding a reason for another hour of Jan—"why don't you go up and take a shower. All your clean clothes are up there in a pile. I'll make us something to eat. I think you need to eat something before you go."

Why is he staring at me like that?

"We can part friends that way," I say. "No more harsh words or angry recriminations. They're not needed, are they? We both understand how things are. But, hell, we've always been friends as well as lovers. And I always loved that . . ." I smile. Trembling, I reach up and kiss him gently on the lips, gently touch his scratch, stroke his mustache. "I love you."

I turn away from him to go and prepare the dinner, but he catches my arm, pulls me towards him, holds me tight in his arms, nuzzling his face in my neck.

"I love *you*, Lady. I've never stopped lovin' you. It doesn't mean that I don't love you . . ."

After a few moments I pull myself away from him. Smile, caress his face. "Go and get your shower. Everything's up there. I'll make us some dinner." I turn quickly and leave the room.

In the kitchen, I lean against the wall, hot, feverish, out of control. I hear him go upstairs. I've let him into my life again. How am I going to feel when he goes? *Will* he go? Perhaps he won't; perhaps he'll never leave me again, now that it's obvious he still needs me, still wants me, as much as I still need and want him.

316

I know he'd like an omelette; he was always asking me to make omelettes. With lots of cheese in it and mushrooms. I set our places in the dining room, then automatically reach out for a bottle of wine. No, no wine—he doesn't need any more alcohol. I take some water glasses and a bottle of Perrier.

I can hear him in the shower. I rush upstairs, quickly get out of my clothes, splash Bal à Versailles over myself. Why am I doing this? But I want to look pretty for him. I want to let him know what he's going to be missing. I put on the hot-pink silk dress he likes so much: it's strapless, ties in a little knot between my boobs. I quickly slip the emerald studs into my ears, the emerald around my neck. I'm already wearing my sun-angel. And the ring, the new, beautiful ring—I slip that onto my engagement finger. What am I trying to do? Make him feel guilty some more? God, I hope it will!

With my impeccable, fantastic, classy-ass timing, I'm putting the omelettes out onto the plates when he comes into the kitchen. I turn and smile, feeling slightly self-conscious at being dressed up for him. But still . . . he always liked that.

"Why don't you go into the dining room?" I don't know what else to say. He nods, smiles, and leaves me. Well, at least he's looking better, with his damp hair tied back and a clean white tee on and clean jeans.

"It's fresh bread," I say as I take the things in. "Well, yesterday's. I *made* it. Anni, that's Sven's wife, she showed me how," I chat on nervously.

I watch him eat some of the omelette. He's hungry.

"Where's the wine? We always have a glass of wine." He sounds as though he'd never left!

"You've had enough alcohol, Jan. Perrier is better for you."

"Yes, Ma'am." He gulps at the water, bites off a big chunk of bread and makes an approving face. "Tell me about Sverige."

I tell him about my trip. "Oh, Jan, you'd love it there. And Nils would, too. I wanted you to be friends with my Larsson clan, so much."

"You . . . you fucked Kris?" He looks slightly angry. Hell, what business has he to be angry?

"Look, cowboy—I know you told me that if I ever fucked with someone else, you'd kill me. But that was when we were together. And you know I never would have. But *you* walked out on us—*I* didn't!" His angry look deepens into a scowl.

317

"Are you so conceited," I continue, "so arrogant, that you think you are the only man who can pleasure me?"

"Pleasure you?" The scowl gives way to a lopsided grin.

"Yes. And Kris did! I enjoyed it. Kris enjoyed it. My life can't end—though it felt like it at the time—just because you walked out on me. I need someone to love me, to love."

"I know. I'm sorry," he says. Observing him closely, I think he means it.

"That's been my trouble," I say. "Being without a man for so long." He frowns. "On the plane coming home from Sweden, I had a terrible period-ache, and I was so irritable and cranky. And all during the month I remained irritable and cranky. I had a bad—"

"Fuckin' German Airplane disease," he interrupts with a grin.

"Yes." And why are you smiling at him, Solange? "And I've just got over another painful period last week. I think it's extremely psychological again. I think I need a man."

"Why didn't you say so, Ma'am?" Lopsided grin as he rubs the side of his nose. "I'll just get outta my pants!" Laugh.

I glare at him. "I was thinking I'd better wait until I've finished my book before I get involved again. But maybe I won't," I say arrogantly. "Maybe I'll just find someone who *really* wants me and appreciates me." My look is slightly haughty. "It's very strange, you know, Jan, having to get used to the feel of someone else inside me, when . . . when there's only one person I want to feel inside me." From arrogance to sentimentality! "Tell me about your songs, Jan."

He does so. Then he grins. "Hey!" he exclaims. "We're tourin' Europe this year. And when we're in England, I'm goin' to do *The Muppet Show.* I gotta sing 'Remembered Times,' with Miss Piggy. He winks. "Now, that's a sexy lady." Laugh. "And I'm doin' a heavy rock number with Doctor Teeth and the Electric Mayhem. And me and Kermit do a sketch with the Swedish Chef—you know how that guy breaks me up. We're gonna do it in Swedish. Well, I'm gonna talk Swedish, *he's* gonna talk his stupid Swedish." Jan grins, making me smile.

"That should suit you," I tell him, "the Swedish Chef. You being such a Swedish meatball yourself."

"Watch it, Lady!" he grins.

The rest of the dinner passes amicably. I tell him to go into the lounge, but he wants to go into the study. I make some coffee, putting a few crushed cardamom seeds in with the freshly-ground coffee, the way I showed him. Sitting at the other end of the sofa, I tell him: "You're looking better already, *Yahn-Tobias.* See—you really do need me to look after you—and love you." Lopsided smile; but why isn't he agreeing? "Listen, I'll get those dirty clothes washed. I'll take everything to Roy's for you. I mean, I'll be leaving here soon anyway."

"You're actually goin'?" Frown.

"Yes." I tell him about Maman and Rand. "So, I have another house. I'll go between there and Sweden. I *can't* stay here anymore, it hurts too much: having you so close and not being able to be with you."

We look at each other and I pour him some more coffee. He's sitting on the edge of the sofa. I can't resist it. I go and kneel between his legs, put my hands on his face, kiss him.

"*Listen* to me: Don't drink anymore. After all, didn't you tell me when you first met me that you weren't a boozin', pill-poppin' rock star? So don't become one now. A clean-livin' cowboy—remember?" Why isn't he smiling? "It's been very hard for me, Jan. But at least I knew you were doing something you wanted—I thought you'd be happy because of that. To blow all we had, for unhappiness—well, it doesn't make sense. So for God's sake be happy—let me have that, even if I can't have you. Work on your poetry, Jan; you're like me—you want to die creating." I smile, caress his face, then hug myself to him. "Your creativity is the most important thing in your life, Jan. Don't lose it. Don't throw it away. Don't let *anyone* take it from you. Sometimes you have to be very, very selfish to further your own creativity. You *have* to. You know what William said about burying talent. Your creativity—it *is* the most important thing, and so it should be." My eyes fill with tears. "I . . . I just wanted to be the second."

He takes my face between his hands—his large, warm, gentle hands that always feel so sensuous against my skin—and kisses me. . . . Oh, hell, why am I responding? Why do I *always* respond to him?

"What *does* your William say about it?" he asks.

"About what?"

"Burying talent. I don't have a memory for all of your Nobledaddy's works like you do."

"That's not my fault—perhaps you should read more!" I deserve the frown I get; however, I quote for him: " 'If you, who are organised by Divine Providence for spiritual communion, Refuse, and bury your Talent in the Earth, even tho' you should want Natural Bread, Sorrow and Desperation

319

pursues you thro' life, and after death shame and confusion of face to eternity.' "

"Shit!" Jan-Toby Axelsson looks rather taken aback. "They're heavy words the man wrote."

"I hope you've taken heed of them?"

"What's it from? *Jerusalem?* No. *The Four Zoas?* No." He looks puzzled, searching his memory. "It ain't from *Urizen?*"

"No, it's not. It's from a letter he wrote when he was living in Felpham, to Thomas Butts. It's an amazing letter—read it when you get home."

He looks at me intently, wanting to say something.

"Darlin' . . . I've got so many things to say to you, things I've got to tell you. It's just that I—"

"You don't need to say anything!" I interrupt angrily; then feel guilty for doing so. So I say gently: "I understand, Jan." I sit back on my heels. "I think you'd better go now, Jan," I tell him, standing up. "Let me see you out."

Jan stands up, too. Looks around him, taking in the study, and I feel sad. It was our secret haven; we both loved working here so much.

At the front door we both stand looking at each other. I smile nervously, and he puts his hands on my shoulders. It makes me want to melt; I need his touching, all over.

Oh, don't cry, Solange. Not now!

He pulls at one of the curls in my fringe. "Jesus, it looks so pretty. You're so beautiful, Lady . . ."

"Yeah—that's why you're leaving me!"

"You're the one that's asking me to leave, Lady. *I* wanna—"

"Oh, thank you for the ring," I suddenly remember to say, and reach up and kiss him. "But you shouldn't have. You don't have to buy ex-mistresses things. It must have cost so much—it's so beautiful. You didn't have to—why did you?"

"I was in Kazanjian buyin' *Mor* a Christmas present. Thought the ring would go with the other things. I bought those there, too."

"I know."

."And the books—they were so nice, Lady. It . . . Oh, shit! Jesus fuck! *I hate* this! Solange, I need to talk." He looks puzzled, as though he's not sure whether I *do* want him to leave.

"Calm down, darling." I put my hands on his arms. "And drive carefully. And *please* stop drinking." I reach up and kiss him tenderly, the perfect epitome of the dumped ex-mistress. "I love you, Jan. If ... if you ever need me for anything ... well, you know where I am." He smiles one of those lovely pulled-out-of-shape smiles, and I kiss him again. "I *love* you!" Damn! I shouldn't be crying. He's not going to make me cry. He goes to say something, but I can't look at him anymore. I go inside quickly, close the door, lean against it.

Déjà vu: Solange remembering doing just the same, after those first few days we spent together; devastated enough then—but now ... !

I listen for the car starting up. Why doesn't it start up?

Silence. All I can hear is silence.

He must have got into the car by now. Still no sound of car engine. Jan—what are you doing? Why is it that when I close my eyes I feel your presence?

I fling the door open. He's just *standing* there—just as he was the first time. Standing looking at the house, the door, *me*.

"Jan!" I'm crying and I'm running, and he gathers me up into his arms, holds me tight. It hurts, but I don't care. We're kissing.

Jan-Toby Axelsson swings me into his arms and carries me into the house, kicking the door shut. He carries me into the study.

Jan-Toby Axelsson, his hands firm, warm, deft as he tugs at my dress and pulls it down so that it slithers around my ankles. He sinks to his knees and gently pulls my panties down, kisses my pussy hair ... pushes me back onto the sofa.

I feel him everywhere as I lie in a euphoric haze. I moan softly as I feel his mouth on me, so creamy and waiting. His lips, his tongue, his teeth, his beard—they all feel so *good*. So *right*. So peaceful, so perfect. I close my eyes, his fingers providing a beautiful, sensuous fullness inside me.

Solange, whimpering. Solange, crying, moaning—a gentle scream. "Inside," I beg. "Inside—please, inside!"

Through my dreamy, hazy eyes I watch him quickly get out of his clothes. He's kneeling in front of me; pulls my legs up around him, pushes into me.

The first time—it feels like the first time: I was so nervous then as he undressed me, undressed himself. "I want to eat you," he said, and he did. How could it have been so good? But it was. And then I took him inside me, where he's stayed ever since. As soon as I felt him inside me I knew it was *him*, that it would only *ever* be him. Solange, filled up with Jan cock, Solange, forever filled up with Jan.

321

Not for long, though. That beautiful low moan of his, as he comes.

He holds me to him, kisses me. Whispers, with a faint laugh: "Better?"

A haze of unreality. Dreamy and creamy and so very eager. Nothing matters anymore. Jan is back with me.

He carries me upstairs, and we cuddle together in bed, me almost lying on top of him, the way he likes. Me, tightly enclosed in his arms, the way I like.

I think I'm trembling. No, I'm not. I'm crying.

"Ssh . . ." He rolls us over so that I'm lying flat; supports himself on one hand, touches my body with the fingers of the other. Gently, very gently. Rubs my pussy hair with the flat of his hand. My tummy. Touches my boobs, smiles. Touches my nipples again, making them stand up.

I listen to the surf—so loud. The surf and Jan—what more could I possibly want?

We're kissing. It feels like he never left. Will he? I don't care anymore—he's with me *now*.

I lie on top of him, with his beautiful, hard, muscular body beneath mine. I always loved lying along him. I kiss his fuzzy chest, move so that I can kiss my way down to that line of fuzz to his tummy button, stick my tongue into it; he laughs. I kiss my way up and down it again, and he laughs again.

I know what he wants, and I give it to him. He comes with a groan of sated pleasure.

I climb back into his arms, see the contented smile on his face, kiss him. Together, cuddling the way we always cuddled, we fall asleep.

Jan gets up; it wakes me. I watch him go into the bathroom; I smile as I listen to him peeing. I'm still smiling, sleepily, as he comes back to bed and pulls me into his arms, tells me he loves me.

I think we want each other again.

We cuddle and kiss for a long time. So warm and close.

"Jan . . . we have to talk, don't we?"

"I can't talk. Not now—it's not the time. I just *want* you. I needed to see you, so much." He leans over me, pressing me beneath him. Solange doesn't care about talking, either.

He looks at me, gently feels my breasts. "My beautiful sweet delight."

I close my eyes, and I feel his mouth on my nipples, one and then the other, sucking them like a hungry baby. "Your beautiful tits, I've missed them." he whispers, and sucks hungrily again.

"Make love to me," I say, just before he kisses me. "Be gentle, though," I whisper against his mouth, "remember, I used to be a virgin."

"Am I allowed to eat a used-to-be virgin?" he asks, a laugh in his voice.

"Gently. Very, very gently . . ."

Jan eats me gently. But I don't come gently: It's an impossibility to come gently for Jan. It is, veritably, the little death, an exquisite torture, physically and mentally. Even when he just looks at me, I come: a spiritual orgasm. I'm in a dark dream world, a black unconsciousness from the little death, as Jan kisses the insides of my thighs, as he says, "My beautiful sweet delight." And then he delights me again.

Jan inside me. Jan coming. But Jan wants to stay inside me; he does, while he feels for my sticky little button. He pulls me into his arms, and I'm crying, sobbing, clinging to him, with my arms around his neck, as he tightly holds me.

"Please don't leave me anymore. Please don't leave me anymore."

"Ssh . . . shh . . ." Jan kissing me.

"Please! Please don't go away again!"

"Ssh . . . shh . . ." Jan kissing me.

"I *love* you."

"I love you, darlin'."

"Please don't leave me anymore. I've been so desperately unhappy."

"Ssh . . . So have I, darlin'. Who says I'm goin'? I don't want to leave you. I never want to leave you." Jan kisses, Jan caresses. Jan, soothing me, loving me. And I'm falling asleep . . .

No . . . that's Jan's voice. Yes . . . it's Jan's voice. But I'm so *sleepy.*

"Darlin' . . . I just want you to know . . . What I needed to say to you . . ."

Why am I so sleepy? What's that he's saying? Oh, I feel so good, lying in his arms. Jan's arms. Safe, in Jan's arms . . .

*   *   *

I awake. Suddenly. I'm startled; I sit up quickly.

Startled. Because I'm alone. I'm *alone!*

"Jan!" Why do I feel Jan? I thought I heard him call my

323

name. I glance at the clock: it's just after eleven in the morning.

"Jan?" My voice hardly above a whisper.

Perhaps it *was a dream?* It must have been. I kneel up, stare down at the bed. No, hardly a dream. I feel so sticky. And the bed is stained.

I suddenly relax. Of course! He's having some coffee. It reminds me of that first morning; he was having coffee then, too.

In the bathroom, I notice his old clothes in a pile on the floor. Of course, he'll be in clean ones.

"Jan?" I call out as I rush downstairs. Gulley is in the kitchen, sitting on the table in the sunlight. I rush into the study and into the lounge and through it onto the terrace but no Jan. I suddenly feel very cold. In desperation I rush to the front door, fling it wide open. . . . No car.

"Oh, God!" I feel sick. I rush upstairs into the front guest bedroom, which overlooks the front of the house from which I can see down the road. Still no car, but then, what did I expect?

Back in my own bedroom I get slowly onto the bed, wobble slowly up and down. Of course—I'm crying.

Oh, Solange! You stupid, *stupid* bitch!

I rub between my sticky legs, touch the come stains on the bed. They're cold.

Oh, no! I couldn't have let this happen to me!

Maybe he's just gone to pick up a paper?

Oh, Solange—you're daydreaming again, aren't you?

Maybe he's just . . . gone.

I hear a car . . . the front door open. My heart pounds as I smile, "Jan . . ."

"Solange?" Miriam's voice echoes through the house, and the smile vanishes.

"Oh, God . . ." I look up at the ceiling. "You fucking *bastard!* Go hide in your fucking clouds again!"

Miriam bounces into the room. "Hi, baby. You *should* have stayed for the *rest*—"

She stands still, looks around, looks at me as I kneel on the cold, cold come sheets.

"*Smells* like a fucking *brothel* in here!" she comments brightly, then claps her hand over her mouth and giggles. "Phil's not in *there*, is he?"

I stare glumly at her. "No. Wait. He *came back*. Then . . ."

Miriam, aghast. I think she's got the picture. Her look turns into one of fury: yes, she's definitely got it. *"You stupid little bitch!"*

She's suddenly by my side, kneeling on the bed too, shaking me.

"Stop it!" I call out. *"Stop it!"*

We look at each other—kneeling and wobbling.

"He was here when I got back . . ."

"Oh, baby . . ." She hugs me, maternally.

"I thought . . . I thought . . ."

"I can *imagine* what you *thought,* baby. Are you *still* so fucking *naive?* Haven't you *learned* your lesson *yet?* What are you *doing* to yourself over that *dude?* You've let him *use you* again!"

"No. It wasn't . . . I've just woken up. He was *gone!* And he said . . ." I'm crying.

"Solange! He just *needed* to get *laid,* that's all! That's *all* he ever *needed* from you! You *know* how to get his *rocks* off—that's *all!"*

"Make some coffee, please, love," I ask, not totally convinced.

19

"Are you sure you're all right?" Miriam interrogates me again for the umpteenth time.

"Yes. Promise. I'll call you as soon as I'm there."

We hug and kiss, and Miriam sees me through the gate for the plane to New York.

I call her from New York. Everything is fine. And I call her again from Cannes, from the Carlton.

Of course, I recognize just what I've done to myself. But I also realize that I can't blame anyone *but* myself. I've been over and over the things Jan said to me before we made love, while we made love, and after we made love. I begged him to stay, and all he replied was: "Ssh . . ."

He said he'd been unhappy too. And he said, "Who says I'm goin'? I don't want to leave you." But they were empty words he knew I needed to hear.

Solange talked to her beautiful Maman while Miriam made

325

her coffee. Explained everything: explained that what she was going to do was just go away and write.

And so Miriam helped me pack and got me onto a plane, and only Miriam knows where I am now. Only Miriam is *going* to know where I am, from now on. I don't want *anyone* to know where I am. Not Maman. Not Marie-Claude. Not Matthew and Chris. Not Justin and Anna. Not even my Larssons.

No one. *I* don't even want to know where I am.

*   *   *

I've been here for a week. It's been nice sitting out on my balcony, reading lots of books—in French. So good to be reading in French again.

I've just finished talking to Miriam on the phone. She had so much to tell me today, but even that didn't upset me. She'd called Maman to tell her I'm fine. Maman and Rand understand my wanting to be by myself—as long as I'm all right.

Of course I asked Miriam whether Jan had been in touch, just in case there had been some weird mistake and he hadn't really left me. But she said, "No—what else d'you *expect* from that *asshole?*" However, she did say he'd seen Marie-Claude and Jed, and wanted Marie-Claude to tell Miriam to tell me he hoped I was all right.

And Nils, he too talked to Miriam; he was rather upset that I wanted to be alone, when I could have come to Texas to be consoled; but considering the circumstances, he understood. So I guess that by now everyone knows the circumstances of that night. I'm sure that Miriam will have given everyone a delicious mouthful of adjectives about it.

*   *   *

To walk around Cannes again feels strange; my Maman and Rand so near and yet unreachable. I decide to rent a house. Then I can work and have Gulley over with me too. And Miriam can come and go as she pleases.

But where? Not just here. Dangerous. I don't want to bump into Maman or Rand or any other old friend. No, further down the coast.

I rent a car and drive down to Le Lavendou, hunt around the house rental agencies. Everything's so terribly expensive. Still, I have the money. I even have my French bank account.

I find it: a beautiful little house on a cliff. Small, just two bedrooms. A high fence runs around the property, and there's a tiny patio that overlooks the sea. In the garden are vines, vegetables, fruit trees, all meticulously kept. *Oh, yes!* I rent it for six months, paying the whole amount at once, then drive back up to Cannes and immediately get on the telephone to Miriam. She's as excited as I am.

The first evening in my little house I spend on the patio: eating shrimp and salad, drinking a bottle of Dom Perignon, and trying very hard not to think about the evening with Jan.

I'm no longer upset or unhappy, though, and I find this very strange. Perhaps it really didn't mean all that much to me? But I know it did; it meant *everything* to me, and I'll always remember it and all the other times we had together.

Maybe I'm hoping he'll realize that while he's imprisoned he'll never be happy. And that he doesn't *really* have a son anyway. Maybe then he'll leave her.

I call Miriam and find myself asking her whether Jan has been in touch. No, she answers disdainfully—he's obviously getting himself laid elsewhere. I ask Miriam to bring Gulley and some books that I need. She replies that she's just in the middle of a delightfully delicious relationship with a deliciously delightful little chick who's about to depart for Canada, so could I possibly wait a few days?

I'm feeling like a naughty schoolgirl playing truant. It's giving me an emotional lift, this being in hiding. Miriam tells me that everyone is fine; they all wish me well, are glad that I'm happy and working. Of course, Miriam is enjoying every minute of this charade. She's blatantly *encouraging* me to play the game of hide but don't come seek. She says that she and Janis have just a few days left, then she can come over with Gulley.

I drive into Cannes, raid the record shop, buy a few dozen albums. Over dinner, I listen to Jan's second: *Remembered Times Of Yesterday.* The title track is so good.

I go and sit on the terrace, stare up at the moonless sky. The cool, starry night soothes me. *The heaventree of stars hung with humid nightblue fruit. . . .*

*   *   *

Miriam is arriving with Gulley today, and I've just realized that I'm four days overdue with my period.

327

I check my Swiss calculator and my diary to find the error. But there isn't any: I'm late. My cycles are *exactly* every twenty-six days—never miss—and I'm *late!*

Of course: my period started before Christmas, ended on time. And my fertile period, according to my calculator, was between December 29 and January 5. And—of course, what else!—Jan-Toby Axelsson made love to me on January 2. Oh, and on January 3 as well; all night.

Of course, this could only happen now! But wait. Don't panic. Maybe it's the upset, the change of location, all that's happened in the last few weeks. You're just late, Solange; that's all it is.

* * *

I hug and kiss Miriam. And Gulley meows and protests to be let out of his basket. All the way home in my new little white Peugeot, Gulley perches on the back of my seat behind my shoulder, meowing in my left ear, while Miriam constantly chatters in my right ear. Yes, Miriam assures me, Elena has come to stay the whole month she's away. Janis decided not to go to Canada; instead, she's moved into Miriam's Venice apartment for now. For the rest of the way home I listen to Miriam extolling Janis' sexy tits and cunt! I, of course—true to form—don't tell Miriam my fears about being pregnant.

Gulley settles in well. I'm glad the fence is eight feet high and has barbed wire on the top—Gulley-proof! He's taken a fancy to one of the shade trees. I think he likes being back in France.

Jan, Miriam says, is back in L.A., recording.

"Jan didn't contact me *at all?*"

"Only asked Marie-Claude to tell you he was fine and that he hoped you were fine." Miriam sniffs disparagingly.

I'm disappointed. But what did I expect!

"I don't wish to know about anyone until my book's finished." The first run through, anyway. I figure that if I work hard, that should take me through until about June, when the lease of this house is up. Then I plan to return to Malibu, sell the house, then return to France to live in the house Rand and I had.

Miriam and I spend a restful four weeks. She decides to stay an extra week. And me—well, my body, that is—it decides not to have another period. But I'm still not thinking about it, still telling myself it's the upset and the change.

Of course, I know that it's not upset or change. Just like I knew before, when I was pregnant by Johnny. How strange: I didn't feel pregnant then but somehow, now ... Yes, I think that's why I've been feeling so contented. Solange is grown up this time. Solange can handle being pregnant this time. Solange *wants* to be pregnant this time.

That's right, Solange—start off with Jan's baby. Then? Well, there's Matthew and Johnny and maybe Kris? Why *not* a little brood, Solange? I think you'd love it!

Miriam finally returns to California, leaving a weird silence behind her. The first few days without her incessant chatter, I find myself making quite sure, now and then, that I haven't suddenly gone deaf. Dear Miriam ... She asked me whether I was sure, really *sure*, that we couldn't have some sort of a *relationship* together. Why was it that I almost felt that I was betraying her, when I explained my feelings to her? Explained that I'd always love her as a friend, as a sister, but that I could never have her as a lover. I need a man for a lover, Miriam. What I meant, of course, was: I need Jan-Toby Axelsson for my lover.

By the time the middle of March comes and I've missed my third period, I decide that I should buy one of those home pregnancy-test kits—not that I really need the confirmation. I guess that makes me ten weeks pregnant.

Gulley sits watching me. I feel like a scientist as I impatiently wait the two hours for the result to show—a dark ring.

That night, the cool evening, I sit out after dinner, wondering what to do. Solange, you're going to be a thirty-four-year-old unmarried mother—I hope you realize that. With even bouncier boobs. And, knowing *your* luck, maybe even with shorter legs!

But why not? I mean, your man's walked out on you. Your mother's married your ex-husband. Your best friend married a Texan. Your secretary wants to fuck you. What more could you ask from life?

I'm giggling ... why the fuck am I giggling? I gently, very gently, press my hand to my stomach. A baby. *Jan's* baby. A tiny Jan-Tobias Axelsson, and it *is* a son, I just know that. Not that I'd mind a daughter; it's a son.

Do I tell Jan? Oh God, no! He couldn't handle that, *another* son. Where would he consider his duty lay then?—to his wife and son, of course. *Mistresses* and sons don't count.

"Hey, you up there! Hiding yourself in your fucking clouds! You're surely having a giggle over this one, I bet. And William, darling ... I sure fucked this one up! You've always helped me make it through my life, so help me make it through this. What have you got to say about that?

> Sweet Babe, in thy face
> Soft desires I can trace.
> Secret joys and secret smiles
> Little pretty infant wiles.

"Thanks, William, you're right. Having Jan's baby isn't fucking anything up. It's a sweet delight."

Gulley comes and sits on my lap. "Gulley—you're the man in the family." He purrs. "We're going to have a baby to look after. You're going to have to help, too." He blinks, but continues to purr, unruffled.

* * *

The first of May—such a lovely warm day. I celebrated: went and had another hole put in my left ear. I have a tiny diamond stud in it. I wonder what Marie-Claude will say.

Solange, sitting eating an ice cream sundae, watching various people trip past her. So many handsome men; so many beautiful girls. There's a group of men near me, drinking and talking and laughing; they're girl-watching, too. So many *thin* girls; I'm very much aware of the girls' thinness. Men in France like their girls *thin;* a woman can never be rich enough or thin enough, it's said. I surreptitiously glance down at my bouncy pair. I wanted them shrunk; I've ended up with expanding ones. Solange with visions of being carried off into space, hanging there suspended by two enormous boobs. . . . I'm only four months pregnant and they've grown two inches! I was always slightly paranoid about my bouncy pair—especially living in France with all this *thinness* surrounding me. French *haute couture* doesn't cater to bouncy boobs; it never has and never will. (But at least maternity fashion is for us bouncy chubettes). Now, my paranoia is no longer just slight. By the time the baby comes and I'm feeding him, I know my boobs are going to be around a sixty-D. And afterwards, when the eighteen months or so of nursing are finished, gravity will set in and my nipples will soon point the way to Australia.

Still, I'm pregnant and having *Jan's* baby. I'm extremely happy about it, even though I suppose I shouldn't be. Me, an unmarried mum. In the pudding club. Knocked up. A bun in the oven. And, as Reg would say, lumbered! All those awful derogatory euphemisms for being pregnant. Having a baby: a beautiful, miraculous wonderment.

I go around in my own secret little world, happy and contented. Especially now that I can feel the baby. He turns somersaults and flipflops. We have a conversation every night before I fall asleep.

I finish my ice cream and walk slowly home along the seafront. I'm thinking about the doctor, Doctor Dubois. I went for an amniocentesis test today. I was a bit afraid of it, but as I'm nearly thirty-four, I decided I'd better have one. I have to wait four weeks for all the test results to come in. Four weeks to the beginning of June. I'll be nineteen weeks pregnant then. And it's then that I have to move out of the house: The owners are coming down for the three months' season. So I'll take all my things along to my house on Cap d'Antibes, then Gulley and I will go back to California to sell the house there.

I reach home, cuddle with Gulley as we sit out on the patio in the shade of an awning, stare at the gently swaying trees, at the ruffled sea. Solange, swallowed up by landscape.

I sit thinking about the baby. I'm always thinking about it—well, when I'm not remembering all those beautiful loving times Jan and I spent together. I like remembering those, and I think baby Jan would like that. He'll always know how much I loved his daddy.

I daydream: me and little Jan (about four). He's got long, untidy, dusty-blond hair like his daddy; his daddy's beautiful eyes, of course; his daddy's long legs, too (anything but my little legs!). Solange and little Jan at a Jan-Toby Axelsson concert:

"It's so nice that we can come and see Daddy like this, Maman."

"Isn't it, darling."

"Isn't he *good*, Maman?"

"Oh, yes, darling. Your daddy's *exceptional*." (Ain't that the truth!)

"Do you think we could go and see him after the concert this time, Maman? It would be nice to meet my Daddy." Little Jan looking up at me, a beautiful little look, almost heartbroken, on his face: a puzzled look. He gives me a tiny lopsided grin and rubs the side of his nose.

Solange cuddling her son, comforting him. "Not this time, darling. Maybe one day. Until then, we'll just play his albums and come to his concerts."

331

Jan-Toby Axelsson: a big, shiny hero to his son and his ex-mistress!

...And, daydreams aside, I do have the problem about telling Jan. *Do* I tell him? And if so, *when?*

I've decided that baby Jan will be born in Sweden. I'm going to get in touch with my Larsson clan when I return to California, ask them if I can come there. I'll feel safe having my baby there; he can be born at the house, as all the Larsson children were. Before, I always thought of our babies being born in Texas; that's what Jan wanted—his children born Texans. But I can't just go to Texas and have a baby there on my own. I can't tell Marie-Claude, even. So I thought of Sweden, and Jan's Swedish heritage of which he's so proud. So at least baby Jan will be Swedish. I think Jan would approve of that.

I did so want Jan to be with me, though. We'd talked about it—him with me, on his parents' ranch, holding the baby as soon as he was born, a perfect Leboyer delivery. It makes me very sad that he won't be there to see his son born; he'd have liked that.

He missed seeing Andy born. He was on tour, and Andy arrived early. He told me about it one night as we were cuddled up in bed. We'd been reading *Finnegan's Wake* together, but Jan was getting horny. I said, "Maybe we'll make a baby this time. It's my fertile period." And Jan said, "Hey, I wanna be there when he's born. I mean, to hold him while he's bein' born." And we talked about that. The prospect seemed exquisitely delightful to me. It still does.

Melissa hadn't gone on tour with him when she was pregnant. She stayed at home with her parents, on their ranch. But Andy arrived early, over one month early. Jan was furious, not about that but because he wasn't even told that Melissa had gone into labor. In fact, his parents weren't even told, and they lived quite nearby. It was only one week later, when Melissa-Sue had left the hospital with Andy, that she phoned Jan and told him he had a son. She hadn't wanted anyone around except her mother; she told him that she hadn't wanted to worry him, spoil his tour for him.

He was tiny, Jan told me. Most babies are, I said. But he was bigger than I thought, he said, bein' premature an' all. And Melissa wouldn't feed Andy herself. And he was such a cute little fucker. Jan smiled his lovely Axelsson smile as he thought of baby Andy, his beloved son. And I kissed him ... and made love to him.

332

I think I need to see that lovely Axelsson smile as he looks at *our* baby. But I won't, though.

* * *

Doctor Dubois looks extremely solemn as I sit before him in his office. He has a folder in front of him, my folder. The results of the amniocentesis test.

He suddenly smiles. He has white hair and blue eyes; his skin looks soft, slightly wrinkled. He'd make a lovely grandfather.

"The tests are totally clear." I giggle and clap my hands together. "Of course, that's what I expected—but it's always wise to check."

"Oh, thank you, Doctor Dubois." I'm crying, wiping away my tears with a delicate finger.

"Now, my dear: the big question."

"Yes?"

"Do you wish to know the sex of your child? Some women do not; they feel it takes something away, already knowing the sex of the child."

"It's a boy," I say.

"You would be disappointed if it were not?"

I see the slight smile on his face. "No, not in the least. But I just *know* that it is a boy."

"You are right, Madame."

* * *

I leave the little house and drive to Cap d'Antibes. Gulley burrows among the things in the car, meowing and protesting.

I'm going to miss that little house. It got me through a tough time. And I wrote some terrific words there. *I* was burrowing: into my book, the security of my work.

Now my house at Cap d'Antibes feels strange, empty, lonely. It seems funny that Rand and Solange no longer live here. An odd couple, they were.

"This is where we're coming to live," I tell baby Jan, gently touching my tummy. Gulley darts here and there, remembering and repossessing the house where he grew up.

I'd have liked to have gone and seen Maman and Rand, but they've gone to Japan for a few months. They both sent me their love. I'm so glad they've found some happiness together. I really do think they'll make a go of it.

"*We're* going to make a go of it," I tell baby Jan. I feel him turn a somersault. Five months! I still can't believe that I have a five-month-old baby growing inside me. Oh, how I'd love Jan to feel his son kicking inside me. He never felt Andy either, as he was away touring, and the few times he did see Melissa then, she was edgy and touchy, not wanting any contact. How strange, but I suppose it affects women differently. Me, I'd want Jan to touch me continuously, feel his son continuously.

Jan touching—a forever touching. A forever love I feel for this man. . . . Solange, little Ms. Sentimental-Ass again. Glad she's little Ms. Pregnant-Ass!

* * *

I'm feeling very tired by the time I get out into the concourse at L.A. International. Miriam is there waiting for me, grinning like a maniac.

"You're getting *fat*," she tells me, cheerfully accusing, as she cuddles me.

Ain't that the truth! I'm in an *extremely* billowy peasant dress. It's a beautiful shade of amethyst—to match baby Jan's eyes. And I'm wearing dark violet suede boots. I'm looking very good. My hair has grown, too, and I have it parted in the middle again; I'm just going to let it grow and grow.

It's strange to see L.A. drift past me instead of France as I gaze out of the car. Miriam's chatter bounces around the car like a load of high-speed ping-pong balls; I only vaguely listen. Justin's inquiring about my book. Maman and Rand sent a card from Kyoto. Marie-Claude hasn't called for a few weeks; she's too happy and settled in Texas now, anyway. And *him,* he's just gotten a new album put out.

I ignore her. I don't want to hear about *him.*

I go and stand on the oceanfront terrace. I feel a warmth. I'm glad to be back, to be home. Home? I suppose it isn't anymore, not really. After all, I am going to sell it. I feel a confining sadness.

"You know, you *have* put on *weight,*" Miriam tells me brightly.

"I know . . . I want to talk to you about that."

"It's all that French *bread.* And all that scrumptious *ice cream.*"

"Mm . . . plus a little something else."

She brings coffee. "I got the *decaffeinated,* like you *asked,*" she tells me. (No drugs of any description for Solange while pregnant—not even caffeine). I watch Gulley rushing around

like a maniac, chasing imaginary shadows and mice, happy to
be home in his other home.

"*Listen,* Solange—I've got to *talk* to you."

"Yes?" What's this? She sounds very serious, and she looks
serious. Her face wrinkles up when she's serious, and she
looks like her grandmother—who's a lovely, feisty old lady.
"What? Must be something heavy."

"It's Jan . . . he's just . . . *divorced.*"

"*What?!*" Solange, shocked. Stunned. "*Why didn't you tell
me?*"

"*Down,* girl! That ain't *all* of it." She quickly looks around
her, back at me. Squeezes my hand compassionately. "He's
got himself another *chick.* I *mean,* it's *serious.* I mean . . .
that's why he divorced *Melissa.*"

"*What?*"

"*That's* why I didn't *tell* you. I *didn't* want you *upset.*"

My eyes flood with tears. I'm trembling. "You mean—he
actually *divorced* Melissa for another . . . ?"

"*Yeah.* When he *wouldn't* do it for *you.* The *asshole!*"

"But . . . What . . . ?" I gaze helplessly at Miriam.

"When he was *recording.* Tracey *Rivers*—he met *up* with
her. You *know,* that little *singer?* Shit, she's *nineteen.* Very
tall and *slim.*"

I'm still shaking. Is it rage or sadness? Both, I think. "You
mean he was willing to . . ." I sniff hard. I'm feeling sick. I
never expected this, never in a million billion years did I
expect this. "But . . . what about *Andy?* He's the most important thing, for . . . Does he see him, then?"

"*I* don't *know.* I don't *think* so, from what *Marie-Claude*
said. I don't think he *cares* much, *now.* Not *involved* like he
is with this *new* little *chickie* of his. They *all* went to the
Bahamas together." Miriam smiles triumphantly. Let's face it,
she's enjoying telling me all the bad news about Jan-Toby
Axelsson. She's pleased to be proved right, pleased she can
say "I told you so."

"Who did?"

"*Jan* and *Tracey.*" She rolls her eyes heavenward. "*And*
Marie-Claude and *Jed. Joel* and a girl. *Nils* and some chick.
All his *band* and his *roadies* with girls. And *Roy* and a girl.
And that *friend* he has, Billy *Wilson.*" She gives me a sly grin.
"The beginning of *last month,* for a few *weeks.* There was a
photo of them in the *National Enquirer.* And in *Rolling
Stone. And* in *People.* I *saved* them to *show* you." She smiles.
"I *told* you, didn't I, that if he *loved* you enough, he'd have

335

gotten out of his *marriage* for *you*. I *told* you he was just *using you*."

Oh yes, you told me, all right!

"They're getting married?" I'm trembling again. Tears in my eyes again.

"I don't *know* about *that. Rumor* has it that it's *pretty heavy*."

"Rumor?" I stare irritatedly at Miriam. She's still looking so pleased about the whole thing. Surely she knows she's hurting me?

"I've *heard* they're gonna *tour* together."

"She's joining his band?"

"Not *exactly* . . ."

"Not exactly? *What* exactly, then?"

"You know: *he'll* do a set. *She'll* do a set. *They'll* sing a few *together*—*staring* at each other and *coming* all over the fuckin' *audience! Jan* and *Tracey*—two little *lovebirds* working and *singing* together. *Yuk!* It's so *sickening!*"

Jan singing love songs with a girl? That doesn't sound like Jan, singing sweet slushy duets. But I guess when you're in love . . .

"You *know*," continues Miriam, ploughing on undaunted through my raw emotions, "I figure *that's* where she *wins out*. I mean, *you* couldn't tour and *sing* with him, could you? *You're* just a *writer!*" She takes both my hands, smiles gently down at me. "I'm *sorry*, Solange. I *truly* am. But you *had* to be *told*."

"You didn't have to enjoy telling me," I snap back. I stare coldly at Miriam. Coldly, but resignedly: She was right. I can't run away from that any longer.

"You know . . ." I say, mostly to myself, "When Jan came, and we made love . . . I was sure that he was telling me the truth, about loving me and wanting me. It was just that . . . his head . . . He was in such a state, over Andy. It's just . . . I thought . . ." I don't know what I thought, what I think. I don't know what to think anymore; perhaps it's not even worth trying to think. "The love we had . . . I was so *sure* . . . it was only Melissa's blackmailing hold over him, because of Andy. I know it wasn't that he loved her. He's never loved her, I know that. It was his love for his son. Oh, Miriam . . . I thought we had so much in common, Jan and I. . . . We enjoyed that so much."

"I always *told* you he was *using* you. He's an *asshole!*" Miriam says brightly.

"No, he *isn't!* He's a beautiful, gentle person. So creative.

336

And kind, and sensitive. It's ... I guess I just couldn't offer him what he really wanted. This girl ... she must have something ... he must have seen something in her he *really* wanted and couldn't be without. She must have touched him in a way I wasn't able to. But I'm pleased that at least he's got himself free from Melissa. And he didn't really have Andy, anyway. Not as a son—as a son should be."

I'm crying, sobbing. Where's all my diamond hardness gone now? I'm brittle glass again, shattering into thousands of splinters.

Miriam holds my shoulders and I manage to calm myself. "I must ring Marie-Claude."

"Oh, why *bother?* She's a *Texan* now—Marie-Claude *Brackett.* She can't be your *friend* like she *used* to be."

This starts me sobbing again, because I feel she's right. Marie-Claude is in a different world now, with different loyalties. I couldn't go and see her and Jed, not with Jan so close. Even Nils I couldn't go and see. It would be too awkward for everybody. Perhaps they're all hoping I'll just stay away, that I won't get in touch with them again. And maybe that's for the best. . . .

Miriam gives me some tissues; I blow and sniff, wipe my eyes. Then I stare desperately at Miriam, and cry out, "I'm *pregnant!*"

"*What??!*" Miriam does a perfect doubletake, stands staring at me. "Did I *hear* you *right*, girl?"

"Yes. I'm pregnant ... twenty weeks."

"But ..." Right before my eyes, her astonished look rapidly transmutes into one of anger. "*Twenty weeks?*" She skips over the calculation, intuitively. "*You mean*, it's *when* ..."

"Yes. When Jan came, that time."

"Oh, *baby*, I didn't *know*. All those *things* I've said ..." She hugs me.

"It's all right. I wasn't going to tell him, anyway. I don't think he could have handled it. But *especially* now—I'd never tell him now ... now that he's happy with someone else."

"Oh, *shit!* I didn't mean to *hurt* you. I didn't *know!*" she wails, an anguished look on her face.

"It's all right, Miriam. All right now. I've resigned myself to it. It's a boy—I had tests. I mean—I'm happy I'm pregnant. I always wanted Jan's baby. He's *my* baby. We'll leave for France. . . . It's only that ... only that my ego's shattered over him and this Tracey. That's why I'm upset. That's all."

"Why the *fuck* didn't you *get* an *abortion?* It's *still* not too late. I know a *great* doctor—I'll get it *set up.*"

"No, Miriam! I don't *want* an abortion—he's my *son.* I never even considered an abortion. It's Jan's son—*Jan's* son and *my* son . . ."* Even now, a warm, loving glow makes its way through me. Little Ms. Sentimental-Ass, delighted to be having the son of the man she loves, even if he's a man she'll never see again.

"Solange, you're not *listening!"* Miriam's chiding wakes me from my reveries. *"Listen . . .* while we're *at* it. I'd better *tell* you *now."* Why is she smiling one of her secretive little smiles? *Now* what? What else hasn't she told me? *"Howie,"* (I breathe a sigh of relief—it's not more about Jan, anyway.) "He *wants* me to go and work for *their* organization. *Tour* with them. So I'll *go,* as soon as *you* go off to *France."* Miriam flashes me a bright smile.

"You want to leave?" An astonished Solange.

"I *told* you I *didn't* wanna live in *France.* It's so *boring* there. Nothing's going *down* there. And, *well . . ."*—she looks slightly guilty, for the first time—"well, I've *loved* working for you, but even *that* was getting to be kinda *boring.* I'll be *touring* with Howie."

"Well, you must do what you want, Miriam, what's right and best for you." What else can I say? I don't want to say anything else. To me, now, it's Miriam's future that's kinda *boring.*

"Anyway, you *did* say there *couldn't* be anything *between* us, so it's *your* fault really. I'd of *stayed* then, of course."

"Of course, Miriam."

"So I thought I'd *better* just *tell* you." She smiles brightly again, as though expecting my approval. *"Justin* can get someone to handle your *mail.* And you'd *easily* find someone to *type* the *manuscripts.* You'll be *happier* in France—I mean, you're not *at all* American."

"Yes . . . I'll be much happier in France," I echo.

"No *rush,* of course. I've told *Howie* I'll be there the *beginning* of *July.* Oh, I'm so *excited* about it!"

"Yes . . . That's good, Miriam. I'm sure you'll be much happier. And obviously, less *bored."*

"And *you'll* be in *France*—you'll be much *happier* there. And you'll have your *baby.* See—*everything's* worked out *fine* for the *both* of us."

My baby . . . Yes, I've got my baby. Only . . .

20

Why am I awake so early? Did I sleep at all? I must have, for a little while anyway. I wasn't at all tired last night, even after all that flying and the time change. I just couldn't sleep. Normally my attitude to that is: I haven't worked hard enough; or, I haven't loved hard enough. I did work, though. It felt like *very* hard work, flying home and on top of that having to listen to Miriam telling me all about Jan yesterday. No, the problem's obviously the loving, and I need Jan for that.

I'm hungry. I tiptoe downstairs.

I take a can of fruit from the fridge, grin at the eight remaining cans. Am I expecting them to grin back at me? They should: I raided the supermarket after Miriam's tirade, and when I returned she said, "They having a *bargain* sale? *Twelve* cans of the *same?*" Yes, twelve. Solange is on a *craving* binge.

I open the can, hear a scurrying sound behind me. Gulley agitates around my feet, rubbing himself against me. I swear he can hear the can opener from right down the end of the garden! I give him his breakfast, then see to mine. I pour the juice into a tumbler, then empty the segments into a sundae glass. Curling myself up in a corner of the study sofa, I drink the juice quickly, then eat the small, limp, cold segments of mandarin orange with my fingers. Gulley comes in through his cat-flap, sits and washes his face.

Solange: numb and tired, unable to think. Unable to reason. Unable to ... anything, except cry—that she can always do. . . .

Jan. My beloved Jan-Toby Axelsson. Jan-Tobias Axelsson, Yahnilill: my chauvinistic, motherfuckin' Texas cowboy—*divorced*. Jan leaving Melissa-Sue and Andy—but for another woman, not for *me*. How *could* he do that? We had so much in common. Gave so much to each other. Learned so much from each other. What the fuck's the matter with *him*?

I chew on another segment of mandarin orange, but it

doesn't inspire me. Maybe Melissa-Sue relented and agreed to Jan seeing Andy? No, she'd never do that; it'd be utterly contrary to her bigoted, spiteful, hypocritical, bitchy nature!

Tracey Rivers must certainly have something exotic to offer, or is it just that they can tour and work together, as Miriam said? Tracey's a singer, not like introverted little Solange, sitting all alone reading her books and typing her words. . . . But Jan told me once that Melissa was too young for him, and Tracey Rivers is three years younger than Melissa. He's old enough to be Tracey's father! And he also told me that he needed an intellectual equal, that that was what he loved about our relationship. That *can't* have been just Texan owlshit, surely? And, according to Miriam, Tracey didn't even finish high school. It must be love, exotic infatuated *love*, all right!

Admit it, Solange—you're jealous! And after admitting it, don't think of it anymore. It's over. Finished. He has a new life now, a new love now. You have a new life now, a new love now. And my new little love does a flip-flop. He's awake and doing his early morning exercises. You may have taken yourself away, Yahn-Tobias Axelsson, but you've left something very precious with me. Such a sweet delight.

Jan—why aren't you here for your son? He's going to need you. I also need you, you bastard!

Oh, hell! I feel like I've been on the run for months now, and it *is* months—about ten months, altogether. My life since I met Jan feels like it's become *The Perils of Pauline*—or perhaps, *The Saga Of Solange!* No, go back to France, Solange. Bury yourself in your work. Bury yourself in words, in other people's words too. You know that's where you belong, where you're safest: in words. Yes, I can always bury myself in books.

I stare at my sundae dish. I'm still hungry, but the craving is allayed for now. I go and look at my manuscript folders. I guess I'd better stop feeling so bloody sorry for myself and start to *work*. Miriam has to start typing up this first run through. I turn some pages. So many corrections and changes —I hope she can read them.

Baby Jan starts to kick. "Hello—awake properly, are you?" I gently touch my tummy, look at my boobs, which are standing out even further these days. (And they're starting to leak already.) Still, I knew my bouncy boobs would come in handy one day! And Doctor Dubois said I should have an easy delivery due to my wide hips. Solange, daydreaming:

working at the typewriter while having her labor contractions. Solange stopping for five minutes to give birth to baby Jan. Washing him, bundling him up, putting him in his little basket, so that she can return to her work. Solange: epitome of motherhood, built like a peasant, baby suckling at her breast while she edits her day's work.

I put some Wolfgang Amadeus on the stereo. "Now he knew how to create beautiful music," I tell baby Jan, and he flip-flops in agreement. "I guess we should go and buy your daddy's new album. At least we can buy his albums. . . ."

Baby Jan and I go and get ourselves some more mandarin oranges. Back in the study, Gulley comes and sits on my desk and watches me idly picking at the segments of fruit. He glares at me most indignantly.

"You're quite right, Gulley. I've really fucked it up, haven't I?" I touch my hand to my stomach. "What do you two guys think, then?"

Gulley purrs and baby Jan flip-flops. "You don't have to be so unanimous about it. I've got to get myself straightened out. I mean, it's Sunday. And on Wednesday. I'll be thirty-four. I've got to be straightened out for that, haven't I?"

I eat the rest of my mandarin oranges. "I'm *going* to do it, you guys. I'm going to make this a very special, *special* day. The day Classy-Ass reigns supreme. The day I get my act together. I mean, I *can* do it. I've never been a helpless female. And besides, we have each other." Wolfgang Amadeus finishes, and I listen to Debussy's *La Mer*.

My special day. I smile to myself. A Solange day. My Mandarin Orange Sunday. "Yes—that's what I'll call it, guys. So I can forever celebrate its memory, every year. The day Solange got it together. Her special day, her Mandarin Orange Sunday." Baby Jan flip-flops, Gulley purrs.

"You know what I *really* want to do? I want to talk to Jan. I want to tell him just what I think of him and his lies. Do you realize that for the first time I'm really *angry* with that chauvinistic, motherfuckin' bastard of a cowboy?

"You know, guys . . . I *am* going to get in touch with him! Call him. *Wherever* he is."

I glance over at his desk. Oh, Jan. You know I don't hate you, don't you? And yet you must have known what it would do to me. You must have known, just telling Marie-Claude to tell Miriam to tell me you 'hoped I was all right,' what that would do to me?

And why, *why* did you walk out like that? *Why* didn't you contact me? Miriam would have told you where I was. You

341

could have, so easily. But now you're with this little disco chick who's young enough to be your daughter, singing slushy love songs with her and, in Miriam's words, coming all over the fuckin' audience!

I guess Miriam was right—you *were* just getting your rocks off.

Wait a minute! Doesn't all that sound rather weird to you? Jan and Joel, Wilb and George and Dan—playing *disco?* Jan *hates* that mindless junk. So do the rest of the band. They'd never do that! I mean, he might like fucking the chick, but he'd never fuck his act up, he's too proud and conscientious about it. What *is* all this?

But Miriam said ... Miriam showed me the actual clippings. Miriam would have known if Jan wanted to contact me. Miriam wouldn't ...

Miriam wouldn't ... *Would* she?

No, that's stupid. Impossible. Ridiculous. After all, you saw those clippings, didn't you?

But what did the clippings actually say? Only things like, "Rumor has it ... Seen together ... Are they ... ? Will they ... ?" And, "We're just friends because my manager is handling her." (That's a quote from Jan.)

Those garbage weeklies! They'd say Burt Reynolds was fucking the Queen of England if they thought they could get away with it.

But Miriam said ...

Miriam said? Miriam, who hates Jan? Miriam, who hates *men?*

Miriam!!! Yes, I think you'd just better talk to her when she turns up today, Solange!

I go into Miriam's office. God, what a mess! She's never let it get into this state before. I glance through the pile of opened letters on the desk, and smile as I recognize a few of my weirdo regulars—Dawson still wants to come and suck my toes.

I glance at an album down by the side of the stereo: Tracey Rivers. Shit, she looks so *young*, so tall, and she's so slim. Big blue eyes, long dark hair hanging down her back; she's very pretty. I'm sure Jan enjoys himself fucking her—I can understand why he's fallen for her. My little legs and bouncy boobs obviously lost out to all that length and slimness.

What's that, tucked away *behind* the stereo? It's an album of Jan's. One I've never seen before. *It's his new one!*

I pick it up, stare mesmerized at the cover: such a

beautiful photo of Jan's face. The title is *Lover Lady:* of course, that's the song he was working on when we were together. But why has he used *that* as the title track? The song was about me—about *us.*

I notice, unbelievingly, Jan's handwriting across the front of the album cover. It's dated, May 20. (But that was only *three weeks* ago . . . !) And it says—no, I don't believe this—"To my Lover Lady—came back to me, darling. Wherever you are, call me. *Why* won't you call me? I need you. I love you.—Jan."

What the fuck is this? *Why* didn't Miriam give it to me?

Tears fill my eyes as I look at the album cover (a double one). On the back, a photo of Jan, Joel, Wilb, George, and Dan. They're sitting out by the pool—*my* pool. Nils took the photo last year.

And inside—no, I don't believe this, either!

Inside: various photos, with printed captions in Jan's handwriting. A photo of Jan and me: "Me and my Literary Lady." Joel took that one when we were in San Francisco last year. And another of Jan and me, with Jed and Marie-Claude, that Roy took in his garden. And then some more of Jan and the band with George's, Dan's, and Wilb's kids. One with Nils and Axel. And lastly, a photo of me—just me, with Jan's scrawl underneath: "My Lover Lady." It's the one of me sitting leaning back on my heels, holding Gulley Jimson. But I'm in my black lace teddy—and you can see my nipples peeking through the lace and a shadow of my pussy hair. The bastard, using that one! Well, at least he didn't use one of my nude ones (but I wonder if he's shown them to anyone?) I *do* look good, though. Oh, Solange . . .

But what *is* this? Is this the man who heedlessly ditched you?

An extremely confused Solange takes the album back to her study, plays it. And plays it again.

It's so *good.* "Lover Lady" sounds so good with the band. And there's one, soft and gentle, called "The Special, Secret Places Of Your Mind." It's beautiful. And he starts off side two with "Sun Angel Blues." That's about how his special little sun-angel of the sea has gone from his life. And he can't find her. . . . And why am I crying my eyes out?

But the last one is called "The Lady She Has Gone." I listen to Jan singing:

> I was almost down to nothin'
> when the lady came along.

I was almost down to nothin'
      when she heard me sing my song.
But I took our dreams and smashed them—
      this fool still ain't gettin' wise.
And now, I'm back down to nothin'
      and the lady, she has gone . . .

I listen to the rest of the song. Listen—and cry. And eat the rest of my mandarin oranges.

"This fool still ain't gettin' wise . . ." Jan's voice echoes through my mind. Foolish!—that's surely what I must have been because it's plain and obvious that something *is* wrong, has long been wrong. Obvious even to stupid little Ms. Dumb Ass!

Foolish . . . What did my beloved William say about foolish: keep on with the foolish and maybe someday you'll hit wise! Something like that.

You're right, William. But maybe it's too late—maybe I'm never going to hit wise!

You've got to handle this, Solange, and quickly.

But Jan walked out on you. Yes, he did . . . and now there's tall, slim Tracey.

But *is* there Tracey? And *did* he walk out on you?

Of course he did. Didn't Miriam say that he'd never even bothered to contact you? Didn't Miriam say . . .

Miriam!

I stare up at the ceiling. "You fucking bastard! You've come out of your clouds again, haven't you? Been interfering again, haven't you? I bet you're having a fuckin' good laugh. *Asshole!*"

Okay, Solange, calm down!—But I don't want to. I'm so *angry!*

How do I do this?

Roy. Yes. Talk to Roy. After all, Jan could be with Tracey. And if he is . . . if he's found himself some happiness . . . you'd have no right to disrupt that.

But at least I can find out what's happening.

And Miriam? I'm going to kill that little bitch!

* * *

The buzzer sounds for the front door. Solange, frightened for an instant, but frightened of what? Of what Roy might tell her? But that's stupid. She already knows that Jan's left her. And what could she hear that's worse than that? That he's in love with another woman?

344

As I walk to the door my burnt orange caftan swirls and moves around me, a silken creation. Does it show that I'm pregnant? I stand up as straight as I can. No, it just appears that I've put on weight. (I hope!)

Standing before me, one smoothie dude—Roy, immaculately dressed in a gray vested suit, with matching gray snakeskin attaché case.

I dig my hands into the side pockets of my dress, hold it out from me a little (pregnancy camouflage).

Mr. Panache speaks: "Well, you've decided to return to us at last, have you, Solange?" He touches my shoulder and gently plops a kiss on my cheek.

"It's good to see you, Roy." I lead the way into the lounge. I can feel his curiosity probing my back. I can also feel his irritation. He was just leaving for an appointment when I called.

"Can I get you some coffee, Roy?"

"No, thank you, Solange." He flings his briefcase onto a chair, sedately places himself in a corner of the sofa and drapes an arm along the back. I'm being stared at. I sit defensively in the other corner, curl my feet up under me, spread my dress cautiously around me—there, who says I look pregnant? Roy doesn't seem to have noticed, anyway.

"Where the *hell* have you been? Why the fuck wouldn't you call *Jan?* Do you know what you've been putting him through?"

Solange is speechless for a moment. "Don't you shout at me!"

"I'm sorry . . . but *do* you realize what you've been putting Jan through? Why, *why* did you run out like that? *Why* wouldn't you return his calls? *Where the fuck have you been?*"

Solange is angry. *"Roy!"* Such cool anger, though. "I don't know what's been happening. That's why I asked you here. But for a start, you've got your facts wrong. It was Jan who walked out on me. I *never* walked out on Jan."

"D'you mean running away and refusing to get in touch with him *wasn't* walking out on him?"

"I've never refused to call Jan. You want to get your facts straight, Mister Kane. It was Jan who came here to get his rocks off—and then *left!*"

Solange and Roy, glaring at each other.

Roy shrugs slightly, sighs slightly. "Well, *where* have you been? Let's get that one sorted out, for a start. Because there's a *lot* needs sorting out around here."

"I've been in France. I rented a house so that I could have peace and quiet to finish my book. I got back here yesterday." I realize that I'm clenching my hands tightly, so I look down and make sure they relax. "And I came back to some *great* news."

"Oh? What was that? What 'news'?" He's looking puzzled now, for the first time.

"News that Jan is now divorced. And, that he divorced Melissa for the new lady in his life, the lady he took to the Bahamas. The lady he's going to tour with and sing with now. The lady who obviously means so much more to him than I ever could, because he divorced Melissa and left Andy for her. Something he'd never do for me? *That* news!"

Roy's mouth is open. "Where the hell did you get all that idiotic crap from?" he finally manages to ask.

"That's what I want to discuss with you, before I ring Jan up and let him know just what I think of him," I tell Roy.

"Did *Miriam* tell you all that? It must have been Miriam."

"Of course she did. She's kept me informed all the time."

"What, exactly, *did* she *inform* you?" Roy asks scathingly, getting up and pouring himself a large Scotch. He stares at me and sips, watchfully, awaiting my answer.

I quickly explain all Miriam told me. "But," I add, "I just this morning found Jan's album in Miriam's office—hidden there. With his writing on it, for me. And the album's so *good,* Roy. And now ... now I don't know, I'm totally confused. What he wrote on it to me—and the album itself: *why* would he do that, when he left me? And when he's with Tracey now? I can't make any sense of it at all."

"No wonder—it doesn't make any sense. Because it's not sense. It's not true, either. He's *not* with Tracey. Oh, there were a few reports, but you know what the press is like. He hasn't fucked her since last year, when you were in Sweden. And she came to the Bahamas with *me.* She's trying to get to the top, she'll fuck anything. But Jan—he was keeping himself too smashed to worry much about chicks. I had a hell of a time—"

"I don't believe you!"

"What d'you mean, you don't believe me? You weren't there, lady, so don't you start telling me what happened and what didn't. No, Tracey has nothing going with him. Never did have. He doesn't have anything going with anyone—only with *you ... !*"

"Roy, I don't *understand* ..."

346

"I think that dikey little secretary of yours has been doing a number on you—very systematically—for months and months."

"Oh, no, she *wouldn't!*" But, what other explanation is there? After all, you already realized that it *was* Miriam. You're going to have to believe it! "Jan really isn't working with Tracey? He's *not* involved with her?"

"Jesus Christ, Solange, can you imagine Jan and the band playing with a fucking chick that sings that moronic disco muck? I only handle her because there's money in it these days. I don't even like her much, except that she's great at getting horny."

"But he divorced Melissa—is *that* true?"

"Yes. Months now. But he divorced her for *you.*"

"Roy, Jan walked out on *me.* So don't tell me that! *That* doesn't make sense, either."

"He *didn't* walk out on you!"

"Oh, I see—you mean, he hadn't really gone when I awoke that morning? And I assume you know what morning I'm talking about?" Roy nods solemnly. "Where was he, then, if he hadn't walked out?"

"Solange . . ." Roy takes my hand and holds it between his long, thin ones. "Yes, he went, but it wasn't what you thought."

"Oh, I *see!* Leaving me like that wasn't really leaving. How stupid of me to think he'd left me because he left me, when he hadn't really left me, he'd only *left* me!"

"Solange, I wish you'd just quit this. Just *listen,* will you, please?"

"What else am I to think?" I continue, ignoring him. "He came to me, Roy. And Jesus, you should have seen the state he was in. I fed him and looked after him. Loved him. And we made love—all night, we made love. And I thought . . . he said . . . but when I awoke he was gone. He'd just walked out. I was here the rest of the day. He didn't come back—of *course* he left me."

"No, Solange, it wasn't quite like that. I know—"

"This doesn't make any sense, Roy," I interrupt him. "Not at all does it make any sense."

Roy impatiently ignores me. "Why wouldn't you talk to him when he called you? *Why?* He was so upset, because he realized he'd gotten onto the plane without saying anything to you. He realized, then, what you must be thinking. So why didn't you speak to him then? He could have explained it, gotten it all sorted out then and there, saved all this—"

"Roy! I don't know what Jan told you, but he *didn't* ring me. Where did he go, then? Back home to Dallas?"

"Yes, that's right. But he *did* ring you—I was there. And you refused to talk to him."

"I did not!"

Roy and Solange, confronting each other with angry disbelief. And then, simultaneously, it begins to make sense. All of it. Well, most of it.

"Miriam!"

"You mean—you *didn't* say you wouldn't talk to him?"

"Of course not. I didn't know he'd rung me. Of *course* I'd have talked to him. I was in such a state when I awoke and found him gone—I'd have been relieved, glad, to have sorted it all out."

"I'm gonna kill that fucking little butch. *Jan* is going to kill that . . . that bitching cunt, as he'd say. *Butching* cunt!"

I'm crying, no I'm not, I'm laughing. I don't know what the hell I'm doing anymore.

"He *rang* me? But why—why did he *go* like that?"

Roy squeezes my hand. "Look—he came to you because he realized he just couldn't go on anymore as he was. He didn't *want* to go on anymore like that."

"He didn't say anything about that to *me*," I snap. "I said so many things to him—some horrid things, too. But he never said that. Nothing like that. Only that he needed to see me, and that he *couldn't* talk."

"Yes, well . . . but I was there when he left, Solange. I'd spent Christmas and New Year's with Axel and Kirsten—so I know. Melissa *knew* he was going to you when he suddenly announced that he had to get back to L.A. We all knew why, of course, and we were glad. He said he wasn't going to take any more of all that shit. And that he didn't know why he'd *been* taking it—he must have been crazy. And that he had to repair the damage he'd caused, before it was too late—that's if it wasn't too late with you already. But of course, Melissa came out with all the old garbage: if he goes, he'll never see Andy again. And Jan said he couldn't give a fuck, because he didn't have Andy for a son anyway, so what was the point? And then he left for L.A. Me, Kirsten, Axel, Jed, Marie, Nils—all of us—we were so *relieved*. It's like we had the old Jan back—the *real* Jan back. You must know we'd all been on at him all the time."

"Why didn't he tell me all this?" I answer my own question, "Oh, Roy, he was in such a state."

"I know, love. Anyway, the next afternoon, when he came

back, you should have seen the state he was in then. He said that he was on the plane home before he realized that he hadn't told you he was going, and especially, that he'd be back again. He'd rung you from the airport as soon as he landed, but Miriam had told him that you wouldn't speak to him. As soon as he hit the house he was on the phone again. Nils and I were trying to piece together what had happened. But again you wouldn't speak to him. I mean, that's what *she* said. He even hung on while she went and spoke to you—so *she* said."

"But I didn't know! I was just . . . I was crying my eyes out all morning because Jan had gone."

"That bitch! Well, after that, Nils rang, and I rang; and then later, when we called up again, Miriam told us you'd gone away and wanted to be by yourself for a long time, while you finished your book. And she said you *never* wanted to see Jan again, for what he'd done to you. Darling, hey, stop crying. We're going to get it all worked out." He kisses my cheek, smiling. "Look, it's obvious that Miriam has caused the most horrendous fuckup. So let's just sort it out."

"He never said he was staying. He never said he'd come back to me. He did say there were things he had to tell me, and I shut him up. But then, after we'd made love, I begged him not to leave me. He said: 'I don't want to leave you.' And I thought . . . But he was gone when I woke up. And I was worried for him, because he was in such a state, Roy. He looked *awful*."

"I know, baby. That's why he came to see you."

"But why did he go?" I shout at Roy, in desperation, anger, confusion, and God knows what else.

"He said . . . and he's spoken about it so often since, continuously, in fact—I think Nils and I know every little detail. He said that when he woke up with you he realized that he'd *really* gotten himself back again. And then he felt ashamed for treating you the way he had. Of treating *himself* the way he had. And all he wanted to do was to go to Melissa and tell her where to shove her visitation rights. He said he was so *angry* that all he could focus on was telling Melissa to go fuck herself. The plane had just taken off, and the chick brought him some coffee and was chatting to him, when he suddenly realized he'd left without telling you." Roy gives a subdued laugh. "He said he looked at his watch, eleven it was, and he suddenly called out—very loud, mind you, and it embarrassed him—'*Solange!*'"

A cold, tingly shiver passes through me: it was eleven when I awoke—and I thought I'd heard Jan call me.

"Anyway, he got off the plane and called, but Miriam told him you wouldn't talk to him." Roy sits back, swings at his drink.

"You mean . . ." I'm crying again. I'm trembling. I can't believe what Roy's just told me. "You mean—he *hadn't* really left? He *had* come back to me?"

"Of course he had! He said . . . I'm sorry, Solange, I don't want to embarrass you or anything, but he talked about it so much—he said you, your loving, your sex . . . he could never have left you again. And he couldn't understand why he had."

"Oh, Roy . . . It *was* so good. That's why I couldn't understand . . . We needed and loved each other so much. He said he loved me. But when I awoke to find him gone . . ." My eyes fill with tears again. *"Miriam!!"*

"I sincerely hope you're going to fire her."

"She was my friend."

"With friends like that . . . !"

"I still feel so confused, Roy."

"Look, let's get going right now. Jan's in Dallas, I'm on my way there. Talk it over. Oh, God, he'll be so pleased to see you. He's been fucking impossible, a basket case. And turning into an obnoxious alcoholic."

"Jan's still *drinking?*"

Roy puts an arm around my shoulders. "Darling, all I know is that Jan loves you. He's been going through hell over this. We'll go to Dallas right now, and you can both talk it all out. You can make love for the rest of the week, until you leave on tour with him—and then you can fuck your way around Europe. How does that grab you?"

"Mmm."

"Jed and Marie and Nils are going on the tour with us, so you'll have all your friends with you. And you and Jan can make a baby—he's depressed because Marie and Jed are having a baby—"

"Marie-Claude is *pregnant?*" I giggle happily, clapping my hands together in delight for my beautiful friend. We always did things together—like sisters.

"Yes. Just four months, I think. But Jan . . . he says you tried so hard. He's happy for the both of them, of course, but he wants you, and for *you* to have his baby"

"I am!"

"What?" Roy looks totally puzzled—most uncharacteristically, for such a smoothie. So I stand up and hold my dress to me, to show off my bulgy outline.

"My God—you *are* pregnant. *You're* pregnant, too!"

"Mm . . ." I nod enthusiastically, smile a beatific madonna smile.

"You mean . . . ?" Roy's face shows incredulity, astonishment, pleased surprise, and finally a broad smile. "From that night?"

"Of course! There's been no one else since—or for quite a time before, come to that. And it's a boy—baby Jan-Tobias. I had tests done in France." I'm giggling happily again.

"But then . . ." He looks puzzled again, "I'd have thought . . . It's even more ludicrous that you didn't get in touch with him. With his *baby* . . ."

"No, it made it worse, much worse. Don't you see? I thought he'd walked out, anyway. And as far as I knew he was still with Melissa and Andy. He couldn't have handled *me* being pregnant. I'd never have pressured him, either, into anything—that's no good. Look how Melissa pressured him into marrying her because of Andy. He'd had all that once; he didn't need it all over again. And it's not my way—I'm extremely independent, Roy, you know that; and Baby Jan and I can manage. I'm still not sure whether . . . I mean, he has Andy . . . Look, I wouldn't want him to think I was pressuring him, because I wouldn't."

"But he wouldn't think that!" I sit down, and Roy takes my hand in his. "You . . . having Jan's baby!" he says. It seems to have really surprised him. "He's gonna kill you, little lady, for not getting in touch with him."

"But what else was I to do?"

"Well . . . No—I can see it from your viewpoint, too." He nods, decisively. "And now, I'd better just be getting you to Dallas. They have a concert there tomorrow. They always do an annual Dallas concert. And before that—today—Kirsten is giving Jan an early birthday party, as he'll be away for his actual one."

"I don't know—the idea scares me."

"Solange!"—Roy getting impatient with this dithery female—"This whole thing is all sorted out now. Why don't you accept that, and just accept all the goodies you really have? I don't understand really, at this point in time, what's holding you back."

I stand up and walk over to the window, still unsure. Why?

I stare out of the window at the few fluffy clouds smudged, like a child's finger paintings, here and there in the sky. "Jan may feel different now. It's been so long."

"But he doesn't. That's what I've been telling you," Roy says patiently. "You don't feel differently about it, do you? No. So why should he?"

I stare at him, unconvinced; I fidget. I come back and sit next to him. "Melissa won't let him see his son, then?" Solange, recalling Jan's perennial irritation, the irritant still in place. "How is he, now that he can't see his son? It must be killing him."

"He doesn't have a son, though," Roy says, poker-faced, but with a hint of triumphant smugness in his voice.

"I know that's what Melissa wants. But Andy *is* his son—there's no way around that, is there?"

"Yes, there is. It was all a con game. Andy's *not* his son, in actual fact. No way."

"But how . . . ? I think I must have missed something, Roy. How could Andy *not* be his son?"

"By being someone else's." Roy's smugness is really triumphing now.

"Someone . . . *else's?*" I echo disbelievingly. After all, Melissa—a Baptist-reared virgin . . .

"Yes. Jan found out the answer when he told Melissa to go and get fucked. She told him the truth, for the first time."

"*What* truth?"

"We all thought he'd been born a month premature. But he wasn't—in fact, he was late, if anything."

"What? How . . . ?"

"Yes. She'd pulled a real fast one. It all came out then. Red Freely, that's Bill Freely's son—Bill's Andrew Cantrell's foreman, and Red worked for Cantrell too. Well, it appears that Red and Melissa had been making it for some time. *He* was the one that popped Melissa's cherry, not Jan as she later convinced him. But she wanted Jan—he was a *star* and made a lot of money. She'd already missed a period by then, and she knew darn well that she was pregnant by Red Freely." Roy grins, wryly. "He's called Red on account of his hair. And he's got freckles all over his fucking nose—just like Andy does. I mean, shit, Andy *does* look like him. But Melissa being redheaded too, she got away with it, the little bitch! So she used being pregnant to hook Jan—like old Groucho used to say, God love him, 'Hook the schnook is the name of their game.' And Jan fell for it."

"You mean . . ." I can't think lucidly. "After everything

352

we've been through...Jan giving everything up for his son...*he doesn't actually have one?*" I'm suddenly giggling, hysterically. Crying. Laughing. How could this ever have really happened? I look up at the ceiling—I *know* how it happened. Old Nobodaddy again, the fucking asshole: I bet he's sitting up there in his damn clouds, laughing his head off! Nobodaddy's revenge, all right. He *showed* us, didn't he, that we have to ask his permission to have a bit of happiness and love!

"Are you quite sure of all this, Roy? I mean, she could have just been saying that, to get back at Jan. Us ladies don't like being rejected."

"No. We checked the hospital records, saw the doctor. Axel and Kirsten insisted, and Andrew Cantrell insisted too, come to that. The blood tests and all the stuff they can do now—Jan couldn't have been Andy's father, it's a biological impossibility. And that's why she didn't want him near her while she was pregnant. He was touring, but she didn't even want to see him on his time off, especially towards the end. We just put it down to one of those female things, glands, hormones, stuff like that. Of course Jan would have realized how pregnant she actually was if he'd seen her sans clothes. You know, Jan and the Axelssons didn't even see Andy until a week after he was born! Oh, Melissa and Charlene explained it away—and we believed their reasons. That bitch Charlene, she knew what was going on, right from the start. But she obviously figured Jan was a better catch for her precious daughter that the foreman's son."

"I thought they were Christians?" I say, genuinely puzzled, not at all sarcastic.

Roy grins, without comment. "Anyway, the divorce went through without a hitch, and of course Jan didn't have to pay a penny. Andrew Cantrell was extremely embarrassed about the whole fucking scene. He'd only come down heavy on Jan because he'd thought...Well, anyway, Red Freely had to marry Melissa-Sue. He's only a year older than she is. Andrew's made Bill a partner, and given Red a hand in running the place too, so that his precious daughter isn't married to just the foreman's son. Poor dumb little bastard, Melissa and Charlene will eat him alive."

"Has Jan seen Andy at all?"

"No. The Cantrells won't let him. He wanted to put some money in a trust fund for him, but they wouldn't even have that. I think that's best, really. A clean break; Jan has no ties there now, nothing. It hit him pretty hard at first; he really loved that little boy. But at the same time, he was so relieved. Then, when he looked back at it all, he was fucking angry with himself for being taken in like that—and what's more, for giving you up, with all you two had going. And on top of it all, he couldn't find you and he thought you didn't want him anymore. So, Solange, he needs you, very much he needs you. And, by the looks of it, young lady"—he glances down at my tummy—"you need Jan."

"Oh, Roy, I couldn't agree more." I turn, startled, as the door is flung open. Miriam bounces into my room.

"Solange, I—" She stops, with a horrified look of realization at Roy and me; it took her only a split second to compute the situation. She stares down at her feet, knowing that I now know everything.

"Please join us, Miriam," I say very coolly. She looks uncertain. "*Now*, Miriam," I watch her intently as she comes down into the lower section and stands a little way away from me.

"Do you realize what you've done?" Roy shouts, unable to keep quiet any longer. "You little bitch, it's *despicable!* Solange is your friend, as well as your employer—and this is how you've treated her."

"I was *only* . . ."

"You shut your lying little mouth," Roy points a finger at her for emphasis. "You lied—lied, systematically and deliberately. There's no way you can justify doing that. No way you can justify what you've put Solange through—not to mention other people, too."

"I *did* what was *best* for *her!*" Miriam screams at him. "*You* didn't *see* her after that *bastard left.* I *didn't* want her *hurt* anymore! She doesn't *need* that fucking *asshole!*"

Roy cuts her off. "You're nothing but a jealous, spiteful little butch of a dyke! *You* couldn't have Solange, so you were making sure no one else could."

She looks pleadingly at me. "*You* didn't *see* what he *put* her through. *He* didn't *care, I* did. So *don't* blame *me!*"

I give Miriam a cold, cold stare as Roy subsides, and I eventually say, "You lied to me, Miriam. Lied."

"I *wanted* to keep *you* from being *hurt!*"

"What!" I scoff. "What about all the pain you were causing me? And Jan's album—how could you hide it? How *could* you do that?" Miriam's coffee-colored skin is looking rather pale. "I asked you so many times if Jan had called."

"I *didn't* want anyone *upsetting* you again."

"How dare you make my decisions for me!"

354

"I *don't* have to *stay* around here to be *insulted!* I know when I'm *not wanted!*"

"Miriam! You were my friend, my friend. How could you be so . . . so *specious?* I'll never trust you again. In fact, I want you to go—*now.*"

"I *was* leaving *anyway,*" she angrily flings back.

"Excuse me a minute, Roy." I get my checkbook, write Miriam a check. "I think that's fair enough," I say, holding it out to her.

Roy is up and looking at it, calculating. "But that's three months' wages," he protests, now the smoothie manager again. *"One* would have been too much, in view of the fact that she'd resigned."

"It's okay, Roy," I say, and to Miriam: "If you need a reference, contact me. I can honestly say you got the manuscripts and letters handled very well. But I was also paying you to answer the phone. *Responsibly.* You'd better think about that, when you start your new job."

"I suppose you'll be going to him now?" she replies, ignoring what I said and staring hard at the check, as if afraid that the writing will fade out and vanish.

"Yes, I will, now that I understand what really happened. Miriam, *why* did you do it? I still don't understand. I've always been good to you. I've never treated you as just another employee. You were a *friend,* So why . . . ?"

"Because she's a fucking bull dyke, that's why," Roy savagely interjects.

"Please, Roy!" I glare at him. "Miriam, take your things, and come back for any you can't manage now. I'll contact Elena, and she'll be staying here."

Miriam looks baffled, apparently still trying to compute a way out. "I was *only* doing what I *thought* was *best* for you—why won't you *believe* that?"

"I'll never believe that, Miriam—and you're not so stupid as to think you can kid me about it either, are you? You know damn well that *Jan* is best for me. And you know damn well that what you did was spiteful and childish." I glance around the room to avoid her eyes for a moment; I feel so awful—I've never had to fire anyone before, and I hate it. "You were my friend, Miriam. I trusted you, I really did."

"He *won't* marry you, or even *stay* with you, you know. He likes *young* chicks too much."

I watch her turn and leave. And then I cry.

"Come on, sweetheart, let's get you to Dallas and Jan," Roy says briskly.

I pull myself away from him, feeling real terror at the idea. *Why* do I feel so terrified and confused? Baby Jan flip-flops and kicks, as though telling me to stop messing around and get to his daddy.

Then I realize with sudden clarity just what's holding me back. "I can't, Roy."

"You *can't*? Why not? *Now* what is it?"

"Catch-22."

"What?"

"Catch-22. Well, a little one. A tiny one. A Texan one—a *semeye*-Catch-22. At least Jan would appreciate that."

"What the fuck does that mean?" Roy's exasperation with me dissolves into laughter.

"Well, I wanted to marry Jan and have his baby. But now . . ."

"Now?"

"Well, I can't marry him because I *am* having his baby."

Roy shakes his head, in a sort of dazed amazement. "Jesus Christ," he says. "For an intelligent lady, you sure are dumb."

"It makes immense sense to me. Jan thought he had to marry Melissa because he'd made her pregnant; she trapped him. So he'd think I was doing the same thing, now—*making* him marry me because I'm pregnant, using it to trap him. He thought it was his duty before—I know he'd feel the same way again. But that's not what I want, Roy. I don't want to pressure him—I want him to want *me*. I want him to love me for *me*, not because he thinks it's his *duty* because it's his son."

"Solange! He does love you. He wants you to have his babies. He'll be delighted. You don't have to pressure him—he'll know you're not doing that, anyway."

"You really think so?"

"Listen, he's made two dumb-ass stupid mistakes: leaving you in the first place, and then forgetting to talk to you that morning. Don't go on punishing him by refusing to be with him when he wants you. He's always wanted you, he just couldn't handle the shit he'd stuck himself in. . . . Come on, we're going."

"But I can't just go without packing. Without getting Elena here to stay with Gulley."

"Well, *call* her; then get packed."

"You're really sure Jan *does* want me?"

Roy hugs me, kisses me, laughs. "He does want you—I swear it," he says. "But, tell you what—I can prove it to you.

I've just thought of the best way of doing it—I'll tell you as we go."

As we drive down the Pacific Coast highway Roy says, "I sure do have a nice surprise for Jan's birthday. You'll be the best little present he could possibly have." He leans across and gently touches my tummy. "And him—he'll be the best little present Jan could have, too."

"Oh, Roy," I say, feeling almost confident now, "he *will* want us, won't he?"

"Of course he will. All he does is talk about you. He's so proud of you as a writer, and he's delighted that you understand him as a writer, that you understand what his creativity means to him. Melissa never had the faintest idea . . . D'you know what that fucking bitch did to him?" he says angrily. "When Jan left for L.A. that day, she went and got Andy and left, because she knew he was going to you. In Jan's room, when she was getting Andy, she noticed Jan's poetry folder on the desk. So she took it—and burned it."

"She *what?!*"

"Yes. You can imagine what that did to Jan."

"But why would she do a thing like that?" Solange, horrified at the idea that anyone could destroy the words Jan took so much pleasure in creating.

"She said she was affronted by the photos of you that Jan had stuck inside the covers."

"Oh, hell!" Jan had stuck photos of me in there, all right—in the front, one of me in my teddy, and on the back cover, one of me, just me. All me. Beautiful little naked me. "So she *destroyed* his poetry? Everything he'd created?"

"Yes, she did. And Jan cried. I mean, he *wept*. That was his life's work. I was doing a deal with Solly to get some of the poems published. Jan said he could never do all that again."

"Oh, God! How spiteful! I know how upset I was when we were burgled and they took my manuscript." My eyes fill with tears: I feel Jan's loss almost as he must have felt it. Solange and Jan—empaths. "Oh, Roy, I . . ."

Then a memory flashes brilliantly before me, neon, lit. "Roy! Stop the car! We've got to go back."

"Back? But we're on our way . . ." Roy looks at me as though afraid he has another basket case on his hands.

"Back! I've just remembered something. When Jan was off on his last concert, I wasn't feeling too well. So I stayed at home while he did his sound rehearsals."

"Sound checks."

"Yes. Oh, do turn *around*, Roy." He obediently makes a U-turn. "Well, I was looking through his poetry," I continue. "He was working on one called 'Reflected Lights of Mirrored Love.' Oh, Roy, it was so fucking *good*. So damn literary. I mean, writing poetry, it's so different from his songs."

"I know. He's tried to explain that to me. But what . . . ?"

"Well, I thought I'd like to have a copy of it. So while I had the time, I copied it. I photocopied the whole folder, on Miriam's machine. That's why we're going back—we can get it, take it to Jan for his birthday."

"Jesus Christ, Solange! No way can you tell me that you two aren't meant for each other! No fucking way!"

Solange, this *is* your special day, after all. Your little Classy-Ass *has* reigned supreme!

I grin at him. "Ain't that the fuckin' truth?"

21

The airport is crowded. I never realized that airports were so crowded on Sundays. Especially on special Sundays—Mandarin Orange Sundays.

Roy takes my elbow and guides me through the gate, giving me a smile because he knows how nervous I am. Actually, I've got a touch of the eager-terrifieds. What if . . . what if . . . what if . . .

Well, this is it. Solange is at last in Texas. And it has to be Texas: There are so many cowboy boots and hats at the airport, it couldn't be anywhere else.

We collect our luggage and Roy grabs a porter. Someone, tall, lean, and suntanned, is waving at us; he helps the porter pack the bags into the Mercedes. Roy tips the porter and introduces me to Jim Rodriguez, who works for the Axelssons.

"Is it far?" I whisper to Roy.

"About an hour or so, but that's close, for Texas."

I stare out at the countryside, the bright, bright afternoon, but I don't take anything in. All I can do is think—think of

Jan. What if . . . whatif . . . whatif . . . Roy chats to Jim, and Jim chats to Roy

"Your first visit to Texas, Ma'am?" Jim asks me, with an amiable smile into the driving mirror.

"Yes."

"Someone sure is going to be having a mighty good party." Jim grins broadly; Roy laughs; baby Jan flip-flops; and me, I find that I'm even blushing slightly.

"Axelsson territory, Ma'am," Jim finally announces with another amiable smile. The car goes under a huge archway, between open, white-painted gates, into a long, long drive-way.

"It's so *big!*" It seems to go on as far as the eye can see. But then, I've never been on a ranch before. The house we gradually approach is huge and white. A second floor terrace runs around it. There are a dozen or so cars parked in front of it.

"Everyone's around the back, most likely," Roy tells me, giving me a hug. Dear Roy, he knows how I'm feeling. "Kirsten made the party outside on the terrace—Jan likes that."

"Oh . . . !" Solange, little Ms. Nervous-Ass. "I'm scared!" I announce as I step from the car. "Do I look all right?"

Roy smiles gently; he knows that I mean my question, I'm not just fishing for feminine compliments. He takes my shoulders. "You look beautiful," he reassures me, and kisses me on the cheek, then hugs me again to calm me down.

Do I? In my strapless sundress of dusty-pink silk, with suede boots to match. And I'm wearing my sun-angel, my eagle, and my bear-claw like talismans. Also my engagement ring—I hope we still are engaged. And of course, in the beauty case I'm hanging onto so tightly, my beloved William's words: I always carry them around like a good-luck charm. But even so, I'm feeling nervous.

"What's that? It's got *horns* on the front." It's white, but it's not a cow, it's a Cadillac. "Don't tell me—it must be Jed's?"

Roy laughs. "He's got a horn on the front, too."

"Ain't that the truth!"

Two huge German Shepherds come and say hello, backing me up against the side of the car. Jim whistles and pulls them off me. I say hello back, and they wag their tails. They're Jan's—he's told me all about them. They're called John Wesley Hardin and Billy the Kid. They've even been on an album cover with him.

"I'm scared, Roy. What if . . . what if it all goes wrong?"

Okay, little Ms. Scaredy-Ass, just get your act together, *Ma'am!* How could it possibly go wrong, when you're doing something right for a change? You've come to Jan, and that's just as it should be. Something he'll love you for. You're his Literary Lady, his Lover Lady. His little Ms. Classy-Ass. And this is the day you're making everything go right, remember? So how *can* anything go wrong today? Of course it can't! Not today—your special day: Your Mandarin Orange Sunday.

* * *

Roy takes my hand and leads me through the house into a large room, a huge, long lounge with beautiful modern furniture, and with thick rugs and a Persian carpet on the floor. I grip the big, flat, gold-wrapped package to my boobs. My attention goes to the patio outside, where there are voices. The French windows have heavy white voile curtains, which make us invisible to the people outside. I hang onto Roy's arm, become a little girl again. "I'm scared, Roy."

He gives me another comforting hug. "Listen, it'll go all right. We'll do it just as I suggested. That way you'll *know,* without any doubts, that Jan wants you for you, not just because you're having his baby. No semeye-Catch-22. It'll go fine, just you see. I'll go and get Marie-Claude first—okay?"

"Okay. But don't you say anything, mind."

"Okay."

I look around the room while I wait. I think, suddenly, of Maman and my Larssons: how pleased they'll be. I *must* call them. Jan and I can explain everything *together.*

I go over and sit on the long black leather chesterfield, perching on the edge. A photo on the end table is of the Axelsson boys: a little Nils about ten, a little Jan about eleven, and Axel who must have been about thirteen, all in football uniforms. They all look so blond, clean and shiny. Three little Innocent Angels.

"Solange!" I turn. There before me—no, I don't believe it! But it is—Marie-Claude Leboux, metamorphosed into Mrs. Jed Brackett, a Tex-ahn. I stare at her in amazement: Marie-Claude, her hair down to her shoulders, and wearing jeans tucked into amazingly embroidered cowboy boots with pointed toes. She has a blue and white checkered puffed-sleeved maternity top that hides her tiny bulge—and yes, the whole effect is topped off with a white cowboy hat and aviator sunglasses.

"Marie-Claude!" I run to her and we hug and cry. She throws her hat and sunglasses onto the sofa and cuddles me. Laughs. Cries. Holds my hands. We stare at each other, and then we burst out laughing again, hugging again: Solange and Marie-Claude in *Texas!*

"You are pregnant, *ma chérie?*"

"Yes . . . And you too? You are pregnant, also?"

I never realized that Marie-Claude and I could say so much to each other in such a short space of time. Talking in French helps, of course, but we've gone into overdrive, light-speed. Within minutes everything is told and understood.

"Mon Dieu!" She's hugging me. I'm hugging her.

We both point at each other, giggle, and say almost in unison, "You've got another earring!" We hug and kiss—we always did do things together. And we touch each others' tummies—our babies.

"Jan—he will be so pleased. He has been so unhappy, *ma chérie.*"

"I still feel so scared, Marie-Claude, in case he won't want me and baby Jan, after all this time."

"He *will!* He never stops talking of you. When he couldn't find you . . . Oh, darling!" Hug and cry again. "And you came now, for a surprise," Marie-Claude giggles, "as Zhed says, 'snuck in, lower than a ratt-lair.' "

Roy joins us. "Ready to put my fantastic plan into action?" He quickly explains to Marie-Claude.

"Roy. Marie-Claude." Kirsten Axelsson smiles at me. She is slim and beautiful: I know she's sixty-two, but she doesn't look it. Her white-streaked blonde hair is in plaits, which are coiled around the back of her head—so very Scandinavian. And her eyes are beautiful: large, dark, amethyst eyes.

"Solange . . ." She gathers me into her arms, then looks down at me. "A baby. *Jan's* baby?"

"Yes—a son."

She hugs me again. "Yahn-Toby—he will be so happy; he has been so miserable. He is outside. Shall I get him?"

Roy quickly explains again, and she smiles. "Jan's son. Everything will be fine now, Solange, you will see. Now that you are to be with Yahnilill." She kisses me tenderly on the cheek, and my eyes again flood with tears. Solange is going to love having Kirsten Axelsson for her *Mor.*

"Come on." Roy leads me to the French windows. "Marie

will help when the time comes, won't you?" Marie-Claude nods enthusiastically, then tells Kirsten my news.

"And you won't mention I'm here—or the baby?" Roy grins and nods.

Marie-Claude puts her arm around me, and Kirsten holds my hand on the other side, as the three of us stare out unnoticed.

And I'm still feeling so *scared*. Baby Jan gives a comforting flip-flop and a little kick: "Get on with it! I want to meet my daddy!"

"Where are they?" asks Marie-Claude. "There!" She points across the terrace. And I dare a look.

I see Jed. And Nils—he's sitting on a chair, but he has *legs*. "He's learned to use his legs," I say to Kirsten, who smiles delightedly. And I see Joel talking to Billy Wilson and Tom G. Watson.

Oh . . . Oh, God . . . now, now I see Jan. I start to tremble uncontrollably, and my eyes fill with tears; I stand absolutely transfixed; I don't know what to do.

Jan's in black trousers and a white, tight-fitting shirt. And his hair is even longer now; he has it tied back with a leather thong. I stare. What if . . . what if . . . what if . . . He laughs with the man next to him. It's obviously his father: the same great build, tall and muscular; hair of the same color, but Axel Axelsson's has gray in it

Roy goes over to Jan. Jan hugs him, Axel hugs him. The warmth of it makes me smile. Jed and Nils—who's walking so well with his crutches—join them.

"Oh God, I wish I could hear them properly," I say. Baby Jan flip-flops. Roy, animatedly, telling Jan, Axel, Nils, Jed—and now also Joel and the rest of the band, Billy, Tom G. Jan sips his drink. Jan stares at Roy. Everyone looks at everyone else. Roy nods enthusiastically, and adds something else.

"Miriam did what?" Jan roars (I could hear *that!*). Roy goes on. *"What?"* Jan drops his glass, and it smashes into hundreds of pieces on the flagstone.

Jan-Toby Axelsson grabs Roy's shoulders. "Where's Solange? *Where is she?"* Roy answers. *"Why didn't you bring her?"* And I know what Roy says to that: That I wanted a bit of time to myself. "We're going! *Now!"* Jan shouts.

Jed, full of grinning excitement, shouts, "That's it, Jan-Toby, ole buddy—rope her tighter'n a runaway calf at brandin' time. Whoo-whee!" I giggle: Solange is going to need her little Classy-Ass roped!

But Roy grabs for Jan and continues to talk. It's Marie-

Claude's cue. "I'll go," she says, "and Kirsten can ring the terrace number." When Kirsten has punched out the number, she hands me the phone, and I see Marie-Claude pick up the terrace phone on its first ring.

"Solange? *Tu es prêt?*"

"Oh . . ." I'm trembling as I hold the receiver to my ear. Kirsten keeps a comforting arm around my shoulder. "Wait —just a minute!" I'm watching Jan talk excitedly to Roy. "Just a minute, Marie-Claude." She waits patiently. We stand silent, phone receivers in hand.

Jan shouts: "Where's *Mor?*" and looks around him. He touches his father's arm. "I've *got* to go and get her. *Now!* I've got to. She thought I'd left her! I've *got* to! *Mor* will understand, *Far.*" His father hugs him closely, a great bear hug, and nods, smiling. And Jan kisses his cheek. I smile to see such warmth and love between father and son. That's how it will be—and the thought fills my eyes with tears—between Jan and *his* son. If I can just get myself through this . . . !

"Marie-Claude . . ." *Am* I ready now? What if . . . what if . . . what if . . . But this is your *special* day, Solange. Yes. *"Oui, bien sûr, je suis tout prêt."*

Marie-Claude turns so that she's looking at them all—at Jan, who's talking of going with Jed in the plane to fetch me.

Slow motion, everything's in slow motion. How nice—free, light and airy . . . I stare at Jan: all I can see is Jan. All I can feel is Jan. He *didn't* walk out on me! He *did* want me! He *does* want me! It's over: this ghastly, terrifying nightmare, it's *over*. I smile—still in slow motion—as I stare at Jan's back.

Marie-Claude's voice startles me. I hold the phone up to my ear.

"Zhahn . . . !" I see Jan turn to where Marie-Claude is. "Someone to speak to you."

"I can't talk on the fuckin' phone, little darlin'. Come on, Marie, we're goin' to leave for L.A." He beckons impatiently; Jed goes over to his wife.

"C'est important!"

"Marie . . ." Jan, so impatient. "I *don't* wanna speak to *anyone.*"

Marie-Claude giggles as Jed grabs her in his arms. "So, I will tell *Solange* that you do not wish to speak with her?"

"What?" Jan spins around and stares at Marie-Claude.

"I'll tell Solange to ring back, then?" Fits of giggles.

Jan-Toby Axelsson is across the terrace in a flash, grabbing

363

the phone from Marie-Claude. I step back a pace or two from the window curtain; I don't want him to know I'm in the house.

"Solange? *Solange?*"

Of course—what else?—little Ms. Classy-Ass is immediately reduced to tears as she hears her man's voice over the phone. Baby Jan gives me an encouraging kick. "Jan . . ."

"Jesus *fuck!*" I'm crying, and I hear Jan sniff. "Solange . . . Roy's just explained. Oh, Solange! I never meant to *leave* you. I *said* I was stayin'. I didn't leave you!

"Jan . . . !" I'm crying in earnest now.

"Oh, God, little darlin' . . . *I couldn't find you!* Why didn't you come over with Roy?" I can't even answer, just sniff and cry. Baby Jan gives me the strongest kick ever. "Answer Daddy, Mama," he's saying.

"I just . . . I just needed to speak to you on the phone, before I saw you. I needed . . . oh, Jan!"

"I'm comin', darlin'. Right now." I watch him shifting excitedly from one foot to the other. Jed, Nils, and Joel crowd around him. His father stands beside him with a broad Axelsson smile on his face. And Kirsten still has her comforting hand on my shoulder.

"You want . . . to come and get me?" I ask hesitantly.

"Darlin'—I *love* you."

"Oh, I love *you.*"

"I'm on my way. Oh, shit, I can't even *talk.*" He laughs; I watch Joel hand him a drink, and over the phone hear him slurping it. I giggle: Bourbon and branch water, I bet. "Jesus *fuck,* I can't discuss all that's happened over the phone. I'll be with you as soon as I can. Then we can . . . It's your birthday on Wednesday. I've bought you so many presents. We'll get married on your birthday. We'll—"

"You want to marry me?" Solange, elated to hear him say it again. Baby Jan excited. We join each other in a flip-flop. "You haven't exactly asked me. Not this time around, I mean."

"I'm on my knees." I see him drop to his knees on the flagstones. "Literally, on my knees. For my Literary Lady. Ask anybody."

Joel grabs the phone. "He's on his knees—say yes! Put him out of his misery!"

Jan grabs it back. "You will marry me, won't you? On Wednesday? Here at home? We can get married on Wednesday. I'm not letting you go again. Solange?"

I watch him stand up and slurp his drink. "Yes, I'll marry

364

you. Of course I will, Jan darling." Kirsten hugs me and I'm crying again, grinning too, and baby Jan gives me another resounding kick (his daddy always did like football, didn't he!). "Jan?"

"What, darlin'?" But before I can answer, I see him grinning around at everyone as he shouts, "We're getting married on Wednesday."

"Jan ... I keep on remembering when we made love that last time. I haven't made love since—so I keep on remembering. I'm always remembering. I should have realized ... we loved each other so much. Do you remember?"

"Remember? I've been doin' nothin' else but rememberin'." He bursts out laughing.

I burst into loud sobs.

"Solange—listen, darlin'. I need to talk to you so much, we've so much to say. But I've gotta get you. I've been so fuckin' miserable. I know it's been a fuckin' mess, and it's my fault, but I'm just so fuckin' glad we're together again. Oh, Solange, we're together! And that's all that matters now. Just you and me—together!

And a little someone else, I think to myself. "Jan?"

"What, darlin'? Hey, we're all gonna leave now. Jed and Marie—hey, they're havin' a baby. We'll make a baby. And Nils, he'll come too. We'll all come to get you. But what? Quick! I wanna come to you. What, darlin'?"

"There's someone ... there's someone I'll want you to meet."

"What ... 'someone'?" Jan, highly suspicious.

"The new man in my life."

"What!!"

"Umm ..."—Baby Jan kicks: "Get on with it, Mama."—"Your *son.*"

"What?" Jan roars, incredulously. Everyone looks startled, except Roy, who's grinning a pleased smoothie grin.

"Well, not for another four months, actually. But you can say hello—he's started to kick a lot."

"He *what?*"

"I said—I'm *pregnant!* You're going to be a *daddy!*" Joyous giggles from Mama Solange.

"Jesus *fuck!*" He looks around him. "She says she's *pregnant!*" he shouts to Nils, Jed and the others.

"I had tests."

"She had tests," he repeats to them.

"It's a boy."

"It's a boy? She's having my baby—and *it's a boy!*"

"Baby Jan."

"Baby Jan," he echoes to everyone. They immediately start to whistle, cheer, and clap.

Tears well up in my eyes and I know that I can't *not* touch him for another second longer.

"Solange!" he shouts down the phone as Nils and his father hug him. "Solange—" I put the phone down on the table. He's standing with his back towards me, out on the terrace. "Solange," he calls. "Answer me, Solange!"

I grab Kirsten's hand and walk my classy-ass through the curtains.

Solange, in full view—feeling unutterably shy as all now stand still and look at her. Startled looks. Smiling faces.

"Why isn't she answering? She's crying—I bet she's crying," Jan says. (For once he's guessed that wrong.) He sees that all the others are looking my way, with big smiles on their faces. "What the . . . ?" He spins around quickly, does a double take. *"Jesus fuck!"* For the second time that afternoon, Jan-Toby Axelsson drops a glass onto the paving, heedless of it smashing.

I'm totally unaware of anyone else; my world contains only Jan-Toby Axelsson.

"You beautiful bitch . . ." I see the tears in Jan's eyes. Or is it the tears in my eyes again? Hell, I don't think it matters. Not anymore.

He rushes the few feet across the terrace, scoops me up into his arms, and swings me around and around as he kisses me. Then he sets me down, looks at me. Holds my shoulders. Runs his hands up and down my arms. Kisses me—hugs me—kisses me. Looks at me again.

"God—you look so *beautiful.* So soft and round."

"Twenty pounds rounder."

He laughs. "My beautiful sweet delight."

I throw myself into his arms again, and he swings me around, then places me down. "Careful, be careful, little darlin'," he says, looking down at my tummy. "Jesus fuck," he says in an awed tone. I take his hand and press it to my tummy, because baby Jan is kicking impatiently to be introduced to his daddy. "I feel him!" Jan roars in delight.

"I love you, Jan," I say breathlessly in between kisses. "I *love* you!"

"You do, huh?" he says.

"Sure do, cowboy!"

"I love *you,* little darlin'."

"You do, huh?"

"Sure do, Ma'am!"

There doesn't seem to be anyone left in the universe. We're not even aware that everyone is standing so quiet, just smiling and watching us.

Jan-Toby Axelsson rubs the side of his nose, puts his hands on his hips, looks up at the sky. I look up there too and smile. Are we both thinking that Old Nobodaddy has finally left us alone and gone back into hiding? Or perhaps even wished us well, for a change?

I look at the blond fuzz on Jan's chest and kiss it, touch his sun-angel and his bear claw, smile, as he touches mine in return.

He takes my face in his hands and kisses me tenderly, and all the onlookers burst into loud cheers. And of course—what else?—I'm crying again. Warm tears for my warm Jan.

"Hey . . ." he says, my face still in his hands, his face so close to mine. "You're cryin'—and you ain't even come yet." He kisses me tenderly, and I smile back at him through my tears.

"I'm sure that's something you'll soon rectify?"

He pulls me to him, buries his face in my neck and says: "Ain't that the truth, Ma'am." He laughs. "You beautiful bitch—I've got a fuckin' hard-on!"

I fling my arms around his neck and press myself up against him as he wraps his arms around me. "You think I haven't noticed, cowboy?" He laughs and kisses me again. And this unmarried mama, his Literary Lady, has more than a touch of the eager creamies.

"Wait!" I say, remembering another piece of happiness I've brought him.

"What?" he asks.

"Wait. Just wait." I quickly rush into the house and return with my gold-covered present. "Happy birthday!"

He reads my inscription on the front: "To Daddy Jan, from Mama Solange and Baby Jan-Tobias Axelsson."

"We're having a baby!" he shouts joyfully as he rips the foil away.

"I didn't pay much for the gift," I tell him with a cheeky grin. "I just made a copy of something valuable. But seeing as you haven't got one anymore . . ." He looks totally puzzled for a moment, holding the blue folder in his hands. I reach up and kiss the side of his beard. "Open it, then," I tell him with impatient excitement.

He opens it, stares at the first page. Gives me an amazed glance. Flips through a few more pages. I swear his mouth is hanging open. "Jesus *fuck!*" He stares at me with a vacant, dazed expression. "Jesus fuck, it's my poetry . . . all of it!" His eyes glisten with tears as he leafs through more pages. "It's my poetry. You've given me back my poetry . . ."

Nils takes the folder from him as he stands there just looking at me. I fling myself into his arms and we cuddle and kiss for a long, long time . . . feeling ourselves a part of each other again.

And then he looks at me, with that puzzled look I saw when I first met him: that *beautiful* puzzled look of his that I love so much. He gives me a gentle, lopsided grin, and I reach out and caress his mustache. He bites gently at my finger, kisses me, and then feels his son kick a happy, excited kick.

I don't know exactly what Jan-Toby Axelsson is thinking . . .

. . . but it sure looks good from where I am!

ABOUT THE AUTHOR

ANGELIQUE DURAND was born in London where she went to stage school and college, studying English literature and drama. She has been an actress and singer and has had songs and short stories published. She is now devoting her time to writing novels. Her main interests, besides literature, music, and the theater are Egyptology, vampires, the occult, and men (not necessarily in that order). At present, she is living with a friend in Virginia.

A Special Advance Preview of
the breathtaking opening pages of

Tides of Love

the new novel by the bestselling author

Patricia Matthews

Chapter One

The wind, carrying a burden of cold salt spray, cut vicious-
ly through the dark night, and Marianna Harper, lowering
her chin into the wide collar of the man's coat she wore,
turned her face away from the blow.

Her hands, deep in the coat pockets, were already numb,
and despite the gum boots, her feet ached from the chill
and the wet.

The storm had been raging since late afternoon, whip-
ping the waves into huge, jagged combers that tore at the
Outer Banks as if to destroy them. The wind was at least
sixty knots and howled along the sandy beaches with a
terrible frenzy.

Inside the hut it had been uncomfortable enough—with
the leaking roof dripping sour, cold water and the wind
blustering through every chink to chill one's flesh and make
one's bones ache—but now, in the roiling dark, at the water's edge, it was sheer torture, and only Marianna's fear
of Ezekial Throag and the others kept her at her post.

From the direction of the roaring sea, she could hear the
sound of a ship's bell tolling wildly. It had the shocking
sound of a cry for help.

For a moment Marianna felt a stab of pity for the poor
souls on the ship that was about to be bilged on the shoals.
She usually tried not to think of such things, for these
thoughts brought her only confusion and discontent; but
sometimes, like now, while she was waiting and her mind
was not occupied with her tasks, she couldn't help but
think of the people out there, about to be drowned; or, if
they were spared by the sea, to be bludgeoned by Ezekial

Throag and the others. After all, they were people like herself, and she could not help but wonder how they must feel, how afraid they must be, as the ship's back broke beneath them.

Marianna knew well enough what Ezekial Throag and the others would say to such thoughts. They would say that she had gone soft, and they would tease and torment her. But just the same, she often felt that what they did, what they were doing, was very wrong.

She also often puzzled over how Ezekial Throag seemed to know when a ship was due; he was almost never wrong. It was a shivery thing—almost as if he possessed some frightening mystic sense that informed him of ships passing close to the Banks.

Marianna peered out from the rock behind which she was crouching for shelter against the biting wind. About two hundred feet south along the beach, she could see the yellow glow of the huge, whale-oil lantern flickering in the windblown sand and spray.

It was this light that the ship would be heading away from, thinking it a lighthouse warning. As they steered away to avoid the light, the ship would run aground on the treacherous shoals, the bottom would be ripped out of the vessel, and passengers and cargo would be spilled out into the icy waters.

Then Marianna and the others would go to work. All of them—men, women, and children—would wade into the surf and pull to shore that which they had destroyed and killed for. It was the way they made their living. They were wreckers.

Suddenly the ship's bell sounded startlingly near, the sound borne on a gust of wind, and then, even through the storm's roar, Marianna thought she heard the final death cry of the ship, a moaning, roaring sound of rending metal and tearing wood.

Along the beach great fires suddenly blazed, springing up at Throag's thundering bellow. It was the signal. She must now go to work.

Closing her mind to all thought save that of the task ahead, Marianna took her hands from the comparative warmth of her pockets and plodded toward the water's edge, peering through the gloom for the sight of floating chests, crates, or other goods.

The water was icy, and she dared not go too close to the surf, or she risked being sucked into the sea herself.

There! A keg bobbed toward her, rolling on the white foam of a comber.

Deftly Marianna snagged it with her pike, grasped it, and wrestled it up on the beach to a spot where it would not be reclaimed by the waves. She could see the dim forms of the other wreckers along the beach as they all scurried about their tasks.

As she left the keg on the sand, Marianna sighed softly to herself. When it was all over, when they had gathered all that they could for the time being, they would return to the huts, and she knew what would happen then.

After a wrecking Jude Throag was always randy as a goat. He would want to have her, tired and wet though she might be. Of course, he took her almost every night, anyway, but after a wrecking—which seemed to excite him in some mysterious way beyond her understanding—he was always insatiable, taking her three or four times, pummeling her body and bruising her flesh until she felt that she simply could not endure it.

Sometimes Marianna wished that she could have remained a child. Things had been so much simpler then. She had had only to do her duties and mind her tongue, and she had been left alone.

But now—now that had all changed. Last year she had turned fourteen, and her body had begun to alter. Her bosom had swelled, fine fuzz had appeared on areas that had been bare and neat before, and her bottom had grown fat.

When that had happened, the men had started to notice her. Their attitude toward her had changed; no longer did they call her child and shoo her off, but made ugly, vulgar jests when she was near and pinched her. How she hated the pinching!

And then she was fifteen, and Jude—Ezekial Throag's son and second in command—had singled her out for his. With no fancy flourishes, Marianna's mother had told her on her fifteenth birthday that she was to be Jude's woman.

The idea had frightened and repelled her. Jude was old, at least thirty, and big and swaggering and rough-talking. Besides, he already had a woman, redheaded Jenny, who had been with him for several years.

But her mother had shaken her head. "Jenny's to go," she said firmly. "Jude told me himself. He wants you, girl. You should be glad. He's the leader's son. He's strong, and when Ezekial goes, Jude will take his place. You will be the leader's woman."

Her mother's lips had spread in an awful smile, and Marianna knew that there was nothing she could do.

And so, she had been given to Jude Throag, and he had casually and brutally deflowered her in the bedroom of her mother's hut, while the others drank and laughed in the other room. It had hurt, and Marianna had not liked it. She could not understand why redheaded Jenny had cried and looked at her, Marianna, with venom in her eyes. Surely, Jenny should be glad to be let off, to have someone else take her place.

Later Marianna had tried to talk to Jenny, but Jenny left the mark of her hand on Marianna's face and stalked away. One of the other women, Old Mary, had finally explained to Marianna that Jenny was jealous and unhappy at losing Jude to another woman.

Marianna could not understand it then, and she could not understand it now. Of course she had known about sex—you couldn't live the way they did and not see everything that went on—but somehow, this knowledge had never really touched her. Somehow, she had never thought that she would be involved in it herself. And it was so awful! She was so small, still not much taller than she had been as a child, and Jude was so huge, particularly that part of him that she had begun to think of as his weapon —for that was the way he used it, like a ram, to batter her down, like a club, to pound away at her. She was always sore, always tender, there below.

Now she drove her iron hook into a small crate that the waves had just tossed up onto the beach and pulled it shoreward, grunting, thinking of the further punishment her small body would absorb that wild night.

The wind had quieted, only occasionally making a lunge at the hut, and the rain had all but stopped.

Inside the main room of the Throag hut, a fire roared, sending warmth and cheer around the room and into the cold bones of those assembled around it. The air in the room was rank, but Marianna, being accustomed to it, did not notice it particularly. She drank her tot of rum, like the rest, and prayed silently that Jude would consume so much that he would be rendered incapable of performing his will upon her.

The other Bankers were laughing and singing rough songs, telling tales, discussing how it had been out there tonight for them, gloating over the catch they had made.

Marianna sat as quietly as she could, hoping to go unnoticed, hoping to be left alone. She was deadly tired and, despite the fire, still chilled to the bone.

Sitting pressed between the malodorous bodies of Old Mary and her own mother, Marianna tried to make herself as small as possible so that it would be easy for Jude to overlook her.

Jude waxed expansive under the influence of the rum and was talking in an animated fashion to his father.

They looked so much alike, Marianna thought, Ezekial and Jude Throag. Despite the fact that they were father and son, they seemed not much apart in age. Ezekial, like his son, was a huge man, with a barrel chest and heavy, muscular arms. His coal-black hair was still not touched with gray, despite the fact that he must be well over fifty years of age, and his eyes showed a feral cunning and more fire than did those of his son.

Marianna both feared and hated Ezekial Throag. He ruled the little band of wreckers with a heavy and awesome hand, taking the best of everything for himself and his son, cowing the others with his great strength and brutal temper.

The men said that he was a good organizer and that without him, they would not fare nearly so well as they did. He was clever, was Ezekial Throag, and always scheming new ways to lure the ships onto the shoals and new ways to salvage the loot from the wrecks.

So, although the men grumbled among themselves, they did his bidding. They did better under his leadership than did many of the Bankers, and so they were willing to put up with a certain amount of abuse.

Marianna, almost dozing from the effects of the rum and the fire, suddenly felt her arm seized. Before she was completely alert, she found herself on her feet and then clasped in a pair of hard-muscled arms.

She opened her eyes to see Jude's face grinning down at her in drunken lust. She shut her eyes again and sighed. Jude laughed and lifted her high.

"Well, it's good night to you all, mates. I'd love to stay up with you, but you know how it is when a man has a new woman," he said crudely. "With a new woman, a man's appetite grows apace!"

Marianna heard the coarse laughter and ribald remarks as Jude turned with her in his arms.

She opened her eyes slightly to see Jenny glaring at her and turned her head away, only to meet the gaze of Ezekial Throag. He was looking at her with his strange, gray-green eyes, and he was smiling slightly through his thick black beard.

Marianna felt herself shiver. He was staring at her in much the same way that Jude looked at her, and this recognition shook her to the core. In their society the strong took what they wanted, and Ezekial Throag was the strongest man of all. Still, Jude was his son; and if he had a soft spot at all, it was for Jude. Surely he would not take his own son's woman!

But the thought of Ezekial's smile remained with Marianna and made her unusually subdued as Jude strode with her into the small inner room that held their pallet . . .

It was a thin, pale light that greeted Marianna's eyes in the morning, seeping slowly in through the small, grimy window set high in the wall, and she knew that the storm had been followed by fog. . .

Experiencing the excitement of the hunt, Marianna headed toward the now peaceful whispering of the sea, still not discernible through the smothering bank of fog. At the water's edge it was a bit clearer, but she realized in exasperation that it was going to be hard to see anything that had washed up unless she practically fell over it.

She started along the beach and in short order found another small keg like the one she had discovered last night, a large crate that she could not budge by herself, and a beautiful amethyst flacon, sealed, and, miraculously, unbroken.

She turned the flacon back and forth between her hands,

feeling its smoothness; seeing, even in the fog, the light that seemed captured in the brilliant glass. She had never seen anything so lovely and had never imagined having something of such beauty for her very own.

Gazing around to see if she was observed, she quickly put the flacon into the inner pocket of her coat. She would have to hurry now, the others would be stirring soon. She would see if there were any other small or manageable items, and if not, she would return to the large crate with a crowbar and see what was inside. Once there had been a chest with women's clothing, beautiful goods, which the women had fought over and then parceled out, piece by piece, among themselves.

Marianna had been too small then to have been awarded a share, but she remembered still a swatch of blue velvet, bluer than the summer sky and softer than the down on a baby gull.

Patting the bulge the flacon made in the coat pocket, she moved on, squinting through the swirling fog. Suddenly she tripped over something low and yielding on the sand.

Swearing under her breath, she caught her balance and looked down. A long, dark form lay sprawled at her feet, shrouded in seaweed and flotsam.

Leaning closer, Marianna let out a soft cry. It was a man, she could see his face now, pale through the kelp.

At that moment the fog thinned, and a pale wash of light showed the figure more clearly. No, not a man, but a youth. Not much older than herself, and beautiful as a woman.

Shocked, Marianna stared down at him, a great and sudden sadness washing over her. So young he was, and so beautiful! Had he died in the storm, drowned, or had Ezekial Throag, Jude, or one of the other men, bashed him with their great clubs? It was no matter, Marianna supposed, but she hoped that he had drowned. It somehow seemed more fitting.

Still, it was a pity that he was dead. She would have liked to see the color of his eyes. . . .

The youth stirred. His head raised slightly, and his eyelids fluttered.

Marianna felt her heart begin to hammer with fear and excitement. She felt a mixture of emotions difficult to sort out: delight that this beautiful youth was not dead, and dismay that he was alive. Throag would not like the fact that there had been a survivor of the wreck, and he would remedy that oversight at the first opportunity.

Marianna stood poised for flight, uncertain as to what she should do. Then the youth groaned, and she stopped thinking as instinct took over.

She dropped to her knees on the sand. Brushing the kelp away from his face, she put her arm under his shoulders and raised him. His eyelids quivered again and then opened, leaving her looking down into the bluest eyes she had ever seen, bluer even than the scrap of velvet she had long admired. He stared at her uncomprehendingly, then opened his lips, as if to speak.

Marianna parted her own lips, as if in response. Oh, what a pretty mouth he had! She had never seen such a mouth on a man.

His eyes began to show awareness, and she found herself talking to him as she might a child, words of comfort and kindness. "There, there. 'Tis all right now. You're alive. You'll be fine, you will. There now."

He swallowed, and the movement caused him to wince in pain. "Where?" he croaked in a dry voice.

Marianna glanced quickly back over her shoulder, hoping that none of the others would happen upon them, and then back at the young man. She whispered, "Your ship sank. You've been washed ashore on the Outer Banks."

He stared at her, confusion mirrored in his eyes. "The Outer Banks?"

"Shh-h—yes. Just off the Carolina coast. The islands."

The youth closed his eyes and grimaced as if a sudden pain had seized him, and Marianna, concerned, brushed the damp hair away from his forehead. It was smooth and cold to her touch, and she shook her head in dismay. He had lost his body heat, and the cold might very well take him, particularly if he stayed out here in the wet.

But *what* was she to do with him? The sensible thing, of course, would be to tell Jude or his father. She shuddered, for she knew what they would do—club him once or twice, smashing that beautiful face to a bloody pulp, and then toss him back into the sea. Somehow, she knew that she could not let that happen. But where could she take him? She would have to hide him, and on the barren, windswept Banks, hiding places were in short supply. Also, every man, woman, and child knew one another. There were no outsiders. It seemed an impossible task.

And then she thought of Old Jack's hut. Stuck away it was, in a tiny cove, away from the main settlement, for Old Jack had been a sour and uncooperative man, who liked to be off by himself. Old Jack had died last week, of old age and old rum; but the shack was still there and unoccupied, for none of the others wished to live that far from the main group. She would take him there, make him as comfortable as she could, and see what happened. Marianna knew that she was taking a grave risk. But she had no love for either Jude or his father, and she felt something, even if she couldn't put a name to it, for this lad.

"Can you move?" she asked. "Do you think you can walk?"

The youth's eyelids fluttered open. What thick lashes he had, she thought, almost as thick as her own.

He swallowed. "I don't know," he said in a shaky voice. "I'll try."

He kept on staring at her in the most curious way, a strange expression on his face, until Marianna began to feel uncomfortable.

"C'mon now," she said sharply. "Let's try it then."

He smiled, a slow, weak smile, but one that sparked his features with a sudden light and charm that took her breath away. "You're beautiful" he said in hushed wonder. "So beautiful. Like a sea princess."

Marianna felt herself blushing furiously, the heat tightening her face. "C'mon now," she said again, "there's no time for such talk. We must get you up and away from here, if you're to stay alive."

His expression changed to one of puzzlement. "Why? What do you mean?"

"There's no time to explain. Just believe what I say and *do* what I say."

He nodded and with an effort raised his upper body.

"That's a good fellow," said Marianna, putting her hands under his arms. "On your feet now."

This took a bit more effort to accomplish, but in a few moments the youth was standing, leaning on Marianna for support; and although he was very shaky, she thought that she could get him to Old Jack's hut.

Slowly they moved off. The youth's weakened condition made him uncoordinated, and it was like walking a great baby, Marianna thought.

The fog had not lifted, but Marianna was sure that she could detect sounds of life from the direction of the cluster of huts. The others were up and about now, and soon they would be coming down to the water's edge to search for salvage.

The walk seemed to take an interminable time, and the young man grew heavier and heavier as they drew nearer to the shack. But despite her small stature, Marianna was both strong and tough. She managed to get the much taller and heavier youth to the gray, wind-scoured shack and inside, where she had him lie down on the rough pallet that had belonged to Old Jack.

There were no covers or quilts—Old Jack's few belongings had been scavenged by the wreckers—so she removed her heavy man's coat and placed it over the stranger, tucking it around him.

His face was very pale, and his eyelids looked thin and blue, almost transparent. "Are you all right?"

"I'm not sure," he said through chattering teeth. "So cold, I'm so cold." He shivered. "My wet clothes . . ." The words trailed off.

Of course, she thought. They must come off. Why hadn't she thought of that already?

She removed the greatcoat and began to take off the wet clothing that was plastered to his slender frame. It was fine material, she could see. Gentleman's clothing—a velvet vest, a fine linen shirt. Carefully she peeled the garments off one by one, feeling a vague embarrassment as she did so, although why she should was a mystery, since the sight of the nude male body was no novelty to her. The Bankers were far from a modest lot, and they lived a communal sort of life. Long before Jude had taken her, Marianna knew what the male form looked like; yet somehow this was different. Perhaps it was because this young man was so alien a creature, so different from the men she had seen and know.

His shoulders were broad and well formed, she saw as she lifted the shirt over his head, but his chest was smooth and hairless as a girl's. Dropping the shirt onto the dirt floor, she tentatively moved her palm over the skin; so smooth—and so cold that it was amazing that there was life within. Quickly she covered his chest with her coat, arranging the heavy garment so that it only covered the upper body, and then bent to the task of removing his breeches.

Gentlemen's breeches they were, too, of fine fabric and excellent fit. With a rising sense of curiosity, Marianna undid the waist and began to pull them down. He was so different from the other men, would he be different there, as well? Or would that part of him be as ugly as Jude's weapon?

The breeches slowly peeled away, showing linen drawers, an item she found a wonderment. A leather purse fell onto the ground with a jangle. The catch opened, and Marianna glimpsed the glitter of gold coins. If Jude or his father saw those coins! Hastily she snapped the purse closed and returned it to the breeches.

Then the underdrawers joined the pile of clothing on the ground, and his lower body lay pale and exposed to her gaze. She knew that she should cover him, yet she hesitated, fascinated by the sight of his thighs, muscular, and larger than she would have thought, and his well-formed legs and well-developed calves. Here also he lacked much body hair, except at the joining of his thighs, where a bright, golden patch of wiry hair nested his male organs, which were drawn up and shriveled from the cold. They appeared pale and harmless, nothing like the dark, threatening dangle that was Jude's, even in repose.

Somewhat reassured, Marianna pulled the greatcoat over him, again tucking it around his cold body.

He tossed his head. "So cold," he muttered. "So cold. Help me!" His eyes flew open and stared into her eyes. "I'm going to die, aren't I?"

The question was voiced calmly enough, but Marianna felt an unaccustomed lump in her throat. The coat was not enough, she realized. Covering would keep in body heat, but this youth had no body heat to keep in. She must not lose him now. What *was* she to do?

And then she knew. She must give him her own warmth. She had seen it done before. Quickly she climbed onto the pallet next to him, placing her body close to his, touching him from shoulder almost to toe, spreading the greatcoat over both of them.

As she snuggled close, he groaned and turned to her, instinctively seeking her warmth. Her arms went around him, and she felt the cold smoothness of his back under her hands. The only thing warm about him was his soft breath on the top of her head.

Marianna lay there stiffly, holding the strange youth tightly, feeling awkward and chilled. But slowly, very slowly, warmth began to creep over her, coming from her body, through her clothing, and going out to the young man. She could feel it she thought; like an ocean current, moving gradually outward from her body to his. Gradually his body warmed under her hands, and his breathing slowed until she knew he was asleep.

Marianna lay next to him for a long time, feeling something that she had never before known or experienced—tenderness.

Marianna's rescue of sensitive, passionate Philip Court-
wright plunges her into a turbulent love affair with him.
But then she meets the dynamically forceful sailor Captain
Adam Street.

Read the complete Bantam Book, now available wherever
paperbacks are sold.

The wonderful new novel by the author of
KRAMER VS. KRAMER

Steve Robbins has a heart-wrenching dilemma.
His wife has found a satisfying career of her own.
His kids have grown up. And the job he is so good
at has lost its challenge. Caught in the mainstream
of modern marriage and success, Steve wakes up
one morning to realize that his dreams—everything
he's longed for—have come true . . . and they're not
what he really wanted at all. So Steve goes back to
where the dreams began. And he starts searching for
the one thing he left behind . . . happiness.

THE OLD NEIGHBOR-HOOD

By AVERY CORMAN

(14891-5) $2.95

Discover A New Romance

With these four just-released titles from Bantam Books

Family Affairs

Catherine Gaskin

From illegitimate daughter of the family cook, through two marriages to rich, powerful men, Kelly rises to the highest circles of London society. She finds her marriages tainted by intrigue and tragedy and her destiny tied to her three stepdaughters. Still, she searches for the fulfillment every woman needs. And as she searches, every woman will recognize Kelly Anderson's emotions as her own.

(14718-8) $2.95

A Woman's Age

Rachel Billington

"Remember those old-fashioned novels that we used to walk into as if into a house full of genuinely interesting people, and spend a week or two listening and be sad to leave? This is one of them....," said the *New York Times*. A moving, romantic saga of four generations of women in love with life, *A Woman's Age* tells a rich satisfying story of 20th century Western woman.

(14142-2) $3.50

Tides of Love

Patricia Matthews

"America's First Lady of Historical Romance" brings you
a ravishing new novel. Marianna was once a member of
the Wreckers—a callous group of men and women who made
riches by luring ships ashore and looting them. Now, her
attempt at a new life in beautiful Sag Harbor is threatened by
her entanglement with four men from her past.

(01328-9)   (5¼" × 8¼" large format edition) $5.95

MANDARIN ORANGE SUNDAY

Angelique Durand

Solange delaMer is a rich, talented novelist who writes
about a poetic witch named Pandora. And, she's very
liberated. Follow her as she romps through one outrageous
adventure after another. That is, until she meets a gorgeous rock
star named Jan-Toby Axelson who is everything she's
ever wanted in a man.

(14709-9) $2.95

THE LATEST BOOKS IN THE BANTAM BESTSELLING TRADITION